THE
GRYPHON

PAULA GROVER

 FriesenPress

Suite 300 - 990 Fort St
Victoria, BC, V8V 3K2
Canada

www.friesenpress.com

ISBN
978-1-5255-3860-5 (Hardcover)
978-1-5255-3861-2 (Paperback)
978-1-5255-3862-9 (eBook)

1. FICTION, FANTASY

Distributed to the trade by The Ingram Book Company

Prologue
From the Journals of Tale Weaver,
at her home in the Forest Lake Nesting Site . . . . . . *v*

PART ONE
Sunsky of the Mountains

Chapter One
Opinicus *1*

Chapter Two
Eye of the Storm *6*

Chapter Three
Nightsky *9*

Chapter Four
Homewinds and Hippogryphs *13*

Chapter Five
The Oracle *19*

Chapter Six
Gryphonic Heresy *24*

Chapter Seven
Gryphonic Court *32*

Chapter Eight
The Third Heresy *44*

Chapter Nine
Between Ground and Sky *55*

Chapter Ten
The Valley of Outcasts *68*

PROLOGUE

From the Journals of Tale Weaver, at her home in the Forest Lake Nesting Site

I am Tale Weaver, the wingless kryphon scribe and the teller of this tale.

I have seen the events that I have described through a vision, which has made it possible for me not only to see the actions of Sunsky of the Mountains, but to hear her thoughts as well. I have recorded them as though they were happening in the present, as indeed they were during my vision.

I received this vision from my sister, the gryphonic oracle Truth Speaker. I believe that she facilitated it from a higher source, and so it is that a flightless kryphon who lives far from the action in her Forest Lake nesting den may tell the story of a winged gryphon who lives in the mountains.

The reign of Sunsky represents a new age for the gryphonic peoples, one which we of the Forest Lake nesting site have predicted for many generations. We live in a sacred retreat for mystics, sages, oracles, hermits, rovers, and other creatures rejected by their societies. We all reside together in a haven of peace, but we are aware that the outside communities may not comprehend our purpose. Instead, they might mistrust or even fear us, and this is the reason for the secrecy which surrounds our location. In the new age, however, we hope that such secrecy will be unnecessary.

This is the story of how Sunsky and her family gradually overcome their doubts and fears until they are ready to leap into a new beginning, one that will shake the entrenched traditions of Gryphonia to its foundations.

THE GRYPHON

PART ONE

Sunsky of the Mountains

CHAPTER ONE

Opinicus

The gryphon stands magnificent upon the precipice, staring down at the valley below. She shimmers in the morning sun, her golden feathers rustling slightly in the gentle mountain breeze. She cocks her head, her reddish beak as sharp and hard as the mountain rock upon which her leonine body stands. She is stalk still except for her tail, which swishes like that of an agitated cat. Her aquiline forearms present a contrast to her rear feline body, with talons as razor-sharp as her avian beak.

The creature's name is Sunsky. The oracle has perceived her as the highest and deepest of all gryphon citizens, and she will become the leader of Gryphonia after the old queen passes. For the first time in her life, however, she is uncertain of her destiny. Last night she dreamed of a winged horse. Among the two-legged hopha creatures (known in some spheres as humans), a winged horse in a dream is a miraculous sign, but the gryphons view horses as enemies and therefore stigmatize them with a negative symbolism. A horse with wings is an especially bad omen.

"What does this mean?" she ponders. "For my reign, my future mate, and our progeny?"

As if in answer, a yearning screech pierces the air. Sunsky looks in its direction and her heart lifts for a moment. It is Dreamspinner, the mighty opinicus, come to mate with her.

Dreamspinner flies down from the sky, his outstretched forelimbs breaking his flight as he lands atop the mountain beside his beloved gryphon queen. Although the two beings belong to the same species, they are sexually dimorphic in that they exhibit different physical traits. They are opposite in their forearms: while Sunsky's feathered appendages are equipped with the talons of an eagle, those of the opinicus resemble the front paws of a lion.

Dreamspinner throws back his golden-brown feathered head, opens his beak, and shrieks a love-song to the heavens that is undecipherable to any but the gryphonic beings.

"O queen of the sun and sky! I come in search of you, to entreat you to be my one true mate!"

Sunsky remains silent. She remembers her dream, and her heart is troubled.

"O mighty opinicus king!" she answers. "I need more time to make my decision. I have of late had some worrisome dreams that cause me to question my worthiness to be the premiere queen. You should have only the best and the greatest to be your mate and that may mean choosing another."

Dreamspinner squawks in surprise, fluffing out his head feathers with great indignation.

"O queen, o sun and sky of my desire! This response rips my lion heart as your talons ravage prey. How could you ever think yourself unfit to be premiere queen, unworthy even to be my queen? I will have no other! It is I who am undeserving of you. Perhaps you have another in mind. If so, he can be no greater than I can. If he thinks in all his arrogance that he is better, I will fight him for you!"

Sunsky screeches her objection.

She extends her talons as she replies. "There are none for you to fight, mighty Dreamspinner! None but my shadowy nightmare, which I am too afraid to name."

"Afraid?" Dreamspinner replies in disbelief. "How can a gryphon queen, with such a courageous eagle-lion heritage as yours, ever entertain fear? I, the lion-eagle king, am your complimentary opposite. No nightmare can ever chase me from you. Fear not, my love!"

Sunsky is silent for a long while. She looks away from him toward the distant skies. Perhaps her dream is only what it appears to be: a mere fantasy, a simple imagining that represents her anxiety about her approaching courtship and reign.

She feels a tremor of excitement in the lower leonine aspect of her body. Her aquiline head and forelimbs remain still, her eyes piercing the distance as if hoping to penetrate the future's mystery. And yet, no answer comes to her from the sky. Her tail twitches from side to side as Dreamspinner's claws run gently up and down her body.

She twirls around, her beak tweaking Dreamspinner's tail playfully. Dreamspinner laughs, giving her a return tail tweak.

The two winged creatures toss and tumble with each other on the mountain peak, pecking each other passionately until Sunsky feels sufficiently receptive to Dreamspinner's amorous advances. This will be the third mating between her and the opinicus king, and the possibility of a pregnancy looms closer.

Her heart is lighter as Dreamspinner's seed enters her body.

"If this mating produces gryphlet chicks, my worries are over," she thinks happily. "For how can the nightly winged horse of my dreams intrude himself upon a pregnant gryphon?"

She asks the gryphonic oracle for the birth of a gryphlet chick or even that of an opiniclet cub, if the sun in the sky so aligns itself. The live-born gryphlets and opiniclets are revered as prophets and leaders of the future, primarily because they will soar high above their wingless brothers and sisters, that subset of gryphonic beings known as *keythongs* and *kryphons*.

If life does not bless Sunsky and her mate with winged offspring, even the emergence of wingless hatchlings from her eggs will be a source of solace. Of course, they will immediately surrender any such youngsters to the Council of Keythongs, which will sterilize and train them for a life of service to the Great Winged Ones.

Dreamspinner interrupts Sunsky's reverie with a peck on her shoulder. He lifts his head and looks at her sharply as they lie together on the mountain bedrock. He senses her thoughts.

"Fret not, my queen, over the form our young will take. We are bound for live birth chicks or cubs! That is certain. Our royal bloodlines cannot produce anything but the greatest."

"Aha," Sunsky rebukes him gently, "no keythong or kryphon eggs have been fertilized by you, ever?"

Dreamspinner squawks, his feathers rustling.

"Maybe just a few," he admits, "although my wingless offspring are strong, intelligent, and they will be councilors one day rather than simple servants."

"I see," Sunsky responds quietly.

She says no more to him, and they remain together in blissful silence. Sunsky stays beside him for as long as she can, but finally the responsibilities of the gryphon rock castle bid her to end the peaceful interlude and return home. She quivers slightly as she stands up.

"Must you go so soon, my queen?" Dreamspinner asks.

"Yes. I have been away too long. It is time. And now, you must fly to your own territory. Remember, I have not yet made my decision."

"*When* will I have your final answer, my queen of the sun and sky?"

"When the sun in the sky so aligns itself," Sunsky answers. She leaps into the air, her giant wings beating powerfully.

CHAPTER TWO

Eye of the Storm

Sunsky flies over the mountain peaks. She has flown farther than she originally intended. She knows her kryphon nanny, old Egglight, will not be pleased. Ever since Sunsky was a young gryphlet, she enjoyed flying off into the skies on her own adventure. Egglight, although wingless, flew into a foul temper whenever the young princess left without permission, which was quite frequently. In the past, Sunsky delighted in teasing her by flying away, knowing that the wingless kryphon was incapable of following. The elderly nanny could do nothing but slash the air with her talons, shrieking in frustration.

Kryphons, the wingless females, are born of an egg, as are their more numerous keythong brothers. The kryphons, who are not of noble birth, are most often employed as nannies to gryphlet princesses, along with some of the lower-ranking gryphons that serve as winged nannygryphs.

Egglight always makes a habit of angrily dispatching the winged nannygryphs to retrieve her charge more swiftly, but Sunsky seldom consents to return without a rousing game of mountain hide and seek. When she finally does return home, nannygryphs flying at her side, Egglight's screeched scolding is a deafening experience.

Sunsky laughs as she thinks of it now but realizes that, as a queen on the threshold of adulthood, she can no longer afford to play such games. She will need to demonstrate her responsible nature, and arriving home late from a freedom flight is no way to prove herself worthy of the queenship.

She knows she will receive not only a mandatory reprimand from Egglight but also a lecture from her mother, Skystar. "At the age of eighteen sun revolutions, you ought to know better," the matriarch will say.

Sunsky will need to restrain her rebellious screeches and learn to control her temper. It is a rigorous discipline for a young princess accustomed to doing what she wants when she wants.

"I am not fit to be premiere queen," Sunsky tells herself. "I cannot possibly take over the reign from my grandmother Heartsong at my present state of maturity!"

And yet, if the elderly Queen Heartsong passes on, she must be ready to take over the reign. Her mother may advise her, but she cannot assume the reign on behalf of her daughter.

When gryphons in line to the Stone Throne are related, as Sunsky and Skystar are to Heartsong, the passing of the reign must skip one generation. This is according to a piece of legislation known as the *Gryphonic Code*.

Thus, it is Sunsky and not Skystar who will be premiere queen.

"Skystar is so much better suited to reign," Sunsky opines. "I am far too often flying away to the mountain peaks and getting lost. I am too young for such an honor."

While she frets in her mind about the reign, she realizes that the wind has blown her a long way off course. She descends into the territory of the lower mountains.

"Oh, what a fool I am!" she chides herself. She sees that the sky is so dark that it is like the night.

She fights the rising currents of air to no avail. A spiral of wind pulls her down into the darkness. She suppresses a squawk of panic and forces herself to remain calm. She has entered a storm that she does not have the strength to battle. Sunsky has no choice but to abandon herself to the inevitable pull of the vortex.

As she falls into the whirlwind, she can no longer hold back her fear. She screeches in terror as the tornado drags her down, faster and faster in a circular motion, further into the raging storm.

She views her life as a great panoramic drama before her. She sees herself from the time she was birthed as a gryphlet in front of her noble father, Sun Quest, to her early training by Egglight and Skystar. The vision ends at this foolish present moment, and she fears that she will die never having proved herself as premiere queen and never having birthed her first gryphlet.

She becomes quiet inside as she dreams of her majestic king, Dreamspinner. She feels the warrior wind slowly subside as it spins downward into a gentle whirlpool of calm. It deposits her into the center of peaceful silence that is the eye of the storm.

CHAPTER THREE

Nightsky

All is dark. As Sunsky awakens, she feels the cold stone surface of the mountain press against her furred body, a stabbing pain in her right wing and warm breath upon her. Slowly, she arises, her eyelids opening to a terrible sight. As she turns her feathered head toward the source of the warm breath, she jumps up in shock, bolting a few steps before stumbling and falling. She screeches loudly at the dark, winged nightmare before her. It is the winged horse of her troubled dreams.

The horse speaks in a high-pitched voice, but she cannot understand him.

"O, dark and horrid cave bat!" she cries. "Finish me off now, while I am wounded, and let me not see the light of morning! Since my own foolishness has led me to this, I deserve to be devoured by you. I surrender to you as I succumbed to the gale!"

The horse does nothing. He looks at her, his eyes gentle and his ears pointing forward in great interest. Sunsky flops about helplessly, feeling even more foolish. It is night, and she cannot fly in the dark. In addition, she realizes that her right wing is broken, with both wings missing feathers.

She squawks miserably at the irony of her situation. When morning breaks, Egglight will immediately dispatch a squadron of search gryphons to find her. The elderly kryphon will not know, however, that her winged charge is now as equally tied to the ground as Egglight has been all her life. As she considers her ridiculous condition, Sunsky feels ashamed of herself. She wishes this black horse demon would finish her off, because she would rather die than be found by her sister gryphons in this humiliating flightless state.

The horse continues to irritate her by doing nothing. He watches her through the darkness and into the first rays of sunlight. As the sun rises, so do the vultures, screeching their deathly taunts. Sunsky lies still, preferring to conserve her energy. The vultures will have her when she dies, if death deigns to come and rescue her from this horrible predicament. Her heart is heavy as she realizes that, although injured, she is nowhere near the end of her life. There is nothing left but to wait to see if the search gryphons will find her and carry her back with them to her worried family. If they do not find her, she will probably die slowly, for flightlessness to a gryphon is in itself a kind of death.

If I am lucky, she thinks ruefully, *a predatory animal will dine on me. This stupid horse does not seem to be fulfilling his role as my devourer.*

In a sudden burst of anger, she snaps at the quietly watching horse. "What is wrong with you? Why don't you just kill me? Don't you know that horses are the enemies of gryphons?"

The horse says nothing but comes near and nuzzles her hind leg. Sunsky hisses, stretching out her talons to chase him away. He retreats, turning his attention to some nearby buzzards that have landed. He bounds toward them, flying furiously in their direction and chasing them away. Sunsky is chastened and after that does not object when the black horse nuzzles her leg.

As the days and nights pass, the horse brings her small rodents to kill and eat. He gently picks up the animals with his mouth and places them before her, where her claw-like forearms ravage the animals. She devours them hungrily.

As the two beings share time together, Sunsky eating meat and the horse grazing on mountain grasses and plants, telepathy is birthed between them.

The horse's name is Nightsky, she learns. He is well named, for he is her opposite in every way. He is night to her day, a gentle plant-eater as opposed to the savage predator that is Sunsky the gryphon. He is as patient as the mountain rock, while she spends much of her time fretting and squawking impatiently about her inability to fly.

"In time," Nightsky reassures her through telepathic transmissions, "you will fly again. Remain calm. Let the eternal silence heal you."

Sunsky rustles her remaining feathers, but she can do little because it is too painful to walk with the burden of a broken wing. Instead, she abandons herself to the silence. The more she permits the stillness to enter her mind, the clearer the communication between her and Nightsky.

As the evening falls, she even allows herself to experience the ever-growing attraction between them. Repeatedly, she allows his advances upon her. She delights in his gentle equine lovemaking, his quiet manner so different from Dreamspinner's furious pawing and cawing.

Dreamspinner. Guilt clouds her thinking once again. How can she be his lover again after having mated with a winged horse? The anxiety that haunted her dreams returns.

"Fret not, my Sunsky," the dark horse says, nuzzling her as they lie side by side the next morning. "I will be your lover. You can stay here for as long as you wish."

Sunsky trembles as she feels his warm body next to hers, cozily nuzzled in a cave of tree branches, one that he fashioned for her in order to protect her from the elements and predators. He chased away the wolves and gargoyles, his wings lifting him above the growling beasts when they tried to ravage him with their claws. Sunsky is now in awe of him. She is deeply in love with Nightsky, her one-time enemy turned lover.

As time passes (she knows not how long), her wings heal under his gentle ministrations.

Can I now fly? She asks herself, and if so, should I not leave Nightsky and return to my family, my own people?

Her heart grows heavy. She realizes that it is time. She thinks of her parents, of her grandmother, the great Queen Heartsong, and of her sister gryphons. She knows she must return to her responsibilities. She cannot leave her family alone with their worries over her disappearance.

Nightsky, knowing her thoughts, is similarly heavy-hearted. One day, he nuzzles her and walks away, over the mountain. With a groaning screech, Sunsky makes five clumsy attempts to propel herself into the air. She practiced beating her wings for the past few days, and she is now strong enough to walk.

Finally, after a few short bursts of flight, she manages to propel herself into the air long enough to glide amongst the currents. It is now time to leave Nightsky and sail home.

CHAPTER FOUR

Homewinds and Hippogryphs

Just as the warrior wind dropped her on the lower mountains, so the gentle air currents carry her back home. With a soaring heart, she recognizes the peaks of the gryphonage, the place where the gryphon castle beckons her to return. Her wings are aching, as they have for the past few days. She sought refuge in the branches of mountain trees by night and glided the currents by day. She paused only long enough to catch whatever miniature prey her weakened condition would allow.

As she slides into her home territory, she gathers all the strength that is in her to bellow loud and intermittent screeches. It is not long before her screeches are joyfully returned. A flock of search gryphons, accompanied by her parents, Skystar and Sun Quest, soar towards her. Skystar positions herself under Sunsky's left wing while Sun Quest supports her right. Her heart bursts with happiness as she wearily accepts her parents' support. They guide her landing upon the smooth terrace, which wingless workers have painstakingly chiseled from Rockcastle Mountain for the royal families.

The kryphon nanny Egglight bounds toward her, forgetting in her deep relief to scold the prodigal princess for her foolish flight of fancy. Many of her sister gryphons, among them her biological sisters Mountain Rain and Cloudhopper, are there to greet her.

"Sunsky!" Mountain Rain exclaims. "Thank the oracle you've returned! We thought you'd been killed by that devilish windstorm."

Sunsky, weakened from her long voyage, can only coo her gratitude to her family for their love. Her elder sister Cloudhopper hops about clumsily as her wings beat in excitement, all the while knocking over the many statues that line the terrace.

"The lost one has been found!" her father Sun Quest announces. "We must have a feast tonight in my daughter's honor."

"No, Sun Quest!" Skystar admonishes him. "Can't you see that she is in no shape for a celebration yet? She must spend the night in the physician's den."

Sun Quest rustles his wings in impatience, but he knows his first mate is correct in her assessment of their daughter's condition.

Skystar brings Sunsky into the healer's den, where Light Healer orders her to lie on a mat. Exhausted from her long journey, she collapses into a long sleep. During her rest, she dreams of Nightsky, his form this time a welcome and pleasant dream rather than a nightmare.

As she awakens much later, she has almost forgotten that gryphonic society strictly forbids any such mating with a winged horse. Still, nagging thoughts bring the old fears back.

"No one ever has to know," she tells herself as she stretches her limbs.

"Aha, you are awake, Sunsky," Light Healer says. "I have made some proto-gruel for you to improve your strength."

"Yrrrr—aaaaaaaa—kkkk!" Sunsky gags in disgust. "I hate proto-gruel."

Nonetheless, Sunsky knows that to grow stronger, she needs to eat the mushy, squalid gruel. Light Healer places a platter of the stuff in front of Sunsky and she reluctantly takes it in.

"I have some good news for you, young queen," the physician says. "I know your parents will be pleased as well. I ran some tests on you while you were sleeping. You're disease-free and you have a live-birth opiniclet prince in your womb."

Sunsky sits bolt upright on her haunches. She almost forgot about her last mating with Dreamspinner! The dreams of Nightsky have been so vivid. She squawks her surprise.

"I know it's a bit overwhelming, your first live birth," Light Healer continues, "but you'll do fine with Skystar and Egglight beside you. By the way, you've laid two eggs and they are resting unbroken in your pouch. Too early to tell if they'll mature into full keythongs or not."

Sunsky stares at Light Healer in surprise.

Two eggs? She has not even noticed them in her pouch. It must have happened on the long journey home.

A thought suddenly emerges from her mind. *Surely it cannot be possible. Could Nightsky have fertilized one of my eggs?*

She knows that a horse and gryphon can produce a hybrid creature known as a *hippogryph*. The hippogryph is born of egg, as are the keythongs and kryphons; but unlike them, she has wings. Nonetheless, Sunsky knows that in spite of their winged status, gryphons push hippogryph hatchlings away to the edges of society, where they live as outcasts.

"Nonsense!" Sunsky tells herself. "Hippogryph hatchings are very rare. Nightsky cannot have fertilized my eggs. They are keythong eggs from Dreamspinner and nothing more. I must celebrate the upcoming arrival of my opiniclet prince!"

She chases all thoughts of hippogryphs from her mind. As she gains strength over the next few days, she welcomes visitors to her healing den.

"What news!" her closest sisters, Mountain Rain and Cloudhopper, cry as they bound in to see her. "An opiniclet prince in your womb, Sunsky?"

"Yes," Sunsky replies excitedly. "I must see the oracle as soon as I leave this dull old den. I must consult her with regard to the young one's name."

"Our father Sun Quest is planning a big celebration for you, Sunsky!" Mountain Rain gushes. "He is thrilled about his new grandson."

The sisters caw delightedly.

"Father Sun Quest never stops planning celebrations for me, it seems," Sunsky says ruefully. "But I wish he would plan one for both of you instead. He spoils me too much."

"I'll say," agrees Mountain Rain. "Cloudhopper and I don't mind, but Talona becomes very jealous."

A cloud of anger passes through Sunsky at the name of her archenemy and rival. Talona, the daughter of a ruthlessly ambitious gryphon, Soundringer, is also her half-sister. Sunsky and Talona fought each other from an early age, usually over the excessive amount of attention that their father, Sun Quest, showered upon the daughters of Skystar while at the same time ignoring his lone daughter Talona.

"My opiniclet pregnancy will cause Talona to shed all her feathers in a rage," Sunsky muses. "I hope Dreamspinner has at least given her a full birth pregnancy."

"'Fraid not, Sunsky!" Cloudhopper informs her. "I heard it was just a few keythong eggs for Talona."

"There's justice for you!" Mountain Rain exclaims. "She doesn't deserve the honor of a gryphlet or opinicus birth."

"Stop it, both of you!" Sunsky chides them. "No point going around gossiping about her, as Talona's mother Soundringer does about me and Mother Skystar."

Mountain Rain groans at the mention of the name Soundringer, also known as the *gossip queen*.

"We're learning bad habits around here, Sunsky," she laments ruefully. "I wish you would let Cloudhopper and I tag along on some of your flying adventures."

Sunsky squawks, "No way! You'd never have survived my past ordeal."

She puffs herself up with pride.

"By the way," Sunsky asks, "did either of you congratulate me on the two keythong eggs that rest in my pouch?"

Mountain Rain and Cloudhopper roar in laughter.

"Sunsky," Mountain Rain says in between chuckles, "you're too much."

To her surprise, Sunsky's heart sinks as they deride the keythong eggs. *If this is their attitude toward keythongs, how would they react to news of a hippogryph egg? Wait! How can I be thinking of Nightsky and a possible hippogryph egg by him?*

Sunsky feels both shock and excitement at this thought. If it is true that she is carrying his egg, then her whole life as she knows it will be over. Mating with horses and conceiving a hippogryph are completely against the Gryphonic Code. Section nine specifically forbids any such pairing. It stipulates that any gryphon who conceives a hippogryph must either abandon the hatchling to the Valley of Outcasts or suffer banishment from gryphonic society. She cannot consider becoming premiere queen, taking Dreamspinner as her mate, or even living in the gryphonage if she keeps and raises a hippogryph hatchling.

The thought of having to leave her family terrifies her. At the same time, she is excited at the prospect of returning to Nightsky and spending time with him in their mountain forest den. Sunsky shakes her head.

I must be daft! What on Gryphonia am I thinking?

Suddenly, she stands bolt upright, surprising both her sisters and Light Healer.

"I must go to the oracle immediately!" she announces to the flabbergasted trio.

CHAPTER FIVE

The Oracle

Sunsky waits impatiently at the mouth of the oracle's cave. She must wait to see the oracle because there are ten other gryphons waiting to speak with her, all anxious to enter into Truth Speaker's presence.

"None of them have my family ranking," Sunsky thinks imperiously. "Truth Speaker ought to see me first."

Truth Speaker does not, however. Instead, she takes her time, seeing each of the low-ranking gryphons and treating each one as though she were the premiere queen.

At last, it is Sunsky's turn. She struggles to contain her irritability and her ego, for she knows that Truth Speaker looks askance at self-aggrandizement. She bows her head, waiting politely for the revered prophet to address her. To Sunsky's trepidation, the oracle peers intently at her but does not say anything. Does she see something wrong with her, something unacceptable?

After a long pause, Truth Speaker addresses her gently. "Sunsky, daughter of Skystar and Sun Quest. Come into my chamber."

The young gryphon meekly follows. They enter into a beautiful candlelit chamber, its walls adorned with gryphonic paintings and stone artifacts. Centuries-old carvings of famous heroines and heroes line the sides of the pathway into the oracle's private quarters. Sunsky sits in the middle of the room and waits, her heart beating rapidly.

Truth Speaker is silent for a long while, her eyes closed. Sunsky tries to quell her jangled nerves, shutting her eyes in imitation of the oracle. She feels as though a windstorm is whirling through her head.

Finally, after what seems an eternity of silence, the oracle speaks. "I see that you have mated with two different males."

Sunsky twitches her wings while her heart hammers out its anxiety. *Does the oracle see my mating with Nightsky?*

"Calm, my dear, calm," the oracle soothes her. "You are a strong and compassionate gryphon. You have much turmoil and change ahead of you, although I feel deeply that you will endure it. Do not fret about the future, but take each moment as it comes."

"Truth Speaker, my oracle," Sunsky pleads, "tell me about the young I carry within my pouch."

Truth Speaker pauses before answering. "Within your womb, my young gryphon, I see an opiniclet prince, a beautiful young male with wings that shine in the sun. He is strong like his parents, and eventually he will grow to be as brave as you and your mate Dreamspinner. It will take time, however, as I see him being raised by two very stubborn opinicus males."

"What?" Sunsky exclaims in surprise. "How can this be, my oracle? You know the gryphonic law requires all winged youngsters to be raised by at least one gryphon and an opinicus. You say he will be raised by two males, but what about a gryphon? Who will be the female involved in his upbringing?"

"I see two gryphons in the background," she replies, "but they are not from the prince's maternal line. There is none of his maternal line around him."

Sunsky flaps her wings, crying in horror. "None? But what of my parents, Skystar and Sun Quest? What of my grandparents, the Premiere Queen Heartsong and her opinicus king, Lightning Bolt?"

"Sunsky," Truth Speaker says softly, "you must calm yourself before I continue. Feel your heartbeat to calm your mind."

Sunsky turns her attention immediately from her racing mind to her pulsating heart. As she listens to its beat, her wings and thoughts grow still.

Truth Speaker recommences her prophecy. "Now, my young Princess Sunsky, listen to your heartbeat whenever you feel anxiety. You do not need to panic. You have asked me specifically about the young in your pouch, not the young in your womb. Most gryphons want only to know the fruit of their wombs and care nothing for those in their egg-pouches. You are different: you have compassion for those erroneously dubbed lesser beings. Compassion is the sign of a gryphon who has learned to love beyond form. You will need this quality when you hear the news that I must give you about one of your eggs. Light Healer will not have noticed it yet, even with her multitude of physical tests, but one of your hatchlings is a hippogryph. The other is a keythong, the wingless son of Dreamspinner."

Sunsky feels dizzy. She tucks in her head, fighting the rising panic within her breast. *Feel your heartbeat! Feel your heartbeat,* she furiously commands herself.

Truth Speaker waits until Sunsky has settled. "Fret not, my princess, for your hippogryph daughter's wings will shine in the moon's light. She will become a great queen among her own people, as you will of yours—eventually. As for your keythong son, he will go on to be the king of the wingless. He will be a creature of great wisdom, and he will mate with a kryphon queen. They will produce many young, including some gryphons and opinici."

Sunsky is confused. *What in Gryphonia is Truth Speaker going on about? Perhaps she is mistaken. Perhaps she is having a bad day. Keythongs and kryphons do not mate! They do not bear young, hatched or live.*

The sterilization of keythongs and kryphons at birth is a legal requirement to ensure that the wingless do not become too numerous. This lesson has been repeated to Sunsky and other winged youngsters for centuries. The power dynamic must stay as it is, with gryphons and opinici ruling over keythongs and kryphons. Even when they ascend to the loftiest perch for their kind and earn the right to serve on the Council of Keythongs, the wingless ones are still not permitted the same rights as gryphons and opinici. *Is it not written within section five of the Gryphonic Code?*

"Calm, my dear. Calm," Truth Speaker whispers as Sunsky digests this strange information about her offspring.

In addition to the potent keythong, it seems that her two other offspring will be equally unconventional. What is she to make of the hippogryph queen, the one whose wings shine in the moonlight just as the wings of her son shimmer in the sunlight? According to the oracle, however, her prince will grow up without his mother!

"Please, oracle, I must know!" Sunsky cries in forlorn misery. "Am I to raise any of my progeny, or will I be thrown in prison for mating with a winged horse?"

Her own words shock her. She has never voiced her fateful action aloud to another gryphon before this.

"My dear," replies Truth Speaker, soothing Sunsky's feathers gently with her beak. "I know this must fill you with a deep and terrible loneliness, but you have a choice to make. Either you abandon your daughter to the hippogryphs of the valley, thereby retaining your right of ascension to the gryphonic throne, or you forego the privileges of your royal birth and live as a wing-grounded outcast, raising your daughter among the hippogryphs."

Sunsky stares at the oracle, speechless. She drops her head.

"What am I to do?" she wails. "Oh, Truth Speaker, I was a fool to mate with Nightsky!"

Truth Speaker unfolds a protective wing around Sunsky and sits with her as she cries long and bitter cawing sobs.

CHAPTER SIX

Gryphonic Heresy

Sunsky sits alone in the mouth of her cave. The sun shines down on her head, pouring warmth on her skin, penetrating through the soft down of her feathers. She lies still, listening to the steady beat of her heart. She has been resting in silence for most of the day. She knows that everyone is worried about her. They do not understand why she does not want a celebration. Her father, Sun Quest, is particularly puzzled.

She watches as he flies down onto the rock terrace below her chamber.

"Sunsky, my daughter!" he bellows. "Come to me."

Dutifully, Sunsky rouses herself. She knows she cannot sit still forever. Truth Speaker has bought her some time over the past few days, telling her family that she needs a home rest for spiritual reasons. Now, however, the time has come to tell her family the truth. She flies down to greet her father with dread in her heart.

"Hello, Father Sun Quest."

Sun Quest is in no mood for niceties today. "Tell me when, O daughter, we may celebrate your safe return and the upcoming birth of my royal grandson!"

Sunsky attempts to collect her thoughts. *Feel the beat of my heart*, she thinks feverishly.

"Come, my princess, my soon-to-be queen!" Sun Quest roars, leaving her no room to ponder. "Dreamspinner has been driving Mother Skystar and me insane with his continual screeching to see you. Why do you keep him from his queen and son? Surely, this spiritual rest must be over by now. Why does the oracle test our patience so?"

Sunsky hesitates to tell her father the truth. Should she tell Sun Quest now, or should she seek a private audience with her mother? If she tells him now, he will become hysterical. If she tells him later, however, he will also become hysterical. If she fails to tell him at all, he will be both heartbroken and hysterical when he finally finds out. For that matter, Dreamspinner will be even more heartbroken. *Dreamspinner! My dear would-be mate who can now never be my mate.* It is possible that she could keep from Dreamspinner the real reason that his love must be spurned, although she cannot keep it from Father Sun Quest. She knows she must tell him, but not without Mother Skystar present.

"O, my Father!" Sunsky says finally. "I have a terrible truth to tell you and Mother Skystar. You must bring her here to me. No other family members for now. My poor father, there can be no celebration for me."

"What madness is this?" Sun Quest booms. "No celebration for you at the upcoming birth of a prince? I will not have it! What is so *hippogryphin'* terrible that you cannot tell me without all this anxious trepidation?"

At Sun Quest's use of the gryphonic cuss-word "hippogry-phin'" Sunsky bursts into screeches, wails, hoots, and mournful caws. Sun Quest is startled and sings out his mateship song as a signal to his queen, Skystar, that she should come immediately. Within moments, Skystar has touched down onto her daughter's private terrace.

"Whatever is the matter, Sun Quest?" she asks worriedly. "Why is Sunsky so upset?"

"She has some terrible secret to tell us," Sun Quest replies, "some reason why we may not celebrate the upcoming birth."

Skystar lets out a cry.

"Oh, no!" she laments. "Don't tell me there is something wrong with our young prince? Some deformity, perhaps?"

Sunsky pauses to listen to her heart once again. She gathers all her strength, closing her eyes for a moment to center her thoughts and swirling emotions. She needs to confide in her parents. It is tearing her apart to live alone with this terrible secret.

"Mother Skystar, Father Sun Quest. My opinicus prince is not the reason for my pain, as he is of course a joy to me. I feel him kicking in my womb every so often, and I will be pleased to hand him over to you so that you might attend to his needs. I will not be able to raise him myself, but I would like to choose his name based on the words the oracle gave me. She said his wings would shine in the sun. Therefore, I give him the name *Sun Wing*."

"Excellent choice, my daughter!" Sun Quest agrees. "And if you want us to do so, we will be honored to raise him for you as you adjust and train for your upcoming role as premiere queen. Was this the terrible secret? I think you could easily perform both the queen and mother roles, but if you are concerned, Skystar and I will raise young Sun Wing. This, however, is no excuse to deprive us of a celebration in your honor!"

Skystar looks intently at her daughter. "No, Sun Quest, it's something else. Tell us please, Sunsky. Keep us no longer in suspense."

Sunsky waits a moment before she replies. "My parents. What I have to tell you will break your hearts, but say it I must. After I was grounded by the windstorm, a beautiful, black winged horse cared for me and brought me small animals to eat while my wing mended. Without his care, I would certainly have perished. And so, I mated with him to show my gratitude for his saving my life."

The two parents appear stunned and do not reply. Sunsky wishes they would scream at her or tear their claws into her—anything but this agonizing silence.

Finally, Skystar regains her speech. "This alone is not cause for great alarm, my daughter. Other than the oracle and us, it is wise to tell no one about the matter. Mating with these winged beasts is, well, not as rare as you might think. I myself had a chance encounter with one, and I was deeply enchanted with him. I might have continued the courtship, but Sun Quest drove him away."

Sun Quest's wings flutter nervously as he speaks. "Yes, I did indeed drive the monster from her, but I must admit that in my youth I also mated once or twice with the odd wingless mare. These kinds of indiscretions happen quite frequently, daughter. No need to go around screeching them to the mountain tops."

Now it is Sunsky's turn to stare in stunned silence. She never knew Skystar and Sun Quest had even entertained the idea of mating with a horse, let alone actually doing so!

"Listen, my dear," Sun Quest continues. "It happens to the best of us. We know how deeply honest you are, but a courtesy mating with a horse is not the worst you could do. I myself did far worse in my courtesy mating with the vicious gossip queen, Soundringer."

"Sun Quest!" Skystar rebukes him sharply. "I know Soundringer is a chore to deal with, but please don't compare her to a horse. Remember, you have a daughter with her."

"Please don't remind me of that spoiled young brat," Sun Quest laments ruefully. "Talona and her mother have been the bane of our existence. We must not let them know of this indiscretion of Sunsky's, for they would use it to wrestle the premiere queenship from her!"

Sunsky listens to her parents' banter with shocked horror. *They are not taking this at all seriously!*

"My parents!" she screeches, finally finding her voice. "You do not seem to understand. I can never be the premiere queen. I have a hippogryph egg within my pouch!"

Another stunned silence greets her admission, until Skystar once again finds her voice. "Sunsky, are you absolutely certain of this? Light Healer, the physician, said nothing about it!"

"Light Healer did not know," Sunsky replies. "The eggs were not mature enough to tell. She assumed, naturally, that they were both keythong eggs..."

"Then perhaps they are!" Sun Quest interrupts angrily. "Hippogryph hatchings are very rare. It is much more likely that the eggs are Dreamspinner's keythong sons or kryphon daughters. This... this... winged horse creature can surely not have impregnated any daughter of mine!"

"One of the eggs is Dreamspinner's—a keythong son who will mate with a kryphon and have many young—or at least that's what the oracle says," Sunsky explains. "She also says that the second egg contains a hippogryph who will grow up to be a queen among her kind."

Sun Quest and Skystar look at each other incredulously. They leave her side for a minute to confer with one another. Sunsky nervously awaits their answer.

After much muffled squawking between herself and her mate, Skystar comes to stand beside her daughter. "Sunsky, your father and I have been discussing this issue, and we both agree that it is most serious."

Sunsky bobs her head in assent. She needs no convincing to view the matter as serious.

"Father Sun Quest and I wish to accompany you to Light Healer's den. We must learn for certain the identity of the egg. You know how skeptical Sun Quest can be about spirit knowledge, even if it does come from the oracle."

"Yes, Mother," Sunsky agrees. "But I know that the oracle speaks the truth. I must either abandon the hippogryph or the premiere queenship."

"You cannot abandon the queenship, my princess," Skystar responds sharply. "No hippogryph is worth that much."

"But I must ensure her well-being!" Sunsky asserts, her heart aching for the young hatchling.

"Sunsky," Skystar whispers, drawing her daughter near to her. "It is gryphonic heresy."

"But what about you and Father mating with horses?" Sunsky retorts angrily. "Is that not also heresy?"

"Yes, of course, but we were lucky! Our matings did not result in offspring."

"Aha," Sunsky chides her saucily. "Then it is really only heresy if there is physical evidence of the deed."

Skystar screeches at her daughter and bats her with flapping wings, but she knows Sunsky is correct. The matriarch quiets at last and then concedes. "All right, all right. Now let's go to the healer with no more fuss."

Sun Quest and Skystar fly with their daughter to the physician's den, where Light Healer greets them. "Sun Quest and Skystar. Congratulations on the conception of your daughter's opinicus prince."

"Light Healer," Skystar whispers, dispensing with all niceties, "we come to you in the strictest of confidence. Please check Sunsky's eggs thoroughly. Tell us if they are healthy keythongs or not."

Light Healer, although puzzled by the request, senses the urgency in Skystar's voice and does as she is told. She bids Sunsky to sit on the examination table and uses her medical equipment to probe within the young gryphon's pouch as she examines more closely the contents of the two eggs. At once, she makes a rasping noise.

"What is it?" Skystar asks anxiously.

Sunsky does not need to ask what it is, because she already knows. Light Healer slowly confirms what the oracle already told her.

"One of your eggs contains a hippogryph," she says, checking her results again, "and one an ordinary keythong."

"Kill it!" Sun Quest commands angrily. "Destroy the hippogryph egg. This *creature* cannot compromise my daughter's future!"

To Sunsky's immense relief, Light Healer stands between her and the family patriarch.

"No, Sun Quest!" the physician screeches. "I am a healer of life, not a destroyer! As long as Sunsky remains in my healing den, I will not allow her eggs to be touched. Hippogryph or not, this is still a life, and it is my duty to protect it!"

Sun Quest screams his rage while Skystar attempts in vain to calm him.

"I will not let the egg be destroyed, Father Sun Quest!" Sunsky cries. "Light Healer is right."

Skystar urges Sun Quest to retreat with her from the healing den for a while. There is much squawking and screaming until the parents return at last, utterly dejected.

"Very well, Sunsky," Skystar says. "When the hippogryph is hatched, we will help you bring it to the Valley of Outcasts, where we will find another hippogryph to raise it for you."

A sinking feeling descends upon Sunsky, but she dares not tell her parents what is running through her mind.

CHAPTER SEVEN

Gryphonic Court

Skystar and Sun Quest try to keep the news about the hippogryph egg a secret, but inevitably, the rest of the community hears about it. It is virtually impossible to keep a secret within gryphonic society. For one thing, Light Healer is obligated to release to the Gryphonic Council the number and kind of life forms that each gryphon produces. It is the law, as all youngsters must be accounted for by the community and their educational path prepared for them, depending on whether they are born gryphon, opinicus, keythong, or kryphon. There are no plans made for a hippogryph, other than to abandon it in the Valley of Outcasts.

Light Healer delays as long as possible the release of information about the hippogryph egg because Soundringer, infamously known as the gossip queen, is a member of the Gryphonic Council. When the physician finally does relinquish the data, she makes a special request that the council keep it confidential. The other members agree, and all keep it to themselves—except, of course, for Soundringer. The queen of gossip feels it her duty to trumpet the news far and wide, to every mountain top and beyond, whether or not the community members want to know. The situation is now at a point where no one in the community can ignore it.

Soundringer can barely keep the glee out of her voice, greeting Skystar in mock concern whenever the council gathers for its daily business. "How is Sunsky today, Skystar my dear? She'll need to keep up her strength for the new addition!"

Skystar ignores her, and she does not tell Sunsky what a pest Soundringer is at the meetings. Sunsky remains sequestered in her den, awaiting the birth and hatchings. The oracle visits her regularly and encourages her to engage in silent meditation. Together, she and Truth Speaker listen to their hearts beat. At times, Sunsky can feel the hearts of her three offspring beating in unison.

The rhythm is soothing, calming. As the time passes, various members of her family come in to sit with her—Mountain Rain, Cloudhopper, Sun Quest, Skystar, and the kryphon nanny, Egglight—each in his or her own way offering unconditional love to her.

She cannot help but feel guilty for all she is putting them through. They all have such high hopes for her, yet the more she listens to her hippogryph daughter's heartbeat, the less she feels that she can ever abandon her to the Valley of Outcasts.

The oracle feels her hesitation in this area, but she is the only one to do so. The others all believe that Sunsky will do as she must to secure the premiere queenship. Truth Speaker offers her quiet support as Sunsky's determination to raise her daughter grows with every passing day. Still, she tells no one of her decision.

One afternoon, the elderly Heartsong, the current premiere queen and Sunsky's own grandmother, pays Sunsky a visit. She lies down beside her granddaughter and gazes at her for some time with compassionate eyes. Sunsky feels comforted.

"O, Granddaughter," Heartsong says at last. "I must know of your intentions."

These words catch Sunsky by surprise. She has not yet voiced her true intentions.

"Wh…what intentions, Grandmother Heartsong?" Sunsky falters, hesitant to tell her grandmother what she is planning to do.

Heartsong is silent for a while. "My granddaughter. I must know your intentions for the premiere queenship. If you do not choose to accept it, the next in waiting, your half-sister Talona, will."

Sunsky opens her beak in shock. Talona, her nasty nemesis from their younger days, is next in waiting! Sunsky has all but forgotten. If she gives up the queenship, many gryphons fear what the sulky, spoiled Talona and her mother Soundringer will do in such a powerful position.

Sunsky pauses, closing her eyes as she considers her position. Finally, she says to her grandmother, "O Queen Heartsong! My heart is torn. I wish to fulfill my commitment to the gryphonic community, but I fear that I cannot abandon my daughter."

Heartsong is quiet for a long time.

"I need to go back to the council and tell them that I sense hesitation," she states at last. "My granddaughter, I am devastated to tell you this, but the issue may need to be decided through Gryphonic Court. If it was solely a matter for my own decision, I would gladly give you the queenship and the right to raise your daughter within the gryphonic community. I must, however, listen to the views of others. I cannot make a unilateral decision about this. Do you understand?"

Sunsky nods mutely, astounded by her grandmother's generosity of spirit. *If she were to make the decision alone, she would allow the young hippogryph to live among gryphons with no loss of my queenship.* Sunsky can only marvel at this idea. *If only the Gryphonic Council would agree to such a just decision!* She knows her grandmother is sincere, but it is unlikely that even the elder's deep wisdom will persuade the others in the community. Sunsky gives Heartsong a gentle peck on her beak.

"Thank you, Grandmother Heartsong. I will follow my own heart's song."

Heartsong returns the beak peck and envelops her granddaughter in a loving, winged embrace.

The fateful day of decision dawns at last. After days of arguing, the Gryphonic Council summons her to appear before it in court to judge her fitness for the role of next in waiting to the Stone Throne and for the crime of conceiving a hippogryph chick. Due to the seriousness of the situation, the members of the wider gryphonic community will also witness the proceedings.

Sunsky trembles as she enters the crowded cave chamber of the Royal Gryphonic Court. She immediately hears jeering hisses from her half-sister, Talona. "My, how far the mighty one has fallen, Sister Sunsky!"

Sunsky glares at Talona but otherwise ignores her nasty nemesis.

I have bigger things to worry about than a bratty, spoiled gryphon princess, she thinks imperiously. She looks away from Talona and keeps her gaze trained upon her grandmother, who sits with dignity upon the Stone Throne. Heartsong's loyal king consort, the opinicus Lightning Bolt, stands with equal dignity beside the monarch. Surrounding the royal couple are her parents, Skystar and Sun Quest, along with Talona's mother, Soundringer, and seven other high-ranking gryphons. Sunsky shivers nervously, wondering how the council will respond to her.

No one utters a single peep as Sunsky waits, anxiety gnawing at her stomach, before the twelve councilors. Finally, after what seems an eternity, Heartsong addresses the crowd. "Members of the council and people of the wider community! We all know why we are here. I will not break hearts by screeching the crime to the skies, but I will acknowledge it: my own granddaughter, next in waiting to the Stone Throne, went astray amidst the furious mountain winds and mated with a winged horse."

The chamber is filled with witnesses from the community who are here to observe the court proceedings, and all ruffle their feathers uncomfortably. There is an uneasy silence as the throng awaits the queen's next statement.

Sunsky feels strangely calm, her heart beating in unison with her family members. She feels a deep connection with Grandmother Heartsong, the physician Light Healer, Egglight the kryphon nanny, the oracle, and with every gryphonic being attending the solemn assembly, including even Talona and Soundringer. She decides within her heart, if not her mind, that she will stay with her daughter in the Valley of Outcasts. She senses her own soul hovering above her as an ethereal presence, yet she remains grounded in her body. She is now at peace, having surrendered to her fate. She listens resolutely to Queen Heartsong.

"A hippogryph egg is the unfortunate result of the mating, and so my dear granddaughter, the gem of my soul, must make a terrible decision."

All eyes are now on Sunsky as the white-feathered old queen motions to her to approach the throne. Sunsky moves closer, her leonine body relaxed and her avian mind focused.

"Princess Sunsky, daughter of Skystar and Sun Quest. You are charged with gryphonic heresy because you mated with a winged horse and created offspring with him. Will you tell the court how you plead?"

Sunsky draws herself up proudly. She bows before the queen and says in a clear, booming voice, "O noble Queen Heartsong and honored members of the Gryphonic Council: I plead guilty to the charge of gryphonic heresy, for I did indeed mate with a winged horse and have willingly accepted his progeny as my own!"

A muffled chirping greets this announcement.

"Silence!" bellows Heartsong. "Let my granddaughter speak her piece. Do you have anything to declare before all of us, Sunsky, before the council begins its judicial process?"

Sunsky hastily rehearses a suitably tragic reply before she makes her declaration. "Yes, honored queen! I would first like to apologize to my immediate family, especially Mother Skystar and Father Sun Quest, and to you, Grandmother Heartsong and Grandfather Lightning Bolt. I also express my regret to the greater gryphonic community that I, through a thoughtless indiscretion, have forfeited my claim to the Stone Throne. I am no longer fit to be anyone's queen, and that includes my own cherished mate. I am so sorry, Dreamspinner, especially since I carry our young cub Sun Wing within my womb. I fear that I shall never know our prince."

An enraged screech arises from the crowd as the opinicus Dreamspinner lifts himself above the others and flies over to the spot where Sunsky is delivering her apologetic soliloquy.

"No, Sunsky!" he wails loudly. "No, my queen, I will have no other—only you! I care not one feather for the mating with a winged horse, nor do I care about the unhappy hippogryph. Let it hatch, and let it be cast away! Afterwards, you shall return to me, and I will be king to your queen. O, leave me not, cruel gryphon!"

Sunsky is angry with herself for not having spoken to Dreamspinner personally before coming to court, but she was so preoccupied with her decision. Although Father Sun Quest has likely spoken with Dreamspinner, it still must come as a shock to the poor young opinicus.

Grandmother Heartsong, however, will have none of Dreamspinner's lamentations. "Dreamspinner, son of Wing Dreamer and Windsinger! You are hereby banished from these proceedings for your unruly behavior. I call upon your father, Windsinger, and your stepmother, Stormspeaker, to account for your behavior and escort you back to your own den. There you will stay for the next three days."

Heartsong motions to Dreamspinner's parents to approach the throne. Father Windsinger flies forth and perches before the queen, but his mate Stormspeaker stays where she is. Instead, Thundercloud, the grandfather of Dreamspinner, joins his son and grandson.

Thundercloud nods to Windsinger, as if authorizing his son to speak on his behalf.

"O, Queen Heartsong! We do not wish to defy you, but my father and I have raised Dreamspinner, rather than my second mate Stormspeaker. I wish to spare her the embarrassment of this moment, since it is Thundercloud and I who are at fault for Dreamspinner's unruly behavior. We confess that we have raised him without the guiding wing of a mother gryphon. My original mate, Wing Dreamer, was not there to raise young Dreamspinner; and my next mate, Stormspeaker, naturally did not wish to raise an opinicus that was not hers. I am heartily sorry to have ignored the law, O Queen!"

The assembled throng cackles its surprise and horror at this second heresy as Queen Heartsong flaps her wings in rage. "It is against the Gryphonic Code to raise any winged young one with no gryphon present to guide the process! Two opinici may *not* take on the sacred task of raising a prince. Your rash deed forces me to uphold the law and confine you all to your dens until further notice."

Windsinger hangs his head in obedience to the queen, but Dreamspinner and Thundercloud stare back at her defiantly. "I refuse to leave, my queen!" Dreamspinner squawks childishly, as Thundercloud administers a stern peck on the head to remind him of his place.

"Queen Heartsong and King Lightning Bolt," the elderly opinicus says. "I, Thundercloud, admit my wrongdoing, but I believe it was for the right reasons. My son's first mate, the biological mother of Dreamspinner, was banished to the Valley of Outcasts. You may remember that she was expelled for the same crime of which young Sunsky is guilty. Wing Dreamer was not brought before a court as her rank was too low, but she disgraced our family nonetheless. Her treacherous deed so enraged me that I declared soundly: *no gryphon shall raise my grandson, Dreamspinner!* I declare the same for my great-grandson, the unborn cub of Sunsky. I demand the right, along with my son and grandson, to raise young Sun Wing! He must be free of the horse-tainted gryphon that begat him, and that includes her horse-loving parents as well."

Sunsky's heart freezes as terror grips her. *Dreamspinner's biological mother was banished for hatching a hippogryph? Dreamspinner never mentioned this!*

Queen Heartsong glares at the rebellious old Thundercloud, while Father Sun Quest and Grandfather Lightning Bolt forget their places on the council and fly at Thundercloud furiously. They tear his grey body with their claws, plucking his head feathers out with their beaks. "Our prince will not be taken away from us!" cries Sun Quest. "How dare you insult my daughter and our family? Thundercloud, you impudent brute!"

The throng thrashes about in a madcap manner, some yowling for calm, others roaring their support for Sun Quest's family, and still others shrieking their support for Thundercloud and his clan. Heartsong surveys the insanity while Sunsky sits forlornly in the middle of the melee, cawing at her father and grandfather to stop attacking Thundercloud. Dreamspinner joins her by screaming at his own guardians as they strike back at the other two opinici.

A piercing, ear-splitting screech echoes authoritatively across the chamber, and the fighting stops immediately. The throng falls silent as Heartsong takes wing, flying first at her mate

Lightning Bolt and then at Sun Quest, chasing them back to their places while giving each of them a sound nip on their tails.

"Have you forgotten that you are councilors?" Heartsong says menacingly. "Step into line, both of you!" Sun Quest and Lightning Bolt obey her sheepishly. She turns her attention to Thundercloud, her anger hidden behind her steely gaze. "You and your family have disrupted these proceedings. I apologize for the behavior of my mate and my daughter's mate, but it does not diminish the arrogance and rudeness with which you spoke. I intend to satisfy none of your demands without the permission of Sunsky, the mother of the opiniclet prince in question."

"Excuse me, Great Queen!" Thundercloud explodes, barely concealing his contempt. "If Sunsky is to be banished, my family gets first claim to the baby prince."

Heartsong flies at him angrily but avoids nipping him. "Because of your age, Thundercloud, I will not punish you physically. You, however, are in contempt of this court. You and your entire clan are henceforth excluded. The council will decide whether Sunsky is to be banished, not you. Now go, before I tear each of you impudent thugs to shreds with my talons!"

Thundercloud beats his wings in warning. "If you do not banish her, Heartsong, I shall issue a charge of nepotism against your family. It is the opinici who must raise royal princes, not gryphons!"

Thundercloud takes wing in a fury, leaving the council to soar above the crowds into the sky. Windsinger and his mate Stormspeaker follow him, hustling the reluctant Dreamspinner away from the court to be imprisoned in his own den.

Heartsong bellows to the crowd, "Now, let me address you on the subject of who should raise opiniclet princes: It is mandatory that *both* a gryphon *and* an opinicus are present for the rearing of *any* young winged one, gryphlet or opiniclet. As long as I am queen, that rule stands, and it is reinforced by section three of the Gryphonic Code."

A cheering cacophony greets Heartsong's words, providing proof that the old queen has not lost her authority. "I hereby declare that the two older opinici, Windsinger and Thundercloud, are to be restricted to their dens as an example to young Dreamspinner. He disrupted out of youthful innocence, whereas the other two ought to have known better. In order not to be guilty of the charge of favoritism, I also declare that my mate, Lightning Bolt, and my daughter's mate, Sun Quest, are to be similarly confined to their quarters until after the court proceedings are finished."

A murmur of approval ripples through the crowd, prompting Lightning Bolt and Sun Quest to bow their heads in obeisance and depart from the court. There is, however, one lone squawk of disapproval from Soundringer as she lifts her right wing in a gesture of respect for the queen. "Noble Queen! May I speak?"

Heartsong bobs her head, giving the gossip queen permission to speak. Soundringer bows to the monarch in an exaggerated manner. "Your Royal Greatness! I believe, begging your pardon, Lightning Bolt and Sun Quest should be permanently excluded from this council. They have reflected their bias in this matter and have shown by their aggressive behavior toward poor Thundercloud that they do not deserve to be on this council."

Heartsong closes her eyes for a moment. Sunsky taps her talons on the stone floor nervously. She knows that her grandmother insists upon fairness. The crowd cries at Soundringer to perch and keep her beak shut, but she does not stand down. She stands before the crowd eyeing them with an icy, challenging glare.

"Silence!" Heartsong shouts above the din. "I am afraid that Councilor Soundringer is correct. I give you my apologies for not acting in fairness. My gratitude to you, Councilor Soundringer."

Soundringer puffs out her breast in pride, gaining confidence as she replies to the queen. "O, Your Greatness, I was only doing my duty. If I may, my queen, I would also like to suggest the replacements..."

"No!" Heartsong cuts her off. "You are not bias-free yourself, dear Councilor! The decision on who shall replace these two shall be given to the oracle."

Truth Speaker steps forward to address her. "My queen. Because these four excluded opinici have departed the council chambers, there are no other winged males with the required experience and rank. According to council rules, however, there must be at least two males on the Council of Twelve. Therefore, we must choose two males from the Council of Keythongs."

The crowd rustles its feathers collectively in surprise. Keythongs on the Gryphonic Council? None has ever heard of it! It sounds to many of them like a third heresy.

CHAPTER EIGHT

The Third Heresy

After a short recess, the court reconvenes. Sunsky hears many muffled chirps among the other gryphons that Truth Speaker must have lost her mind. Keythongs on the Gryphonic Council? Surely, Heartsong will not allow it.

Heartsong does allow it. She is not alone in her approval of this decision; Soundringer enthusiastically and somewhat oddly supports her. Sunsky feels some trepidation about the support of the gossip queen. She knows that Soundringer has a number of keythong brothers and sons on the Council of Keythongs, the most influential of whom is her elder brother, a councilor named Mudstone. Will Soundringer make behind the scenes power plays to replace Councilors Sun Quest and Lightning Bolt with two keythong brothers loyal to their overly talkative sister?

Sunsky shivers before remembering, as always, to consult the wisdom of her heart. The oracle's voice speaks softly inside: *Let go. Let go of any need to control these proceedings. Let the process continue as it is, without judging it good or bad.*

It is difficult, Sunsky realizes, *but I must keep calm and return to the center of my soul whenever anxiety threatens to overwhelm me.* As she travels deep within herself, the windstorm of worry in her mind quiets to a gentle breeze. She sends a silent prayer of hope into the skies for Dreamspinner and his excluded family, together with her dear father and grandfather, both of whom have lost their places on the council defending her honor. Sunsky feels a momentary stab of guilt but lets it pass.

A respectful silence falls over the throng of gryphonic beings assembled in the court. Members of the Council of Keythongs are also present, lying respectfully apart from the assembled winged beings who are their social superiors.

Heartsong addresses the assembly. "Honored members of our community, both winged and wingless. Today there was an unfortunate incident of violence as we gathered here this morning to judge my granddaughter. I trust no more such incidents will occur. Because of the delicate nature of the council appointments, the next two males to join the council must be keythongs. To ensure minimal bias, I have asked our respected oracle to make the appointments. Truth Speaker." Heartsong motions for the oracle to come to the front of the chamber.

Truth Speaker proceeds quietly to the front and then surveys the expectant crowd for a moment. "I, Truth Speaker, have been asked to appoint two keythongs to the council. To be fair, I must appoint one keythong from Heartsong's line and one from Soundringer's. Therefore, I call the two most experienced individuals to the Gryphonic Council for purposes of this deliberation. I call upon Mudstone, the elder brother of Soundringer; and Ground Paw, the son of Heartsong and Lightning Bolt."

Truth Speaker steps down from the stage as the two distinguished keythong councilors step up. Both Mudstone and Ground Paw genuflect in front of the oracle as they ascend the steps, bow a second time to Queen Heartsong, and yet a third time to the assembled gryphons and opinici. Heartsong returns their gracious gesture. "Welcome, Councilors. You have been briefed as to the reason the keythongs have been called in?"

"Yes, most high and distinguished queen," Ground Paw replies.

Mudstone says nothing but nods to the queen and his sister. Soundringer eyes him approvingly as the two wingless beings join the Gryphonic Council, each taking a place at either end of the semi-circle of gryphons.

"Now then," Heartsong declares. "Let's waste no more time. Sunsky, step forward, please." Sunsky feels a momentary flutter of panic in her stomach but lets it go as best she can. She steps up to the center stage before her regal grandmother. "Sunsky, the council has heard your apologies to your family and the community. Is there anything else that you wish to say before the judicial process begins?"

"Only that my intention for my baby hippogryph is to raise her myself. I cannot abandon her to the Valley of Outcasts."

A horrified pause greets this announcement. Skystar looks directly at Sunsky with her beak open, obviously wanting to speak but knowing that she cannot interrupt the proceedings again if she wishes to remain on the council. Sunsky returns her gaze in an attempt to convey reassurance to her mother, but it does not work. Skystar ruffles her feathers in agitation.

"I see," Heartsong replies, unflinchingly. "Is there anything else, Sunsky?"

"No, Queen Heartsong."

"Very well," the old queen concludes, permitting a touch of sorrow to enter into her words. "Since you have decided to raise your hippogryph daughter, then I'm afraid that ascension to the throne is impossible."

Skystar shrieks at this pronouncement. "No, Mother Heartsong! Please, do not allow this. It is not an option, you know that!"

Heartsong bestows upon her daughter a severe gaze. "You are out of turn, daughter! Do not make me remove you as I have done with your mate and mine."

Skystar looks in desperation to Sunsky, who can only stare back helplessly. Soundringer takes advantage of the situation and eagerly raises her right wing. Skystar glares at her, but the queen gives her the stage. "My fellow gryphons, you have all heard Sunsky's intentions. She will throw away the queenship in order to raise a *hippogryph*. She is not fit to reign!"

An angry howl greets Soundringer's words, but she is unmoved. "I'm sorry, but I'm afraid I must be the one to stand up and tell you the things that you don't want to hear. Let us waste no more time on this farce of a trial, but let us vote now to banish Sunsky and clip her wings. Let the miscreant raise her daughter in the Valley of Outcasts. This is the only sane response to such an insane intention. I also move that my daughter Talona, the next in waiting, be readied for the reign in Sunsky's place."

The cacophony that follows her statement is enraged and hostile. Heartsong yells for peace before earnestly addressing her granddaughter. "Sunsky, will you not change this rash decision? You are the next in line to the throne. Are you sure you want to give up this most important duty?"

Sunsky hangs her head momentarily and then brings it up again to state, with as much courage as she can muster, "I bow to my rival, Talona. Let her take over my reign when the time comes."

A great victorious whoop erupts from Talona and her family, and Soundringer barely manages to contain her delight.

"Very well," Heartsong replies gruffly. "Then you leave me no other choice. The vote is on whether or not to banish Sunsky. Are there any defenders?"

Skystar steps forward, raising her right wing. "Please, Heartsong, my queen and mother! Order Sunsky to do the right thing. Only you have the power to do so!"

"That would be an abuse of my power," Heartsong counters. "Sunsky has the right to make her own decision—section four of the Gryphonic Code reinforces this."

"Oh, blast the Gryphonic Code!" Skystar screams. "Sunsky, my daughter, don't do this to us. Don't do this to your own people, who put their trust and faith in you!"

"Mother Skystar!" Sunsky replies, forgetting to ask the queen for permission to speak. "Before I am worthy to reign over other gryphons, I must first protect my chicks. Section seven of the Gryphonic Code says so."

At once, a heated debate arises among the ten gryphons on the council as to the interpretation of the seventh section of the Gryphonic Code, for nowhere does it mention hippogryph chicks. The two keythongs, Mudstone and Ground Paw, remain silent in the midst of the arguments. Finally, Heartsong calls the debate to a halt. "Enough! My granddaughter has the right to protect her own offspring, no matter what form it takes."

"But, Mother Heartsong!" Skystar objects, neglecting to address her properly. "Sunsky can ensure the safety of her hippogryph daughter by handing her over to another hippogryph to be raised! Would that not be better for a hippogryph chick, to be raised by its own people?"

"Sunsky *is* this hippogryph's only family," Heartsong answers. "The hippogryphs do not usually adopt castaways. I have learned this recently from my keythong son, Ground Paw, who knows more about hippogryphs than any of us. Is that not so, Ground Paw, the son of my egg clutch?"

Ground Paw stands, his gray body glistening with experience, his avian head cocked to one side. He bows to the queen. "O Queen Heartsong, mother of the egg out of which I have sprung. It is true what you have said about the hippogryphs. I have occasionally dealt with them to negotiate the boundaries of their territory and ours. They are most suspicious of outsiders and might care for a young hippogryph left alone in the valley, or they might not. One never knows with these beasts."

"What, based on your knowledge of the creatures, is the best thing for Sunsky to do to ensure her daughter's survival?"

"O, Queen," Ground Paw answers. "I, the Wingless One, stand ready to serve the winged. My own belief is that it would be best if Princess Sunsky, O blessed niece of my heart, was to give her daughter over to the hippogryph queen named Night Lover so that she may love and raise the chick. I have reason to believe that Sunsky's chick and this one called Night Lover share the same father."

Squawks of surprise from the assembly greet this piece of news. Sunsky's heart leaps. *Does my keythong uncle, Ground Paw, know Nightsky? Should I give my chick over to this Night Lover?*

Sunsky raises her right wing to ask a question. As Heartsong nods to her, Sunsky cries, a little too excitedly, "Ground Paw, my uncle! Tell me, who is Night Lover's mother? Does she inhabit the Valley of Outcasts?"

Ground Paw appears startled. He is accustomed to orderly proceedings, but this has been anything but orderly. He responds to his niece in a shaky voice. "Princess Sunsky, I fear to name the mother but since you ask, I am bound by honesty to tell you. I must inform the council that Night Lover is the daughter of Wing Dreamer. She is the same gryphon whom Thundercloud named earlier during his shocking outburst. He ruthlessly banished her to the Valley of Outcasts for bearing the offspring of a dark, winged stallion known as Nightsky."

Sunsky's heart leaps up at the mention of Nightsky's name. *Wing Dreamer, the mother of Night Lover, is also Dreamspinner's mother! The same whom Thundercloud banished for mating with a winged horse.*

"O, my Uncle Ground Paw!" Sunsky interjects. "Night Lover is then the half-sister of my hippogryph chick, she whom I name Moon Wing, to compliment her opiniclet brother Sun Wing."

Caws burst forth from the crowd in response to Sunsky's words, but this time not all voices are approving. Soundringer raises her right wing and barely gives the old queen time to nod her assent before she jumps into the conversation. "Moon Wing! The sister of Night Lover and the daughter of Sunsky and Nightsky. My dear, I am getting confused. Sister gryphons, to what low place have we sunk as a society when we speak the names of hippogryphs as though they were gryphons themselves? There can be no more of this. You all know we cannot let this stand. If Sunsky is not punished for her willful act of disobedience, other young gryphons will also get it into their heads to mate with this horrid equine being, Nightsky. Let us vote now to banish Sunsky for the crime of equinophelia!"

A few cheering hoots are heard among those jeering at Soundringer, a sign that the throng is losing its sympathy for Sunsky. She bows her head to the good opinion of the community. *Let them banish me, for I am ready. I will not abandon my newly named daughter, Moon Wing. But what of my prince, Sun Wing? Will Windsinger and Thundercloud raise him with no gryphonic authority present, as the oracle predicted?*

"We have not yet heard from the other keythong, my brother Mudstone," Soundringer calls out, refusing to let up. "Mudstone, what say you about the traitor Sunsky and her progeny?"

Heartsong glares at Soundringer for her impudence, but she motions for Mudstone to speak. "Your opinion, Mudstone? Should Sunsky leave her daughter with Night Lover to raise, as your fellow councilor Ground Paw has advised?"

Mudstone stands and bows respectfully to the gryphons. "My queen and my gryphon sister, Soundringer. It is my opinion that Night Lover will have no particular interest in raising her infant half-sister. Hippogryphs, like the horses that begat them, are selfish beasts. They know nothing of service to the community. I believe that Sunsky's chick, Moon Wing, will survive only if Sunsky is there to defend her."

Trills, cackles, chirps, and wails greet Mudstone's pronouncement, but the keythong stands proud, staring iron-eyed at the throng.

Sunsky is angry at Mudstone's supercilious attitude. What does he know of horses or hippogryphs? His judgments certainly do not describe Nightsky. Nonetheless, the keythong seems to be siding with her on the idea of raising Moon Wing in the Valley of Outcasts. Sunsky puts away any thoughts of what might happen in the future and tries to focus only on the present.

"Granddaughter," Heartsong calls. "We have heard the opinions of the two grounded ones who know the hippogryphs best. Now, I give you one last chance. What say you? State your intentions clearly, for it will affect the outcome of this trial and your future role as premiere queen."

Sunsky stands, her heart pounding furiously. She listens quietly to its beat until she feels inner tranquility. She is full of sadness for what she must do to her family and full of joy at the decision she has made on behalf of her daughter. "O, Blessed Queen, I have come to a difficult decision of the heart. Since there is no one who can ensure my daughter's survival, I must be the one to care for her. I know this excludes me from the premiere queenship and possibly even my own society, but this is the choice I make."

Heartsong gazes at Sunsky in a manner that is both sad and compassionate. She sits in silence for what seems an eternal moment. Finally, she steps down from the throne and wraps her large, graying wings around her granddaughter. Mother Skystar joins the embrace, and Sunsky feels their love blazing into her soul.

Heartsong disengages from the pair and slowly returns to the Stone Throne. In a weary, heart-broken tone, she announces to the council and the surrounding community: "Sunsky, the daughter of Skystar and Sun Quest, has made her decision. She has renounced the throne."

A heavy, sullen mood descends upon the throng. No caws, jeers, cheers, or feather ruffling greet Heartsong's words, only an empty lull. Soundringer holds her wing up to speak, but Heartsong quiets her with a glare. "I would like to remind my people and my council that I am not dead yet. I shall remain in my position as premiere queen while Talona, the next in waiting, prepares herself. I will be fully involved in her training until the event of my death."

The monarch looks sternly at Soundringer, who bows, her eyes glinting with an air of poorly concealed mockery. She holds her wing up again, and this time Heartsong allows the councilor to make a triumphant announcement. "My Queen, I welcome your help in my daughter Talona's training. I would also like to invite all of you to a special celebration in Talona's honor. The next in waiting must be celebrated!"

A deathly hush greets Soundringer's invitation. Sunsky cannot see, but she can feel Talona's jeering, jealous gaze burning into her. She moves closer to Mother Skystar, who puts a protective wing around her. Sunsky realizes the enormity of what she has just done and how many gryphonic beings she has let down. She closes her eyes as she hears her grandmother's response. "Soundringer, I understand your joy at your daughter's appointment; however, any announcement regarding a celebration of Talona's new responsibilities must wait. The council has another unhappy duty to perform. We must decide whether or not to banish my granddaughter Sunsky and my great-granddaughter Moon Wing to the Valley of Outcasts."

Sunsky burrows herself deep into Mother Skystar's breast as the pair envelops each other in their own soft, feathery wings.

CHAPTER NINE

Between Ground and Sky

Sunsky and her sisters sit quietly in the darkened family den of Skystar and Sun Quest. Their father has been restricted to his den for the duration of the council meeting. Mountain Rain and Cloudhopper have each taken turns bringing him food and cheer, but he refuses. The two gryphon sisters reluctantly comply, leaving Sun Quest alone with his dark mood as they await Skystar's return from the council chamber. Sunsky wishes that she could say something to lighten the hearts of her two sisters, but nothing comes to mind except worrisome questions. *Will they banish me? Will this be the last time that I will be with my family?* As if in answer, Mountain Rain and Cloudhopper gently caress her leonine body with their beaks and wings.

The beleaguered young mother feels her heart divide into two pieces. While one half languishes in deep grief at the prospect of losing her family, the other leaps in deep joy at the thought of raising Moon Wing. As she considers her choice, many questions nag her mind. *Will the hippogryphs accept us? If not, our only alternative will be to leave the valley and go in search of Nightsky. But where in Gryphonia will I find him? I only met him by chance after the winds deposited me in the lower mountains. The likelihood of finding the exact area is nil, not to mention the foolishness of traveling with young in my pouch. Will I simply make do with being an outcast among outcasts? I suppose I must, if Moon Wing is to have any chance of survival.*

"Sunsky! Are you listening to me?" Mountain Rain's voice intrudes upon her reverie.

"Er... sorry, Rain. I was just thinking."

"Obviously," Mountain Rain replies in irritation. "Sunsky, you've got to stop thinking about this and start dealing with it. Are you sure you want to go to the Valley of Outcasts? It's still not too late to change your mind. Cloudhopper and I will go with you to find this Night Lover character and you can just give her the unhatched egg. She'll know what to do with it more than you will. You can send us right now to the council, to give word of your new intentions. We can speak on your behalf, apologize to the council..."

"No!" Sunsky answers decisively. "I am going to the Valley of Outcasts, just as soon as Sun Wing is born. I shall leave him with Mother Skystar, if the council agrees. If not, I shall give him to Dreamspinner and his family, although he will no doubt be raised only by Thundercloud and Windsinger."

Cloudhopper squeals. "Oh, Sunsky! How can you be so cruel to your own little son?"

"It's far crueler to abandon Moon Wing to the blasted valley. If she has to go there, then so do I. Besides, Dreamspinner and his family have the right to raise Sun Wing, especially after all the devastation I have caused them."

Cloudhopper coos mournfully in response, but Mountain Rain glares at her sister.

"What about the devastation you are causing our family, Sunsky? Or does that enter into your *hippogryphin'* mind at all?"

Sunsky beats her wings in rage and attacks her sister. The two gryphons fly at each other, screeching and ripping each other's feathers out. Cloudhopper tries in vain to separate the pair by placing herself between them, but they roughly push her out of the way. When at last the melee subsides of its own accord, the sisters fall exhausted onto the den floor and close their eyes.

She awakens to find her mother prodding her. She glances at Mountain Rain, whose bare patches of skin betray the fact that Sunsky savagely ripped the feathers from her own sister. She realizes that she must appear in the same ragged fashion to Mother Skystar, who regards them in stern silence. Sunsky feels a heavy sense of shame descend upon her.

Skystar puts a wing around each of the sisters and draws them near to her. Cloudhopper moves into the circle as well, and the four gryphons sit quietly for a while before the matriarch informs them of what took place at the council meeting. "My daughters, the council has come to a decision. I fought hard against it, but in the end the idea of a hippogryph being raised among us was too much for most gryphons. The vote favored banishing our Sunsky to the Valley of Outcasts and clipping her wings."

"But why clip her wings?" Cloudhopper asks. "She will need her wings in the valley to escape predators, such as mountain lions and gargoyles!"

"I know, Cloudhopper, my gentlest daughter," Skystar replies softly. "It is senseless, but Soundringer would not let it go and she convinced the others of its necessity. Grandmother Heartsong and I, however, managed to insert a few stipulations.

First, I will be the one to clip Sunsky's wings, and no one else. Second, Sunsky will not be leaving home until she gives birth to Sun Wing. Light Healer says that the live birth should occur before the two eggs hatch, and we argued that Sun Wing must be born here in the mountains. The council agreed with us, although after deliberating for some time, they decided that Dreamspinner's family should raise Sun Wing. We are to surrender him to Windsinger and his mate, Stormspeaker, immediately upon birth."

Sunsky's heart sinks, but she knows that this is inevitable. "The oracle told me that Sun Wing would be raised by two opinici and that there would be two gryphons involved, but only marginally."

"I believe the oracle is correct," Skystar confirms. "I managed to secure for myself visitations with Sun Wing; but my mate, Sun Quest, and Heartsong's mate, Lightning Bolt, are barred from ever visiting him. In addition, I am forbidden to speak to Sun Wing about his mother or her family."

Sunsky's sides heave at this terrible news. *Will Sun Wing be raised with no gryphon fully participating in the process of his education?*

"Wait!" Mountain Rain cries. "How can they do this to us? Are they not breaking the Gryphonic Code by allowing two opinici to raise Sun Wing?"

"I know your outrage, Rain, my outspoken daughter," Skystar replies wearily. "Officially, it is Windsinger's mate, Stormspeaker, who will participate in raising the young prince, not Thundercloud."

Mountain Rain cackles mirthlessly. "Stormspeaker! Everyone knows that she will not nurture a cub which is not hers! Surely, the council knows that it will be arrogant old Thundercloud who will raise our prince, along with his spineless son, Windsinger! Sun Wing will grow into a squawking mess, like Dreamspinner."

Sunsky snaps her beak at Mountain Rain for insulting Dreamspinner and his family, but she knows that her sister is essentially correct. *Dreamspinner will be pushed away from any involvement in Sun Wing's education by his aggressive father and his even more aggressive grandfather. No wonder poor Dreamspinner is a squawking mess! Thanks to me, my mate will also be a laughing stock in his own society. If only he could attach himself to another gryphon.*

"Mountain Rain!" Sunsky exclaims suddenly, startling them. "You must take Dreamspinner as your official mate. Train him how to behave properly, so that his grandfather and others will take him seriously. With you as his mate, Dreamspinner might be able to challenge his father's claim to the prince, and you could both raise Sun Wing!"

Mountain Rain beats her wings in rage as she offers her retort. "I have no power, my sister! Our family, in case you haven't noticed, has been disgraced by your actions. Even if Dreamspinner was willing to take me as his first mate, which he clearly isn't—he insists upon you—I would never be given permission to raise Sun Wing because my rank is too low. My birth was never slated by the oracle for queenship, any more than that of our sister Cloudhopper. You are nothing but a foolish dreamer, Sunsky. Unfortunately, your folly has ruined our family."

Sunsky bows her head to her sister, defeated. Skystar chirps an angry warning to Mountain Rain, and the young gryphon relents, speaking more softly this time. "Sunsky, I'm sorry. My words to you have been harsh."

"No," she replies, "you are right, Mountain Rain. I no longer deserve to be a member of this family. After Sun Wing is born I shall go to the Valley of Outcasts and trouble you no more."

Mountain Rain loses her patience and squawks, infuriated at the statement. "No, Sister Sunsky! You will always be a part of this family, no matter what idiotic thing you do. You won't get rid of us this easily, you know. Cloudhopper and I will visit you in the valley to make sure you are all right."

This time, it is Sunsky's turn to squawk in fury. "No! You will *not* visit me and put your own futures at risk. You will disown me and secure your own positions in gryphonic society."

Mountain Rain screeches in reply, letting forth a volley of gryphonic cuss words.

"*Silence!*" Skystar screams. "There will be no more fighting between you. I will visit Sunsky and no one else. The council has given me its reluctant permission to do so, as long as I am discreet. I also need to inform you of another piece of sad news: Grandmother Heartsong, as long as she remains in the position of premiere queen, is forbidden to have contact with any of us. An exception has been made for me, while I am in my official capacity on the council. Unfortunately, your father has lost his position on the council permanently."

All three young gryphons screech in protest, but they know there is nothing they can do about any of it. If Grandmother Heartsong is to remain in power, she will be forced to shun them, and that means the wider gryphonic community will follow suit.

"Oh, we might as well all go to the Valley of Outcasts!" Cloudhopper laments ruefully. "We will have more friends among the hippogryphs!"

No one bothers to screech at this piece of blasphemy. A feeling of defeat dwells within them all, and they huddle close together.

When the fateful day finally arrives and Sunsky gives birth to Sun Wing inside Light Healer's den, she is permitted at least one precious gaze at her infant son. Light Healer has cleansed him of afterbirth and he sits, beautiful and innocent, on his leonine haunches. He makes a cawing noise, infantile and rasping, as his tiny wings flutter. A ray of sunlight penetrates through the window of the healer's den and settles on the baby opiniclet's wings. Sunsky coos at her son in delight, forgetting for the moment her status as a pariah. The little one immediately toddles over to her, his beak reaching up to hers to be fed. In an instant, the tiny being is snatched away by an impatient old opinicus. Thundercloud has been waiting outside the den all day, refusing to give up his prize.

"Thundercloud, be careful," Light Healer warns, but he ignores her. He holds Sun Wing in his strong beak by the scruff of his neck. The gray-winged opinicus departs, flying into the distance with the tiny miracle. Sunsky lets out an inconsolable cry as her heart breaks. She is joined in the lament by her sisters and mother.

After giving the family a respectful distance so that they might grieve, Light Healer returns to the healing den offering words of comfort. "Sunsky, Skystar, Mountain Rain, and Cloudhopper. I want you to know that I will be checking on young Sun Wing's progress. It is my duty as a physician, so Thundercloud cannot refuse me. I will do my utmost to make sure that this young one receives the proper nurturing."

The young gryphons nod their thanks to Light Healer, too saddened to respond verbally. Skystar puts their feelings into words. "Our gratitude to you, Light Healer, is eternal. You have been more than kind and respectful of us throughout this difficult process. I too will be checking on Sun Wing periodically, and I will be reporting to Sunsky on his condition."

Light Healer lowers her voice to a whisper. "Listen, Sunsky. If Sun Wing is not being properly cared for, I can issue an order for him to be returned to Skystar and her family."

"That won't be necessary," Sunsky says sorrowfully. "Thundercloud and Windsinger have experience raising opiniclets. They will neglect nothing."

"But if the gryphon Stormspeaker is not involved in Sun Wing's education as a full participant," Light Healer says, pressing her point, "the Gryphonic Code is very clear. There must be a gryphon fully involved in the raising of young winged ones, as well as one opinicus."

"No," Sunsky states flatly. "It will be too confusing for young Sun Wing if a great feud erupts between two families over his custody. Thundercloud will not give him up without a fight and that will destroy us all, including Sun Wing. I cannot allow that to happen. Besides, the oracle foretold that Sun Wing would be raised by two opinici."

Light Healer shakes her head in response. "The oracle's words are not written in stone. These prophecies can be changed."

"No," Sunsky replies firmly. "We must learn to live with this sorrow, for Sun Wing's sake." She knows by the pained, wordless look in her mother's eyes that she will abide by her wishes, no matter how painful it might be to do so.

"Well," Light Healer says after a period of silence, "I am going to extend your stay at the healing den. The loss of your son has been traumatic, and I believe that you are in no shape to travel to the valley today."

Sunsky staggers to her feet in protest. "No, the council's order was clear. I am to go to the valley immediately after the birth. Besides, I must arrive there before Moon Wing hatches. She is not safe within gryphonic society."

Light Healer growls in protest. "I will protect her, Sunsky. You cannot travel in your present condition. I have checked the eggs. They will not hatch for at least another few days. You have time to rest, at least one more day."

There is a chorus of agreement from Sunsky's sisters. Light Healer adds, "There is one more important duty that you must perform for your offspring. Have you forgotten Dreamspinner's keythong son, the second egg? It will most probably hatch before the hippogryph does. You must have him sterilized and handed over to your keythong uncle, Ground Paw, for training as an eventual servant councilor."

Sunsky's heart experiences another painful stab. *No*, she thinks, *I have already given up one son. I will not give up another.* She remembers the oracle's prediction for her keythong son: *He will become a king and will mate with a kryphon, who will bear many young.* She knows that she cannot yet speak this blasphemy, so she replies, "Yes, Light Healer, of course. I will speak with Uncle Ground Paw before I leave."

Light Healer and her sisters persuade her to stay at the healing den for one more day. She fervently hopes her wingless son does not hatch during this time. At Light Healer's request, Ground Paw the keythong councilor is summoned to the healing den, where he bows to Skystar and her daughters.

"Sister Skystar," Ground Paw greets the gryphons, "my blessed nieces, Sunsky, Mountain Rain, and Cloudhopper. I, Ground Paw, the Wingless One, am at your service."

Sunsky, startled at her keythong uncle's arrival, asks her family to leave so that she may have a private audience with Ground Paw. Skystar looks at her daughter suspiciously, but she grants the request and motions the two sisters to follow her out of the den onto the outer terrace.

Ground Paw appears flabbergasted by Sunsky's request. Never has he been in her presence alone, nor has she been in his. As he waits for her to address him, Sunsky feels sorry for the old councilor. This is bound to be a shock to his system of rules, obedience, and service; yet Sunsky knows this may be her only chance to keep her second son.

"Ground Paw, my uncle," she says softly. "First of all, I must ask you to keep all that I tell you confidential. According to the Gryphonic Code, I am allowed certain stipulations regarding my keythong son."

Ground Paw is mute for a moment and when he speaks, his voice is trembling with terror. "Surely, my niece, you will not order the young keythong destroyed, just as he is about to hatch?"

Sunsky is horrified that Ground Paw thinks that she would destroy her own young. She then realizes that he is referring to an ancient clause in the Gryphonic Code that permits gryphons to destroy their keythong eggs if they are becoming too numerous, but only during the early stages of formation.

"No!" Sunsky responds. "You don't understand. I wish to

keep my keythong son. I have just given up my opiniclet son, and I do not wish to repeat the process. I want Moon Wing to grow up with a brother her own age, for there may be no one else with whom she can grow and share chickhood experiences."

Ground Paw's beak gapes wide open in shock at the heresy of Sunsky's suggestion. Finally, he manages to speak. "My blessed niece, this would be against the Gryphonic Code."

"No, it wouldn't," Sunsky snaps. "Section seven of the Gryphonic Code clearly states that I may take extreme measures to ensure the safety of my young."

"But this young one is in no danger if you give him over to me to raise and train, my princess. He is keythong! He must be sterilized by Light Healer and given over to my care, as I am the eldest keythong brother in our family line. We have been following this method of training keythongs for thousands of sun revolutions. It is written in the Gryphonic Code, and it is clear on the subject of the maternal separation needed to train the wingless for a life of service to the winged. It cannot be changed by such liberal interpretations. I am heartily sorry, my niece, but I cannot go along with such an outrageous suggestion."

Panic rises within Sunsky. She grasps for an argument to support her claim. She calms herself before feeling the presence of the two eggs in her pouch. Finally, she says, "My respected elder, Ground Paw. My son—my keythong son—is slated by the oracle herself to become a great king. He will mate with a kryphon, take her as his queen, and he will have many young, both winged and wingless. Therefore, I cannot sterilize this keythong. He must be raised by me in the Valley of Outcasts. I'm sorry, Uncle. I know this must be a shock, but I order you to cede training over to me."

"Niece!" Ground Paw yowls in horror. "I cannot do this! The others will not allow it."

"I order you to be quiet about it, Ground Paw!" Sunsky says, before adding more gently, "Please, Uncle Ground Paw. This could be the beginning of a grand new reign for the keythongs and kryphons! A reign in which they are not sterilized but are given back their full rights to reproduce. Haven't you ever dreamed of what life might have been like had you not been denied your natural birthright to mate? Perhaps you would have made love to a gryphon queen and sired young!"

Ground Paw is now shaking in fear. "No, my niece!" he splutters. "No, I have never, ever dared to dream such blasphemy!"

"Well," whispers Sunsky slyly, "now's your chance. Dare to dream, Uncle Ground Paw. Perhaps a medical solution can be found so that you can regain what was stolen from you at birth."

"I am too old to dream, cruel young gryphon." Ground Paw hisses at her, forgetting for the first time in his life to use his courtly manners.

"Then, cruel old keythong," Sunsky retorts, "allow my son to dream, if you will not. Cover for me, please!"

Light Healer enters the den, interrupting their less-than-hushed conversation. Sunsky inwardly chides herself for speaking her intentions so loudly.

"Is there something wrong, Ground Paw?" the physician asks. "You look as if you've just heard the heresy of all heresies."

Skystar and her two daughters follow Light Healer into the room, sensing that something is amiss. Ground Paw ruffles his head feathers slightly, and then composes himself once more.

"My mighty gryphons," he says, bowing to them. "Sunsky and I were just agreeing to the terms of the young one's transfer."

"What?" Skystar exclaims heatedly. "What are these terms? You don't need terms for the transfer of a keythong, for the oracle's sake!"

Ground Paw and Sunsky look at each other helplessly.

"Young Sunsky." Ground Paw falters, struggling both to obey Sunsky's order to be silent and to preserve his own honesty. "She wishes to keep the young keythong with her for a while before she gives him over to us. She wishes for Moon Wing to have a companion."

"Not a good idea, Sunsky!" Light Healer protests. "It will make it more difficult for the young keythong to be trained properly for his role."

Sunsky suddenly rises above them all in a screaming, flapping rage. "My son will have a different role than the one forced upon his predecessors. The oracle has said so! My son will be the missing link between gryphon and kryphon, keythong and opinicus, the egg-born and the live-birthed, the winged and the wingless, ground and sky! I therefore give him the name Groundsky, the unsterilized keythong. Groundsky, King of the Keythong, who will mate with a kryphon and produce many offspring, both winged and wingless."

The four other gryphons and one keythong look at her, stunned. "You're mad!" Mountain Rain cries, "You've lost your brains as well as your feathers, Sunsky!"

"*Blast your rules!*" Sunsky yells as she flails angrily within the den, knocking over scrolls and instruments until finally she bolts outside, taking wing and leaving her family behind her. Unbeknownst to her, Mother Skystar follows at a discreet distance.

CHAPTER TEN

The Valley of Outcasts

As Sunsky flies in a gradual downward spiral toward the valley, she reflects upon her life. Memories of herself as an innocent gryphlet princess flood her mind. She remembers being fed by Mother Skystar, playing a game of air-tag with Father Sun Quest, playing hide-and-seek with her sisters, and teasing old Egglight, her kryphon nanny. What a treasure she is leaving behind, she thinks sadly, as she glides the gentle mountain air currents. She wishes that she had not left them all in such a rage, for now there will be no opportunity to say good-bye.

She shakes her thoughts and memories away from her. *I must leave the past behind,* she thinks. *I cannot allow myself to become anxious about the future. I must remain in the present moment, as the oracle taught me.*

Sunsky attempts to concentrate on her flight by reminding herself that this will probably be her last. Mother Skystar did not speak about the dreaded duty of clipping her wings before she left, but Sunsky decides that she will honor the council's decision by not flying. When she lands in the valley, she will choose to remain grounded of her own accord. She shifts her attention from the future back to the blowing mountain winds, the sight of drifting cloud cover all around her, and the icy chill that bites at her feathered skin and leonine body.

The air warms slightly as she descends, until she finally lands in a lush green field. The field stretches as far as she can see, portions of it covered with groves of trees. Sunsky regards her surroundings, amazed. She has never traveled this far down from the Mountain of the Skies. She lies down on the grass for a rest, unsure of what to do next. She imagined the valley as being crowded with hippogryphs, crying out to her to come and live with them. She dreamt this vision on numerous occasions; but as she looks around her, she finds the valley deserted.

Her thoughts are interrupted by a powerful rush of wings, as a being lands directly behind her. Sunsky is startled and turns around to face what she expects will be a mad hippogryph that has come to carry her off. Instead, it is her mother Skystar. Sunsky's beak opens wide in surprise.

"Er...good afternoon, Mother Skystar," Sunsky says haltingly.

"Good afternoon, indeed!" Skystar exclaims gruffly, her eyes glinting with anger. "Not when I've been following you for the better part of a day, trying to catch your attention. Did you think I would let you fly off, just like that?"

"Oh yes, you need to clip my wings," Sunsky replies lamely. "Council's orders."

"Council can be blasted to the stars!" Skystar thunders. "I took on the dreaded duty of clipping your wings specifically so that I could neglect it."

Sunsky shakes her head in opposition, holding out her right wing. "Mother Skystar, you must clip my wings—otherwise, you and our family will get into trouble!"

"Listen, my little chick, I have news for you: we're already in queen-size trouble as it is. A bit more won't make much difference." Skystar pushes Sunsky's wing down with her talons.

"All right," Sunsky concedes. "Then I will behave as though my wings are clipped and I will not fly while I remain in this valley. In fact, with you as my witness, Mother Skystar, I take on a new name. Henceforth, I will be known as Sunground rather than as Sunsky."

Skystar is furious at the very mention of the new name. "I was the one who named you, and in my world your name will always be Sunsky. You must never agree to ground yourself, my precious daughter of the sky. You were born to fly, for you are a gryphon. You must therefore use the wings that are your birthright."

Sunsky shakes her head wordlessly, committing herself internally to her new name. It will help her relate to her unhatched keythong son, Groundsky.

"Who will teach Moon Wing how to fly?" Skystar asks, as if sensing her thoughts. Sunsky does not answer her mother. She does not know how she will teach Moon Wing to fly. In fact, she does not know how she will teach either of her offspring much of anything.

The younger gryphon envelops Skystar in her wings and the two remain close for a long time, until Sunsky finally speaks the dreaded words that are in her mind. "Mother Skystar, if you will not clip my wings, then you know that you must leave."

The gryphon mother is stubborn and refuses to leave until the young have hatched. Sunsky decides that it is wise not to argue, and the pair takes refuge in the woods. Skystar helps her daughter to fashion a nest out of branches and leaves, similar to the one that Nightsky made for her when she was grounded after the windstorm.

Nightsky. She tries not to think about him, yet she wishes fervently that he could be here to see his daughter hatch. *He probably doesn't even know that I am carrying his chick or even that I am capable of bearing a fertilized hippogryph egg,* she realizes with great sorrow. The more she thinks about the forbidden stallion, the more she dreams of his return. She wonders if he mates mostly with the wingless females of his kind, whom he once referred to as mares. *I suppose that the mares only birth their young, like most uni-mammals. We gryphons are unique from other species because we are avian mammals blessed with the ability to house and hatch our eggs in pouches or to carry our young within our wombs and birth them. But what about the hippogryphs?*

Sunsky taps her lower belly with one talon as she considers the hippogryph within her. Moon Wing is unique because she is a biological trinity, having within herself the life code of three different beings: the eagle, the lion, and the horse. The leonine characteristics, judging from the few sketches that she has seen of hippogryphs, are recessive. The hippogryphic beings in the portraits possess the head and forelimbs of an eagle and the rear body of a horse, in addition to their huge, magnificent wings.

As she settles into the newly constructed nest, Skystar preens her head feathers. "Sunsky, you're thinking of the hippogryphs, aren't you?"

Sunsky is surprised that her mother has so easily sensed her thoughts. "Why yes, I've just been considering their odd tripartite nature."

"Well," Skystar replies. "I have a feeling that we're going to get the chance to study them more closely."

Sunsky turns her head in alarm and follows Skystar's gaze. To her shock, she sees a group of hippogryphs standing behind the grove in a semi-circle, surrounding them and watching the pair silently. She and Skystar stare back at them, mesmerized. One hippogryph stands out in particular: She has an avian head covered with golden feathers and a rear equine body as black as the night skies.

Nightsky! Her heart leaps as she remembers her Uncle Ground Paw's tale about a hippogryph named Night Lover, the one that is the daughter of her beloved Nightsky.

Sunsky attempts to send a greeting telepathically, as she learned to do with the winged stallion, but Night Lover does not acknowledge it. She continues to stand proudly, peering at the two gryphons from behind the trees.

"Why don't they do something?" Sunsky whispers. "All they do is just stand there, mutely looking at us. That's what Nightsky did when I first met him, and it drove me insane."

Skystar caresses her daughter with her beak. "Patience, my dear, you can't expect them to overcome their mistrust immediately. Give them time."

Sunsky is frustrated, but she does as her mother suggests and focuses on her unhatched young. She cultivates patience by reminding herself that hatchlings do not follow a rigid schedule but will arrive in their own time. Sunsky and Skystar can do little more than wait and watch their neighbors as they come and go. They notice that there is always at least one silent sentinel who remains behind to stand guard over the gryphons.

One day, the hippogryph standing guard is the individual that Sunsky believes to be Night Lover. She stares at them, as usual, and Sunsky stares back without thinking about anything.

Suddenly, a message shoots into her mind like a bolt of lightning: "*I am Night Lover.*"

Sunsky is startled. She sees in her mind's eye a horrendous image of an opinicus savagely tearing a gryphon's flesh with his mighty paws and beak until he finally kills her by ripping out her throat. Behind the gryphon, a small, dark hippogryph youngster screams in terror as a flock of adult hippogryphs rush at the opinicus, chasing him away in a feathery fury.

Sunsky feels deeply disturbed by the image. *Is it Night Lover who is sending this thought?* She does not attempt to send a return message, fearful of keeping her mind open to further telepathic communication from the daughter of Nightsky. *Is the murdered gryphon supposed to be an image of me and the little hippogryph my future offspring, Moon Wing?* She desperately hopes not, but she needs to know. There are, however, no more messages or visions that day.

"She is Night Lover," Sunsky finally reports to her mother. "She told me so with her mind, and I think she sent me some kind of warning about a dangerous opinicus."

"Yes," Skystar agrees. "I heard her voice too, and I saw the image of an opinicus killing a gryphon."

"What do you think it means, Mother Skystar?"

Skystar pauses. "The opinicus in the image looked a lot like old Thundercloud—when he was younger, of course. I do not think he would possess the strength to carry out such a heinous crime at his present advanced age. I would not be surprised to learn that he killed Night Lover's mother, Wing Dreamer, some time after she was banished to the Valley of Outcasts. After all, he did express a great deal of vehemence toward her at the court hearing and toward us, calling us horse lovers. The vicious brute."

Sunsky's mind reels in shock as she recalls Thundercloud's words to the Gryphonic Council: "*I demand the right, along with my son and grandson, to raise Sun Wing! He must be free of the horse-tainted gryphon that begat him, and that includes her horse-loving parents as well.*"

She shivers in horror, remembering how Thundercloud ripped her precious son away from her after his birth. *Can the grandfather of Dreamspinner really have murdered Wing Dreamer? And if he did, will he or his son Windsinger repeat the process with me?* She knows she must be very careful not to allow Dreamspinner to approach her in the valley, for it is unlikely that Thundercloud will have told him about the nefarious deed. *Poor Dreamspinner!* Sunsky laments on behalf of her once-lover. *He would be devastated to know that his own grandfather killed his mother, Wing Dreamer!*

It makes sense, however, that Night Lover would wish to warn them about what befell the last gryphon matriarch to inhabit the Valley of Outcasts. Nonetheless, she has trouble believing it, and she pushes it out of her mind so that she can focus on the two precious lives within her egg-pouch.

The two gryphons wait for the days to pass, with hippogryphs constantly standing guard over them. Sometimes, Night Lover is present at the post; and at other times, various individuals from the herd watch them. Always, there is silence.

One day, however, the keythong egg begins to crack inside her pouch, and Sunsky feels the little creature's beak working at the shell. She does not say anything or make any movements. She does not completely trust these hippogryphic beings around her keythong baby. She signals quietly to Skystar that the egg is cracking, and Skystar discreetly explores the pouch with her beak, gently assisting the keythong cub in his efforts without doing too much for him.

In order for the egg-born to develop strength, they are encouraged from the time they hatch to be industrious and not expect much outside help. In fact, this is the first time that Skystar has ever assisted in a keythong hatching. Other than physicians, gryphons almost never deal with the hatching of an egg. The egg is most often surrendered just before it hatches, to be incubated by a kryphon surrogate. When a hatching occurs, the task of attending it is normally assigned to a kryphon or a keythong.

Sunsky feels the little one struggling to penetrate the shell, and she focuses intently on loving messages toward the infant keythong. "Come, Groundsky, my keythong son, come into this world and emerge as the prince that you are."

Sunsky knows that "prince" is a word reserved for opiniclet young only, but she uses it nonetheless. Once Groundsky's reddish beak emerges from the shell, the rest of him follows swiftly. Mother Skystar's talons hold the pouch open to reveal a tiny, wingless cub. He is a golden-brown ball of fur and head feathers surrounded by broken pieces of white eggshell. As he shakes the shell off his body, Skystar restrains herself from cleaning him, as she would do for an opiniclet.

When Sunsky looks at her questioningly, she responds, "Keythong young eat the shell and surrounding membrane shortly after they are born. It contains the nutrients they need until the caregiver can make up the vegetable gruel for the little thing. My brother Ground Paw told me about this aspect of the hatching. This is why I needed to stay with you for the emergence of your young, for I and my elder siblings have knowledge that you do not."

Sunsky feels tremendous gratitude and love toward Skystar for her knowledge, patience, and courage in staying with her for these hatchings. She fervently hopes that her mother does not get into trouble back home for doing this.

Skystar senses her thoughts. "Sunsky. Fret and fuss no more about affairs back home. You will need your energy for the challenge of raising these two hatchlings."

"Thank you, Mother Skystar," Sunsky whispers, amazed at her mother's great compassion toward her and these two small creatures that the rest of gryphonic society considers lesser beings.

Skystar caresses her daughter with her beak before she takes command of the situation. "Now, let's get down to the business at wing. Groundsky will need some nutrients when he finishes eating the eggshell. I don't believe we have the proper vegetables to make the usual mash, so I will need to hunt down some rodents. We will need to chew and regurgitate the meat so that he can eat it."

Sunsky marvels at her mother's practicality, as it emerges victorious over the decorum of social tradition. In ordinary circumstances, a keythong or kryphon is never fed meat, for this is only the privilege of the winged.

"Will meat harm keythongs, Mother Skystar?" Sunsky asks.

"No," Skystar replies. "They are the same beings as us, basically, except that they are born of egg and have no wings."

Skystar wastes no more time in speaking, but instead disappears into the woods to hunt for small prey. Sunsky watches the hippogryph guard worriedly as her mother leaves. The guard stares ahead and makes no move to stop Skystar.

The gryphon matriarch comes back with two rodents in her beak. Sunsky devours the prey, readying her belly to regurgitate the meat bit by bit into Groundsky's hungry little beak. It is not long before Groundsky has digested the eggshell, and Sunsky begins the feeding. She reaches into the pouch with her beak until she can feel the little one's miniscule head poking about in search of a meal. She provides it to him by carefully, bringing up the meat bits into his open beak a little at a time so as not to overwhelm the newborn's body. *Thank the oracle for Mother Skystar*, Sunsky thinks as the older gryphon continues her forays out into the surrounding forest, seeking more prey for the mother and her ravenous cub.

Sunsky is surprised at how often Groundsky needs to be fed. She previously believed that wingless cubs required less care than winged ones, but she now realizes that this belief is a myth. Sunsky worries about how she will cope when Moon Wing, a much bigger creature, hatches. *What in Gryphonia do hippogryphs eat? Do they eat vegetation like a horse, or meat like a gryphon? Do they eat both?* Sunsky does not know the answer to any of these questions, yet somehow she must muddle through it. Skystar surely will not be able to stay much longer, as they will become suspicious of her long absence back home.

Skystar soothes her during the night-time hours, quietly telling her not to worry. They each take turns regurgitating meat into Groundsky, within the safety of his mother's pouch. As the days pass, however, Sunsky feels her cub's restlessness. He is preparing to leave the pouch and venture out into the world, as the ever-growing, gigantic hippogryph egg increasingly pressures him to depart.

One night, Groundsky finally makes his exit, squawking angrily as he bounds from the confines of the pouch. Sunsky is at a loss. *What will I do now? Will Groundsky wander off? I must protect him from the hippogryphs, but what about Moon Wing?* She knows that she may need the help of the hippogryphs in order to raise the equine being properly. She ruffles her feathers in frustration.

"Calm, my daughter, calm," Skystar says. "It will be all right. If the hippogryphs wished us harm, they could easily have attacked us by now. They are more numerous, and we are obviously nesting our young. I believe that they are waiting for the hippogryph to be born."

"So," Sunsky murmurs, "hippogryphs do have a sense of community, like gryphons! Councilor Mudstone was wrong. They are not 'selfish beasts', as he put it."

"I do not believe so," Skystar replies. "I have been watching them, as they have watched us. I believe they are as anxious as we are, wondering if we are here to harm them. My sense, though, is that their anxiety has lessened as they have observed our actions."

"Do you think there's any danger of them harming Groundsky?" Sunsky asks.

"Be calm, my daughter. I will stay a while to find out."

"But you must go back, Mother Skystar!" Sunsky exclaims. "You cannot delay any longer!"

"I will ensure the safety of my chick and grand-chicks first!" Skystar declares firmly, ending the debate. Sunsky knows better than to argue with her, and she is secretly relieved that Skystar is not leaving yet. She is doubtful about her own abilities to raise the two young ones in this strange, foreign land.

As the days pass, Groundsky becomes more energetic. He darts and dashes around the trees, exploring his environment. He often comes perilously close to the observing hippogryphs, but as always they do nothing.

Skystar is required to be a temporary nannygryph to Groundsky, since Sunsky cannot move far with the huge hippogryph egg in her pouch. The egg of a gryphon begins as a soft, gelatinous substance that grows and hardens within her pouch, just as the fetus grows within her womb. Nonetheless, she had no inkling that the hippogryph egg would grow to such an enormous size. She wonders if Moon Wing will ever hatch. *This is worse than pregnancy*, she thinks. She is impatient now and wants to move so that she can help Skystar with the growing cub, but it is not possible.

"I am amazed at the busyness and energy of Groundsky," Sunsky says to Skystar during one of his brief naps. "I never realized that keythong young could be like that."

"Remember," Skystar cautions, "Groundsky is not like other keythong cubs. He has been fed meat, for one thing, instead of vegetables. Most importantly, he has not been sterilized as he was supposed to have been. There is an age where keythongs can no longer safely be sterilized and Groundsky, judging by how fast and strong he has been growing, will reach that benchmark soon. If you wish to have him sterilized, now is the time, my daughter. I will ask your Uncle Ground Paw to come and perform the task for you—but then, he will want to take and raise him among keythongs. Once he has been sterilized, we cannot refuse Ground Paw his own great-nephew to teach and train."

"No," Sunsky replies firmly as she watches her sleeping son. "I will keep him with me, unsterilized. The oracle foretold that he will be a king among the keythong and sire many young."

"I'm not sure how he will be a keythong king," Skystar answers dryly, "when he will have no experience of keythong culture. Nonetheless, I bow to your wisdom in this, my daughter."

Since the council's fateful decision, Skystar has argued little with her about her choices. She is amazed at her mother's generosity in being willing to let go of maternal authority. At the same time, she is afraid of her new freedom. What will happen when Skystar leaves? Sunsky wonders if she is fit to raise her young with no older gryphon to help her. She will then truly be Sunground the grounded gryphon, caring for her ground-son and moon-winged daughter. *What will happen to them?* Sunsky can think of no answer as she peers at the shadowy trees in desperation.

Suddenly, she feels a jolt of energy shooting through her mind and body.

"I am here," a voice says inside her mind. "I will help you raise the hippogryph choal."

Sunsky looks out into the woods, calling, "Night Lover! Is it you?"

As usual, there is no immediate response. Sunsky considers the words that have entered her head. She understands them but is unfamiliar with the term *choal*. The word must be a combination of "chick" and "foal", the equine term for an infant horse.

"I will help you to raise and protect Moon Wing," the voice says. "I will not harm any of you."

"Thank you," Sunsky says in her mind, trying to send a thought-message in return. There is no reply to her expression of gratitude, but Sunsky realizes that Night Lover must be so attuned to her mind that she knows the name of her *choal*, Moon Wing. She feels peace descend upon her after hearing Night Lover's comforting message. *Will Night Lover really help me to raise Moon Wing?* Sunsky still harbors doubts, but she tries to free herself of them. She does not have the luxury of fretting over her chick-rearing skills or lack thereof.

One night, with the moonlight shining down upon her, it happens. The dreaded yet hopeful moment arrives when Sunsky feels Moon Wing's hind legs thrashing at its eggshell nursery. The novice mother is unsure of what to do so she simply waits. Skystar bounds off into the woods to find Night Lover. She does not have to go far.

Night Lover, who previously kept her distance from the gryphons, thunders onto the birth scene before Skystar has even had time to communicate the situation to her.

Sunsky looks at her looming figure and feels a momentary sense of terror. The hippogryph's front talons are huge, her equine body much taller than either of the gryphons. Night Lover shows no signs of dominance but instead lies down, with her hind legs tucked under her enormous body. She looks at Sunsky's swelled pouch, with Moon Wing thrashing about inside, and she signals her intent to go inside the pouch by pointing a talon at it. Sunsky nods her assent, and Night Lover wastes no time. She reaches into the belly-pocket with one forearm and forces the great egg out of the pouch, guiding it with her other arm. Her claws grip the egg tightly, ripping it out of the pouch and into the moon's light. Sunsky feels a searing pain as the egg finally exits, her pouch torn and bleeding in the process. She feels alarm as well as pain. She understood that egg-born youngsters were to remain in the pouch until they were strong enough to come out.

Is it safe for Moon Wing to be out of the pouch so soon, she asks herself.

"She must come out," Night Lover's words speak inside Sunsky's mind once again. "She will die if she doesn't."

Night Lover helps the *choal* to break open her egg prison by pecking at it with her beak, but Moon Wing has already driven a mighty hole in one side. Skystar, receiving Night Lover's thought as well, offers her a crudely woven blanket of leaves to wipe the shell and liquid from the infant hippogryph. Night Lover takes the offered blanket with her deft talons, wiping off the gelatinous blue fluid from the choal's body and from the inside of her beak-like mouth, so that all parts of her can breathe freely. The two gryphons are surprised by the amount of fluid inside the egg.

Moon Wing shakes herself, making several awkward attempts to stand. Before long, she arises on her back hooves and steadies herself with her aquiline arms, shaking but proud. Moon Wing's head feathers and wings are a beautiful black-gold color and true to her name, she stands illuminated by the full moon's ethereal light. Her hind body is as black as midnight, like that of her older sister, Night Lover.

Sunsky marvels at her daughter. She had no idea hippogryph chick-foals were so large. Moon Wing at birth stands almost as tall as herself and Skystar. Sunsky's pouch, unaccustomed to carrying such a heavy load, is bruised, bloody, and sagging. Mother Skystar is already attending to it, wiping off the blood with cleansing leaves that she had collected while her daughter was nesting.

"Your pouch is ripped, Sunsky," Skystar says. "You will need to rest awhile."

Even as her pouch screams its pain, Sunsky is grateful that the huge creature has safely exited. She also feels disappointed that she will not immediately participate in the care of her choal. Night Lover and Skystar are strict nannies and will not allow Sunsky to do anything until her wounds heal.

It is not long before Moon Wing is steady enough on her hooves and forearms to walk about, exploring her environment. Hippogryphs move similarly to gryphons, using their hind legs to propel themselves forward and their shorter avian arms to steady the body, as in the manner of an Earth kangaroo. Unlike a kangaroo, however, they do not hop but instead use their wings to help balance their large bodies.

Moon Wing is voracious, eating leaves, grasses, and bark from the trees, in addition to drinking milk from Sunsky's leonine mammary glands. Normally in gryphonic society, the milk of the mother is extracted, combined with either meat or vegetable matter, stirred into gruel, and eaten by the caregiver before being regurgitated into the youngster.

Modern gryphonic beings nurse their young through suckling only if the physician deems the chick or cub too weak to take in other forms of nourishment. In recent times the gryphons have fashioned both an instrument to extract milk from the mammary glands and one to protect the leonine teats from the chick's sharp beak. Gyphonic beings possess an inner suckling mouth within their beak, but the parents must train the chicks to open their beaks wide and not bite down while suckling.

Sunsky has no nursing instruments with her, so when Moon Wing pokes her beak into her mother and begins to suckle, it is a very painful experience for the young nursing gryphon. Night Lover is always there, however, to soften the pain. She inserts her talon in between Sunsky's teat and Moon Wing's beak to teach the young one to use only her inner suckle-mouth on the teats and not her outer beak. Soon the young one learns to nurse properly, with her mouth and tongue extracting the milk while her beak, with its tiny sharp teeth, stays wide open to avoid contact with the teats.

Night Lover strokes the young hippogryph gently as she nurses, while Skystar does her best to engage a squawking, jealous Groundsky. The young keythong cub has not been welcoming toward his new sister. He makes repeated attempts to copy her suckling techniques by tearing at Sunsky's belly with his by now razor-sharp beak. Every time he does so, he is sternly disciplined by Skystar.

"This little cub is stubborn!" an exhausted Skystar proclaims. "He needs to learn that he is to be fed by regurgitation only. His sister Moon Wing will need all the milk that your body can produce."

Sunsky nods, feeling more like a feeding station than a mother. She feels a sense of guilt, recognizing that her milk was supposed to have been for her body-born son, Sun Wing. In order to feed him, it will now be necessary for Sun Wing's opinicus caregiver to obtain milk from another nursing gryphon and combine it with the meat-gruel mixture that will nourish the winged infant. This milk-sharing practice is common in gryphonic society, as gryphons do not always produce milk with every birth. There are many milk substitutes, such as that extracted from domestic mountain goats that gryphons keep and tend. Sunsky fervently hopes that Sun Wing is being fed the milk of a gryphon rather than that of a goat.

She pulls her attention back to the present once again. *I must keep my mind focused on what is happening in front of me,* she thinks. *Pining for Sun Wing will not bring him any closer to us.* Instead of thinking about her opinicus son, she studies her nursing daughter. She is definitely as energetic as her keythong brother, Groundsky. She is already dashing madly about in imitation of him. Soon, they will be playing tag with each other. When this happens, it means that they are ready to leave the nest and she will need to teach them their hunting, foraging, and for Moon Wing at least, flying skills. Then, Sunsky must take over, hopefully with the continuing help of Night Lover. She knows through the sorrowful pang in her heart that Mother Skystar will soon return home.

Indeed, the time comes when Sunsky's birthing wounds are healed well enough for her to rise from the nest and assume Skystar's former caregiving responsibilities. Both gryphons are saddened, but Skystar knows that she has stayed away from the rest of her family for far too long.

One day, as the two young ones are napping, Skystar caresses each of them gently with her beak before enveloping Sunsky in her wings. They both feel their hearts breaking. Finally, Skystar chirps good-bye to her daughter and takes wing so that she may return once more to her family in the mountains.

PART TWO
Sunground of the Valley

Chapter One
The Quest for Nightsky. 91

Chapter Two
Groundsky 104

Chapter Three
The Banishment of Grass Hopper 114

Chapter Four
A Song for Great Heart 121

Chapter Five
Reunion 128

Chapter Six
Escape 135

Chapter Seven
The Hiding Spot 143

Chapter Eight
In Search of Moon Wing 154

Chapter Nine
Captivity 163

Chapter Ten
The Hopha 179

THE
GRYPHON

PART TWO
Sunground of the Valley

CHAPTER ONE

The Quest for Nightsky

Gryphonia is alone among the stars, an oasis of life in a galaxy riddled with dead worlds. The natural satellite wraps around its fiery light-bearer in countless, orderly revolutions, the lives of its inhabitants utterly dependent on the solar behemoth.

Timeless the planet dances its rotations between day and night, revolving around the sun on its orbital journey.

From the planet's surface, a small creature looks up at the night sky and observes her insignificance in comparison to the entire universe. She is capable of making this comparison only when she separates her mind from the whole of creation. When she allows herself to be swallowed by *the whole*, she knows that she is an intricate part of the eternal web of life. As this small being looks into the stars, her mind is crowded with awe and wonder at the space above her, as it has been from her youngest days. She longs for a *deeper whole* that is already present within her. At this time of uncertainty, she has confined her own understanding of the world to the cold, hard ground. She no longer uses her magnificent wings for flight.

The golden-feathered gryphon appears much larger and more fearsome as one draws near to her. Her rear leonine body has fur that shimmers, shining gold, under the star-lit sky. Sunsky was once a princess in line to the Stone Throne, the highest office in all of gryphondom, but now she is a lone pariah. She has given up her inheritance to raise her two young ones in the Valley of Outcasts. She has not flown since she arrived here seventeen sun revolutions ago; and her name, the one she bestowed upon herself after arriving in the valley, is Sunground, the grounded gryphon.

There are those who still refer to her as Sunsky, but her days of flight and freedom in the skies are gone. This is not because she cannot use her wings but because she opts to remain on the ground. She chooses her flightless condition as a kind of reprimand to herself for having engaged in a forbidden mating with the winged horse, Nightsky. The one rash act caused much turmoil for her family.

Nonetheless, the valley has been a great vehicle for learning. Sunground has developed a worldly wisdom that one can receive only from the ground. She lives as an outcast among outcasts in the valley, raising her hippogryph daughter Moon Wing and her wingless keythong son, Groundsky, beside the local clan of equine-avian beings.

Although the hippogryphs of the valley have tolerated Sunground's presence, they have never accepted her as a full member of their society. She can hardly blame them for that, as gryphonic society has for ages ruthlessly shunned hippogryphs and the gryphons that have borne them. The last gryphon to inhabit the Valley of Outcasts was murdered savagely by one of her own family members.

She pushes the horror of Wing Dreamer's murder out of her mind and distracts herself instead with thoughts of Dreamspinner and his endless love songs to her. Full of rapturous romance, Dreamspinner still laments: "O, Sunsky, my queen! Take me as your one true mate and I will live happily with you and your youngsters as a family without stature! What do I care for stature, after my true love was banished for loving her chicks too deeply to abandon them, just as my dear mother Wing Dreamer did? I stand in awe of your courage, you who have boldly raised our wingless son, Groundsky, as an unsterilized and free keythong. Please, let me join you!"

Dreamspinner has always deeply touched Sunground's heart with his unrelenting proposals to her, although she firmly refuses in every instance. Sometimes she is gentle with him and at other times quite violent, chasing him away with her beating wings, her lacerating talons, and her sharp beak. Nonetheless, Dreamspinner never gives up. Inevitably, his angry grandfather Thundercloud found out about his clandestine professions of love, and he banished him from his own family, including his son, Sun Wing.

Sunground's feathers ruffle slightly at the thought of Sun Wing, and she wonders how he is faring. She has not seen her first-born son since his birth seventeen sun revolutions ago. Dreamspinner has likewise heard nothing from his family, because he joined his erstwhile mate's own marginalized brood after his expulsion by Thundercloud. This banishment was one of Sunground's two biggest fears for her lover. The other was that he would one day find out that his own grandfather killed his mother, Wing Dreamer. Neither Dreamspinner nor Sunground's sisters have been for a visit in recent sun revolutions, however, and Sunground is glad for this small mercy. She hopes that Dreamspinner is concentrating on raising the two gryphon chicks that he sired by her sisters, Cloudhopper and Mountain Rain.

Meanwhile, Sunground fills her days by caring for her two young ones. She is eternally thankful that Night Lover, the hippogryph daughter of Nightsky and the late Wing Dreamer, is present to help her raise Moon Wing. Otherwise, she would have been completely lost in the attempt to raise a hippogryph filly on her own.

"Mama!" Moon Wing says, cackling at her mother. "You should have seen how well I did in flight class today! Sister Night Lover said that I'm ready for a flight to the lower mountains. I do wish that you would dispense with that silly order to remain grounded and come fly there with me."

Sunground looks fondly at her daughter, marveling at how grown up she has become in such a short time. At seventeen sun revolutions, she already stands high above her mother. The young hippogryph's equine hindquarters bestow her with a height that Sunground, with her smaller leonine hindquarters, does not have.

Sadly, Sunground realizes that Moon Wing is coming into her adult phase and will be ready to mate soon. She has been keeping company with a young winged colt named Pegasus, a fully equine being whose white coat is a contrast to Moon Wing's midnight-black coat, a trait she inherited from her father.

"Perhaps," Sunground suggests gently to her daughter, "I would be one too many. Are you not traveling there to see Pegasus, Moon Wing?"

Moon Wing lets out a cry, a curious cross between an eagle's screech and a horse's whinny. She rears up on her hind legs, her large forearms flailing in the air, her talons outstretched, and her beak open. She is a fabulous, terrifying thing to behold.

"No, Mama, not Pegasus! He comes to the valley all the time. I'm talking about going to search for Papa. I want you to come so he will recognize who I am."

Sunground stares at her daughter in shock. She has not seen Moon Wing's father since that fateful time seventeen sun revolutions ago when he cared for her, after she received an injury to her wing from the fierce windstorm. She has never found her forbidden lover, Nightsky, but she has told Moon Wing many tales about the mysterious winged horse. The stories instilled within the youngster an insatiable desire to meet her equine father.

"Moon Wing," Sunground says gently to her daughter, "I do not know where to find Nightsky."

"Oh, Mama!" Moon Wing protests. "You have never even tried to find him. Sister Night Lover says that she used to come upon him every once in a while near the lower mountains, and Pegasus tells me that the lower mountains are his mating territory. That was the very place where you were grounded by the windstorm, and where you met Papa. I want to try to find him now, while I still can. In another sun revolution, I will be big with *choal*."

Sunground lets out a quiet, cooing sound. *To think, I will soon be a grandmother!* An image of her own grandmother, Heartsong, comes into her mind, and she feels a deep sadness. None in her family has been allowed to have contact with Grandmother Heartsong while she holds the office of premiere queen. Sunground shivers as she realizes that soon, her vicious half-sister Talona will take over the reign, aided by her interfering mother, Soundringer.

"I must not fly, Moon Wing," Sunground replies. "You know that."

Moon Wing shakes her head impatiently. "But why must you listen to that silly Gryphonic Council, the one that rejected us? Rebel, Mama, rebel against that ridiculous order, as Grandmother Skystar once urged you to do!"

Sunground shakes her head firmly. "No, Moon Wing, I must not."

A wingless keythong bounds in, jumping up on Moon Wing playfully before he climbs the nearby branch of a tree. He lets loose a roaring caw, propels himself into the air, and lands on the ground with a thud. "Rug-a-bug!" he roars angrily. "I will accompany you to the lower mountains, Moon Wing, just as soon as I learn to fly."

"Groundsky!" Moon Wing responds. "You *can't* fly. You don't even have wings, my keythong brother." Groundsky roars in protest as Moon Wing giggles.

"That is quite enough, Groundsky," Sunground scolds. "No one is going to the lower mountains. Nightsky will not be there, and I don't want either of you running into any gryphons."

Moon Wing screeches in irritation. "I don't care about those ridiculous gryphons! I want to see my father. Groundsky has seen his father many times. Why can't I?"

"Because," Sunground explains angrily, "it could be dangerous. Groundsky has not seen his father Dreamspinner that often, because of the danger to our family if Talona and Soundringer find out."

"Talona and Soundringer!" Moon Wing snaps in contempt. "I care not for them or for some silly danger. Dreamspinner and my aunts, Mountain Rain and Cloudhopper, have visited ever since I can remember and this danger you speak of has never bothered them. You fret far too much, Mother Sunground!"

Sunground realizes that she cannot hold Moon Wing back from her quest much longer. *My daughter is becoming more willful and independent as each day passes*, she thinks. Moon Wing flaps her wings in frustration and flounces off to play with Groundsky. Sunground spots Night Lover, elder half-sister and mentor to Moon Wing, approaching her from the woods. The gryphon mother is lonely for the company of another adult and cheerfully welcomes her visitor. "Greetings, Night Lover. How may I be of service?"

She has long since learned the hippogryphic dialect well enough that they no longer need to communicate through thought messages, although Night Lover continues to send telepathic signals to those around her to supplement the verbal language.

"Greetings, Mother Sunground," Night Lover replies politely. The hippogryph is twice Sunground's age, but she still pays her respect by calling her "mother", in recognition of the fact that Sunground gave up everything to raise her daughter in the Valley of Outcasts.

The other hippogryphs permit Sunground to live in their territory because of her connection to Night Lover, who was recently named premiere queen of the hippogryphs. They are, however, far less tolerant of the opinicus Dreamspinner when he ventures into the valley. They are suspicious of him because he is the grandson of the terrifying, murderous Thundercloud.

Ever since Thundercloud murdered Wing Dreamer, the hippogryphs have been especially fearful of any winged gryphonic male. This is yet another reason that Sunground prefers Dreamspinner's visits to be as brief as possible, since she has been unable to deter him from coming to see his wingless son Groundsky. Although Moon Wing has no fear whatsoever of Dreamspinner—in fact, she calls him "Uncle"—his visits have caused her jealousy in the past.

Maybe this is what has fueled Moon Wing's desire to find Nightsky, she muses to herself as Night Lover ambles over to her slowly. Sunground peers directly at the black hippogryph.

"I understand," Sunground says cautiously, "that Moon Wing wishes to make a flight journey to the lower mountains to visit her father Nightsky."

"That is correct, Mother Sunground," Night Lover replies. "She is now ready, and I am willing to accompany her there."

"But Night Lover, elder sister to my daughter, it is most unwise, is it not? Her chances of finding Nightsky are very slim."

"Whether or not we find Nightsky is not the point," the older hippogryph explains. "Moon Wing must make the attempt as part of her journey into full adulthood."

"I see," Sunground answers. "I suppose I can understand that, as I embarked upon a similar flight of folly as a young gryphon. It was the ill-advised adventure which led to my mating with Nightsky."

"And is that something you regret?" Night Lover asks. "Is that why you oppose the journey?"

Sunground is taken aback by the question. Surely, she cannot regret the birth of her beloved daughter, Moon Wing! And yet, the cost to her family has been so high. Had Sunground not mated with Nightsky, she might now be the Premiere Queen Sunsky, with Dreamspinner as her king consort, together raising their opiniclet prince Sun Wing.

"No," she thinks furiously, "*I must not think of what might have been. It will drive me mad.*"

Night Lover, using her telepathic ability, has already sensed Sunground's emotional confusion on the matter. "I'm sorry, Mother Sunground, it is unfair of me to ask such a question. I know you love Moon Wing passionately, but you must let her spread her wings. This is something that she has wanted to do for many sun revolutions."

"I know," Sunground replies ruefully. "She has wanted to find her papa ever since she was old enough to understand where she came from. It's just that I fear for her safety, Night Lover. When my sisters come on their visits, they report to me that Talona, the next in waiting, is impatient to take over the reign from my grandmother Heartsong. Heartsong is holding on for as long as she can but when Talona takes over, it may become more dangerous for us here in the valley. I am fearful for any hippogryph wandering out of our territory but especially Moon Wing, who has not been raised to fear gryphons."

"That is good," Night Lover counters, "for fear is not an environment in which to raise a young *choal*."

"I know," Sunground replies, "but fear can be necessary when it helps us to stay out of unnecessary danger."

Night Lover says no more, for she knows that Sunground needs to be the one to make the final decision; or perhaps Moon Wing will decide if she takes matters into her own talons and partakes of her quest without permission.

Sunground knows only too well that Moon Wing, like her when she was young, will be stubborn and willful enough to embark on the journey of her own accord. Would it not be better simply to allow the journey to go ahead, supervised by Night Lover?

"After all," Sunground muses ruefully, "I cannot accompany her, for to do so would be to break my oath and use my wings!" Moon Wing, of course, is very impatient with this notion of having to repent through flightlessness. She continuously argues with her mother over it because she sees it as an insult to the hippogryphic people.

"Do you regret having committed the transgression of my conception and my birth?" a hurt Moon Wing once asked her. Sunground had no answer for her then, or now. What can she tell Moon Wing? Hippogryphs are considered outcasts by the gryphons and hatching one is a serious transgression. Nevertheless, she knows Moon Wing is right, and she certainly does not regret her daughter's birth. She feels blessed by the choal's arrival into the world and has told her so many times. Paradoxically, however, her guilt at abdicating the queenship responsibilities and handing them over to the dreadful young Talona has clouded her thinking on many occasions.

After considering the matter for some time, Sunground finally comes to a conclusion. She will allow Moon Wing her journey as long as it is supervised by Night Lover and as long as they both promise to go no further than the lower mountains.

When she hears of her mother's decision, Moon Wing is ecstatic. She races around the woods, chasing her half-brother, Groundsky. Sunground watches them with Night Lover.

"You have made a good choice, Sunground," Night Lover reassures the mother gryphon.

"I hope so," Sunground murmurs.

"I know so," Night Lover responds confidently. "Moon Wing and I should begin our journey tomorrow at first light."

"So soon?" Sunground asks, more to herself than to anyone else. She knows, however, that the sooner they leave, the sooner they can return. It is best to get the journey out of the way as quickly as possible. Or is she being naïve to think that Moon Wing will simply go on a small journey and be content with that, especially if she finds nothing?

"This will be a journey that Moon Wing will be on all of her life," Night Lover says softly to Sunground, having sensed her thoughts. "The object of the journey may change, but the life quest will remain the same."

"What?" Sunground exclaims, dismayed. "What do you mean by that, Night Lover?"

"I mean that Moon Wing will always need to quest after something, be it her father, her lover, her vocation, or her own spirit knowledge. The life quest never ends for any of us. Certainly, you do not expect the daughter of the former Sunsky, Queen of the Skies, to do anything less?"

Sunground ruffles her feathers at the mention of her former name. "Please do not call me that, Night Lover. I am not the queen of the skies. I am not the queen of anything."

"Perhaps that is the problem," Night Lover counters. "Maybe you need to stretch your wings a bit. You could come with us, you know. I think it would mean quite a lot to Moon Wing and it would be good for you, as well. Did your mother Skystar not encourage you to keep using your wings before she left?"

"Yes, she did, but I cannot do that. I made a choice, many sun revolutions ago, and I must pay the price for that choice. You know that, Night Lover."

"No," Night Lover states in a flat tone. "I do not know that, Mother Sunground. Your choice to bring Moon Wing into the world was the right one. Stop punishing yourself for it! You owe the Gryphonic Council nothing."

"No," Sunground retorts, "but I do owe my family something, and if I am caught flying it could be a disaster for all of us, especially when Talona takes over. She is almost certainly in training for the premiere queenship and gaining power by the day."

"Is she not being trained by your wise grandmother, Heartsong?" Night Lover asks quietly. "Do you have no faith in your sister that you think that she cannot learn from Heartsong's wisdom, as you have?"

"Talona is not my sister, only my half-sister," Sunground snaps. "Please, Night Lover, bother me no longer on this topic. I trust you with my beloved daughter. My flightlessness is about me, not her. I cannot go with you, in all conscience, although I wish that I could."

Night Lover leaves Sunground quietly. The mother gryphon feels a deep sadness, for she knows that she was the one to end the conversation between her and Night Lover. She is angry with herself, as there are few adult beings with whom she can converse here in the valley. After Skystar left many sun revolutions ago, Night Lover had been her only adult friend. Although her sisters and Dreamspinner come to visit occasionally, their visits have been infrequent by necessity. Sunground knows that she will be lonely without Night Lover here.

At least she still has the comfort of her keythong son. She knows that she cannot remain despondent while watching the youngster's antics. Moon Wing and Groundsky gambol towards her, cawing their laughter and drawing her into their raucous play. Night Lover joins in as well, and the four of them chase each other about, whinnies and caws abounding.

CHAPTER TWO

Groundsky

The morning light arrives very soon—too soon for Sunground's liking, although Moon Wing has risen well before the sun. Sunground and her keythong son Groundsky watch with sadness as an excited Moon Wing bids them farewell and springs into the dawn sky with her elder half-sister, Night Lover.

"Oh, rug-a-bug!" Groundsky exclaims cheerlessly. "Why can't I go, Mother Sunground? And don't tell me it's because I have no wings!"

"All right, young one," Sunground retorts. "I won't say anything about wings, but I will say that I need you to stay here with me, because I can't go on this flight of fancy."

"Oh, Mother Sunground!" Groundsky replies. "You could go if you really wanted to do it. There's nothing wrong with your wings. But then, if you did go, I would probably be left behind. No matter, I'm working on a solution to my unwinged state."

Sunground chuckles a caw, in spite of her melancholy mood. The pair plays together in the morning sunshine before catching some rodents for breakfast. As they sit contentedly under a shady tree after their meal, the quiet of the day is suddenly shattered by a piercing screech. A large opinicus plummets clumsily into their company.

"Papa!" Groundsky chirps, running forth to greet the mighty Dreamspinner. "You haven't visited us for so long!"

Dreamspinner. Sunground's muscles tighten, as they always do whenever her former lover intrudes upon their exiled lives.

"Hello, young outlaw, my gallant keythong son!" He looks tentatively at Sunground, as if expecting her to chase him away, as she has done on occasion whenever he has become too amorous. Sunground simply peers at Dreamspinner, unsure of how to deal with him today.

"Dreamspinner," she greets him finally, her tone weary. "For what reason have you intruded upon our exile?"

Dreamspinner bows reverently to her and addresses her by her old name, a habit Sunground finds most disconcerting. "Oh, my Sunsky, my queen-in-exile! How can I begin to tell you what is in my heart? But alas, that must wait until a better day. Today, I have come to you to talk about an urgent matter. It is about our keythong son, Groundsky."

Sunground's heart flutters in fear. *What does Dreamspinner want with Groundsky? Then again,* she reminds herself, *he is Dreamspinner's son as well.* Ever since Dreamspinner was banned by his family from seeing Sun Wing, Groundsky is the only son with whom he can maintain communication. Sunground relaxes her tightened muscles.

"Groundsky," Sunground says gently to their son, "why don't you run and play for a bit while I speak with your father?"

"No!" Groundsky exclaims, surprising his mother. "Moon Wing is not here for me to play with, for one thing, and for another, I am old enough to understand what decisions are to be made concerning me. I will stay here and know this urgent issue."

Dreamspinner looks at his son with pride. "Groundsky is right. He will need to hear this, anyways."

"All right," Sunground concedes cautiously. "What is this urgent matter?"

Dreamspinner cocks his avian head, regarding them both fondly but with a look in his eyes that suggests fear. "The queen in waiting, Talona, is most anxious to run her agenda through the Gryphonic Council. Queen Heartsong is doing her best to stop her, but she is ailing. We are all terrified of what will happen when Talona gains full power. Even her mother, Soundringer, is beginning to show anxiety."

Sunground feels her surroundings swirling around as her heart grows cold with fear. Grandmother Heartsong is ailing! She closes her eyes for a moment and remembers to listen to her beating heart for a minute to calm herself.

"Listen to your own heart's song," a wise voice advises inside her mind. "I will always be found here."

Dreamspinner pauses a minute, sensing that Sunground needs time to find her still point before the approaching storm. He waits until she opens her eyes before continuing his report. "Talona's agenda is to ensure that the gryphons remain in power. She wants to have all renegade keythongs tried and put in prison. Soon, all keythongs and kryphons will be legally required to register as servants or as servants-in-training under a qualified elder. That is already the social custom of Gryphonia, but the official registration aspect of it has not yet been enacted as law. Oh, my dear son, Groundsky, you must go to your keythong great uncle, Ground Paw, for training. You must also sign a contract promising to remain celibate, since you have not been sterilized at birth."

"What?!" Groundsky cries in disgust. "Leave the hippogryphs? Leave Moon Wing and my mother for a life of slavery to the gryphons? Never! Let them put me in prison. I'd rather that than to bow my head to tyranny!"

Sunground lets out a screech of agony. She feels a strange mixture of pride and an overwhelming sadness at her son's rebellious attitude. "Oh, Groundsky! Truly, you are your father's son. It is, however, foolish to place yourself at Talona's mercy. Your father is correct. You must go as soon as possible to Uncle Ground Paw. He is on the Council of Keythongs, and he can protect you only if you are wise and cooperate."

"Cooperate!" Groundsky snaps contemptuously. "Cooperate with those blasted gryphons, the ones that took flight from you and would take my ability to reproduce from me? No! I wish to mate with a hippogryph and be part of this society. As powerless as the hippogryphs are, they are free. I will not be a keythong slave!"

"*Groundsky, son of Dreamspinner and Sunsky. I declare in all honesty that you will not be a slave among the keythongery!*"

For the first time in his life, Groundsky faces another keythong: it is his Great Uncle Ground Paw. He pecks at his father angrily. "Did you lead him to us? I thought you were on our side!"

"I am!" Dreamspinner explains, backing off slightly from Groundsky's fierce beak. "And so is your Great Uncle Ground Paw. He is here to help you, Groundsky, and your mother as well. If you do not go with him, Talona will persecute and imprison your mother for failing to have you sterilized and trained when you were a young cub."

Sunground beats her wings, her feathers flying in all directions. She will have to give up a son yet again. She realizes that, ironically, when she refused to give him up seventeen sun revolutions ago to her Uncle Ground Paw, she was only ever putting off the inevitable.

"Sunsky, my niece," Ground Paw addresses her in a respectful tone, but Sunground interrupts him.

"I am called Sunground now, Uncle," she informs him. "I changed my name when I took it upon myself to remain grounded for the rest of my life."

"Ah, yes," Ground Paw says. "Sunground, I mean. I know how difficult this is for you. I have tried my best to keep your refusal to sterilize Groundsky a secret, but questions were asked at the Keythong Council about why my great nephew was nowhere to be seen. As you know, Soundringer has sons and brothers on the Keythong Council. Now that old Mudstone has died, the chief among them is Talona's older brother, Growlclaws, the son of Soundringer and Thundercloud. Growlclaws is a fierce presence on the council. He is more terrible even than old Mudstone was. He has made both Soundringer and Talona aware of Groundsky's absence in our society, and I suspect that this soon-to-be-enacted law is in response to that."

"Rug-a-bugger! Talona, Growlclaws, and Soundringer!" Groundsky caws. "I knew I should have gone with Moon Wing. But maybe, Mother Sunground, we should all just run away from this intolerable situation."

"No," Sunground tells her son sadly. "There is nowhere to hide from the Gryphonic Council. They will control our lives one way or another. Groundsky, my son, I ask you to go with your Great Uncle until I can think of an alternate arrangement.

We must ensure your safety, and right now Ground Paw is the only one of us with enough power to do so."

Old Ground Paw draws himself up proudly upon hearing Sunground's remark.

"Yes indeed, young Groundsky, and if you agree to come with me now, I will make sure that you receive the best of treatment. As I announced to you earlier, we keythongs and kryphons are not slaves. We have freedom and we have our own council, which in many ways is the equal of the Gryphonic Council. We do have a responsibility to the rest of the society, however. That society includes all gryphonic beings: gryphons, opinici, keythongs, kryphons, both the winged and the wingless, both male and female, both the sterilized and the procreative ones. We must not run away from our responsibilities, my great nephew."

As Ground Paw speaks, his gaze rests on both Sunground and Groundsky. *Ground Paw no doubt intends this last part of his speech to be directed toward me as well*, Sunground realizes. She cannot blame her uncle for believing that she has shirked her duty towards gryphonic society. Nonetheless, she feels hurt by the inference. Does Ground Paw think that Groundsky has been raised by her to be irresponsible? Sunground knows her choice to raise him away from other keythongs was unwise at best. Is it now also considered traitorous among the keythong councilors?

Groundsky breaks into her thoughts with a terrifying roar. He rears up on his hind legs angrily. "Not being able to mate, to reproduce! Is that what you call freedom, Great Uncle Ground Paw?"

Ground Paw is obviously taken aback by his great nephew's rebellious behavior. "This is the result when we fail to sterilize keythong youngsters," Ground Paw mutters, more to himself than to anyone else.

Groundsky growls. "And I suppose that you will sterilize me if I go with you?"

"No," Ground Paw says. "We will not do that to you. You have my word. It is too late to operate on you anyways, under keythonic law. All that you will need to do is to take an oath of celibacy, much as your mother has taken a private oath to remain grounded in spite of her unclipped wings."

Sunground ruffles her feathers. *How did he know about my wings remaining unclipped? Surely Mother Skystar would not have told him.* She wonders whether Talona has been sending spies to watch her family and listen in on their conversations. She shudders at the thought and quickly brings her attention back to the present conversation.

"What if I refuse to take an oath of celibacy?" Groundsky thunders at Ground Paw. "What if I tell you that I intend to mate with a hippogryph and to stay here where I and my family belong?"

Ground Paw hisses, aghast at such a notion. "A keythong and a hippogryph? I have never heard of such a pairing!"

"Of course you haven't," Groundsky exclaims. "Keythongs and kryphons are all sterilized at birth; but I was not, and I have mated with a young hippogryph already. She may be pregnant with my choal as we speak. If so, it will be a live birth, since hippogryphs have the lower body of a horse and therefore no egg pouch."

Sunground listens to her son in shock. *Groundsky, a father?* She has never considered the notion that a keythong might actually be capable of impregnating a hippogryph. *But then again,* she remembers, *Groundsky is different from most of his brethren in that he remains unsterilized.* She searches her memory to remember his hippogryph friends. *With which one of them would he have formed an intimate bond?*

A picture comes to her mind of an energetic, joyous, grey hippogryph whom Groundsky has on many occasions chased after, with Moon Wing flapping overhead. The little hippogryph is the great granddaughter of old Queen Grass Grazer, who specifically retired from the queenship to turn the responsibility over to Night Lover.

Grass Grazer's family is not related to Night Lover's line, Sunground learned recently from the new queen. They have a different sire, an old winged stallion named Grey Tree of the Valley. Since Grey Tree inhabits the same valley in which the majority of hippogryphs reside, the daughters of Grey Tree and his relatives are conceived in the womb and born of hippogryphs. By contrast, the hippogryph daughters of Nightsky and his relatives are conceived mostly with lower-class gryphons that live in the nether regions of the mountain, within the traditional mating territory of Nightsky's family. These youngsters are hatched from eggs and discreetly given over to the hippogryph clan. Once they are either born or hatched there is little difference between them, and so the ever-practical creatures do not give preference to either one in their society. The hippogryphs determine their leadership based on individual merit as opposed to family lineage or individual rank. It is, as far as Sunground is concerned, a much fairer practice than the one conducted by gryphons.

Although the queen has educated her on the workings of hippogryph society, Sunground has still not socialized with any hippogryphs other than Night Lover. Unlike her son Groundsky, she is unaware of the other individuals in the herd. She has kept her distance to show respect for the beings and shame at her own society for shunning the hippogryphic people.

Sunground turns her attention back to the matter-at-wing. Groundsky is squawking at Ground Paw and Dreamspinner.

"Groundsky!" Sunground exclaims. "Enough. We do not know for certain that a keythong can produce offspring with a hippogryph. As far as I know, a hippogryph is produced with either a gryphon or hippogryph as the mother and a winged stallion as the father."

"No," Groundsky counters. "An opinicus and a wingless mare may also produce not only a hippogryph, but a hippopinicus as well. Grass Hopper told me she has seen one. They are like hippogryphs, only they have two front limbs that are leonine, not avian. That means that an unsterilized keythong may quite possibly mate with a hippogryph and produce either a wingless hippothong or hippokryphon—*or* a winged hippogryph or hippopinicus. Four possibilities. Not bad for a wingless sire, eh?"

Sunground shakes her head, her mind reeling in possibilities. Amid the bravado, Groundsky mentioned the name "Grass Hopper". This must be the name of the energetic young hippogryph whom he has been courting.

"Groundsky!" Sunground responds at last, realizing that Dreamspinner and Ground Paw are waiting expectantly for her to assert her maternal authority over the argumentative youth. "Groundsky, I do not believe for a moment that you have managed to impregnate Grass Hopper. I think that is all silly bluster on your part, and we do not have time for it. Now, I don't like this any more than you do, but we must not be foolish in our decision making. You will go with your Great Uncle Ground Paw, for your own safety and for the safety of all the hippogryphs as well. We do not wish to attract any more gryphons to this place. Do you understand?"

Groundsky is silent for a moment, as though mulling over his choices. "All right, Mother Sunground," he concedes. "If you and the others will be made safer by my absence, I will go."

Sunground's heart sinks and she makes a sad, cooing sound. "Goundsky, I love you. I don't want you to go but you must, for your own future's sake."

"You will not regret your decision, Groundsky," Ground Paw tells him approvingly. "You will be given the proper education that you missed earlier."

"And you, the keythongs," Groundsky answers him slyly, "will be given an education as well, one that you have all missed."

Ground Paw shakes his head but does not respond to this impudence. After a sad farewell to his parents, Groundsky leaves with Ground Paw. Sunground feels a terrible loneliness descending upon her. Now, even her keythong son has been taken from her. She sobs gently into Dreamspinner's furry breast as he envelops her in his wings.

CHAPTER THREE

The Banishment of Grass Hopper

After a few days pass, Dreamspinner volunteers to go and supervise Groundsky's training. It is unorthodox for an opinicus of high standing to do so, but he is adamant. He so much wishes to do something to relieve Sunground's anxiety and sadness.

Sunground is grateful to him for the love and support that he has shown her over the past few days, but she knows that he must move on. It disturbs her that Ground Paw knew about her wings remaining unclipped. Obviously, it is becoming more difficult to keep secrets from the all-knowing gryphonic people. Anyone spending too much time with her might be suspect from Talona's point of view, so Sunground finds herself encouraging Dreamspinner to go away yet again. It is the last thing she wants, but she knows she must not give him cause to stay. She is far too melancholy for lovemaking and Dreamspinner respects this. In fact, Sunground realizes ruefully that it has been seventeen sun revolutions since she last made love—first to Dreamspinner and then to Nighsky. It has also been seventeen sun revolutions since her last flight into the skies.

The banishment from her society has been so lonely, especially for a gregarious social creature such as a gryphon. In spite of this, Sunground finds herself yet again saying good-bye to Dreamspinner, her first love.

"Farewell, my mighty Queen Sunground," Dreamspinner chants in his formal poetic manner, having finally given in to her new name.

"Farewell, my mighty opinicus, and my gratitude to you is forever," she answers. They peck at each other fondly. She watches as he takes flight, becoming smaller and smaller until he fades into the distant skies.

How I wish that I could fly! It is intolerable, this constant groundedness. Flying is my birthright, yet I made this idiotic pledge to remain on the ground as long as I remain banished from my society.

With a heavy heart, Sunground slowly makes her way back to the shelter. There is no one to whom she can come home now. Groundsky and Dreamspinner have left her, and Moon Wing and Night Lover are still away on their quest.

Suddenly, an idea comes to her. Groundsky spoke of mating with his friend, Grass Hopper. Perhaps under these circumstances, the hippogryph family might permit her a visit to discuss the issue. Her heart flutters slightly as she considers approaching the herd. *What if Groundsky's words are true and he has turned me into a grandmother? No matter how odd the choal turns out to be I am determined to love it, if it even exists.*

She makes up her mind and moves in the direction of the hippogryphs' main territory, the one occupied by old Queen Grass Grazer. She has not traveled long before an elderly grey hippogryph confronts her, barring her from going further.

"What business have you here, Sunground?" she asks, annoyed. "Night Lover and Moon Wing have not yet returned from their journey."

Sunground trembles. Old Queen Grass Grazer is still a formidable presence in spite of her advanced age, and Sunground tries valiantly to maintain her dignity as she blurts out her business. "O Queen Grass Grazer! I am here on an entirely different matter. I have been told by my keythong son that he may have impregnated the young hippogryph named Grass Hopper."

As soon as the words are out of her mouth, Sunground regrets them.

What a fool I have been, she chides herself, *to name Grass Hopper and Groundsky as mates when I do not know if Grass Hopper is pregnant!*

Grass Grazer looks at her intently for a long time before screeching loudly in a dialect that Sunground does not understand. Several hippogryphs arrive at once, including young Grass Hopper. They appear to be having an impromptu conference. Panic stricken, Sunground hopes desperately that she has not endangered either Groundsky or Grass Hopper with her thoughtless words. As often happens whenever she interacts with the hippogryphs, however, her fears prove to be groundless.

"Sunground," Grass Grazer says to her, more gently this time. "My apologies. I did not realize what transpired between my great-granddaughter and your son. Grass Hopper tells me that she is indeed pregnant and that the father is most certainly Groundsky."

Sunground cocks her head curiously. *It is true! Groundsky is a father, and I am a grandmother!*

"There has never been an instance in our herd where a hippogryph has mated with a keythong," Grass Grazer continues. "We mate either with winged stallions or with an opinicus on rare occasions. Thus, we do not know what form this young one will take. Will it be winged or wingless? If it is wingless, then you or Moon Wing must care for it. Winglessness is a dangerous condition when you are a creature hated by the gryphonic tribes. We need our wings to escape. A wingless hippothong or hippokryphon cannot remain within our clan."

The normally joyous young hippogryph lets out a screeching wail, and Sunground feels her heart breaking for Grass Hopper. It reminds her so much of herself many revolutions ago, when she realized that her daughter was to be rejected by her people. An idea suddenly jumps into her mind. "Wait! Grass Hopper and her *choal* will be welcome with me and Moon Wing. Night Lover will guide us in the process, I am quite certain, and I have experience raising wingless ones. Why doesn't Grass Hopper come and stay with me while we await the birth?"

Sunground notices that Grass Hopper shivers slightly at the mention of living with a gryphon. She again regrets her words, but they are well received by the tribe of hippogryphs. Queen Grass Grazer consults with several of the younger hippogryphs, among them Grass Hopper's mother. Finally, the old queen speaks in a dialect that Sunground understands. "Very well, Sunground. Under the circumstances, this is the best solution. Grass Hopper must learn your ways if she is to raise her *choal*, as she wants to do. She will go with you now, to live with you until the birth. If the *choal* is winged, she and the young one will have the option of returning to our tribe. If it is wingless, then both she and the *choal* must remain with you. It is decided."

Before Sunground has time to react to Grass Grazer's words, the herd turns around and walks off into the woods. Only Grass Hopper's mother remains behind to nuzzle her daughter, before she too turns and walks off into the forest. Grass Hopper stands alone, trembling in fear. Sunground's heart leaps. *What have I gotten myself into now? I know not what to say to the young hippogryph.*

"Do not fret, Grass Hopper," she says in a futile attempt to reassure her. "I am nothing to fear, believe me. I am only a shunned and grounded gryphon." Grass Hopper nods mutely and follows her back to the nesting shelter.

The next few days are extremely awkward. Her new charge does not speak much, and Sunground finally decides to stop pushing her to answer questions. Grass Hopper responds well to this strategy and gradually begins to ask her own questions, first telepathically and then verbally. "Mother Sunground," she asks, "when will Moon Wing and Queen Night Lover return?"

"Soon, I hope," Sunground answers, relieved that someone is speaking to her for a change. Silence greets her answer once again. Sunground tries to revive the communication by asking a number of mundane questions that provoke only monosyllabic responses from Grass Hopper. Finally, Sunground decides to address the underlying issue between them. "Grass Hopper, you need not fear me. I am the mother of Moon Wing, and I desire only the best for her, for you, and your people."

Grass Hopper says nothing at first. Sunground waits, letting her words sink in. She closes her eyes and releases the need for a response from the young hippogryph. As she does so, Grass Hopper replies. "Mother Sunground. It is not you I fear but your gryphonic society."

Sunground opens her eyes and listens. "What is it that you fear, Grass Hopper?" she asks softly.

Grass Hopper pauses briefly before responding. "For some time, I have heard the other hippogryphs speculate on the possibility of an attack upon our people by the gryphons and their keythonic allies."

Fear grips Sunground's heart, but she tries her best to suppress it. "Oh, Grass Hopper! Don't fear the worst. I don't think that even Talona, the gryphon queen-in-waiting, would swoop so low; and as long as my grandmother Heartsong has anything to say about it, there will be no attacks."

"But I have heard that the old gryphon queen is ailing. That means only one thing: Talona's reign will shortly be upon us. It is this I fear. What will happen to the outcasts?"

Sunground is startled at how much the young hippogryph knows about the political situation in the gryphonic queendom. She must have given her a querying look, for Grass Hopper is lightning-quick in her response. "We obtain our information from your old caregiver, the kryphon Egglight. She regularly dispatches one of the nannygryphs to the valley to update us on the progress in your society, or lack thereof. We also find informants in your two sisters, Cloudhopper and Mountain Rain."

Sunground stares at her in horror. *Egglight and her two sisters—informants! They could be arrested for treason, and I would be responsible because I was the one to get them into this mess in the first place. No, I will not revert to feeling remorseful about the actions that brought forth my beautiful daughter, Moon Wing. I must not, no matter what happens.*

Grass Hopper seems to realize the impact of her words, for she apologizes profusely. "I am so sorry, Mother Sunground. I ought not to have spoken in so blunt a fashion about our allies."

When Sunground regains her composure, she finally replies. "No, do not apologize, Grass Hopper. It is time that I knew the truth of the matter. I suppose my family is doing it to help Moon Wing, Groundsky, and me. I just hope it does not come back on them in the form of Talona's wrath."

"Fret not, Mother Sunground," Grass Hopper says. "They are keeping it a secret."

Sunground feels her heart sinking as she realizes the naïveté of the youngster's statement. She knows well that no one can keep a secret for long when Talona's mother is in a position of authority. There is little doubt that Soundringer has influenced, if not completely taken over, Talona's training. No one can expect the ailing Grandmother Heartsong to battle Soundringer much longer. If Heartsong is not completely involved in the training of Talona, however, the results might well be catastrophic. Sunground shudders to think of it, but she tries to comfort herself nonetheless. *Perhaps the oracle might have some influence upon her. Let us hope for a more positive outcome.*

CHAPTER FOUR

A Song for Great Heart

Rage of eagle's talon, O lionhearted breast,
sing a carol of love
for the elder gryphon,
a song for Great Heart!
Spirit of Wisdom's divine birth,
ascending on soul wings to the greater height
of a deep home nest
as she of the light feather
sings of infinite love.
The Universal Queen
flies to the skies today,
and she arrives
upon the threshold of eternity.

As Sunground sings the gryphonic *Song for Great Heart*, she feels her own heart breaking. The opinicus Dreamspinner, the bearer of the terrible news, joins her in the song. The dreaded day has finally arrived: The old queen, Heartsong, has flown on to the Eternal Skies.

As Grass Hopper and her young mate Groundsky look on helplessly, Sunground rocks her feathered head back and forth in an attempt to calm herself. She thinks of Heartsong's wise stories, of her gentle clucking that so calmed the active young gryphlet once named Sunsky. Anxiety prevents her from accessing the peaceful feeling of reassurance that Heartsong once inspired. What will happen now that Talona and Soundringer are in charge? She regards her son Groundsky worriedly. Both he and Dreamspinner are now fugitives being hunted by the keythonic law enforcement officers, or *LEOs*. When they are found, they will be arrested.

Groundsky was not among the keythongs for long before he began creating a huge stir of fur with his incessant talk of not sterilizing keythongs or kryphons. With the news of the old queen's passing, Dreamspinner knew that he would need to escape immediately with Groundsky while there was still a window of opportunity.

"Mother Sunground! Father Dreamspinner!" Groundsky says, interrupting his parents' lament. "I am sorry for intruding upon your grief, but we must warn the hippogryph community right now. And we must flee, all of us. The *LEOs* are marching in this direction as we speak, and a squadron of search gryphons will soon join them by air. We have no time to waste!"

Sunground realizes that her son is correct. Grandmother Heartsong would want her to remain strong and act decisively. "You're right, Groundsky. Let us go to the hippogryphs straight away."

Sunground notices that Grass Hopper is no longer with them. The group hears a screech, and the young hippogryph bounds in stricken with panic. "Mother Sunground! I have already warned my people. They are taking to the skies and we would be wise to do the same. Do not fret about Moon Wing, for my people have sent a telepathic message of warning to Night Lover. They will meet her and Moon Wing at the foot of the lower mountains to consult with the queen about the new danger."

Sunground stares at Grass Hopper in horror as she thinks of the danger to her beloved Moon Wing. She knows that her daughter will be safer with the herd of hippogryphs right now, but it still tugs at her heart. She goes within to connect with either Moon Wing or Night Lover, but a new anxiety intrudes upon her concentration. "Grass Hopper, I cannot abandon Groundsky. He cannot fly. You go ahead with your people."

Grass Hopper stomps the ground with her back hoof impatiently. "*You* are my people now, Mother Sunground!"

"Mother Sunground, you must now use your wings! It is imperative," Groundsky declares. "I will follow you by ground. I am very fast, you know. I have four legs for ground-speed. I can outrun the *LEOs*, but only if we leave right now."

"Yes, my great Queen Sunground," Dreamspinner adds. "It is time for you to claim your rightful place in the skies! I will go back to the gryphonic nesting site to rescue your family. Then, your family and I will meet you at the pinnacle of Flight-Quest Mountain."

Sunground gives her anguished consent. She knows there is little else that they can do. At the sound of her clarion call, the beings leap into action. Dreamspinner flaps his mighty wings, taking to the skies in a matter of seconds. Groundsky takes off at a swift run, and Sunground knows that she will need to use her wings to keep up with him.

To her shame, her first attempt at flight falters after so many sun revolutions spent on the ground. She leaps into the air with great majesty only to fall clumsily to the ground with a thud. Grass Hopper waits as Sunground beats her wings in frustration. "Grass Hopper!" she bellows. "Go without me. I will follow along on the ground."

"I will not, Mother Sunground!" she replies defiantly. "If you go by ground, then so shall I, as does my mate, Groundsky."

Sunground lets loose a volley of gryphonic epithets. Her rage intensifies as she tries to beat her wings fast enough to lift her body from the ground. Alas, she cannot. The pair hops along the path in a woeful attempt to catch up to Groundsky, who is no doubt unaware that his mother and mate remain grounded. Gryphons and hippogryphs do not generally use their forearms for long walks. Rather, the leonine or equine hindquarters are designed to catapult their bodies powerfully into the air. Their wings then take over as the main means of transport.

After an hour or so of hobbling along, Sunground stops. *This is ridiculous*, she thinks. *There must be another way to access my flight skills. They have obviously grown weary with neglect.*

Summoning all that is within her, she remembers the oracle Truth Speaker's words and listens to the beat of her heart. The *Song for a Great Heart* grows within her, and it is a wordless song of silence. As Sunground stills herself, Grass Hopper waits respectfully. She is aware of what Sunground is trying to do and says nothing.

Slowly, Sunground's spirit arises from its slumber. She feels the presence of Heartsong grow further inside her until it has gone beyond her physical form. It unfolds around her, just as she was once enfolded by her grandmother's wings as a gryphlet chick.

Behind her, she hears the rustle of paw upon ground and the barking of orders, but it does not deter her from focusing on Heartsong's presence. She feels her wings stir and ever so slightly, they begin to flap. They are soon beating softly, gaining momentum until finally Sunground tenses her haunches and attempts another take-off. This time, she flies a few beats into the air before she falls back down to the ground. She continues onward in determination as Grass Hopper encourages her from behind.

The barking from behind grows louder. Sunground remains calm and gradually covers larger spans of flight. Grass Hopper follows her and when she falls, the young hippogryph hovers overhead until she leaps back into the air. They journey forward in this manner until they manage to put some distance between themselves and the ground-pounding keythong forces that are pursuing them.

After a short rest Sunground and Grass Hopper are finally able to travel in full flight mode, each of them taking turns to swoop low and watch out for Groundsky's progress. Before long, they detect the young keythong running along the path up Flight-Quest Mountain. The trees are beginning to thin as they approach the apex. That means there will be far fewer places behind which to hide from the determined posse of LEOs that are hunting them.

There is also a new danger, Sunground realizes. As they ascend closer to the mountain peak, more squadrons of search gryphons will be patrolling the area, specifically watching for them. They will all be clear targets. *It is ironic*, she thinks, *that we are not only exiled from our people but hunted by them. I would never have thought it possible in the sun revolutions of my youth.*

As the duo nears the peak of the mountain, they hover cautiously over the ground. Sunground sees no evidence of search gryphons, but neither does she see Dreamspinner and her family members. She hopes that they were not captured during their escape.

The pair lands softly by some bushes, trying as much as possible to blend in with the landscape. Groundsky soon joins them, as Sunground marvels at his speed and agility in having climbed the mountain by paw.

"Well, where are they?" Groundsky demands impatiently. "We have the *LEO* brigade on our tails! We don't have time to waste."

"Groundsky, my son," Sunground replies. "We do not know whether Dreamspinner was successful in rescuing our family members. We must wait."

"We have no time to wait!" Groundsky growls. "The *LEOs*…"

Before he finishes his sentence, they hear the trees rustle as five *LEOs* charge into the clearing, their leonine claws drawn. The trio ducks and clings to the bushes, but it is too late. The leader sees them first and leads his pack over to them.

"Groundsky!" the keythong leader thunders. "You and your kin are under arrest for treason, by order of the great and mighty gryphonic queen, Talona!"

Groundsky charges the keythongs, biting and clawing at them angrily. He is overpowered after a brief but powerful fight. "Flee, Mother Sunground! Grass Hopper! Flee!" Groundsky cries to no avail.

They simply refuse to leave him in the custody of those loyal to Talona. Sunground flies at the group of keythongs, thrashing them with her wings and tearing at their flesh with her talons. Grass Hopper flies from above, kicking them with her powerful equine hind legs and ripping their furred skin with her talons.

"Halt!" the commanding LEO cries. "You will be named as traitors to the gryphonic queendom if you do not stop your attack upon its loyal officers!"

"Fools!" Groundsky replies. "Open your eyes and ears! Do you not realize that the queendom works against the rights of the keythong people? You are the traitors, not us!"

"Lying rebels!" the commander screeches, reaching his paw into the air to defend himself from another airborne attack. "You disgrace your heritage with these actions. Cease your attack now and you will be treated well, with great fairness."

"Fairness, my tail!" Groundsky exclaims, taking advantage of the distractions caused by his mother and mate to renew his own attack. This time, the LEOs break away from them.

"Let us go and bring reinforcements! These savages are more dangerous than we imagined!" the commander roars as the fugitives escape into the bushes of the lower forest.

CHAPTER FIVE

Reunion

The group of three continues on its trek, zigzagging down the mountain and then up again, searching desperately for signs of Dreamspinner and the family. *This is pointless,* Sunground says to herself. *He is not here.*

At the exact moment of her despairing thought, a large winged presence appears above, and swoops down among them with a crash. "Do not fret. I am here, my love!" the opinicus cries.

"Yes, but Dreamspinner, where are our family members?" Sunground asks, her mind murky with fear and exasperation.

"They will join us later. They have taken different routes to divide the paths and cause confusion to our pursuers."

They continue on, zigzagging endlessly. Sunground cannot stop thinking about her family, and her anxiety threatens to overcome her. Each time she feels her stress levels rising, however, she listens to her heartbeat and hears the quiet cooing of her grandmother, Heartsong, who used to lull her to sleep when she was a chick.

They persist on their journey for the next two days, pausing only to eat bark and leaves for sustenance. There is no time to hunt even the smallest of prey. Eventually, Dreamspinner leads them into a small clearing. There, to Sunground's profound relief and delight, are Mother Skystar, old Egglight, and her sisters Mountain Rain and Cloudhopper.

The reunited family members squawk in joy, flying at each other and rubbing heads together. As soon as there is a lull in the reunion, Sunground realizes that her father is not among them. She asks the dreaded question. "Mother Skystar, where is Father Sun Quest?"

"My daughter Sunsky," Skystar responds, stubbornly using Sunground's old name, "your father Sun Quest has been arrested. Talona brought him before the Gryphonic Council's new Court of Accountability to answer the charges against this family—your wings not being clipped, Groundsky not being sterilized, Egglight and your sisters acting as informants to the hippogryphs. All these things have been discovered, Sunsky. One of us had to go to court and your father insisted that he be the one to do so, even though it really should have been me. I was directly responsible for the decision not to clip your wings, among other transgressions."

Sunground listens in shock. Her fears for her family are coming true. She has always known that at some point, Skystar's role in helping her to birth both her keythong son and hippogryph daughter in the Valley of Outcasts would result in some kind of legal proceeding against her, especially now that Talona is in charge. Because of Skystar's involvement in all of this, it makes sense for Father Sun Quest to go to court in her place, as he cannot be charged with any direct violations except the general (and lesser) charge of complicity in these acts. Nonetheless, it must have been a heart-wrenching decision for

Skystar to leave her mate in such a position in order to escape with old Egglight and her sisters.

"Sun Quest has made a terrible sacrifice in order to set us free," Skystar lamented, "and so has your grandfather, King Lightning Bolt, who went against the order to shun our family so that he could represent Sun Quest in court and offer further protection to all of us. We had quite an argument about it. In the end, though, I knew that I had to go to find you and ensure your safety."

"We all did," Mountain Rain says. "We're here for all of you."

As the rest of the family chirps their agreement, Sunground feels an overwhelming sense of love for them all. They too have sacrificed a great deal to come with her. She gives voice to a song of gratitude to them, as they surround Groundsky and her, all the while preening and cooing at them lovingly.

During this reunion, Grass Hopper has been shyly hiding in the woods, watching them silently. From her perspective, the number of gryphonic beings has increased rather alarmingly. Sunground knows she must not forget the young hippogryph. "My family, I must introduce you to Groundsky's mate."

She beckons to Grass Hopper, gently encouraging her to come closer. When the hippogryph hesitates, Groundsky bounds up to her, playfully nipping her equine hindquarters. Grass Hopper squawks and flaps her wings, chasing Groundsky until he has maneuvered her over to where his mother's family stands.

"This is Grass Hopper, the great granddaughter of the retired hippogryph queen, Grass Grazer," Sunground announces.

An awkward pause meets the odd introduction, as her sisters and old Egglight regard the young hippogryph with a mixture of awe and fear. This is the first time any of them have been so close to a hippogryph, other than Moon Wing when she was much smaller. Old Egglight, the wingless kryphon, has never in her life seen such a creature.

Skystar, who became accustomed to hippogryphs during her stay with Sunground long ago in the Valley of Outcasts, moves closer to greet Grass Hopper with a gentle cooing sound. Grass Hopper backs up warily, the equine aspect of her skittish and nervous among so many gryphons. Egglight joins her, cooing at Grass Hopper encouragingly. Grass Hopper, less fearful of the wingless being, reaches over to Egglight and lightly taps beaks with her.

"You are now a member of our family," Skystar says.

Grass Hopper stands bemused among them but says nothing.

"Fret not over these creatures, my love!" Groundsky says. "They only dine on hippogryph meat every other day."

Groundsky's quip is met with peals of laughter, and Sunground is relieved to see Grass Hopper joining in with her own cackles. She looks upon her keythong son in pride. He has a way of putting everyone at ease with his raucous and silly sense of humor.

"Sunground, you have not yet met your nieces!" Cloudhopper exclaims as two young gryphons land rather unceremoniously in their midst, cawing excitedly at Sunground, Groundsky, and Grass Hopper. The hippogryph backs off slightly, eyeing the youngsters with some trepidation.

"Fret not, love, I'll protect you!" Groundsky bellows, bounding at his two newly met cousins and pecking at their hindquarters until all of them are engaged in a rowdy game of tail chasing. Groundsky even entices Grass Hopper to put aside her fears and join in.

"These ruffians are Rainbow Dreamer, the daughter of Mountain Rain, and Luck Wisher, my own scamp. They are both by your noble mate, Dreamspinner, of course. He is the only one foolish enough to mate with the gryphons in this family!" Cloudhopper explains. "They have been off hunting and have come back empty-taloned, so I see."

Sunground feels a sudden homesickness descending upon her as she realizes that she has missed the chickhoods of her two nieces. "They are Moon Wing's age, aren't they?" she asks her sisters wistfully.

"Almost," Mountain Rain answers. "Though they are a few sun revolutions younger. Speaking of Moon Wing, where is the little mischief maker? We have not seen her since she was a chick—that is to say, a *choal*."

Sunground stifles a screech of worry as she thinks about her daughter. "Moon Wing is a *choal* no longer. She has gone with her elder sister, Night Lover, to seek out her father. I can only hope that the hippogryphs were successful in finding them. They will both be safer in a herd—or flock, if they need to fly."

"None of us is safe so long as Talona reigns," old Egglight says. "I do not know where in my raising and teaching of her I went wrong."

Sunground stiffens at the name of Talona. Egglight has been a nanny not only to her and her sisters, but also to Soundringer's chick. For the first part of their lives, up until ten sun revolutions of age, the four of them had been educated together by Egglight. Talona did not inhabit the same nest-den as her half-sisters but rather lived with her mother Soundringer, who was without an official mate.

Sunground remembers with shame how cruel she and her

sisters were to Talona because her mother, Soundringer, was so despised by their mutual father, Sun Quest. She and Mountain Rain would peck at Talona mercilessly. It is odd that, after so many sun revolutions, she is remembering this right now.

"It was not your teaching that was at fault, Egglight," Sunground reassures her old nanny.

"No, indeed—it is the fault of Soundringer!" Cloudhopper chimes angrily.

"Not all of it, Cloudhopper," Sunground says. "We behaved very badly toward her, if I may remind you."

"But, Sunsky—I mean, Sunground—we behaved badly toward her because she treated us so terribly!" Cloudhopper screeches in their defense.

"Where does the circle of the broken egg end?" Sunground muses ruefully, quoting an old gryphonic proverb. "We hurt her, she hurt us. Where does it all end? I have learned much from my banishment, Cloudhopper, and I can't help but feel responsible in some way for Talona's vicious behavior of late."

Mountain Rain chirps in annoyance. "Sunground, what has happened to your vitality and your sense of self-respect? You are no more responsible for Talona's behavior than any other gryphon, Soundringer excluded. Her behavior is her own responsibility, not ours! Why, we were only chicks back then, for the sake of the oracle!"

"Yes, and so was she, Rain," Sunground replies quietly.

The younger Gryphons interrupt their elders, bounding straight through their group tête-à-tête.

"All right, all right!" Mother Skystar says. "Enough of this horseplay—if you will pardon the pun, Grass Hopper. Remember, my grandchicks, that this is not a picnic. We are

133

at the moment fleeing squadrons of both the ground and sky. We need to keep moving."

"I will no more be drawn up into the sky!" old Egglight protests vociferously. "Squadrons or no, I will keep my weary paws upon the ground where they belong."

"Egglight was flying?" Groundsky asks in amazement. "How?"

"Luck Wisher and I put her in a harness and we all carried her in our talons," Rainbow Dreamer says. "We could do the same with you, if you wish."

"No!" Egglight cries, as Groundsky dances in anticipation of a possible flight. "You must guard and protect your elderly kryphon counterpart, Groundsky, the son of my dear Sun-sky-ground. You are old enough now to take on this responsibility. I trust that Ground Paw has given you at least enough education to help an old kryphon. You and I will travel by land, as the universe created us to do!"

"I will perform my duties with gusto, Egglight, nanny of my mother!" Groundsky replies heartily, proud to be entrusted with such an adult responsibility.

"I'm afraid we must all travel by land now," Skystar says. "And we must go into the forest. I feel the vibration of wings in the air."

CHAPTER SIX

Escape

The gryphonic family struggles through the underbrush of the forest. They have descended from the mountain again to render themselves less visible from above. The journey is extremely slow, as the dense bushes ensnare their bodies and wings. It is especially difficult for Grass Hopper, whose equine hindquarters and large, feathery wings snag frequently in the underbrush. Groundsky and Egglight gnaw the hippogryph free of vines and branches, only to find her stuck again.

Groundsky and Egglight have been extremely busy extricating the other gryphons' wings as well. Their own winglessness has for once been a blessing as they crawl through the undergrowth without the entanglement that their winged counterparts must endure.

"This is ridiculous!" Dreamspinner cries in a rage as he thrashes about in an attempt to break free from a bush. "How can we continue like this?"

"We can't travel by sky, Dreamspinner!" Sunground chides him. "The squadron will capture us for sure."

Dreamspinner grumbles his reluctant agreement, but the others feel his frustration.

"Do we even know where we're going, Aunt Sunground?" Luck Wisher, the daughter of Cloudhopper, asks in desperation.

"Shush, Lucky!" Cloudhopper says. "We are hiding from the air squadron as much as we are running from them."

"Oh, why don't we just fight them?" Rainbow Dreamer, the daughter of Mountain Rain, suggests ruefully. "It would be better than this. We can't even hunt in here!"

"Eat bark!" Morning Rain snaps at her chick. "And stop complaining, both of you gryphlets! Grandfather Sun Quest and Great Grandfather Lightning Bolt didn't risk their freedom for us to allow ourselves to be captured!"

The young gryphlets fall silent at the mention of Sun Quest and King Lightning Bolt, their sorrow evident. The entire family feels miserable, but there is little else they can do except to journey on in this most torturous manner.

Eventually, they come to a clearing and cannot believe the freedom of movement that is afforded them by the simple act of breaking out of the woods and thickets. The younger ones run and jump joyously, tearing around the field chasing one another. The adults cry a warning, but it goes unheeded.

A screech rings out from the skies and two large gryphons descend, their talons outstretched. They are aiming for Groundsky. In the blink of an eye, one of them is upon him, and just as quickly, Sunground, Dreamspinner, and Grass Hopper fly at the attacking gryphon.

The second gryphon sees that the pair is outnumbered and aborts her mission, leaving her partner behind to contend with the battling parents and fearsome hippogryph. Mountain Rain,

Cloudhopper, and Skystar have meanwhile formed a protective circle around Rainbow Dreamer and Luck Wisher.

Grass Hopper quickly falls out of the melee so she can aid the old nanny Egglight as she tends the stunned but otherwise unhurt Groundsky. Sunground and Dreamspinner continue to tear many of the feathers off the attacker, screaming at her in rage. Skystar intervenes, squawking at Sunground to stop the assault.

Sunground slowly realizes what she is doing and backs off from the fight as Skystar pins the gryphon down. "Sunsky, get me a vine from the forest!"

Ignoring her mother's use of her old name, she obeys the order and leaps into the forest to snatch the first vine she can find. She rips it from the tree with her beak and races back to Skystar, who uses her deft talons to tie the attacker's forearms and rear legs together.

Sunground feels a bolt of shock run through her as she recognizes the assailant: an old chickhood friend from flight school named Star Sailor.

"Star Sailor!" she says. "How can you have participated in this cowardly attack on our young ones?"

"I'm so sorry, Sunsky. I mean Sun*ground*, that is," Star Sailor croaks miserably. "As Royal Air Squadron members, we have to obey orders. None of us likes Queen Talona, but we must carry out her commands under the gryphonic law. If we do not, she has made it clear that we will be put to death and our families thrown into prison for life. I must tread carefully for all of our sakes, because my mother, Queenstar, is still chief magistrate and represents one of the last remaining power checks on the regime."

Sunground screeches in astonishment. The death penalty, along with life imprisonment, was abolished long ago and has never been considered by a ruling monarch of the recent past, even in the case of murder. The very idea that Chief Magistrate Queenstar—a staunch friend of Mother Skystar—can be threatened with imprisonment is truly terrifying. She feels an uncomfortable rage welling up inside her against Talona, for what she is doing to divide gryphonic families and friends against each other. She looks at her friend lying on the ground, her talons and paws bound together and her many lost feathers scattered around her. She feels a deep empathy toward her plight. The inner conflict that Star Sailor is experiencing must be similar to her own, many sun revolutions ago, when she was forced to choose between her offspring or her queendom. A stabbing guilt pierces her heart as she realizes that her decision to abdicate her reign has led to this outrage.

"Star Sailor," she says gently. "I am the one who should apologize to you. My decision long ago has caused this crisis."

"No," Star Sailor replies wearily. "Talona herself has caused this. She has had every opportunity to learn from the wisdom of Queen Heartsong, but she has refused. She has deliberately divided the gryphonic families against each other by jailing the oracle."

Sunground feels her heart drop with a thud against her breast. "Truth Speaker has been imprisoned?" She croaks incredulously. "How can that be possible? The Gryphonic Code forbids it, unless the most dreadful of heresies has been committed. Why, an oracle has not been imprisoned for a thousand sun revolutions!"

"Talona has used the heresy clause to charge Truth Speaker," her friend laments, "and the council was too afraid of her wrath to deny her. Even Soundringer was shocked. She even stood against her on it, for a brief period, until Talona threatened to jail her own mother."

Sunground beats her wings in surprise. *Soundringer has spoken against Talona on behalf of the oracle? I cannot believe it.* "What heresy could Truth Speaker have committed?" Sunground asks.

Mother Skystar interjects. "Truth Speaker has long been adamant in her support for you, Sunsky. This has no doubt worried Talona for a long time."

"Yes, but Soundringer, speaking *against* Talona, even for a short period. That is unheard of!"

"No," Skystar replies. "Soundringer has been realizing her mistake in pushing Talona into the queenship position too soon."

"Was there no one else to stand with Soundringer, to challenge Talona's grave error?" Sunground asks miserably.

"Yes," Star Sailor replies, equally as miserable. "The physician Light Healer came into the council chamber to protest the action, and she was imprisoned along with Truth Speaker."

Sunground and Skystar yowl in unison. "How can Talona imprison the physician? She is so badly needed by gryphonic society!" Sunground cries.

"It does not surprise me," Skystar murmurs. "Light Healer has staged many protests on our family's behalf, with regard to our prince, Sun Wing, being raised by two opinici."

Sunground feels yet another thud within her breast as she remembers the first and last time that she saw Sun Wing in Light Healer's birthing den. She remembers the sorrow at seeing her newborn son reach up to her with his trusting beak, waiting to be fed, only to be snatched unceremoniously by Thundercloud and spirited away.

Thundercloud. The name sits heavy within the dark fog of her addled mind. *This one that raises her son is the same opinicus that killed Dreamspinner's birth-mother, Wing Dreamer, for the "crime" of mating with a winged horse and giving birth to the hippogryph Night Lover. Wing Dreamer, she who was banished to the Valley of Outcasts, just as Sunground has been banished. Wing Dreamer, she who was torn asunder by the unforgiving claws of her own son's grandfather. This murderous creature has been educating my dear prince, Sun Wing.*

She wonders with great angst how Sun Wing now appears, he that was once her infant but is now a young opinicus the same age as his sister Moon Wing and his brother Groundsky. *How has he fared under the harsh guidance of Thundercloud?* Sunsky wonders. *Has he taught the youngster to regard his birth mother's family with murderous hate, just as the Old One regarded Wing Dreamer?*

Dreamspinner's stepmother Stormspeaker supposedly helped her mate Windsinger to rear Sun Wing, but Sunground doubts that she ever truly participated in his upbringing. A repressed and rotting rage bubbles up within her at her own society, at the council members for allowing all of this and especially for not standing with Light Healer to protest the lack of a maternal wing in the young prince's life. She beats her wings and begins to screech but is drowned out by her sister Mountain Rain's angry denouncements.

"How can you support such a crooked regime, Star Sailor?" she asks the bound and bedraggled gryphon before them. "You and all the others ought to be de-feathered and fed to gargoyles for going along with this intolerable outrage, for allowing such courageous gryphons and opinici as Truth Speaker, Light Healer, King Lightning Bolt, and our own Father Sun Quest to be imperiled just so you can keep your positions in gryphon society. You deserve to be left here, to be pecked and ravaged to death by the vultures!"

Star Sailor offers no argument, but instead hangs her head in mute agreement. Sunground listens to her sister's words in horror. *If the oracle and the physician can be imprisoned merely for protesting the actions of Talona, then what chance has their father, Sun Quest, for evading prison? Or Grandfather Lightning Bolt, for daring to stand on behalf of Sun Quest and his family?* Terror grips Sunground's heart as she thinks of her father and elderly grandfather in the clutches of this evil regime, but neither can she permit Mountain Rain's condemnation of their friend, Star Sailor.

"No, Rain!" she protests. "We will not swoop so low as Talona. Star Sailor is no different from any of us, for we have all had to accept and tolerate actions that none of us like! How do you think Mother Skystar feels about us having left Father Sun Quest and Grandfather Lightning Bolt in the talons of this fearsome young queen? Let us not be divided further but instead, let's bring Star Sailor along with us as we flee—which we must do soon, if we are to escape the air squadron."

"No!" Star Sailor screeches, suddenly raising her head. "Mountain Rain is right. Leave me to the fate that she suggests. If you bring me with you, Talona will consider my whole family to be sympathetic to the rebel cause and she will punish them. Go now, before the squadron returns! Let me not see the direction that you take."

"She is right, my compassionate queen!" Dreamspinner agrees. "The air squadron will not harm her if they believe she is loyal to Talona. We, on the other wing, will most certainly be joining the brave oracle, the physician, the king, and your father in their prison lair if we do not leave immediately."

"Stop talking and let's go!" Skystar yells, rounding up the young ones and running toward the woods.

Sunground and the others follow suit, racing back into the tangled underbrush only moments before the hapless Star Sailor, left alone with her talons still bound to her hind legs, is obliged to greet twelve incoming air squadron officers.

CHAPTER SEVEN

The Hiding Spot

Soon she hears a voice inside her mind. "*Sunground.*" She halts for a second, startled. This is a voice she has not heard in a long time. She recognizes it immediately as Night Lover's telepathic sound messaging. "*Night Lover?*" she calls into the darkness of her own mind. "*Is that you?*"

"*Come this way,*" the voice commands, without bothering to confirm Sunground's query.

Sunground hesitates. *Will the others think I am mad? Then again, Mother Skystar knows all about the telepathic abilities of the hippogryphs from her time spent in the valley many sun revolutions ago. She will no doubt support me.*

"Hey!" Sunground calls out to her fellow escapees. "I've just had a telepathic communication from Night Lover, the queen of the hippogryphs. She bids us to move in this direction."

Sunground points the way with her outstretched talon. The others chirp cheerlessly but offer no resistance to the new command. They all struggle to turn around and begin the process of stumbling their way along this alternate, tangled route.

"Are you sure it's Night Lover, Sunsky?" Mother Skystar inquires, again reverting to the use of Sunground's old name. "Sometimes our minds can play tricks on us in these kinds of unpleasant situations."

"I am certain," Sunground replies, pecking at a vine that has entangled her left wing. "I feel her presence strongly. I think that she may have been silently guiding us for some time now, through me and no doubt through you and Grass Hopper as well."

Her words are met by groans and grumbles, but the group perseveres. They continue to move along through the vegetation for what seems like an eternity before Sunground receives an image in her mind: It is the image of the mouth of a cave, well hidden by branches and undergrowth.

"Grass Hopper!" Sunground suddenly calls out to the young hippogryph. "Have you received an image in your mind from Night Lover?"

"Yes, Mother Sunground," Grass Hopper replies, pushing and scrambling her way through the entangled vegetation. "It is not far now. I know where we are! It is the hippogryphs' secret hiding spot. They must have fled here after they left our home valley many days ago."

Sunground feels a flicker of hope within her breast. A cave, camouflaged by tangled underbrush, will offer a much-needed refuge from the search squadrons.

Grass Hopper takes the lead now, as she possesses more advanced telepathic abilities than those of the other gryphonic beings. Before long, they come upon a tall, dense hedge, so thick and tangled that it forms a wall. The group naturally shies away from it.

"No!" Grass Hopper tells them adamantly. "It is here."

"What?" Mountain Rain exclaims. "We can't get through that mess, Grass Hopper!"

Grass Hopper does not listen but instead plunges into the brush, thrashing about for several minutes before disappearing. Sunground, without pausing to argue with her siblings, follows suit. She feels an uncomfortable wall of branches surrounding her, threatening to choke her. She thrashes through until she stumbles onto a clear, narrow path leading into the mouth of a cave. She calls for the others to follow and one by one, they each make the momentous effort of pushing their way through to the cave's pathway.

Old Egglight is the last to break through the hedge wall, with Groundsky coaxing and encouraging her every step of the way. She rasps agonizingly as she finally breaks free of it. "This is no voyage for an elderly kryphon!" she groans mournfully.

"Fret not, Egglight!" Groundsky reassures her. "The tangled journey is now at an end. It is time to enter the cave!"

Egglight chirps her displeasure. "I suppose we will now need to stumble our way through the dark?" Her question hangs in the air as the group slowly follows Grass Hopper into the dark cavern. They move slowly, unable to see anything as the darkness enfolds them.

"Keep moving!" Night Lover commands, this time out loud rather than telepathically.

They each feel ice cold water lapping on the pads of their paws, and they stop to drink, their thirst from the long journey overtaking them. After they drink their fill, they step gingerly into the frigid water, their leonine and equine limbs shivering as they wallow blindly along the cave's creek. Finally, when the water is so high that it surrounds their entire bodies and nearly forces them to swim, they hear a loud whinny. A tiny drop of light beckons them from above.

"Climb up, straight in front of you!" Night Lover calls. "You're almost there."

Sunground struggles to climb up out of the water, her aquiline talons scraping and slipping on the rocky edge of the bank. Groundsky and Dreamspinner push her from behind with their strong forelimbs, and with a mighty effort, she pulls herself out of the river and onto some kind of terrace. There is a sharp incline that she ascends, scrambling her way up toward the light. Her rear claws scrape and slip painfully against the muddy rock, but she continues to follow the sound of Night Lover's voice.

"You're almost up!" she cries. Sunground pulls her rear body up onto a higher, well-lit rock terrace. She is able to see many torches protruding from the rock walls, lighting the way down a stone hallway.

The others clamber up slowly, one at a time. Egglight is pushed and cajoled from behind by Dreamspinner and Groundsky, who are the last to arrive.

"Rug-a-bug-bug!" Groundsky exclaims. "What an amazing hideout!"

Night Lover greets the group, urging them further down the stone corridor. The dexterous talons of the hippogryphs have evidently altered the cave for their own use, because many rock carvings of equine beings line the way. The rock statues are black, smooth, detailed in every way, and life-like. Sunground gapes at the statues incredulously. She had no idea hippogryphs were so artistically talented.

The rear hooves of the two hippogryphs cause a "clomp, clomp" sound to echo through the chamber until they at last lead the small group into a cavernous cathedral, with numerous stalls carved out as individual resting places for each member of the herd.

Stalactites line the ceiling of the cave like a grand chandelier. On the ground below, the hippogryphs have evidently used their artistic expertise to smooth the spaces that surround stalagmites, the great natural columns arising from the floor of the gigantic cave. The cavern is filled with moss and every conceivable type of vegetation, strewn in a manger at the center of the room so herd members can eat.

The younger ones run to the center and peck at the vegetation and bark greedily. Even vegetable matter is palatable to a hungry young gryphon. When the adolescents have finished eating, the adults move in, munching on bark as they stare warily at the watching hippogryphs.

The chamber grows quiet, with only the odd clomp of a hoof breaking the stillness. Sunground is accustomed to the silent stares of the herd, but she notices that her sisters and Egglight are twitching their tails nervously.

"Can't they at least say something?" Egglight grumbles. "I'm not sure if these horse creatures are here to save us or to hold us captive."

"They are helping us, there is no doubt," Sunground says. "They have taken quite a chance in leading us here. They do not normally trust gryphonic beings, as you can well imagine." She peers intently at the various hippogryphs, searching in vain for Moon Wing.

"She is not here, Mother Sunground," Night Lover informs her softly.

"What?" Sunground cries. "Where has she gone? I thought you were protecting her!"

"I had been," Night Lover replies. "But the death of the old gryphon queen precipitated a crisis for my people. As their own queen, I was under an obligation to meet and lead them to the safety of the secret cavern. I ordered Moon Wing to follow but in the chaos of the flight, she veered off and moved in her own direction. She later sent a telepathic message to me, letting me know that she was going to find her father."

Sunground screeches in panic. "Night Lover! How can you have let her go? Can you not contact her now?"

Night Lover closes her eyes wearily. "Sunground, please, calm yourself as much as you can. I know this is difficult for you to hear, but Moon Wing is adamant in her determination to find her father. She has gone to the land of the hopha to find him, and she is long since out of my telepathic range."

A deep-seated shock settles in Sunground's chest. *The hopha? No one that she knows has ever seen one of these strange, two-footed creatures. Many gryphons believe them to be mythological characters imagined by the gifted gryphonic tale weavers who have told stories of the hopha for eons. Why would Moon Wing have gone there to find Nightsky?*

In answer to her thoughts, Night Lover explains the situation. "When we came to the lower mountains, Pegasus, the white winged colt, was there waiting for us. He told us that the hopha had been invading the area, and that they were attempting to capture winged horses. He said that they had managed to make friends with Nightsky and had then led him to their land. Pegasus believes that the hopha are planning to enslave Nightsky, as they did with many of the other winged stallions that they captured. Pegasus' great grandfather, old Grey Tree, the mate of the former queen, Grass Grazer, is believed to have been captured by these sly beasts."

Sunground is mute with terror. *Could this outlandish story be true?* She searches her mind for chickhood tales of the hopha. The only thing she remembers about them, other than their two-footedness, is that they are friends and allies of horses. Since the gryphons consider horses as natural enemies, the hopha are therefore foes through their association with them. Sunground remembers Egglight telling her that the hopha prize winged stallions above all else.

As she listens to her pounding heart, she knows that she must leave this protective hiding spot to go in search of Moon Wing. Night Lover, sensing her thoughts, moves closer to her. "You must travel with at least one other," she advises. "The rest of your family will be safe here with us, for the time being."

Sunground thinks furiously. Her two sisters need to stay here to protect their own young ones. Groundsky must stay to tend to his mate Grass Hopper, who is pregnant and in no shape to embark on another journey. Mother Skystar needs to remain in the cave, for the family requires a strong leader, and Egglight is too elderly for such a dangerous journey. That leaves only Dreamspinner to act as her travel companion, as he will surely insist upon doing.

As Sunground contemplates how she will manage to travel to the land of the hopha, she is startled to realize that the old queen, Grass Grazer, is standing nearby listening quietly to their discussion.

"Oh, Queen Grass Grazer!" she says, bowing her head in respect. "Pardon me. I did not notice you there before."

Grass Grazer moves closer to her. "O, brave young Sunground, Moon Wing has done a foolish thing. If you intend to go in search of her, however, I can show you the route to the flatlands of the hopha."

"Are the flatlands not forbidden, O Queen?" Sunground inquires. "And the hopha, do they truly exist?"

"Of course they do," Grass Grazer says. "I have seen them with my own eyes when I went to rescue my mate, Grey Tree, many revolutions ago. I was not successful, of course, and the ferocious hopha kept Grey Tree into old age. They refused to let him go home. I felt him pass on to the Spirit Sky in these last few days and I know that after his death the hopha will be determined to keep Nightsky with them, for they do not easily let go of their treasured, winged possessions. If Pegasus has accompanied Moon Wing on her journey, then he will most likely be captured as well."

Sunground's mind swirls in terror as she thinks of her precious Moon Wing being captured by the hopha savages.

"As for the flatlands being forbidden," Grass Grazer continues, "they are so specifically because the hopha live there. The gryphons have always tried to paint them as mythological creatures, but their own ban on traveling to the flatlands contradicts this. Anyone who has bothered to learn anything about the flatlands will know that the hopha make their home there."

Old Egglight listens intently. She bounds over to Mother Skystar, interrupting her meal and nudging her toward Sunground and the two hippogryph queens. Egglight murmurs to Skystar softly; and the gryphon mother is beside Sunground immediately, her feathers rustling in anxiety. "What is this, Sunsky? What is this ridiculous business about Moon Wing and the hopha?"

Sunground explains the predicament to Mother Skystar, and the rest of the family joins them.

"Rug-a-bug-bug-bug-bug-r-r-r-r!" Groundsky roars. "I will go and rescue Moon Wing from the hopha!"

The rest of the family squawks in a noisy furor. "No one is going anywhere!" Skystar screeches, silencing the din. "Sunsky, my daughter! Surely you know that to fly anywhere, let alone to the flatlands, is suicide! The air squadrons will have filled the skies by now. You will never get there traveling by ground through the thick brush, for you will most likely be apprehended by the keythonic ground forces. I know you are worried about Moon Wing, but you will not save her by getting yourself captured. You must realize this!"

The other family members nod in agreement.

"She will not travel by air or by ground," Grass Grazer says, using the gryphonic dialect for the benefit of the group. "She will travel underground."

Grass Grazer's statement is met with a stunned pause.

"How is that possible, old Queen most wise?" Dreamspinner asks, cocking his avian head in respect. "Surely this cave does not extend as far as the flatlands."

"This cave does not, O young opinicus Dreamspinner," Grass Grazer responds, showing no fear of the gryphonic male as she returns his gesture of respect. "This is a natural structure, altered only slightly by our nimble talons. It has been used throughout our history as a hiding place from our enemies. It does, however, connect to an underground tunnel built many sun revolutions ago by the cunning and clever hopha. These creatures may appear small and weak to us, but their minds cause them to be extremely powerful and adept at altering natural environments for their own use. We must never underestimate them."

Sunground's mind reels. She lies down for a moment, dizzy and nauseated. *How can this be?* She lets out a plaintive whistle as her sisters and mother attempt to comfort her by rubbing their soft-feathered heads against her.

"Has Moon Wing been traveling outside, by air?" she asks. "Do you know, Night Lover?"

The younger queen cocks her head, peering intently at Sunground.

"I sent her a mental message after I realized that she was not with us," Night Lover replies softly. "I instructed her on how to enter the cave system from the area in which we were traveling, since it is not far from this cave. These caves are interconnected, and I hoped that she would travel in our direction so that I could further guide her. I believe she was traveling with Pegasus, who no doubt led her to the great underground passageway of the hopha. The colt learned about it from the tales of old Grey Tree and his adventures in the underground. Moon Wing must have decided to follow the passageway, for I lost contact with her shortly thereafter."

Sunground feels a spark of hope kindling within her heart. If she is traveling underground, perhaps they can catch up with Moon Wing before she reaches her destination.

"Dreamspinner!" Sunground cries, abruptly rising from the ground. "Will you travel with me to find Moon Wing through the underground passage?"

"I will, my courageous queen," Dreamspinner agrees. "I will go anywhere with you."

A chorus of caws scream "No!" but neither Sunground nor Dreamspinner pays them any heed. "Then it is decided!" Sunground booms authoritatively. "O my elder-queen, Grass Grazer, will you lead us to the passageway now?"

Grass Grazer quietly nods her consent, beckoning them to follow.

CHAPTER EIGHT

In Search of Moon Wing

After pecking a fond farewell to their family members, Sunground and Dreamspinner are ready to take the passageway to the flatlands. Skystar and Night Lover insist upon seeing the pair off and accompany old Grass Grazer as she leads them to the edge of the hophas' mysterious tunnel. Two exquisitely carved, stone winged horses stand on either side of the entrance, as if they are guarding it from invading hoards.

"These were carved by the hopha, we believe," Grass Grazer explains. "All of these equine statues have been created by the hopha, at one time or another. We think that they came through the tunnels into the caves and inhabited them for a brief period, while they were empty of hippogryphs. Their art work has inspired us to attempt to replicate it, but we are not anywhere near as talented as they are."

"Then the hopha have access to your hiding spot?" Sunground asks, as her anxiety mounts. Skystar and Night Lover peer at Grass Grazer with the same concern.

"Yes," Grass Grazer replies. "That is one of the risks of this spot, but I do not think that the hopha will come here en masse to attack a group of hippogryphs. They normally send only small groups to watch the cave. They do not enter here unless the caverns are empty, because they are afraid of hippogryphs and other gryphonic beings. Some gryphons or opinici have attacked them when they came to the mountains, so they built the underground tunnels. Hippogryphs, of course, have never attacked them and yet they are still wary of us."

"They don't sound very fearsome, these hopha creatures!" Dreamspinner says. "We may have no trouble entering their territory."

"Don't underestimate them, as I've said before," Grass Grazer says. "They seem small and meek, but they carry ingenious weapons. Some of these can shoot lightning from a distance and kill or stun a living being. I once saw them shoot a gargoyle in such a fashion. The gargoyle was not killed in this instance, but it was rendered unconscious. The hopha put a strange marker in its ear. They did not kill or eat it but simply left it there to wake up on its own. They then entered an odd flying structure similar to a nest-shelter, which lifted up into the air and flew away."

"The hopha fly in nest-shelters?" Skystar asks doubtfully. "How can a nest-shelter possibly fly? It has no wings!"

"I don't know how they do it," Grass Grazer replies. "As I've said, their minds and their dexterity make them powerful. They have a singular talent for inventing the weirdest contraptions."

Skystar shakes her head. Sunground knows that her mother does not like this new adventure, but that is why they need to go now, before anyone thinks better of it.

"Dreamspinner, let's go," Sunground says. "Before we change our minds."

"May the spirit of my old mate, Grey Tree, go with you," Grass Grazer says by way of farewell, as she makes her way back along the passageway to the upper cavern.

Skystar and Night Lover remain, crying mournfully to them as they leave, until finally they are out of hearing range. Sunground feels relief. Leaving her family again after such a short stay with them is weighing heavily on her, but she knows that she must find Moon Wing.

The two travelers descend on a dark path that leads further underground, until it finally levels off into a straight, smoothly chiseled corridor. Gone is the rocky ruggedness of the cave that they had been in previously. As they step out into the passage, their eyes blink furiously at the barrage of light emanating from the ceiling. As their eyes adjust to the brightness, Sunground is surprised to find that there are no torches lit, as there were in the hippogryphs' cave.

"How is this passage lit? There are no torches, no flames, but only flat squares of light."

"It could be glow worms," Dreamspinner suggests. "I noticed them when we were slogging our way through that freezing cave river."

"No," Sunground says. "These are obviously not glow worms. If they were, we would see them as little white stars against a dark night sky. Here, there is no darkness. It is just this dull light from above."

"I don't like it very much," Dreamspinner mutters, "although we have no choice but to follow this odd path."

Sunground coos her appreciation of Dreamspinner to thank him for being so willing to undertake this insane quest with her. Dreamspinner rubs his feathered head against hers in response.

The passageway is long and seems to stretch on forever in drab uniformity. The travelers speak infrequently, involved in their own thoughts. They halt their progress only for brief periods to rest or to eat the cave moss and tree bark that they brought along as provisions. They had packed everything they needed for the trip into a bundle and fastened it to Dreamspinner's sturdy back.

They lose their sense of time and do not know how long it has been since they first entered the tunnel. As the journey drags on, Sunground suspects that they have been traveling for several days, yet they have found nothing but this same interminable tube of stone. Sunground nurses her hope of finding Moon Wing before she arrives at the flatlands, although the sad silence of this place threatens to devour all such hope.

On what may have been the fifth or sixth day, the pair halts abruptly at the sight of sunlight pouring in from above. They race toward the light and discover that it is coming from a large opening in the ceiling of the tunnel.

"I will investigate, my queen!" Dreamspinner proclaims, lifting himself up through the mouth with his wings before Sunground has a chance to protest.

"Dreamspinner!" Sunground calls impatiently. "Where are you? What have you found?"

The opinicus gently swoops down once more to the floor of the tunnel.

"We are now in the flatlands, my love! I have seen lands as flat as a landing terrace, interspersed with some wooded areas, but no mountains. They are now far off in the distance. We have arrived at last in the land of the mighty hopha!"

"What about Moon Wing? Were there any hophas nearby?"

she asks with great urgency. "Did you see any signs of a settlement?"

"I saw some strange structures far in the distance, like the mountains, except square in shape. No sign of either your daughter or an individual hopha."

Sunground feels her heart plummet in disappointment at the news. "Oh," she responds, her tone as flat as the land above them. "Then we must continue our journey through this blasted hallway once more. We must arrive at the settlement."

They have not been traveling long when Sunground senses that they are no longer alone. She stops, remaining still. Dreamspinner cocks his head toward her, curious. He refrains from asking what has so startled her, for he knows better than that. They both remain quiet and listen. Slowly, Sunground creeps back toward the gaping mouth on the ceiling. She startles at the sight before her: a two-legged creature is climbing down into the tunnel. The creature freezes, while Sunground backs away, terrified. *This is the dreaded hopha.*

Dreamspinner joins her, his head feathers rustling as he spies the strange being.

Sunground and the hopha remain locked in a frozen gaze, staring at each other in stunned silence. The creature appears to be a female mammalian, with teats oddly situated on either side of her chest. She is wrapped from neck to toe in a brightly colored cloth bound tightly around her body, which appears barren of fur except for the reddish mane on top of her head.

The hopha speaks to her softly in an indecipherable alien language. Sunground attempts a reply, although the high-pitched tones seem to frighten the weird mammal. Instead, Sunground engages in gentle cooing noises that one would normally use

with young chicks in the nest. This seems to be a more successful sound for the hopha female, who relaxes somewhat. She
continues to coo as the hopha climbs cautiously down the wall
of the tunnel, using built-in rungs that were obviously designed
as climbing aids for wingless, two-footed beings.

The hopha looks intently at the gryphon, slowly enunciating
a series of sounds. "*Jo. Free. Ell. Jo. Free. Ell.*"

Sunground attempts to repeat the noises, lowering her pitch
slightly in order to capture them properly.

"Jophriel," the hopha states emphatically, directing one of
her short little talons at herself.

Sunground understands. This is her name: *Jophriel.* She
makes the sound for her own name, *Sunground*, pointing a
talon at herself. Jophriel tries to replicate the sound but is
mostly unsuccessful in her attempts. Sunground also points
at Dreamspinner, who has backed off to let Sunground communicate more easily with the hopha.

"*Dreamspinner*," she caws in the gryphonic language, enunciating it as slowly as she can. Jophriel again attempts to replicate
the sound, this time with more success.

Sunground wonders if the hopha are telepathic, like the
hippogryphs. She sends out an experimental thought message,
"*where are we?*" several times, but it seems to be of no use. It
appears that the hopha are no more talented at telepathy than
the gryphons.

She attempts to communicate the idea of moving forward
along the corridor by pointing her talon in that direction.

Jophriel appears excited, pointing likewise in the forward
direction of the tunnel and then moving her hands in front
of her face. She utters a sound, "*ha-lo-na*" a number of times

before pointing one of her five talons in the opposite direction, back the way they had come.

Sunground is confused. *Does Jophriel want them to return?* She caws at the hopha, pointing in the direction that they want to travel. If she can convince the two-legged creature to be their guide, it would make any further contact with the species much easier.

Jophriel attempts to replicate the sound of Sunground's caw, flapping her un-feathered arms in a rather comical fashion. She points again in the opposite direction of where they want to go.

"I believe that Jophriel does not wish us to go any further," Dreamspinner says. "She may be trying to thwart our journey to protect us, or her own people, from danger."

"We must convince her otherwise," Sunground counters. "Let's simply continue on our way and see if she follows."

The pair leaves Jophriel behind, ignoring her bleating pleas to return. Sunground does not turn her head to see if the hopha is following them. She can sense her presence, trailing behind them at a discreet distance. They continue in this manner for a few days, with Jophriel never far behind them.

Finally, during one of their rest stops, Jophriel makes her presence visible by striding blithely up to them and showing them the base of her hand, holding it within striking distance of Sunground's beak. The gryphon does not know what to make of this, but she supposes that it is another attempt to halt their journey. *These hopha are certainly stubborn*, she thinks.

In response to her private mental opinion, Sunground receives an idea from her spirit heart on how to communicate their mission to the hopha. She scratches an experimental mark on the stone floor with her razor-sharp talon. She uses the floor as a drawing tablet and scrapes out a crude picture of a hippogryph. She points at it and says in the gryphonic language, "*Moon Wing.*" She then points at her own egg pouch, tracing the path from it to the outer world.

Jophriel is quick to understand. "*Moon Wing,*" she intones, pointing at the picture and then to Sunground's belly. "*Dah-tur, chy-uld.*"

Sunground replicates the sounds that Jophriel has made. "*Daaaah-t-urrr. C-k-k-h-yyyy-u-ll-ll-ddd.*"

It seems that Sunground is more adept at reproducing hopha sounds than Jophriel is at replicating gryphonic noises. Jophriel becomes excited, moving her head in an up-and-down manner, which Sunground imitates. The hopha evidently comprehends that Sunground is referring to her offspring, and she points once again in their traveling direction. The mission is now clear to Jophriel: She understands that they are embarking on a journey to the flatlands of the hopha in the hope of rescuing Moon Wing.

The two-footed being draws a square with a small metallic rod. She draws another image inside the square that is similar to Sunground's pictorial hippogryph.

Sunground stares at it for an instant and then realizes in horror what it means. *The hopha have imprisoned Moon Wing!* She lets loose a terrifying screech, but Jophriel does not flinch. She remains still, as if waiting for Sunground to strike her down. The gryphon glares at her. *If this hopha thinks that Sunground of the Valley is going to demonstrate her gryphonic savagery, she will be disappointed.* She draws herself up proudly, determined not to overreact.

Jophriel speaks slowly and softly to her, imitating the cooing noises that Sunground used earlier. She feels her anger dissipating as she considers the possibility that it may not be Jophriel who is responsible for Moon Wing's imprisonment. There may even be an opportunity for her to lead them to where Moon Wing's jail cell is located. Jophriel, as if sensing her thoughts, motions them forward and now takes the lead quite decisively.

"My queen!" Dreamspinner warns as Sunground hurries to follow the biped. "It may not be wise to trust her. Did the old queen Grass Grazer not warn us of the cunning of these hopha creatures? She could be leading us into a trap!"

"It's a chance that I am willing to take, my opinicus king," Sunground calls back. "Besides, she will be able to lead us to Moon Wing more efficiently than either of us can."

The pair follows Jophriel dutifully through the rest of the tunnel until they arrive at the other end, where the sunlight shines powerfully into the dull shadows of the hopha-cave.

CHAPTER NINE

Captivity

Jophriel leads them through a wooded area. Sunground is relieved to be out of that dreadful, dimly lit tunnel but also feels a gnawing sense of anxiety in the pit of her stomach. In what condition will she find Moon Wing? Sunground knows that her daughter is a strong-willed one, but that may not be to her advantage while she remains in the clutches of the wily hopha.

Jophriel halts suddenly and puts one hand in front of them, a gesture that they have learned means "stop" in the hopha culture. She motions them to go the other way, back into the woods. Sunground notices that the trees have become sparse as they travel further into the flatlands. Soon, they will run out of protective areas in which to hide.

"Jophriel!" a voice rings out, unmistakably one of the hopha. The voice continues its unintelligible message in a tone even lower than that of Jophriel. Sunground senses that it is a male hopha, possibly Jophriel's mate.

Jophriel emphatically puts her hand out in front of her, gesturing to them to remain in the thick of the woods. She then turns and runs in the direction of the male voice, returning its call. After a few minutes, she returns with the male. He is like her except larger, and with a black mane on top of his head. Unlike her, he has some facial fur around his mouth and under his nose. She gestures at him to stay back, and then calls the names of Sunground and Dreamspinner, replicating the gryphonic syllables as best she can. The two gryphonic beings reveal themselves cautiously to this new hopha.

"*Roooo-nen*," Jophriel intones, pointing at the male.

Both Sunground and Dreamspinner repeat the sound to signal to Jophriel that they are willing to accept the presence of the male.

Roonen, for his part, looks at the two gryphonic beings with what appears to be extreme caution, if not terror. Jophriel leads the pair in a symphony of cooing to reassure him. Roonen appears less than convinced. Nonetheless, he does seem to be reconciled to the fact that Jophriel has befriended the two strange creatures. He strides up to her and puts a protective arm around her, confirming Sunground's belief that he might be her mate. Jophriel takes time to acquaint him with the gryphonic sounds that she has learned. His attempts to replicate the sounds are even worse than hers, but at least they have managed to establish some sort of communication between their two species.

The unlikely quartet continues its journey in a weaving zigzag, trying to keep within the safety of thick bush. Finally, it becomes obvious that they can no longer hide amid the bushes if they wish to reach their destination. Jophriel and Roonen worriedly consult each other, speaking in hushed tones.

"This is ridiculous," Sunground says in an aside to Dreamspinner. "The only way that we will find Moon Wing is to be captured ourselves."

"My queen!" Dreamspinner squawks in panic. "You must not allow yourself to be captured! It will do your daughter no good. You stay within the sanctuary of the woods and let me go. I will rescue Moon Wing and escape with her from the hopha prison."

"No," Sunground says. "We will both go. If we are captured, it will not be easy to escape. You know what the old queen Grass Grazer said about the ingenuity of the hopha. We will need to negotiate with them for our release, hopefully with the help of Jophriel and her mate."

Dreamspinner utters a muted screech, shaking his feathered head. "How will we negotiate with them when we don't understand their language?"

Jophriel has stopped conversing with Roonen and stands before them, looking at them in a pleading manner. Sunground begins to give her a reassuring coo, but Jophriel holds up her hand once again. She then brings out what looks like a writing tool and some kind of slate. She draws a picture of a hippogryph in a box, much clearer than her earlier drawing on the floor of the tunnel.

"Moon Wing," she says in the gryphonic language, pointing at her. "Daughter. Child."

"Daw-t-urr. Chy-ulld," Sunground repeats.

Jophriel turns her attention to the slate and with her stick-like implement, draws a picture of two gryphonic beings. She points at them, calling their names before slowly drawing a box around them both, accompanied by a straight line leading to Moon Wing's box.

Sunground utters a comprehending caw, for she knows exactly what Jophriel is trying to tell them. "Yes, Dreamspinner!" she chirps. "Jophriel has had the same idea as me. She will help us to get captured, and then we will negotiate our release."

Dreamspinner gives her a dubious look, as Roonen does to Jophriel. Neither of the males is pleased with the idea.

"My queen Sunground," he warbles. "How do we know that these two hophas will negotiate our release? They may simply capture us and leave us there. It would be a very cunning way to get us to cooperate with their plan."

"I think that we can trust them," Sunground says. "Even if we can't, at least I will once more be with Moon Wing."

Dreamspinner ruffles his feathers in frustration. "That will not do any of us any good!" he wails, before catching himself and turning the wail into a muffled squawk. "Why don't we take to the skies and attempt a flight over to Moon Wing's location?"

"We don't know where she is, for one thing," Sunground replies. "Also, the hopha have flying structures that can probably apprehend or attack us in the air. Did you forget Grass Grazer's story of their amazing contraptions?"

Jophriel and Roonen are staring at them as they converse, no doubt realizing that they are at odds with each other over the seemingly counter-productive idea. Roonen gestures toward Dreamspinner and speaks to Jophriel in an exasperated manner. Finally, Roonen throws up his arms and stalks away out of the bush. Jophriel puts one finger in front of Sunground, as if to say that they would need to wait for a while.

When Roonen finally returns, he arrives in a strange moving

structure. It looks like a cart with round wheels, similar to the ones that keythong workers pull when they are making deliveries. This "cart" however, is far more elaborate and very large. He parks it as close to them as he can get before the trees block the vehicle's progress.

Roonen opens up a door at the back and lifts it upward. He then brings out a ramp, which leads into the rear part of the huge cart-structure. Jophriel brings them as close to the cart as they are willing to come and then points at it.

"Truck," she explains, pointing first at them and then at the rear portion, which yawns open like an inviting cave.

Dreamspinner squawks his refusal, regarding Sunground and Jophriel as if they have gone mad.

"We must go inside, Dreamspinner," she tells him. "Either that, or I will go and you can return to the cave and report to the others what I have done."

"No, my queen!" Dreamspinner protests. "Where you go, I go also."

Dreamspinner charges up the ramp and onto the truck first to prove the truth of his words. Sunground exchanges a few coos with Jophriel and as she peers into her eyes, she feels that her trust in this hopha is well placed. She follows Dreamspinner into the truck with full confidence in her new friend. Roonen lifts the ramp as soon as Sunground has boarded and closes the door, leaving them in darkness.

The vehicle roars and takes off. It feels to both of them as though the ground is moving beneath them, but Sunground's keen intellect tells her that the opposite is true and that the truck is in fact shooting across the ground at an incredible rate. It feels almost as though they are flying, yet every once in a while they feel a slight bump that reminds them that they have not left the ground.

The speed is unnerving to her, especially since she is unsure of their destination. Her earlier confidence in the two hophas dissipates as she considers the possibility of betrayal. She and Dreamspinner are now completely at the mercy of these odd strangers, yet her heart tells her that she has done the right thing.

"I do not like this," Dreamspinner grumbles, echoing her thoughts. "We cannot even be certain of where they are taking us. It is not sane to deliver ourselves into their clutches."

"Quiet, Dreamspinner," Sunground says softly. She does not want to engage him in argument right now but instead turns her attention inward to her heart. She feels the glow of verification regarding her choice and decides to put her trust in herself rather than fretting about whether or not she can trust the two-footed beings.

Time merges into the infinite yet again as the blind voyage hurtles on, bringing them ever closer toward their fate. Dreamspinner has abandoned himself to the inevitability of their capture and sits miserably in the corner of the box, compulsively scraping the side of it with his beak.

Sunground does not know how long they have been inside this dark box, but the sensation of movement is rocking her into a sluggish lull. She falls slowly into a deep sleep, dreaming of Moon Wing. She sees images of her lost lover Nightsky throughout the dream.

"Where is Moon Wing?" she asks him.

"She is here," he responds, "working with us."

Sunground sees Moon Wing in the dream, but every time she draws near to her, the young hippogryph moves farther away. Sunground prepares for flight in order to find her daughter, but for some reason she cannot propel herself into the sky. She feels as heavy as a pack of seeds, and each time she attempts to lift her body into the air she falls to the ground with a dull thud.

As she dusts herself off from her failed attempts at flight, she becomes dimly aware of a sharp poke on her right wing. She gradually falls out of dreamtime and remembers where she is. It dawns on her that the moving box in which they have been traveling has halted.

The door on the box flings open without warning. Stabbing rays of sunlight assault her senses, forcing her to keep her eyelids closed until she acclimatizes herself from the darkness to the light. She hears Roonen setting up the ramp for them to exit the box. Dreamspinner recovers more swiftly and exits first, seeking to protect Sunground from danger in case the wily hopha have betrayed them. His shrill cry pierces the air: "My queen of the sun and sky! Come out and see!"

Sunground opens her eyes warily and stumbles down the ramp. She takes a moment to allow her eyes to adjust to the daylight. As she does so, she becomes aware of a figure in front of her. It is a hippogryph, she realizes slowly. Then, as her vision clears, she realizes that it is not just any hippogryph before her—it is Moon Wing!

"Mama!" Moon Wing calls, as the pair rush joyously together, their wings beating mightily in excitement.

"Moon Wing!" They peck and preen each other lovingly, each hardly able to believe that the other is there.

Jophriel and Roonen watch from a distance as the three beings become reacquainted. Once the ruckus has calmed, Jophriel approaches Sunground. She shows her the picture that she had drawn of the three gryphonic beings in the boxes and gestures to the landscape around them. Various gryphonic beings, mostly keythongs and kryphons, are wandering about foraging for small prey. Sunground looks at her quizzically. This is certainly not a box or a jail cell. There do not even appear to be gates or bars of any kind but rather a very large field of long grasses and woodland, surrounded by stone structures in the distance.

"Jophriel is trying to tell you that you can only stay within certain boundaries," Moon Wing explains. "A force field encompasses this enclosure. It is to protect the hopha from the gryphonic beings and the gryphonic beings from the hopha. If we ventured into their cities, there would be panic!"

Sunground marvels at the calmness and clarity of her daughter. She does not appear fazed by the mysterious hopha nor their odd technology.

"What is a force field?" Sunground asks. "Does that mean that we are forced to stay only in the field?"

After a quick chuckle, Moon Wing replies, "In a way, yes. There is an invisible force at the edges of this area that if you attempt to cross over it, will give you a nasty shock. It surrounds us from above as well, to ensure that we cannot fly out of the area. It's quite effective, believe me. I've tried to challenge the boundaries."

Sunground peruses her daughter with great concern. If Moon Wing has been attempting to escape, then the hopha must be putting great effort into keeping her within the enclosure. Negotiating their release will not be easy, as the hopha must fear the gryphonic people a great deal to keep them in such a captive condition.

"Have the hopha mistreated you in any way, Moon Wing?" she asks protectively, glaring at Jophriel and Roonen.

"Of course not, Mama!" Moon Wing counters. "They have been keeping us well fed on delicious grains and grasses of every sort. They will also bring in rodents for you to hunt within the enclosure. Don't fear them—they won't bite, after all. Their teeth are quite dull."

"We will begin immediate negotiations to ensure your release, Moon Wing," Sunground says. "You and all others here must be freed."

Moon Wing cackles at her mother's statement. "Oh, Mama!" she cries, "We do not want to leave. We are staying here willingly to help the hopha. We must find some way to bring Groundsky here, as well. He will be safe from the gryphons in this place, I assure you."

Sunground and Dreamspinner stare at her in shock. "O, princess of my queen!" Dreamspinner says. "You cannot remain here as a slave to these two-footed trolls! Groundsky and the rest of your family remain in hiding in a secret cavern amid the wooded valleys of the lower mountains. The old gryphon queen Heartsong has died and..."

"I know, Uncle Dreamspinner!" Moon Wing interrupts. "We know all about Talona taking over. She has been attacking everyone, hippogryphs, horses both winged and wingless, renegade keythongs and kryphons, gryphons and opinici who disagree with her, even the hopha."

"What insanity would inspire her to attack the hopha?" Dreamspinner cries. "These creatures have built many ingenious contraptions to protect themselves! Talona would have no chance against them—or at least, that is my guess."

"That is precisely why we have aligned ourselves with them, Uncle," Moon Wing replies. "They can help to protect us from this corrupt regime. Squadrons of gryphons have attacked many peaceful hophas who have traveled to the mountains to perform research. They have managed to fend them off using their stun weapons, but just barely. They have noticed that the gryphons have become more aggressive of late, and we are trying to convince them to do something about it."

Sunground shakes her head vigorously. "No, that would not be a good idea! These beings could damage our society irreparably with these weapons. The old queen Grass Grazer told us that their weapons can kill as well as stun."

"Well then," Moon Wing retorts, "perhaps they could kill only Talona and Soundringer."

"No!" Sunground squawks in horror. "We must not employ violence against our sister gryphons, no matter how misguided and insane they have become. We must negotiate."

Moon Wing looks at her dubiously but does not debate her mother. Instead, she cocks her head in the direction of the other beings in the enclosure. "Come on, I will introduce you to our team!" She whinnies, fluttering over to where a group has gathered, all of them regarding the new arrivals with great interest.

As Sunground approaches the group, she recognizes one of its members, a thin and bedraggled gryphon. "Star Sailor!" she exclaims, reaching forward to give her a loving peck. "How in the name of Gryphonia did you arrive here?"

Star Sailor raises her head only slightly to receive Sunground's gesture of affection, her exhaustion evident. She is missing many feathers, with patches of dark, bare skin lying exposed.

"After you and your family left me in the clearing, the rest of the air squadron members determined that I had betrayed them by allowing you to escape. They pecked me almost featherless to stop my flight, leaving me bound to die at the beaks of vultures," she explains. "I was close to death when the hopha landed one of their flying machines and took me into their custody. I awoke in this odd field enclosure to find myself part of an assortment of gryphonic beings, tended to dutifully by the hopha yet not allowed to roam free."

Sunground is shocked. Star Sailor, the daughter of the chief magistrate and one of the most loyal members of the air squadron, abandoned and left to die by her own troop! She can remember a time, not so long ago in their adolescence, when they had each completed their respective flight schooling. Star Sailor had come to her in great excitement to show her the prize that she had earned: It was the school's highest badge of achievement, an award that would ensure her later entry into the Royal Air Squadron. The pair had celebrated the achievement of her dream just one sun revolution later, together with their families. Chief Magistrate Queenstar had proudly presented her daughter with the Sacred Feather, the special emblem of all Royal Air Squadron members. Young Sunsky was bursting with joy at her friend's accomplishment, and she organized a party for her.

Talona was there and attempted to ruin the festivities by jealously baiting Star Sailor into a fight with her. Star Sailor steadfastly refused to engage her in battle. Talona left the gathering in disgust, screeching furiously about Star Sailor's cowardice, but the young gryphon once known as Sunsky was filled only with the greatest respect for Star Sailor and her ability to exercise calm restraint.

"Star Sailor," Sunground coos. "I am so sorry that we bound your talons and hind legs together. I should have unbound you before I left so that you could have escaped."

"Nonsense, Sunground. If you had lingered any longer to untie me, you would have been captured and quite possibly killed, along with your family. Talona's rage grows more insane with each passing day! I am so ashamed to have worked in her service."

Sunground rubs her head against her friend as a gentle reassurance, while Dreamspinner rustles his feathers from behind them in support. He addresses her in an extravagant manner, stepping forward to bow to their former adversary. "You are safe with us now, daughter of the honored chief magistrate! We shall respect you as always, O Great Chieftain Star Sailor of the Royal Air Squadron!"

"I no longer hold that rank, Dreamspinner," she replies. "But thank you anyways. As for my mother, Queenstar, she has almost certainly been suspended from her duties as chief magistrate because of my disgrace."

"There is no disgrace upon you, Star Sailor, for you have joined all of us in opposing Talona!" Moon Wing bleats. "We are all determined to stop the gryphon queen's madness. We *will* reinstate your mother as chief magistrate."

Star Sailor regards Moon Wing with the air of one who is weary with experience.

"It will not be easy, Moon Wing," she warns. "We do not know for sure that the hopha have any intention of helping us. I believe that they have their own agenda, and that may not include a free Gryphonia."

"No," Moon Wing insists. "I think we can trust them and so does Papa."

Sunground flaps her wings at the mention of Moon Wing's father. "He is here?"

"Yes, Mother Sunground," Moon Wing replies. "So is my mate, Pegasus. They have both agreed to go into service with the hopha. Papa believes that they can help us in the struggle against Talona's regime. He is researching their language, and he is friends with Jophriel and Roonen."

Dreamspinner flaps his wings in barely repressed rage. Sunground can feel his seething need to screech his jealousy to the skies but thankfully, he remains silent out of respect for her and Moon Wing.

"Calm, Dreamspinner!" she coos. "You are and always will be my primary mate. It was only ever a courtesy mating with Nightsky."

Dreamspinner is barely reassured by this statement. Sunground realizes that he must sense the fact that she is not being entirely truthful with him: The time that she spent many sun revolutions ago with Nightsky has always meant a great deal more to her than just a courtesy mating.

Moon Wing is oblivious to Dreamspinner's discontent and breezily presses her point by introducing them to the others on the "team", as she refers to her fellow inmates. There are many keythongs and kryphons among them, one of whom is a saucy young kryphon named Fluff Feather.

"Fluff Feather was not sterilized, unlike most of her sister kryphons," Moon Wing explains. "Her gryphon mother, who hails from among the lower classes, was courageous and refused to comply with the stupid rules of her high class 'superiors'. She raised her daughter in secret, well away from the strict but submissive society of the keythong and kryphon servants. When she grew into adolescence, however, an interfering kryphon councilor discovered their secret. Fluff Feather ran away to escape impending servitude to gryphonic society, but soon after she wandered into the flatlands and the hopha immediately captured her."

"Even so, we wingless ones like it here," Fluff Feather explains. "The hopha do not insist on sterilizing us. We can do what we like!"

"Yes, Fluff Feather," Star Sailor says. "We can do what we like, but only within this small enclosure."

"Oh, humph-a-dumph-dumph, you silly gryphon!" she teases. "You only ever see the gloomy side of things!"

As Sunground listens to this sassy little upstart, she is reminded of Groundsky.

Moon Wing laughs. "Would she not be the perfect mate for Groundsky?"

Groundsky. Sunground hopes fervently that Talona's forces have not discovered the hippogryphs' secret cavern. She stifles her anxiety so as not to upset her eager young daughter.

"Groundsky already has a mate, Moon Wing," she informs her. "It is Grass Hopper, the great-granddaughter of old queen Grass Grazer. She is pregnant with his… whatever it will be."

Fluff Feather snaps her beak in disappointment at this news, but Moon Wing neighs in excitement, having already forgotten about her role as matchmaker for her kryphon friend. "What great fun!" she cries. "I thought Groundsky and Grass Hopper might get together. Maybe Grass Hopper and I will give birth at the same time!"

Sunground cannot help but notice that Moon Wing's equine belly has become larger since the last time she saw her. She presses her beak against it gently.

"Jophriel has examined me with her advanced technological equipment," Moon Wing tells her triumphantly. "Inside is a winged foal—a filly. She is fully equine, as is her father, Pegasus. I feel strongly that she will be both black, like Papa, and white, like Pegasus. I predict that when the time of birth arrives, she will drop into this world by moonlight. I therefore name her Moon Drop."

Moon Drop. Sunground believes her daughter's prophecy without reservation. The thought of her unborn granddaughter fills her with love and awe.

"The daughter of Moon Wing is not a hippogryph?" Dreamspinner exclaims in surprise. "How is that possible? And besides, I understood that all female equines were wingless."

"It looks as though Moon Drop will prove you wrong, Uncle!" Moon Wing retorts merrily. "She will be the first winged mare in history."

It occurs to Sunground that this future being, as a winged horse, will be in far greater danger if she returns with her mother to Gryphonia than she will if she remains captive in the flatlands. A heavy cloud falls upon her heart as she realizes that Moon Wing is right to want to stay with the hopha. They will revere her foal deeply, whereas gryphons will despise the youngster as an enemy.

It is not even certain that the hippogryphs will accept Moon Drop as a full member of their tribe if Moon Wing returns with her to the secret cavern. Sunground remembers ruefully how they responded to the idea of Grass Hopper's progeny being born wingless. They considered any wingless creature primarily as a danger to the whole herd. Although Moon Wing's foal has wings, she would be even more dangerous to the hippogryphic community due to the hatred with which gryphons hold winged horses.

What can we do, then? Sunground asks herself desperately. She feels as though she has come up against solid rock. How can they possibly help their people locked up in this place? Yet, if they do gain their freedom and return, they will most likely be apprehended or killed by Talona's forces. She ruffles her feathers in frustration. It is unlikely that the hopha, with their intense fear of the gryphons, will want to engage the gryphonic government as a whole. As much as she believes that Jophriel has good intentions regarding her charges, Moon Wing is certainly too idealistic in thinking that they will be able to forge a formal alliance with the two-footed creatures.

Even so, Sunground muses, *what other choice do we have?* The gryphon mother is sad as she gazes at Moon Wing, realizing that she and Nightsky are right: The goal must change from negotiating their freedom to the nearly impossible one of attempting to forge an alliance with the hopha.

CHAPTER TEN

The Hopha

Sunground and Dreamspinner have been living in the enclosure for what seems to them an eternity. Gryphons and opinici are accustomed to being free, at least in a physical sense, and to have that taken away from them is like going from the fresh air of a mountain peak into the dank, dark security of an underground cave. They are temporarily safe here, but their lack of freedom to go where they wish or to take to the skies creates within them a deadened emptiness.

"Who are we without our freedom, without our wings?" Sunground muses. "Are we no one? Are we nothing?"

"Oh, cheer up, Mama!" Moon Wing admonishes her. "We need to take up a greater purpose to give our lives meaning in captivity. Creating a dialogue with the hopha is our main task right now, but neither you nor Uncle Dreamspinner has been responding to Jophriel when she has come to visit you."

Sunground realizes that her daughter is right, but she finds it difficult to muster faith in these strange hopha creatures. Jophriel and Roonen, as well as a few other individuals, have come and gone from the enclosure at will while they have all been stuck here ruminating about how best to approach them. The last thing that Sunground wants to suggest to these two-foots is that they use their fearsome technology to attack gryphonic society. And yet, if they do nothing, Talona and her minions will destroy the soul of Gryphonia as surely as the wily hopha ever could do with their fabled weaponry.

"Moon Wing, I have been thinking about this situation for some time now, and I must tell you that I have been coming up empty. Talona is a fierce enemy, but at least we know her. These hopha are unknown entities. We cannot possibly predict what they will do. I fear that we are staring into a deep and befuddling miasma."

Moon Wing clacks her beak in disgust and stamps her back hoof, obviously frustrated at her mother's depressed outlook.

"Oh, Mama!" she cries. "Befuddling miasma, my tail! Stop thinking for awhile—consult your heart rather than your mind. What does it tell you?"

Sunground sits amazed at the clarity of the young hippogryph. Of course she should consult her heart. She has been lost in the miasma of her own mental haze. Closing her eyes, she journeys inside to the harmony of her own heart's song, away from the din and the clanking clamor of her mental processes. She feels a strong emotional pull toward Jophriel. She feels another aspect of herself shrinking back but stays with the feeling that she can trust the hophic being. After she spends time acclimatizing herself to the feeling, she opens her eyes and returns to their physical surroundings.

"You're right, Moon Wing," she tells her daughter. "I need to try to develop communication with Jophriel. I'm not sure how to do that, though."

"Oh, yes you are, Mama," Moon Wing retorts. "How do you think you came here in the first place to find me and the others?"

Sunground allows herself a caw and a chuckle. There is just no way to get around Moon Wing's persistent nudges. She does not need to wait long before an opportunity arises for her to initiate communication with Jophriel.

The hopha arrives that morning with a truck full of various grains and grasses, as well as cages full of rodents. She spreads the grasses out in an arrangement along a trough and then sets the rodents in the cages free. They scurry by Sunground, who has no hunger to hunt at the moment. She is intent on Jophriel. As the others crowd around the troughs or run off to hunt, she moves toward her, stopping at a distance so as not to frighten her. Jophriel, for her part, does not appear frightened in the least. She returns Sunground's intense stare for a moment and then returns to her truck to retrieve a parchment tablet and writing stick. She moves toward Sunground slowly and offers her the stick, placing the tablet on the ground near her.

Sunground pauses to put her thoughts in order. How can she communicate their plight? Slowly, she draws a picture of a gryphon with a sun over its head, the symbol for the queendom. She then draws a cloud and a bolt of lightning to signify the storm in the royal reign. She hopes that these symbols will not be confusing to Jophriel. She shows her the drawing, and the hopha moves her head up and down in what Sunground interprets as a gesture of comprehension. She continues to draw, creating a picture of a gryphon with the sun and storm over her attacking other gryphonic beings, and especially the hippogryphs. She pauses to show Jophriel this stage of the drawing and then goes on to the final stage. She draws a couple of hophas fending off the attack of the "sun storm" gryphon. She is careful not to picture the hophas using their stun weapons but rather draws them as using sticks to defend themselves. Jophriel examines the illustration, nodding her head.

Sunground stops to collect her thoughts. She must be very careful in the way that she communicates this, for she does not wish to convey the idea that she wants the hopha to attack her society as a whole. She takes the writing implement and draws a line between the gryphonic creatures who are being attacked and the hopha. She points at herself and then at Jophriel.

Jophriel mimics Sunground's gesture of solidarity between the two of them, but she does not acknowledge the line drawn between the gryphonic beings and the hopha. Sunground points at the picture, retracing the line with her talon, but Jophriel shakes her head, moving her bare paws in front of her face.

"No!" Jophriel caws. "No, Sunground."

The hopha rips Sunground's parchment from the writing tablet and starts her own drawing on a new parchment. She draws hophas with weapons, firing at each other. She draws a sphere that has broken into numerous pieces. She then draws the picture that Sunground had sought to avoid: a picture of hophas shooting their weapons at gryphons. She imitates Sunground's picture of a sun and storm, but places them above the hopha instead.

"No, Sunground!" Jophriel reiterates. "No!"

Sunground wearily imitates Jophriel's previous head movements to indicate that she understands. Clearly, Jophriel knows her own people well. They would seek to destroy Gryphonia as surely as Talona and her minions, especially if they felt that the gryphons were a threat to their own society. Sunground ruffles her feathers in frustration at their apparent powerlessness. It seems as though they have run into another cliff face.

Sunground lets go of her goal for the time being and studies Jophriel's drawing further. She is curious about the broken sphere. What could it mean?

She points her talon at the sphere and regards her questioningly. Jophriel responds by gesturing to the world around her. She then claps her hands together violently and points at the sphere. Sunground bobs her head slowly. The hopha must have a great capacity for violence, to the point where they can destroy their surroundings. Her lion's body shivers at the thought, but she continues to communicate with Jophriel. The pair spends the entire afternoon learning and teaching words in their respective languages. They also trade written language symbols in order to obtain a higher level of detail within their pictorial communications.

These learning sessions continue, day after day, until finally Sunground and Jophriel have obtained a rudimentary knowledge of each other's language. Sunground learns that the hopha, according to Jophriel, believe that they originated from the sky. Sunground is skeptical. How can wingless creatures originate from the air? Not even gryphons can claim that. Jophriel, however, goes further by claiming that the hopha came from the "Beyond Air," from that place where, according to gryphonic scholars, life is impossible.

Jophriel's assertion puzzles Sunground. How can a life form emerge from that which is not life? Jophriel claims that the hopha flew to the "Beyond Air" in a flying contraption they built to travel among the stars. This, however, makes no sense to the befuddled gryphon. To build the flying contraption, they would have had to begin on the same ground upon which all other living beings had begun their lives. Sunground shakes her head. These mysterious hopha are at times indecipherable. Jophriel gives one of her odd little hopha chortles and promises her a surprise the following day.

As the day of the surprise dawns, Sunground is anxious to learn what it is. Why does Jophriel insist upon the drama of a surprise? Strangely, however, she feels as though she is dancing on the pinnacle of the highest mountain in the land. An aspect of her rejoices deeply, as she once did when she was a chick.

Moon Wing tests her patience by teasing her about the mystery occurrence. Sunground feels as though she is about to burst with impatience until finally, Jophriel and Roonen arrive with the same truck that they had used to transport Sunground and Dreamspinner. The gryphonic beings gather around as Roonen unlatches the back of the truck and brings down the ramp. Sunground quivers with excitement as she hears the pounding of hooves within the vehicle. Roonen clicks his tongue in encouragement, as down from the ramp charges the black winged horse, Nightsky.

Sunground utters a warble of joy and steps forward to meet him, followed at a short distance by Moon Wing. As the pair nuzzle each other, her feathers brush up against his equine coat.

"It is good to see you again, Sunsky," he says telepathically. "It has been a long time."

"Nightsky," Sunground coos. "Father of my beautiful daughter, Moon Wing. I am no longer known as Sunsky but rather Sunground."

"There is no need for you to cloak your real name," Nightsky tells her. "The current gryphonic regime is illegitimate! For you to arrive here, you must have flown. Therefore, you are no longer grounded."

"We came by way of an underground tunnel," she explains, "from the secret caves where the hippogryphs hide. I have flown, but I did not fly here. Besides, I have become accustomed to the name Sunground."

Nightsky paws the ground with his hoof in disapproval. Before he can send her another thought message, however, the opinicus Dreamspinner alights in front of him, screeching in jealousy. He lunges at him with his beak, but Nightsky is quick to dodge him. Moon Wing screams at the opinicus in rage.

"Dreamspinner!" Sunground calls. "You will stop this behavior immediately!"

Roonèn jumps on Nightsky's back, and together they leap into the air and fly at low altitude until they are safely distant from Dreamspinner.

"My queen," Dreamspinner retorts. "You told me that it was only ever a courtesy mating with Nightsky! I can see and feel now that it is more. I will not lose you to him! He is a *winged horse*, for the sake of the oracle!"

Sunground's heart pounds in panic. She must put this in its proper perspective, and quickly.

"Dreamspinner, I would not have survived many years ago if it was not for Nightsky. He was the one who tended to me while my wing was broken. He defended me from the predators! He is my friend, and yes, I do love him dearly; but I love you just as passionately. If you will not back down from your atrocious behavior toward him, I will ask Roonen to have you brought to the tunnel, and you can go back to the caves."

Dreamspinner is chastened, but his muscles remain taut, as if he was ready to leap into battle.

"Uncle Dreamspinner!" Moon Wing cries. "How can you have attacked my papa? If you do not stop, I will no longer refer to you as 'Uncle'. Mama will no longer consider you her chief mate, as she does now. If you do not accept Papa, then *you* will be the loser."

Dreamspinner relaxes his muscles, laying down on the ground in resignation. "Very well, Moon Wing. For your sake, and for the sake of your mother, I will not tear him to pieces."

"You *hippogryphin'* better not!" Moon Wing retorts, using her own species' name as a gryphonic cuss word. "Or *I'll* tear you to pieces!"

"That is enough, both of you!" Sunground cries. "No one is going to tear anyone to pieces! We have much bigger problems than mating jealousy. Have you forgotten the reign of Talona?"

"We should tear *Talona* to pieces, Uncle Dreamspinner!" Moon Wing bleats. "And I'll bet Papa would help us."

"*Moon Wing!*" Sunground scolds, pecking at her hindquarters. "I said, *enough* of this tearing-to-pieces bluster. I doubt that either of you would be capable of such savagery toward our own people."

"But Mama, the gryphons are not my people and neither are they yours, anymore."

"What about Grandmother Skystar and your aunts Mountain Rain and Cloudhopper? And did you know, my chick, that you have two cousins who are just a couple of sun revolutions younger than you? Their names are Rainbow Dreamer and Luck Wisher."

"Oh, yes, I know, Mama! Aunt Cloudhopper told me all about them when she visited once with Auntie Rain. All right, I will make an exception for them and for my Grandfather Sun Quest and Great-Grandfather Lightning Bolt. Really, none of our family count as gryphons, for they have all been sent into exile like the healer and the oracle, and for the same reason."

Sunground is surprised at how much Moon Wing knows about the political situation in Gryphonia and about the plight of Sun Quest and the others, for she had never really discussed any of it with her daughter. She must have learned about it through Star Sailor, Sunground realizes with a twinge of guilt. She resolves to include Moon Wing in future discussions of the inner workings of the regime rather than attempting to protect her through keeping her ignorant of her mother's society. Besides, if she does not hear it from her mother, she will learn about it from someone else.

Sunground feels the presence of a short two-footed being beside her, and she turns her head toward Jophriel.

"Nightsky," Jophriel says, pointing at the winged horse. "Roonen. Go."

Sunground shakes her head. "No, Jophriel! Nightsky stay. Need to speak!"

Jophriel nods slowly, her reluctance evident. She no doubt regrets her decision to "surprise" Sunground and is chastising herself for not having taken into account Dreamspinner's angry reaction to Nightsky.

"Dreamspinner good now," Sunground says.

Jophriel regards Dreamspinner anxiously as Roonen walks toward him. Nightsky stays behind at a safe distance. The two males begin their own conversation, Roonen using the same parchment tablet and writing tool that Jophriel used, to communicate with the offended opinicus. When they have finished, Roonen walks over to the curious females. The two hophas speak to each other in their own language, some of which Sunground is able to understand now. She has, after her many conversations with Jophriel, become relatively adept at comprehending and producing hopha sounds.

It sounds as if Roonen is suggesting that she keep away from Nightsky for the time being. Sunground's heart slumps as Jophriel confirms Roonen's words to her.

"Sunground no Nightsky," she says in plain fashion.

Sunground glares at Dreamspinner as he slinks toward her sheepishly.

"My queen, it was Roonen's idea, not mine. You may do as you please, and I will not interfere again."

Sunground feels a wave of sadness sweep over her for Dreamspinner's sake, and she speaks softly to him. "I'm sorry, Dreamspinner. I know this is unfair to you, but we must be in communication with Nightsky. He is, I believe, living among the hopha outside of this enclosure. He can give us more information about them and what their plans are regarding us. Unless I am mistaken, I think that Nightsky has formed a telepathic bond with Roonen."

Dreamspinner hangs his head and bleats in a mock-tragic fashion. "I have endangered the mission with my behavior, O queen! Therefore, let Nightsky come forth among you and I will banish myself to the outer edges of our enclosure."

Sunground hisses in irritation at what seems to be a manipulative bid of sympathy for him and one of guilt for her. She lets go of her irritation as he trudges away in the manner of a sulking drama king. Although she is annoyed, she understands that the opinicus must come to terms with Nightsky in his own way. Nightsky, for his part, does not approach Sunground because he is afraid of invoking Dreamspinner's wrath once more.

So now I am without either of them, she grumbles inwardly. *What a pain in the tail these males are!*

She watches as Moon Wing confers with her father, wishing fervently that she could join them. She stays where she is, again feeling isolated from her loved ones through her actions of long ago. She collapses under a tree, discouraged. Jophriel strokes her head in an attempt to comfort her, but she does not respond. Finally, Moon Wing approaches and Jophriel makes way for her by joining Roonen.

"Mama," Moon Wing coos softly, "it is all right. Papa has resolved to stay away from you out of respect for Dreamspinner, but I will be the go-between and pass messages between you."

Sunground perks up her head. "You do not need to be our go-between, Moon Wing. Your papa and I can communicate telepathically, if I can rid my mind of its clutter and provide a clear channel for him."

Sunground abandons her discouragement about the situation and travels within to the quietude of her heart. After a period of intense stillness, she hears Nightsky's voice. "I am sorry, Sunsky."

Sunground casts aside her irritation at Nightsky for using her old name. "It is not your fault, Nightsky. Dreamspinner realizes now that he must tolerate your presence. Please, I wish to continue our communication."

Sunground receives a joyous feeling rather than a verbal response, and it is enthralling to her. Once more, to be in the presence of Nightsky! At last, she may communicate with him, even if it is at a distance and through telepathy.

"Sunsky," Nightsky speaks into her mind. "I have been forming a bond with the hopha male, Roonen. I know that you have been building a bond with Jophriel too, and I encourage you to deepen it."

"Moon Wing has told me that you intend to form an alliance of sorts with the hopha, to challenge the Talonic reign."

"Yes, indeed," the winged stallion replies. "If a large group of hophas unite, in concert with all the gryphonic beings that will join us, we may be able to call for a new government. The Gryphonic Code, I am told by Moon Wing, has a section that allows the people to call for a new leader if the present one is not performing her duties properly."

"Section eight," Sunsky responds, wondering how Moon Wing learned about the finer details of the Gryphonic Code. "But that section only deals with a leader who is incompetent or lazy, and it does not instruct us on how to manage a tyrant. Talona will never give up the reign so easily."

"I do not say it will be easy, my love," Nightsky returns. "But there is a glimmer of hope in that *section eight*, as it is called. Even Talona cannot reign if the majority of gryphons oppose her. We would all stand in peace and solidarity, not against her but in favor of you returning to reign in her place."

Sunground's heart flutters in panic. *Has Nighsky gone insane? Does he not understand that she can never reign after giving birth to a hippogryph?*

Nightsky senses her thoughts before she has transmitted even one word. He sends her a wave of reassuring love in order to keep her mental channels clear.

"Sunsky, do not fret. You will have the overwhelming support of the majority of gryphonic beings, I am quite certain."

"Nightsky, my forbidden lover," Sunground replies. "You do not understand. When a gryphon gives birth to a hippogryph, she cannot participate in gryphonic society, let alone take over the queenship. No gryphon would support my becoming queen, nor any other member of my family, for I have tainted them all with my actions long ago."

"But, my love," he replies patiently, "according to Star Sailor, this sort of thinking has changed. Since Talona has taken over the position of lead queen, many gryphons have murmured heresies among themselves. They would rather have you reign as queen, accompanied by your hippogryph daughter, than the violent machinations of Talona."

"That only proves how bad the situation has become!" Sunground retorts, before thinking better of the comment and chiding herself for it. It is not her intent to insult either Moon Wing or Nightsky, but she knows how deeply the prejudice against hippogryphs runs in her society. Nightsky's plan is naïve at best.

"We would have enough support among the kryphons and keythongs," Nightsky explains, "and I believe that Moon Wing can convince the hippogryphs to join us."

"The hippogryphs!" Sunground explodes. "Why, they would *never* support gryphons!"

"They would," Nightsky counters, "because Talona's reign directly threatens their survival as a people. If you were in charge, they would be safe."

Sunground mulls the matter over but is not convinced. It seems to her a veritable suicide mission, but she has been unable to come up with a better solution. *Can this crazy plan that Moon Wing and Nightsky are hatching possibly work?*

PART THREE
The Ground-Sky Alliance

Chapter One
The Peace Delegation 197

Chapter Two
The Space In Between Peace and War 220

Chapter Three
The Quest Begins 232

Chapter Four
Unexpected Allies 257

Chapter Five
Imprisonment 266

Chapter Six
The Tormentors 280

Chapter Seven
Redemption 291

Chapter Eight
The Circle of Gratitude. 320

Chapter Nine
Ground and Sky United 334

Chapter Ten
The Scepter of Rulers 347

THE
GRYPHON

PART THREE
The Ground-Sky Alliance

CHAPTER ONE

The Peace Delegation

Time while in captivity has a way of remaining still, like a silent beast stalking its prey. Sunground does not know exactly how long it has been since they first arrived at the flatlands, but she learned from Jophriel that one-half of a sun revolution has passed, which the hopha call a "*semi-year*."

Moon Wing is now big with foal, just as the plans for a return to gryphonic territory are coming to fruition. It has taken some time, but the "peace delegation" is finally beginning to take form. Jophriel and Roonen have collected a group of like-minded hophas who understand that the mission is not to involve weaponry other than as a last-resort defensive strategy. Moon Wing, Pegasus, and Fluff Feather all want to go to the secret cavern of the hippogryphs (known as the Halona Caverns to the hopha).

"I will be the commander!" Moon Wing snorts, stamping the ground with her back hoof impatiently. "I will lead us to the Halona Caverns!"

"No! I will be the commander!" Pegasus counters. "You must keep your strength for the birth, Moon Wing."

"I don't give an oracle's screech who is the commander!" Sunground screams impatiently. "We will all be going together through the caverns. We cannot possibly go any other way with all the search squadrons on the prowl."

Sunground is concerned about Moon Wing traveling while she is pregnant. Moon Wing, however, is adamant that she must be a part of the delegation. Sunground has decided in concert with Nightsky that she will stay in the Halona Caverns along with the other younger and more vulnerable beings. They have not told her about that yet, and Nightsky believes that it is better to wait until they have arrived at Halona to bring up the subject. Sunground has agreed to tell Moon Wing at that time, while Nightsky will talk to Pegasus. Moon Wing will be much more difficult to convince than her mate: young Pegasus has been visiting her frequently with Nightsky, as he is concerned about her and her unborn filly.

During the time that they have all been in the hopha enclosure together, Sunground has formed closer bonds with the others in the enclosure as well. She and her erstwhile friend Star Sailor have reconciled with each other, and she has proven herself invaluable as an advisor on how to proceed with the crazy peace demonstration. Sunground is surprised that, as a former chieftain of the Royal Air Squadron, she is supportive of the idea. Star Sailor understands, however, that they need to do something to counter the Talonic regime and so far, Nightsky's idea of the peace delegation represents their best chance to accomplish that goal.

Sunground is also getting to know Fluff Feather, the sassy young kryphon who Moon Wing believes will make an excellent choice as a first mate for Groundsky. Sunground wonders how Grass Hopper will react toward the young kryphon, as she remembers with chagrin Dreamspinner's reaction to Nightsky. After spending time with Fluff Feather, however, Sunground has to admit that Moon Wing is right. She can see that Groundsky would find the young kryphon a favorable friend.

She remembers the oracle's prediction that Groundsky will become king of the wingless, along with his kryphon queen. Sunground has great difficulty seeing Groundsky or Fluff Feather in either of those roles but even so, she does not doubt the oracle's accuracy. Sunground has not spoken about her keythong son to the little kryphon, except to remind her that Groundsky has a hippogryph mate who is pregnant at this time. Fluff Feather has heard about the unsterilized keythong from Moon Wing, however, and she is fairly dancing in anticipation to meet him.

The most surprising bond that has taken place within the enclosure is that of Nightsky and Dreamspinner. Nightsky sent telepathic messages of peace to Dreamspinner and in the last while, his efforts have reaped a reward: Dreamspinner came to him and learned his method of communication. Soon after the two beings communicated to each other, Dreamspinner changed his attitude. Recently, he has become supportive of Nightsky, and his jealousy toward him has been receding. The unlikely friendship has astonished Sunground. She never thought that an opinicus could receive telepathic messages, much less respond to them. The two males have of late spent much of their time together, discussing plans for the peace delegation. They have, in fact, bonded so well that Sunground feels put out. She deliberately kept a physical distance from both of them in order to keep the peace between them. Now that they are friends, she feels completely left out of the equation.

Nightsky has reassured her that it is important to build a bond of trust between himself and Dreamspinner, as they will need to work together if the plan is to be successful. Sunground understands this but is still slightly disgruntled over it. She decides to ignore the males and instead spend her time bonding with the others in the group. She has also involved herself in introducing the others to Jophriel and Roonen's language.

The two hophas visit the enclosure frequently but so far, out of all the gryphonic beings, only Sunground, Dreamspinner, and Moon Wing have learned the language of the hopha. The equine beings already have a close telepathic bond with Roonen, while Jophriel is much more interested in establishing bonds with the gryphonic beings. Sunground tries her best to facilitate this, as she knows that they will all need to have some familiarity with the hophic language to function as a cohesive alliance. Jophriel, for her part, has guided groups of hophas around the enclosure in order to introduce them to the gryphonic beings and to teach them some key screech words. Jophriel's gryphonic screeching has improved immensely through tutoring by Sunground.

As well as forming group members' emotional bonds, the physical preparations for the journey into gryphonic territory have begun. The hopha have brought trucks that will transport the wingless among them back to the entrance of the tunnel. Jophriel asked that the winged ones simply fly back, following the trucks. Sunground's wings have again become weak through disuse. She and the others have performed wing-strengthening exercises, taught by Star Sailor, to prepare for the flight.

When the preparations are finally complete and the delegation is ready to move out, Roonen pushes a lever, and the force field suddenly disappears. The low, whiny, buzzing sound that accompanied the force field stops, to Sunground's immense relief. She became so accustomed to the sound that she forgot what it was like not to hear it. She and the others realize what a constant irritant it was to their ear openings, now that they are free of the noise.

At long last, the trucks move out, and soon after the winged ones of the delegation take to the skies. Sunground and Star Sailor watch the trucks closely to follow them to the correct location. It is extraordinarily thrilling to be air-borne once more, and Sunground feels her heart soar as well as her body. Nightsky flies on one side of her and Dreamspinner on the other, with Star Sailor leading the way. Moon Wing has been obliged to travel by truck due to her pregnancy, which annoys her no end. She and Fluff Feather are now traveling together in the same vehicle, so Sunground hopes that the wingless kryphon can give her companion some degree of cheer.

They fly over many magnificent hopha structures. The group cannot help but be awed by the creative genius of the civilization. They have seen tall structures, like mountains, and smaller ones that seem to act as dwelling places for the two-footed beings. Everywhere, there are statues of winged horses, carved meticulously from stone and mounted on large square boulders. As they pass over the inhabited areas, members of the populace look up from their activities and point excitedly at the odd flock overhead. Sunground hopes that they do not become afraid and use their weapons against the group, but Jophriel told her that Roonen chose his route carefully. He forewarned the various communities that there would be a gryphonic fly-over but that the creatures are no threat to anyone. Obviously, he went to great lengths to reassure them, for none of them displays any hostility. Instead, they appear curious, pointing objects at them that they press over their eyes.

"Do not fear, Sunground!" Jophriel says through a device she implanted in her ear opening. "Those objects are not weapons, but…" Jophriel trails off, unable to explain in gryphonic the strange tube-like devices that the hophas are putting over their eyes. Sunground has an idea that the objects are used to aid the people visually. She learned from Jophriel that hophic vision is relatively poor when compared to the gryphon's keen sight, especially at a distance.

Sunground feels exhilarated to be in the skies once more. She dreamed of being able to fly freely for many revolutions, yet she limited her dreaming because she thought it impossible that she would ever feel the wind at her wings again. Although she is thrilled to be in flight after their lengthy stay at the hophic enclosure, her delight is tempered by anxiety over how they will accomplish their ambitious goal of actually dethroning Talona. Nightsky seems to feel as though the gryphons will accept her as Talona's replacement, but Sunground doubts it. Her mother, Skystar, would be a far better replacement, if they were ever in a position to call for a new government. Sunground cannot rid herself, however, of the thought that this is a fool's errand. It is likely that the squadrons loyal to Talona will kill them.

Sunground shakes the thought from her mind and travels inward, where she is reassured by the voice of Grandmother Heartsong: "Fret not, granddaughter of the sun and sky, for all will be well."

Sunground wonders if she is simply imagining this reassuring message from her grandmother, but she knows better at a deeper level of her being. The message is clear: "Trust your heart and it will lead you to the peace which you desire."

Another voice speaks into her center of hearing, interrupting her heart's reverie.

"Sunground! We are arriving at the tunnel entrance."

Jophriel and the other ground travelers have slowed. They have passed through the hophic habitation area and are near to the wooded spot where they exited the underground tunnel after coming to the land of the hopha some time ago.

Sunground gives the screech signal to Star Sailor, their flight leader, for landing preparation. The group glides slowly downward, keeping their eyes on the progress of the trucks. The vehicles stop slightly ahead of the flock, that together comes in for a landing a short distance from the ground team.

Moon Wing and the others are finally set free from their moving prisons, and they sprint about joyously. The hophas file out of their own vehicles, one of which has been carrying a whole herd of them. In all, there are about twenty hophas and eighteen gryphonic beings, along with the two winged horses Nightsky and Pegasus. Their contingent adds up to forty beings, a woeful number when compared to the hundreds that comprise the gryphonic ground and air squadrons. The hophas have their stun weapons, but those are not enough to fend against a troop of gryphons intent on ravaging them all to pieces. Sunground hopes that they will not need to fight, for the result of such a battle would be catastrophic for them.

They wait for the hopha to load all their paraphernalia into one small vehicle that is to travel along the corridors of the tunnel leading to the Halona Caverns. Surely, though, they will need to leave it behind once they arrive at the mouth of the cavern. Sunground cannot imagine it being able to negotiate the stalagmites and other rocky protrusions that are a part of cave travel.

An odd and startling contraption presently joins them: a flying structure that descends with little noise onto the ground. This must be one of the "flying nest-shelters" that the old queen Grass Grazer told them about when discussing the technologies of the hopha. A ramp slides out, similar to those in the trucks except narrower. A relatively large male, his head-fur a reddish color, strides down the ramp and exchanges words with Roonen.

Jophriel explains to Sunground that some of the hophas will travel in the flying structures and meet them at the ceiling entrance of the tunnel, where Sunground and Dreamspinner first encountered Jophriel. This location is to be a home base for the operation. The flying nest-shelters will act as suppliers to the base for the whole group, as well as scouting the area from the skies. Sunground agrees with the arrangement, although she worries that this will leave them with even fewer hophic beings in their ground contingent than she had first imagined.

Perhaps that is a good thing, she reminds herself. *If this plan should go seriously awry, which is possible if not probable, at least there will be fewer two-foots vulnerable to being hurt or killed.*

The pair is distracted from their conversation by the voices of Roonen and the red-tufted male, as the volume of their argument grows increasingly loud and discordant. Sunground regards Jophriel quizzically.

"That is Jack Warford," Jophriel says, pointing to the other male. "He would like to bring in more weaponry. Roonen disagrees with him. None of us wants Warford to go with us, but he is an important leader and he insisted."

Roonen throws up his arms in exasperation and stalks over to where Jophriel is communing with Sunground. "That idiot will only make matters worse!" he exclaims, running his stubby talons over his black face-fur.

In recent days, Sunground's understanding of Roonen's rapid-fire speech has improved. He has been losing his temper much more than usual of late. Sunground now knows that it is because of this *Jack-War-Ford* character.

"Roonen has told me many times that Warford is a 'pain-in-the-butt,'" Dreamspinner interjects, joining the trio. "Even his name means 'battle' in the hophic language."

"Warford is a bloody pain in the butt!" Roonen explodes angrily, "That crazy fool wants to ruin everything."

Sunground's worry mounts as she contemplates the idea of working closely with the odd creatures. She knows she can trust Jophriel and Roonen, but she is less certain about the others, especially Warford.

In spite of her concerns, Sunground leads the way into the tunnel once the truck has entered into it. Jophriel walks beside her, accompanied by a younger hopha female whose facial features are similar to her own but whose long and flowing mane is black like Roonen's. She looks as though she is the adolescent daughter of Jophriel and Roonen.

"This is Halona, my daughter," Jophriel says, confirming Sunground's observations. "She is named for the Halona

Caverns and insisted on coming with us. She will go no further than the caverns."

Sunground speaks the youngster's name, and Halona returns the greeting in an almost-perfect replication of a hippogryphic screech call. She has obviously been spending time around the gryphonic beings as her mother has done, although Sunground does not remember seeing her at the enclosure.

"Halona was the one who found Moon Wing and Pegasus at the mouth of the tunnel," Jophriel explains in the hophic language. "She and Moon Wing became friends and learned to communicate with each other before Roonen discovered what had happened. He transported Moon Wing to the gryphonic enclosure and brought Pegasus home to share Nightsky's pasture. He then banned Halona from coming to see Moon Wing or any of the other gryphonic beings. She was angry with Roonen and me, because she wants to continue her communications with Moon Wing and the others. I convinced him to permit Halona to accompany us on this journey, at least up until the caverns. She is one of the few of us who understands and can replicate the gryphonic language, especially the hippogryphic dialect. I have been tutoring her in the gryphonic words that I have learned from you. She is a quick learner."

Sunground can understand why Moon Wing and Halona became friends, for they are obviously similar in temperament and personality. She supposes that Moon Wing never told her mother about the friendship with Halona because of Sunground's earlier mistrust of the hopha and their ingenious technology.

Moon Wing and Fluff Feather join Halona, and the three adolescents bound ahead with youthful vigor, as if ready to pounce upon the future and make it their own.

"Not too far ahead, Hal!" Jophriel calls, using a shortened form of her daughter's name. Sunground has learned much about hophas and their culture since her exposure to them. She learned that some hophas both celebrate and mourn the birth and death of a special oracle each sun revolution, a male who lived a long time ago. He was said to have brought the concepts of love and compassion to the hophic people at the cost of his own life. A portion of the seer's followers, however, gravely misunderstood his teachings, and they later used them to justify terrible acts of brutality against other hophas who did not share the same beliefs.

Sunground feels disturbed. How is it that a group of people could follow a belief system built on love and compassion and at the same time perform such barbarous acts of violence in its name? She then thinks of her own society and how demented it has become under the leadership of a lone tyrant.

Perhaps gryphons have much more in common with the hophas than we care to admit, she tells herself. *Here we are, on a fool's journey in the company of a mad species, discovering our own madness in the process. Who are we that journey onward in the hope of peace?*

A voice from somewhere in the shadows of her mind answers, *We are the Hopha-Equine Gryphonic Alliance.* Sunground speaks the name aloud to Jophriel, who likes the sound of it. They relay the name throughout the contingent.

A historic new group is born, she tells herself, *the only one of its kind to bring together not only the hopha and gryphonic beings but also the equines, the traditional "enemies" of the gryphons. This hostility toward horses has existed mainly in the minds of gryphons rather than as an actual outward occurrence. It is odd that even those circumstances that are precipitated by some outward action must originate from within. The gryphonic society is therefore suffering from a mental condition, one based upon fear and prejudice. I don't know when it began but at some point in time, the collective mental condition of the gryphons must have rendered its society vulnerable to the machinations of a tyrant. The question is, how will we convince the average gryphon or opinicus of her or his own madness? How do we, as a small band of peace-mongers, show Gryphonia to itself?*

"Do not fret, my gryphon lover," Nightsky answers. "We will prevail, for justice is on our side."

Sunground does not share his optimism. She feels that he is naïve as to the ways of gryphons, perhaps blinded by his love for her.

"Love is more powerful than anything else," he speaks into her mind once again, sensing her reservations.

"I hope you are right," she responds, "but still, I have my doubts."

Nightsky transmits a noise that sounds suspiciously like a chuckle. He gently says, "I will not interfere in your truth-doubt process, but I do urge you to have faith in our newly formed group."

Faith. Sunground repeats the word inside her mind, wishing that she was as certain as Nightsky about the outcome of their mission; but she well knows that being on the "right" side of a dispute is no guarantee of success.

The group continues its trek until they have reached the gaping mouth in the tunnel ceiling where she and Dreamspinner had first encountered Jophriel.

"This will be our base," Jophriel explains. "The truck will remain here with a few of our people, and we will meet the flying nest-shelter further into mountain territory."

Sunground experiences a rush of anxiety flitting through her body. "Mountain territory" means gryphon territory, and she is not looking forward to having to confront her own society.

They stop for a while to rest. Jophriel and Roonen rustle through the supplies in the truck before bringing out seeds and grasses for the equines and chunks of raw meat for the gryphonic beings. The hopha themselves eat a variety of meat, fruit, and vegetables, each arranged on a flat feeding plate.

After they have eaten, the journey through the tunnel resumes. The hopha now carry big bags of supplies on their backs and have fastened the supplies for the equines and gryphonic beings on each creature's back. Nightsky and Pegasus carry bigger loads than anyone since they are among the biggest and most ground-sturdy of the creatures, with their four powerful land-legs.

It seems to Sunground that the trip through the tunnel is not as lengthy going to the caverns as it was when she and Dreamspinner were making their way to the then-unknown hophic flatlands. She recognizes the route this time and is able to wind through it that much more quickly, even though traveling in a large group. She estimates that it has only taken them a few days to arrive at the cavern mouth as opposed to the five or six days it took to travel to the flatlands when they were uncertain as to where their destination would be.

She understands from Jophriel that the flying nest-shelter, or "airship" as the other hophas refer to it, will replenish their home base with provisions when needed.

Sunground is grateful for the hopha technology that allows them to do this. It will also help to bring food to the gryphonic people, who have been hiding in the caverns for so long. Thinking about her family and the others, Sunground again experiences anxiety as she realizes that every time they have to go outside the hiding spot to hunt and gather food for the group of cave-bound refugees, they are at risk of discovery by the government squadrons.

Sunground forces herself not to dwell on it right now. They have arrived at the mouth of the cavern tunnel, and she will need to go through it to inform the occupants of the caverns what has transpired. She realizes that she cannot bring a troop of hophas into their hiding spot without first explaining their mission. She hopes fervently that the hippogryphs and her family will not think that she has gone insane.

After conferring with Jophriel and Roonen, they decide that Sunground and Dreamspinner will go first to inform the cavern dwellers, and if it is safe to proceed then Dreamspinner will return and lead the rest of them to the cavern.

The pair crawls and scratches its way through the rocky cavern tunnel. After having become accustomed to the light and ease of movement that the hophic tunnel afforded them, they both find the dark, craggy cavern to be claustrophobic. Their eyes take time to adjust to the dark, and they bump into the various stalagmites that line the bottom of the tunnel. They grope their way forward, their wings dropping feathers as they flap them in frustration.

"We have been spoiled by the hopha and their tunnel of ease," Sunground notes, remembering how they had disliked it.

Dreamspinner utters a muffled caw by way of response, as he is too busy scratching his way up the passageway to speak. The passage seemed far easier to negotiate when they were traveling down it but now requires a great deal more effort to climb, as it inclines steeply upward.

By the time they have made their way to the upper cavern, they barely have enough vocal strength to screech out a greeting of arrival. At first, there is no answer to their call. Sunground panics for a moment as she considers the possibility that the gryphonic forces have infiltrated their hiding spot. She then notices a small form crouching in the darkness. It steps out into the torch-lit passage and suddenly screams in delight. *It is Groundsky!*

Mother and son rush at each other, pecking one another fondly, and the process is repeated with Dreamspinner. Groundsky gives a whoop of joy, and the rest of the group creeps slowly out of the shadows. He leads his parents to the center of the cavern and announces their return vociferously. "My mother and father have returned! Come forth, one and all to greet them!"

There is a moment of pandemonium as Sunground greets her family members: her mother, sisters, nieces, old Egglight, and Groundsky's pregnant mate, Grass Hopper all rush toward her eagerly. Waiting nearby is the elder half-sister of Moon Wing, the hippogryph queen Night Lover, who steps forward once the hilarity has abated.

"Greetings, Mother Sunground," she says respectfully. "I thought that I had sensed your presence, but I sense too that you have brought others with you, some of them strangers to us."

Sunground looks around her at the expectant group of hippogryphs, many of whom are regarding her with trepidation. She will need to tread cautiously as she informs them of what has transpired and of what their rather grandiose plans entail.

"My family and friends," she says awkwardly. "I have some great news. We have found Moon Wing, and she is here, waiting to enter the cavern. She is pregnant! The father is Pegasus, the white winged colt."

The hippogryphs stir slightly, their trepidation lessened somewhat by the excitement of the happy news. Sunground pauses a moment, letting them take in the joy of Moon Wing's safe return and the upcoming birth. Grass Hopper in particular seems pleased, and her grey equine hindquarters tremble in anticipation of seeing her lost friend once more.

"There is more that you have to tell us, Mother Sunground. Please, do not hesitate. Let us know," Night Lover says.

Sunground's heart flutters in panic, but she knows that she cannot avoid telling them any longer. "My friends and family, I have also brought others with us. Pegasus and Nightsky are traveling with our group, as well as some keythongs and kryphons, one gryphon, and a group of hophas whom we have befriended."

At the mention of the hopha, a cacophony of screeching breaks out among not only her own ever-excitable family but also from the normally subdued hippogryphs.

Mountain Rain, her younger sister, is livid. "Sunground, have you gone mad? You've led a bunch of hophas to our hiding spot! What possessed you to do such a thing?"

"I assure you, they are peaceful!" Sunground explains hastily. "They are no threat to anyone because they are helping us to lead a peace delegation to the gryphons to, uh, convince them to change governments."

Sunground stammers as she attempts to communicate their mission to the skeptical crowd. She not only sounds mad, she realizes, but foolish as well.

"Sunsky," her mother says gently to her, determined as always to use her former name. "Surely you know that such a mission is doomed to failure? Why, you and whoever it is that is naive enough to join you will all be killed by the gryphonic forces before you even have a chance to explain yourselves. If you are seen to be turning gryphons against the government, you will be convicted of treason and put to death. You see, my gentle daughter, gryphonic society has changed. It is not the one that you and I remember. Many dissenting gryphons have already been put to death including, we have learned recently, the oracle Truth Speaker."

This latest piece of news hits Sunground like a bolt of lightning in the midst of a terrible thunderstorm. She reels in shock, screeching her anguish into the darkness of the cavern, its sound reverberating in echoes throughout the chamber.

Her family gathers around her in an attempt to comfort her. Dreamspinner beats his wings savagely, vowing to avenge the death of the oracle, while the hippogryphs back off from the mad peace defenders, receding once more into the shadows of the cavern. Only Night Lover and Grass Hopper remain with Sunground and her family, standing nearby them in stubborn determination.

Mountain Rain speaks when the din has quieted. "So much for our bond with the hippogryphs. Come to your senses, Sunground! Do you think the gryphon who executed the sacred oracle will agree to give up her power? Who would we replace her with if we were successful? You, I suppose."

"Yes!" Dreamspinner answers in a triumphant voice. "My equine brother, Nightsky, believes that our Sun*sky*—not 'ground'—shall be the new queen. I, for one, shall not rest until that day dawns! If we cannot accomplish it by peace, then let us accomplish it by battle!"

"I always suspected that you were stark-raving mad, Dreamspinner!" Mountain Rain says. "But now I know that you are irretrievably insane, as is Sunground! What a pair you two make. And what is this about your *equine brother*, you fool of a male? Why, I thought you wanted to tear to pieces the winged stallion that impregnated your dear and crazy queen?"

"I have had a change of heart, O sister of my queen!" Dreamspinner retorts. "Nightsky and I have made peace, for he is the father of our beloved Moon Wing—the next queen of the hippogryphs!"

"So now you're trying to change the hippogryphs' government as well?" Mountain Rain exclaims in disgust. "At the behest of a winged horse? O, how the oracle must be looking down at us and crowing sadly!"

"No!" Sunground surprises herself with her ferocious response. "The oracle did say that Moon Wing would become a queen among her people. She also said that I would too, of mine—eventually, that is."

Sunground lost some of her ferocity on the last part of her response. Bragging about her daughter's future is one thing, but she feels as if making bold statements about her own queenship goes beyond the boundaries of decency.

"You had your chance to be queen, O *Great Sunsky!*" Mountain Rain screeches in rage. "You threw it away, and now all of us are paying for it. You dare to bring up your ambitions of gryphonic leadership! You are worse than the tyrant, Talona!"

Sunground can only hang her head miserably at her sister's stinging admonishment. She fears that Mountain Rain may be right, and she regrets dreadfully having spoken aloud the oracle's prediction regarding the gryphonic reign.

Dreamspinner, however, shrieks his defense of Sunground, and both he and Mountain Rain argue bitterly until Mother Skystar screeches for peace. "Quiet! I refuse to allow you to blame *Sunsky* for past events! However we arrived at this moment, we are here, so stop throwing blame around, Mountain Rain. Dreamspinner, you will stop your infernal shrieking and bellowing at once. It will do none of us any good, and it is frightening the hippogryphs. We must deal with things as they are, not as they were or how they may be in some as yet undetermined future."

There is a subdued silence, followed by the frightened warbles of the young gryphons, Rainbow Dreamer and Luck Wisher. Mountain Rain bows her head, moving to join their other sister, Cloudhopper, in comforting the chicks. She does not, however, apologize to Sunground for her comments.

The old kryphon nanny Egglight moves close to Sunground, preening her feathers gently with her beak. "It is a wonderful thought, my dear, this peace mission of yours. Truth be told, if you were made queen today I would follow you without question."

Before any of them has a chance to recover, a loud bellow echoes from the other side of the cavern, "My mother *will* be queen of the gryphons, my Papa says so!"

The group whirls around as if it comprises one entity. Out of the darkness emerges the pregnant hippogryph Moon Wing, trotting confidently to them. The other hippogryphs, upon hearing her voice, creep nearer to the gryphonic group. They back off again when they see who is behind Moon Wing: It is the adolescent hopha, Halona, accompanied by the young kryphon Fluff Feather. Further behind them is a bedraggled gryphon with balding patches in her plumage. The group remains stock still as they regard the young hopha anxiously.

"Oh, don't worry about Halona, you silly feathers!" Moon Wing says. "She is my friend. And don't worry about Star Sailor either. She's on our side now."

"Star Sailor!" Sunground caws her annoyance, forgetting for the moment her earlier embarrassed obsequiousness. "How could you have led the young ones here without my signal? I have only just informed the group of our intentions, and they are not happy about it. I told everyone to wait!"

"I'm sorry, Sunground," Star Sailor says. "I did not lead these disobedient rebels here! They led themselves here. Apparently, Halona knew another route to the caverns, and she took Moon Wing and Fluff Feather with her. They left Jophriel and me no choice but to go after them."

At the mention of her name, Jophriel emerges from behind Star Sailor, angrily ordering her errant daughter to move quickly to her side. Halona sheepishly complies as her mother gives her a firm admonishment. Sunground likewise admonishes

Moon Wing, concerned that her rebelliousness has caused her to disobey an order.

"Listen, all three of you!" Sunground screeches. "If we are to achieve any kind of success on this mission, you all need to learn to obey orders. You do not just wander off on your own lark! This could have been a dangerous venture for you."

"Oh, don't be silly, Mama!" Moon Wing retorts. "I knew our families posed no threat to any of us. The best way for everyone to get used to the hopha is to meet one or two of them first."

"*Moon Wing!*" Sunground exclaims. "That is not your decision to make! You are *not* in command of this mission!"

"But Mama, *you* said you didn't give an oracle's screech who was the commander! So I thought, 'all right then, I shall be the commander, at least of the young ones.'"

"Listen to me, you recalcitrant chick," Sunground growls. "*You* are *not* the commander of anyone or anything. We do not have the luxury of such chickish games. We have no margin for error on this mission. Foolishness and disobedience can lead to death, and you need to understand that. Perhaps this would be a good time to inform you that you will be staying here in the safety of the caverns and not going on the mission."

Moon Wing cries out in defiance, but Sunground is adamant. She has the support of Jophriel and the others, as they each echo her statement. She is especially appreciative of the hippogryph queen Night Lover's firm support when Moon Wing attempts to appeal to her half-sister against Sunground's decree.

"No, Moon Wing, you shall not leave this cavern, especially in your condition," Night Lover proclaims. "I must agree with Mother Sunground on this. Have you forgotten that you also disobeyed my order to return at once with us to the cavern when we were on our journey together? You promised me that, if we went to the lower mountains to search for your papa, you would obey my orders. You broke that promise when you went with Pegasus to the flatlands instead of coming with us, after we heard the news of the old gryphon queen's passing."

"I do not regret my actions!" Moon Wing retorts. "I did find my papa, and he helped both Pegasus and me to realize that the hopha are no threat to us. Indeed, he convinced all of us at the enclosure to form an alliance with the hopha in order to challenge the illegal gryphonic reign!"

"Our father has always been a naïve idealist, Moon Wing," Night Lover replies gently. "That is not always an advantageous thing to be, especially in the midst of a cruel dictatorship."

"I think the responsibility of being premiere queen has quenched your spirit, Sister Night Lover!" Moon Wing snorts. "You used to be wild and free, like Papa!"

"Wild and free—within the prison fields of the hopha?" Night Lover retorts. "Moon Wing, I think it is you and Father Nightsky who have been domesticated out of your wild freedom."

Moon Wing screeches, prompting Sunground to position herself between her daughter and Night Lover. "Enough, both of you!" she cries. "I know this is a difficult thing to accept, this alliance with the hopha. I've had my doubts about it, believe me. I do not say that we can blindly trust all hophas, any more than we can blindly trust all gryphons. I do, however, trust Jophriel and her mate Roonen, as well as their daughter Halona."

"Halona, Halona! It rhymes with Talona!" A chickish clucking taunts the young hopha from behind Mountain Rain. It is the young gryphon, Rainbow Dreamer. Halona screeches back in the perfect intonation of a gryphon and is immediately quieted by Jophriel.

Mountain Rain, in turn, gives her daughter a firm nip of reprisal. "Don't you dare say anything to them, Dreamer!" Mountain Rain scolds the youngster. "I don't want you becoming a hopha and horse lover like your aunt."

"Mountain Rain, that was uncalled for!" Mother Skystar cries, leaping into the war of words. "That is an insult to every hippogryph in this room, as well as to our Sunsky. I suggest that we all take time to go within, as the oracle and old Queen Grass Grazer would have wanted us to do."

Sunground suddenly realizes that the elderly hippogryph queen is not present in the cavern. She cocks her feathered head, peering questioningly at both Skystar and Night Lover.

"Old Queen Grass Grazer has passed on, Sunsky," Skystar explains, "She died peacefully in her sleep shortly after you left for the flatlands. She told me that she was ready to join her old mate, Grey Tree, in the Otherworldly Forest."

Sunground feels a wave of sadness pass through her as she ambles over to Night Lover to preen her feathers soothingly. Night Lover returns the gesture and the room falls silent. They put aside all dissent for now in order to honor the memory of not only the oracle Truth Speaker, but the old queen, Grass Grazer, as well.

CHAPTER TWO

The Space In Between
Peace and War

The last few days are fraught with tension as Sunground and the members of her peace delegation attempt to argue in favor of the alliance with the hopha. Night Lover finally calls for a compromise. Sunground and her friends may use the caverns as a starting point for their mission, but they may not use it as a base. All hophas, except for those envoys given special permission to be in the caverns, are to remain in the hopha tunnel. Thus far, Night Lover has granted this special-entry status only to Jophriel and Roonen, although she has tolerated Halona's presence as long as her parents accompany her. Since the young hopha knows both gryphonic and hippogryphic sounding symbols, she has been useful in the daily dialogues between Night Lover and the hophas.

Sunground and Nightsky, meanwhile, have strongly impressed upon Moon Wing that she needs to put her young foal's safety above her own desires for adventure. She agrees, with the greatest reluctance, to stay with the hippogryphs and Skystar's family in the relative safety of the cavern. Moon Wing also insists that Fluff Feather be her attendant and that the cavern dwellers must permit Pegasus, Nightsky, and Halona to visit with her.

The hippogryphs have no problem welcoming Nightsky and Pegasus into their midst, but some of the gryphons clearly feel uncomfortable about their presence. Sunground is annoyed by this, but she reminds herself that her sisters and nieces have never really encountered equines before and therefore will need time to overcome their prejudice. Skystar, having once mated with a winged horse long ago, is far more accepting. To Sunground's delight, she relates well with Nightsky in spite of the difficulties that his mating with Sunground has caused the family. Skystar treats Nightsky as the father of her beloved granddaughter, not as a dreaded winged horse, and Sunground is proud of her for it.

Nightsky, for his part, is nothing but gracious to all present. He respects their points of view, but also offers his own as a gentle challenge to their preconceptions. Sunground acts as a translator for him to the others, speaking the thoughts that Nightsky transmits. Mother Skystar, to her daughter's surprise, requires no translation but rather forms her own telepathic communication with the black horse. Although she accepts Nightsky, she does not concur with his admittedly rash peace plan.

"Nightsky, you are an idealist, like my daughter," she transmits to him. "I once knew a winged horse in my youth who was like that. His name was Mountain Pounder, and he was the same color as you are."

To Sunground's surprise, she is able to hear her mother's telepathic transmissions to Nightsky, although the gryphon mother and daughter have never communicated that way together. She did not realize that her mother possessed such an advanced capacity for telepathic communication, but neither had she ever heard the name of her once-lover.

"Mountain Pounder was my father," Nightsky answers, to Sunground's astonishment. "He died fighting against the hopha, defending my mother and me from capture. Although I loved him dearly, I never thought of him as an idealist. I suppose that he was, though, in his own way. He firmly believed in equine freedom. He believed that the hopha were evil creatures who wanted only to enslave us."

"Was he not right about that, Nightsky?" Skystar asked. "Why is the son of Mountain Pounder trying to form an alliance with the hopha? They killed your own father."

"I know this is difficult for you to understand, Mother Skystar," Nightsky replies. "I felt that fighting the hopha was not the way to deal with them. My father and I had frequent arguments about it. He was concerned that one day they would beguile me, and I would lose my freedom to them."

"And was he not correct?"

"He was a very brave horse," Nighsky laments. "I miss him greatly. I fully believe, however, that his death was an accident and that the hopha did not intend to kill him. He unfortunately chose to attack them first, something no equine has ever done. They defended themselves, and they used their magic lightning to do so. When they realized that they had killed him, they were full of remorse and grief. I could feel their anguish as strongly as I did my own. I formed a momentary bond with a young, black-tufted hopha male, who chased my mother and me away before the other hophas had time to follow. I do not know why but ever since then, I knew that I was going to be a peace envoy to the hophic people through this two-footed youth. The hopha neither captured nor beguiled me. Instead, when the time was right, I chose to go to them and chose to be a servant to them so that I could learn their language and their ways. I wanted to form a peace bond between them and us, to prevent any more injuries or deaths. This was why I came to Roonen many sun revolutions later, when we were both older and ready for the challenge. He and I formed a bond when we were both young, and he is committed to doing the right thing by my people. Since then, my wingless mother, Goldmare, has joined us in the mission and is continuing our work with Roonen's mother Andriel while we are away making peace with the gryphons."

"I see," Skystar responds. "First the hopha, and now the gryphons. Your father had similar plans to create a peace bond with us gryphons, you know. He thought that by mating with as many of us as possible, we would be able to dispel the negative thoughts that gryphons held toward the equines. I think he was able to convince me of the benefits of a gryphon-equine treaty but not my mate Sun Quest. He drove Mountain Pounder away with his sharp beak and fearsome claws. That was the end of the gryphon-equine treaty, I'm afraid."

Nightsky utters a noise that sounds like a cross between a whinny and a chuckle. "Yes, my father would think that mating was the way to win the heart of Gryphonia, but I believe that my plan springs from a deeper kind of love than that."

"Ahh, yes, a deeper kind of love—such as that between you and my daughter? I think that you are a lot more like your father than you realize, Nightsky."

Sunground wants to defend Nightsky's position but refrains from doing so, as she senses that Nightsky has something that he wants to say.

"Skystar," he says. "I know that my actions have brought a great deal of pain and hardship to your family. I apologize for that, although I know that none of us can ever regret the life of Moon Wing, she whom your family loves so deeply. I need you to know that I am embarking on the mission of peace not only for my daughter but also for your people and mine, which includes the hopha. I do not want our people to live in fear of the gryphons, nor the gryphons in fear of the hopha and equines, for that matter. What we are trying to do must seem foolish, I know, but whenever there is tension between peace and war, I believe that there is also a space in between these two extremes that we need to hold. We need to be the space between peace and war, between love and hate, between that which is called "right" and "wrong." Sunground and I, along with Dreamspinner and all the others, are determined to do that. I believe strongly, after what I have heard from Star Sailor, that the gryphons are ready for a change of government. If we can be the catalyst for that change, then peace between all of us may indeed be possible."

"Hmmm," Skystar responds. "I can see that you are persuasive, Nightsky. You have succeeded in seducing everyone who entered the hopha lands into this mad plan—not only our impressionable Moon Wing but also Sunsky, Star Sailor, and even the young colt Pegasus, who I am told was set against the hopha when he and Moon Wing first went to rescue you from them. In fact, you have even managed to seduce the hopha themselves into following this fool's errand, by the looks of things. Only the son of Mountain Pounder could perform such a feat."

Nightsky bows his head before her. "Skystar, I have not convinced you, I know. But I am not only the son of Mountain Pounder, I am also the son of my mother, Goldmare. As a wingless equine, she was not encouraged to look to the skies. Nonetheless, she has always held great dreams of peace between all the beings who share this sacred space."

"No doubt she holds great wisdom, Nightsky," Skystar replies. "But she must be worried about you right now, as I am about Sunsky and the others."

"Yes," Nightsky answers, "but she also realizes that worrying accomplishes nothing. This peace mission is something that we must at least attempt to do, rather than bowing to tyranny."

Skystar reluctantly accepts Nightsky's remark, turning away sadly to rejoin the others.

The preparations for the journey of peace surge ahead in spite of the dire warnings of Sunground's family. Cloudhopper, the elder sister of Sunground, has resigned herself to the fact that Sunground will be participating in this mad mission, and she reluctantly supports her in the decision. Sunground is deeply grateful for this, and she tells Cloudhopper so. She realizes that she has not adequately appreciated her gentle sister in the past, thinking of her as a kind but bumbling clown.

"I want you to know that you are always a deep-heart sister to me, my Cloud," she murmurs to her, using her old chickhood nickname.

"You also, Sunny," Cloudhopper coos. "I know Mountain Rain feels the same, even if she isn't telling you herself. She gets angry with you because she loves you and doesn't want to see you get hurt or even killed."

"I know," Sunground replies, her heart aching for the broken relationship with her younger sister. Mountain Rain has not been speaking to Sunground for the last few days, knowing that if she does, she will again fly into a rage over the "mission of folly," as she refers to it. Rain's daughter, Rainbow Dreamer, has also been keeping a distance from her mad aunt, to Sunground's profound sadness.

Luck Wisher, the daughter of Cloudhopper, comforts Sunground by breaking ranks with her cousin and embracing the family pariah. She gives her a loving peck and even a message of fortune to go with it. "As my name suggests, I am wishing you all great luck with your crazy peace mission, Aunt Sunground."

Sunground's heart is filled with gratitude for this simple gesture on the part of her niece. In addition to the reluctant support of Skystar, Cloudhopper, old Egglight, and Luck Wisher, her keythong son Groundsky has been an enthusiastic cheerleader for the mission.

"Let me come with you, O brave mother Sunground!" he says. "I will defend the peace along with you and my father."

Sunground has consistently refused to allow Groundsky to come along on the mission, even though Dreamspinner has been considering the possibility.

"The answer is 'no', Groundsky. You are wingless, and that could be a problem. You must stay here and protect Grass Hopper and her unborn choal. *That* is your mission, my son. You wanted to be a father, and now you must accept the responsibilities that go along with that esteemed role."

Groundsky unenthusiastically agrees to Sunground's order, grumbling that he never gets to go on missions, as Moon Wing has done.

"Moon Wing will not be going either, my dear Groundsky," Sunground says. "She also is due to become a parent. You and Pegasus will together protect your sister while she carries her foal. Fluff Feather, the young kryphon, will join you in this as Moon Wing's attendant."

The fact that Fluff Feather will be staying on in the cavern cheers Groundsky immensely, as he and the young kryphon have developed a bond. The younger ones have likewise lovingly embraced Fluff Feather, including Grass Hopper, the hippogryph mother of Groundsky's unborn choal.

Grass Hopper and Groundsky have been getting on each other's nerves. Far from being jealous of the attention that Groundsky showers on Fluff Feather, Grass Hopper welcomes it because it allows her to concentrate on the upcoming birth of her own youngster.

"Keep him busy for me, Fluff!" she says. "I want a bit of peace before the choal is born."

"Can I have him, Grassy?" Fluff Feather asks her saucily. "Or are you going to want him as your first mate?"

"No, you take him," Grass Hopper says. "He's a pain in the tail."

Thank the oracle for small mercies, Sunground thinks. *The last thing we need is a mating row between two jealous females. At least now I can depart on the dangerous journey with a relatively peaceful mind.*

She is also grateful that the old kryphon nanny, Egglight, has taken the younger kryphon Fluff Feather under her tutelage, teaching her the necessities of being a birth attendant so that she will have some idea of what to do when Moon Wing begins her birthing process.

Sunground knows that the cavern is the safest place that she can leave Moon Wing and her other family members, so she makes a decision to put aside her fears for them in order to concentrate on the mission. She has gone within frequently to ask Grandmother Heartsong, old Queen Grass Grazer, and the oracle for protection and guidance. She has discovered that Grandmother Heartsong is her guide for the peace mission, Queen Grass Grazer the source of protection for the hippogryphs and her family, and the oracle her inner guide. She has received many reassuring messages from the oracle that have helped her state of mind enormously.

She realizes more and more that, even if she is to perish in this bold endeavor, it will not mean the end of her life. Rather, it will be the passing into another realm and another form. She understands now the futility of worldly power, especially taking the life of another being in order to further that power. Ultimately, if the oracle and the others are capable of sending her messages from the beyond, then Talona's attempt to assassinate Truth Speaker succeeded only in killing her body and not her spirit. Sunground has always known this at a deeper level, but the knowledge is just now beginning to bubble to the surface of her mind.

"I am always here, Sunsky of the Mountains," Truth Speaker's voice says to her, "call upon me when you need me."

Somehow, when she hears the otherworldly voice of the oracle speak her old name, it does not seem wrong or out of place. Will she perhaps redeem herself and return to her old name? Truth Speaker seems to think that no redemption is necessary. Sunground shakes her head and pushes the name "*Sunsky*" out of her mind, in spite of the oracle's specific use of it. She must concentrate on the mission, for it is about to begin. She hears the voice of old Queen Heartsong calling her to it.

The next days are taken up in preparation. The hopha have agreed to post observers near the cavern to monitor the activity outside of it. If any gryphonic squadrons are in the vicinity, the hopha sentinels are to warn the cavern dwellers, and if a breach into the hiding spot appears inevitable the hippogryph and gryphon families are to vacate it and go into the hopha tunnel. There, the hopha will protect them with their powerful technology. It has not been an easy feat to get the hippogryphs to agree to this, but Jophriel and Halona have proven to be excellent negotiators. The hippogryphs have reluctantly agreed to tolerate the hopha and their fearful gadgetry if a security breach occurs but not until it does. Night Lover is still worried about the two-footed sorcerers seducing the group into servitude and bringing them to the flatlands, but Sunground has tried to reassure her that any flight to the flatlands would only be as a last resort.

In the end, Night Lover realizes that they do not have much of a choice but to accept the protection offered by the hopha, for the alternative is to be killed by the gryphonic forces.

As the oddly assorted group of gryphonic beings, equines, and hophas prepare to leave, Sunground presents herself to each of her dear family members to say farewell. When she comes around to her sister Mountain Rain, however, the younger sibling refuses her good-bye gesture.

"Will you not at least give me a peck to send me on my journey, Rain?" she asks her, deeply hurt.

"No, Foolish-Feather, I will not," Mountain Rain replies, "for I am coming with you."

"What?" Sunground squawks, astounded. "No, Rain, you can't! You need to stay here to protect our family!"

She turns to consult Mother Skystar, but the older gryphon bobs her head in confirmation of Mountain Rain's statement. "Mountain Rain insists, Sunsky, and I have given her my blessing. She is coming to help keep you safe and out of all of us here, she is best suited to do that. She also wants to discover the whereabouts of and possibly free your father Sun Quest and Grandfather Lightning Bolt."

Sunground is awash with emotions. *Mountain Rain is willing to accompany me on the journey!* She is speechless.

"I'm *not* coming with you because I believe in this idiotic peace group thing," Mountain Rain asserts. "I'm only coming because I want to save Father Sun Quest and Grandfather Lightning Bolt and the others. And, I guess also to keep your overly naïve tail safe from harm."

"But who will protect our family, Rain?" Sunground says. "Will Mother Skystar not need your help? What about Rainbow Dreamer?"

"Have you forgotten, Sunny? Your trusted hophas are going to protect all of them with their ridiculous talking gadgets and magic lightning. Besides, not all of our family is here. We can't ignore forever the fact that our father, grandfather, the physician Light Healer, and others are in prison. Even if you had not hatched this insane plan with your horse-mate and his two-footed companions, I would have attempted to rescue them. I was hoping to go alone, but Mother Skystar convinced me to go with you and your motley crew instead. As for my daughter, she understands the gravity of the situation. She is going to be nothing but helpful to Grandmother Skystar. Is that not right, my saucy princess?"

Rainbow Dreamer grumbles an affirmative response, adding her wish to go with her mother and aunt. She then gives her mother a sad peck, and they embrace each other with their wings. Rainbow Dreamer hesitates before giving her aunt an additional good-bye peck. Sunground is profoundly moved and grateful for this gesture from the youngest family member. Somehow, it gives her strength for the journey ahead.

CHAPTER THREE

The Quest Begins

They set out on their quest, returning down the rocky crawl-way through which the family first entered the upper cavern. Jophriel and Roonen carry light-shining devices that somewhat abate the murky darkness of the cave. They carefully make their descent, down into the freezing cold water of the lower passageway. The hophas are shivering with the shock of the low temperatures.

"This water is like ice," Jophriel murmurs to Sunground. "I'm glad Halona isn't tagging along, as she wanted to do—or at least she better not, the little trouble-maker."

Jophriel turns around every once in a while to shine the lighted torch—which the hopha call a *flash-light*—back in the direction that they had traveled, as if half-expecting to see her daughter and the other youngsters following them. Sunground understands this impulse all too well, rotating her neck backward with each beam of the light to see if she can glimpse Moon Wing or Groundsky surreptitiously venturing along with the group. Each time they do this, they see nothing, but it fails to satisfy them nonetheless.

"Stop looking back, you two!" Mountain Rain calls impatiently. "We can't be continually fretting about our young back at the nest if we are to make any ground on this journey. *Forward!*"

Sunground knows that her sister is correct, but she is having trouble letting go of her precious family yet again. She goes within to consult the oracle, who once again reassures her that her chicks remain in the upper cavern.

The group slogs its way through the cave river until finally they arrive at the tangled brush that hides the entrance to the caverns. They all plow their way through until they are standing in the outer forest, which is almost as dense as the bush wall from which they have emerged.

As the members arrive, Sunground takes stock of them. There are, besides her: Dreamspinner, Nightsky, Star Sailor, Mountain Rain, ten Keythongs, and two Kryphons from the hophic enclosure. In addition, Night Lover has sent with them three hardy hippogryphs named Joker, Nectar Sipper, and Soul Flower. Their purpose is to replace the young delegates, Moon Wing, Fluff Feather, and Pegasus, who remain behind in the cavern. There are twelve hophas in the contingent, including Jophriel and Roonen. That leaves them with thirty-two delegates marching directly into danger.

Sunground knows that Warford and the two other hophas who are riding in the airship will aid them, but she is not certain yet as to how that help will affect their mission, particularly if Warford becomes aggressive. She worries about the argument that she and Jophriel had witnessed earlier between Roonen and Warford regarding the use of weaponry. However, she must trust in the leadership of Roonen and Jophriel when it comes to the hophic members of the group.

Three of the hophas, including Halona, have stayed behind in the tunnel to provide for the group of cavern dwellers. Another couple named Seth and Sharriel act as sentinels, scouting the area for gryphonic forces in order to warn the group back at the cavern should any breach of the cave entrance become imminent. The hophas connect with each other through a technology that allows them to communicate over a long distance. Sunground and the others have been fitted with tiny devices in their ear openings that allow either Jophriel or Roonen to speak to them when they are outside of normal speaking and hearing range.

Although this technology of the hopha may afford them some kind of advantage, it will not be enough should they run into a large air squadron of gryphons or even a ground squadron of keythongs.

"Twelve of our gryphonic members cannot even fly, Sunground!" Mountain Rain exclaims, echoing her fears. "They are as wingless as the two-foots. I cannot fathom why we are bringing along ten keythongs and two kryphons."

"We will need to split up into teams," Sunground explains. "Some among the keythong/kryphon group will need to engage the keythongery."

"You mean they're going to get arrested by the ground squadrons and brought to prison? They can really engage the keythongery from there," Mountain Rain replies, her sarcasm biting.

"The idea is for them to slip into Keythong City unnoticed and to blend in with the rest of them. They will then go to work informing the appropriate keythongs on the council that a change in the gryphonic government is imminent and that their support will be greatly needed."

"Great thinking! Tell the Council of Keythongs what our plans are so they can inform the Gryphonic Council. That will go over wonderfully with Talona!"

Sunground is growing irritable with Mountain Rain's cynicism. Every time she puts forth a plan of action, her sister claws it down, as though her role in the mission is to be the Vulture of Irony.

"The keythongs no longer have a council, my dears," Star Sailor says. "One of the last pieces of information that I received before my comrades abandoned me was that Talona had struck down the Council of Keythongs so the wingless could concentrate more fully on working for the gryphons. In other words, they are now completely and utterly slaves of the gryphons."

"Thanks for letting us know, Sailor!" Mountain Rain says. "Now that we've brought along these useless no-wings."

"I thought that you already knew about the keythongs, Rain," Star Sailor mutters with some chagrin.

"I see. I would know exactly what is happening, having been in hiding for the past half sun revolution! Sunground and Star Sailor, have you two prepared no plan at all? Why don't we all present ourselves for execution right now?"

Sunground feels herself filling with uncertainty. Mountain Rain is correct—they are ill prepared for this mission.

"Tell them that we will all confront the gryphons together, Sunsky," a familiar telepathic voice advises her. Nightsky watches from a short distance as Sunground repeats what he has just told her, to the derision of Mountain Rain and the dismay of Star Sailor.

"Please, Sunground, we cannot do that!" Star Sailor implores her. "It will be suicide!"

Sunground's mind reels in confusion. *How can I possibly lead this exercise in foolishness? No one seems to know how to proceed.* She cocks her head toward Jophriel, hoping that she has a better idea.

"It sounds as if there is a difference of opinion, Sunground," the hopha says. "You were all speaking rather quickly, but I did pick up that the other two gryphons do not want to stage a group confrontation. How else can we do it, though?"

"I do not know what to do, Jophriel," Sunground admits. "I am a poor excuse for a leader. I cannot possibly take over the queenship."

"Don't worry about taking over right now," Jophriel says, stroking her back. "First things first. The main objective now is to confront the government about its recent acts of violence toward others who are different from the gryphons. We are all in this together. You are not alone."

Jophriel's words and gentle touch reassure Sunground, who goes within for a moment to find her center. She travels through the mental chaos to the eye of her thought storm, where she hears the small, still voice of Heartsong: *Proceed with your plan, Sunsky, Queen of the Mountains! The oracle and I will keep you and the others safe.*

After a few moments of inner calm, Sunground turns her attention back to the waiting group and relays the otherworldly message that she received. Mountain Rain is of course dubious about the voice of Grandmother Heartsong speaking to her sister, but Sunground has found a new confidence and refuses to let doubts distract her.

They travel forward through the thick brush, the hophas all the while keeping in touch with the airship that has been scouting the area and watching for gryphonic squadrons. Nonetheless, their progress is slow. Sunground does not focus on her thoughts of failure but instead derives encouragement from the oracle and Grandmother Heartsong.

They have not been traveling long when they receive a message from Warford aboard the airship. "Jo and Roonen, there is a group of wingless gryphons ahead of you in a clearing. They have some sort of encampment there."

"Those are what the gryphons call 'keythongs,' Warford," Jophriel responds, "They are part of a ground squadron. Don't do anything. Let us talk to them first."

Warford grumbles about it being dangerous to try to communicate with the keythongs but does not try to dissuade them. He probably knows that it would be pointless to tell Jophriel and Roonen what to do when they have already made up their minds.

"This is an ideal time to utilize the talents of the keythongs and kryphons, Sunground," Jophriel suggests. "They could be the ones to initiate the dialogue."

Sunground looks at the group of ten keythongs and two kryphons. She realizes that, other than knowing their names, she has not spent enough time acquainting herself with all of them. How will they react to her sending them back into the group that they had traveled all the way to the flatlands to escape? She calls them out by name.

"O keythongs and kryphons, all twelve of you! Lionheart, Rufflefeather, Stoneworker, Mud Drone, Tagglebrush, Tree Climber, Ground Hunter, Dirt Scratcher, Raindancer, and

Sunservant! Kryphons Day Minder and Squawkcaw! We have a mission for you, but it may be dangerous. We will not force you to do it, but we respectfully request that you engage the keythong encampment up ahead. Tell them of our mission and what it is that we hope to accomplish."

The keythong named Lionheart steps forward. "O, Sunground, leader of our sacred group of delegates!" he intones formally. "I and the others stand ready to give up our own freedom in order to free others in the future realm. I will go to the squadron leaders with the kryphon Day Minder at my side. I was once a law enforcement officer of the Royal Keythonic Brigade, and I will be known to this keythong troop, albeit as a traitor."

The others squawk their willingness to accompany Lionheart and Day Minder, but Lionheart insists that two will be less threatening.

Mountain Rain, as usual, protests their bold plan. "Lionheart, you fool! As a former LEO, you will be arrested."

It seems to Sunground that her younger sister never passes up an opportunity to ridicule the mission and its members. "Mountain Rain, you will shut your beak!" Sunground surprises herself with the force of her words. "We must engage at least *some* of our people. Otherwise, we may as well turn back now in cowardice."

"Best idea you've had so far," Mountain Rain mutters, but she speaks no further.

"If I may, great gryphons," Lionheart replies, bowing to Mountain Rain. "It is true that they will likely arrest Day Minder and me. This is why we must go on our own to deliver the message, leaving the rest of our ten wingless ones room to maneuver." Sunground bobs her head in assent, and the two wingless beings leave at once. The group camouflages itself among the trees, waiting in trepidation. They hear little, other than the chirps and cackles of low-tone conversation coming from the clearing. *That is a good sign*, Sunground realizes, but she still worries about their comrades.

Finally, they hear the sound of paws against ground. Sunground peeps out from behind a bush and nearly lets out a screech of shock.

"My blessed niece Sunground!" a familiar voice says. There with Lionheart and Day Minder is her old uncle, Ground Paw.

"Uncle Ground Paw!" she exclaims, emerging slowly from the bush. "What in the name of the sacred oracle are you doing out here with the ground squadron?"

"Alas, I have, to my dismay, become as you are. I am a fugitive, as are the members of the now-defunct keythonic ground squadron. The nefarious Queen Talona has called for my arrest, as I refused to denounce my loyalty to the family of old Queen Heartsong. I was fully prepared to join your father Sun Quest and the others in prison, but those ground squadron members who were also loyal to Heartsong's line brought me, as well as other council members, teachers, and caregivers, into protective custody. We all escaped into the thickets of the lower mountain. Talona has discharged all keythongs from service in both the ground squadrons and in political office. The regime expects keythongs and kryphons to work only at menial tasks assigned to them, by order of the Gryphonic Council. That once-great council has, in truth, become a council of one."

"And that *one* is Talona," Sunground replies. "The situation is even direr than I thought."

The others begin to creep out of the bush as they hear the news. Mountain Rain greets Uncle Ground Paw, tapping beaks with him affectionately.

"My keythong uncle," she tells him, "you are the last one that I would expect to be a rebel. Am I to understand that the key-thonic ground forces have more or less turned against Talona?"

"Yes, my dear and outspoken niece," Ground Paw answers respectfully. "And if we are caught, it will mean execution for all of us, for we have defied a direct order."

Execution! Sunground shudders at the thought. It has been a very, very long time since gryphonic society sanctioned an execution and then only in the most extreme case. This long period of grace ended with the cold-hearted murder of the oracle Truth Speaker. If the oracle can be killed, then they know that many more may follow, including themselves.

"Ground Paw, what about Father Sun Quest and Grandfather Lightning Bolt?" Mountain Rain asks. "And the physician, Light Healer. Are they still in prison, or..."

She leaves the terrible thought unspoken.

"I believe," Ground Paw replies cautiously, "that Talona is keeping your father and the physician in prison, as she hopes to use their imprisonment to keep dissenting voices at bay. After all, she cannot kill everyone or she would have none to rule."

"And Grandfather Lightning Bolt?" Sunground asks hope-fully, although she knows by his omission of the old opinicus' name what Ground Paw's sad reply will be.

"King Lightning Bolt has gone to join his beloved mate, Queen Heartsong," Ground Paw replies, bowing his head. "The execution of the oracle was too much for his old and ailing heart to bear."

Sunground and Mountain Rain let out a quiet trill of grief, stifling the noisy screech that they both wanted to let out into the mountain skies. They know, however, that they need to refrain from loud vocalizations to avoid being captured themselves.

Sunground feels her heart breaking. She is happy on the one hand that Lightning Bolt and Heartsong are now reunited in the Otherworld, but she feels the loss to her and her family acutely. *First, we lose Heartsong and Grass Grazer, followed immediately by the death of the oracle, and now we learn that King Lightning Bolt is gone*, she thinks furiously. Rage wells up within her toward Talona and herself. *This is not the way it should be! Heartsong and Lightning Bolt should have died with all of their family members present. The oracle should never have died in the way that she did!*

"Sunground," a familiar voice inside her proclaims, "my beloved mate is here with me, as is Truth Speaker. Do not give in to rage and hatred! That is not our way, beloved granddaughter. Especially, do not give in to hatred of yourself. Be full of love, my dearest, and all will be rectified."

Sunground feels the wave of self-recrimination that crouches in the shadows of her mind, ready to pounce upon her heart. She feels her grandmother's words, and the desire to heap scorn upon her own self subsides.

"Ground Paw," she says. "We intend to confront the Talonic forces and call for a new reign under section eight of the Gryphonic Code, which allows us to call for a new leader if the present one is not performing her duties properly. Will the rest of the keythonic ground forces join us in our peace mission, do you think?"

"My dear niece," Ground Paw replies, bowing. "The keythonic group of fugitives that we have now become will follow the granddaughters of Queen Heartsong anywhere, even unto death. We are forever loyal to your line!"

Sunground feels intense emotion welling up in her at Ground Paw's words. Still, she wonders if the keythongs who not so long ago hunted her family will now follow them. She senses that Mountain Rain is thinking the same thing. Ground Paw, seeing their quizzical looks, turns and leaves.

When he returns, a large contingent of keythongs and kryphons follow him.

This is unprecedented! Sunground exclaims to herself.

"My brothers and sisters!" Ground Paw says. "My niece Sunground and her compatriots intend to challenge the Talonic realm peacefully, by means of calling forth section eight of the Gryphonic Code. Section eight, as some of you may know, gives her the right to question a leader's abilities and call for a new government. This mission will, of course, be extremely dangerous and may not end well. I have pledged my allegiance to her, but I cannot do so on your behalf. Which of you wishes to join in this endeavor?"

Sunground and the others stand stunned as one by one, the keythongs and kryphons come forth, bowing before her as they pledge their allegiance to her. She is shocked. *Their delegation has suddenly expanded quite alarmingly!*

"O queen of the ground and sky!" an old kryphon sage, known as Fish Beak, says. "We of the kryphonic sisterhood know of your compassion toward us, the humble wingless ones. Ground Paw has confessed to me all about your refusal to sterilize your keythong son, Groundsky, and your belief that the winged and wingless may one day live as equals to each other. We therefore call on you to be our queen, to take over the gryphonic reign. We, along with our keythong brothers, will support you, even unto death."

Sunground feels a wave of panic and shock roll through her. *The whole band of keythongs and kryphons have not only pledged their allegiance to me and the peace mission but have also called upon me to be their queen!* She knows Nightsky believes that, if they succeed, she should take the role of monarch, but it has never been her true intention. She feels unworthy and is concerned that some gryphons may see this goodwill gesture of theirs as a personal power grab on her own behalf.

She feels the strength of Heartsong and Truth Speaker emanating from inside her, and she understands that this is not about her own personal worth but is much larger than that. Could this be a way to rectify the situation that she created by her abdication of the Stone Throne many sun revolutions ago?

"O brave keythongs and kryphons of law enforcement, the Keythonic Council, and other teachers, caregivers, and sages!" Sunground calls out, trying to keep her voice as calm and as leader-like as possible. "I am truly humbled by your amazing support for our mission. I cannot guarantee that this will work out in our favor. I can, however, pledge to you that if our society calls upon me to serve as your queen, I will do so if it is legally permissible. I promise that I will not run from this responsibility a second time. For now, though, our goal is to challenge the reign by means of a peace march up the mountain. We will march or fly straight into gryphonic territory and we will call upon those gryphons and opinici who want a change to join us."

Sunground surprises herself with the boldness of her own voice. Mountain Rain gives her a questioning look but this time does not attempt to embarrass her with one of her sarcastic critiques.

The two groups unite quietly and continue their march. Soon, they will all be outside the protective thicket, and they will be vulnerable. Sunground listens intently to the voices of hophas through her hearing device in the hope that they might help to protect the new group. She hears Roonen keeping in touch with Warford and the others aboard the airship. He speaks continually into the small gadget that he carries with him. If the strange sounds of the hopha disturb their new keythonic and kryphonic allies, they do not show it. Sunground is amazed at the degree to which they have accepted the idea of a peace group, two-foots and all.

The thinning of the trees and bushes eases their passage as they progress in an upward trajectory along the mountain. *Why haven't the Talonic forces confronted us yet?* Sunground knows it will not be long before they meet a gryphonic squadron.

No sooner has the thought entered her mind then there appears from the sky a squadron of five gryphons. They land in front of the group, screeching mightily at them.

"Outlaws Sunground and Mountain Rain!" the leader calls. "Outlaw keythongs and kryphons, especially Ground Paw, Lionheart, and Fish Beak! You are all under arrest."

Sunground addresses her peers. "O, sister gryphons of the air! I am Sunground of the Valley, and I am leading a peaceful march of protest up the mountain."

"Protesting what, exactly?" the leader says. The young gryphon is familiar to Sunground, but she cannot quite remember her name.

"The actions of the gryphonic government have been a source of great concern," she explains, trying valiantly to stay calm. "We are calling the reign into question. We only wish to speak to Queen Talona."

"A meeting with Talona?" the leader replies in disgust. "Good luck with that, outlaw."

"River Wind!" Sunground exclaims, suddenly recognizing this youngster from an earlier time, when she was a chick of only five sun revolutions. "Do you remember me when I was known as Sunsky of the Mountains? I minded you several times when your nannygryph was ill."

"You are no longer known to me, outlaw!" River Wind retorts disdainfully. "I will call you by no name but will only refer to you as 'outlaw'. You have absolutely no relation to me or to my family."

Sunground can hardly blame River Wind for wanting to distance herself from the protestors. The fear that Talona has been instilling, especially within the younger gryphons, has been great. Mountain Rain, however, is not so accepting of the squadron leader's answer.

"River Wind, you little brat!" she rasps. "You can put me on your *hippogryphin'* outlaw list too! Don't you morons realize what Talona is doing to our society? *You* are the true outlaws, following that monster-bird queen of yours."

"Rain, shut up!" Sunground says.

The last thing they need is to antagonize the gryphonic squadron members. River Wind, however, responds well to Mountain Rain's blunt comments. "If there was a way to disengage from the grip of Talona's claws, we would all do it, Mountain Rain," she admits, as the others in the squadron bob their heads in mute agreement.

"Well, you idiots!" Mountain Rain says, "There is a way! Join our movement and protest the government with us. The more who join, the more success we are likely to achieve."

Sunground is astounded that her sister is now promoting the march that she had previously disdained. River Wind, however, is far from convinced.

"We have our families to think of," River Wind responds. "Besides, we cannot join a group that aligns itself with hophas, hippogryphs, and even *winged horses*." She shivers as she speaks, as though the mere mention of a winged horse would bring on some sort of disaster.

Nightsky looks at the young gryphon with great compassion, but she avoids looking in his direction. The dark winged horse moves farther away so that the squadron leader and her group will not feel so threatened.

"I'm sorry, Mountain Rain," River Wind continues. "I have always respected you in our community, but what you are doing is against the law. You are committing treason by engaging in this activity, and I must report you and the others."

Star Sailor, the former leader of the gryphonic air squadron, steps forward from the group and makes herself known to them. River Wind gapes in astonishment as she recognizes her.

"Great Chieftain Star Sailor!" the young gryphon exclaims before catching herself and returning to her former stance. "I mean, outlaw Star Sailor. I understand that you have turned against us. Why? You were among the most respected of the

Royal Air Squadron. You are the last gryphon from whom we would expect treason. What did these renegades offer you?"

"These lawful and dutiful compatriots of mine offered me nothing but their forgiveness and their loyal friendship when I was in my lowest and most bedraggled state. I did not choose to turn against Talona's regime; it turned against me. Sunground and the others justifiably bound me and left me behind after I attempted to arrest the young keythong Groundsky. The air squadron members found me and immediately assumed that I had collaborated with the so-called outlaws by deliberately letting them go, in spite of the obvious fact that they had incapacitated me. Those fools plucked out my flight feathers and left me there to die. I would have perished, but the hopha rescued me. They brought me to the lowlands, where I was kept in captivity, and I met Sunground's hippogryph daughter. At that point, there was nothing to do but join them. I wish I could say that I had enough courage to choose on my own to join their noble cause, but I did not."

"It is still not too late to return to us, Star Sailor!" River Wind says, obviously in awe of the former chieftain in spite of her renegade status. "You can redeem yourself and take back your former position!"

"There's no going back for me, River Wind," Star Sailor replies. "I am now a renegade. If I go back, I will be killed quite mercilessly by the minions of Talona's regime. You know that."

River Wind lowers her head in sorrow. "It is then my deeply regrettable duty to place you under arrest for treason, Star Sailor. You will return with me to face your comrades, whom you have chosen to betray. I offered you a choice because I believe that the squadron unjustly abandoned you, but now that excuse stands empty. You have disgraced yourself, and I can offer you no defense."

"Take off, brat!" Mountain Rain roars. "You are the one who has disgraced herself, not Star Sailor. You may have noticed that you are seriously outnumbered right now. You and your gang of bandits better propel your little tattle-tails back to that screeching mad dictator of yours and let those with true courage fight for your freedom."

"No, Rain!" Star Sailor says. "I have changed my mind. I will go back with them. I once gave an oath of loyalty to the Royal Air Squadron, and I have a special responsibility to account for what I have done."

Sunground stares at her friend in shock. "Star Sailor! You cannot go back now. Stay with us. They will kill you if you return alone with them. You said as much yourself! Why, there would be no sense in your death, as there was none in the oracle's murder."

"I'm sorry, Sunground," she responds stoically, "but I owe my squadron this much. River Wind is correct! I had a choice and I chose rebellion. This goes against my oath. I must return to face my punishment and to bargain for the freedom of my family members, who must surely be in prison or at least under home den arrest by now."

Sunground's mind grasps for answers to their dilemma. *We cannot afford to lose Star Sailor. I understand the pull of duty to her comrades and her ferocious loyalty to her family members, but I also know that returning now will not help them.*

"Wait, Star Sailor!" she says. "You must not leave us. At this point, you can best serve your family by challenging the government over their unjust imprisonment, as well as the imprisonment and murder of others in our community. We cannot let this stand without attempting to change it. We may all be killed in the attempt, but it is the best hope of helping all of our people!"

Star Sailor cocks her head, as if considering it. She knows that it is probably futile to convince the dutiful gryphon, but it is worth a try.

"I will go back with Star Sailor," Mountain Rain offers. "After all, one of my objectives on this mission of lunacy is to ensure the safety of Father Sun Quest and the physician Light Healer. We cannot abandon them."

"No, Rain!" Sunground counters. "We must not lose more members. We need you here with us!"

Before Mountain Rain can retort, Jophriel interrupts them. "Sunground! I need to talk to you."

Sunground looks at the two-foot in irritation. *What could be more important than convincing their two strongest allies to stay with them?* Nonetheless, she moves away from the group after ordering Mountain Rain and Star Sailor not to fly away yet with the five air squadron members.

"Sunground," she says softly, "we have a problem. A group of gryphons attacked Warford's airship, and he opened fire on them. He only stunned them, but they may have been injured when they fell to the ground."

Sunground restrains herself from letting out a furious volley of loud noises. She feels a strong urge to peck out Warford's eyes, but instead of giving in to her rage she closes her eyes and centers herself by listening to the beat of her heart. Finally, after a moment of stillness, she opens her eyes.

"We must tend to them if they are injured," Sunground replies. "Violence must not be practiced by our group or we will be perceived as an army rather than a peaceful contingent."

Jophriel nods and Roonen joins her. He has the small communication device in his hand, into which he has been speaking with great intensity. Sunground can hear the voice of Warford through the device, arguing with Roonen. "Roonen, you fool! I just saved your sorry backside from those savage bird-cats, and this is the thanks I get? What did you expect me to do, just let them fly at the airship and place all of us in danger?"

"You could have landed!" Roonen explodes. "They wouldn't have been able to get you inside the airship, and then you could have warned us that they were in the area, you troglodyte!"

Sunground does not understand the hophic word "troglodyte", but she guesses that it is an insult. The hophas, like the gryphonic beings, are having trouble maintaining cohesion within the group. Sunground looks back at the air squadron members, who are now arguing with their leader, River Wind. They must do something to prevent these divisions between them. She cocks her head questioningly at Jophriel, who in turn nods at her.

"Stop arguing, you two!" Jophriel says. "Jack Warford, you land immediately and have the medical supplies ready. Roonen and I, along with the physicians Gavin and Indriel Findhorne, are coming to tend to any wounded gryphons. You know this was intended to be a mission of peace."

"Jo, you and Roonen are a pair of idiotic dreamers!" Warford shouts. "None of you is to go near those creatures, do you understand? What we need to do is to convince the gryphons that our forces are superior to their animal blood lust. Our mission is to stop these overgrown *tiger canaries* from attacking any more of our people. We've had our vessel assaulted through no fault of our own. Tell the others that I'm taking over the mission due to your incompetence. We will now be engaging in *Operation Button Your Beak, Birdie!*"

Roonen lets out a barrage of hophic cuss words. "You gargoyle, you used us to further your own agenda! You lied to us, Jack! We told you that our intention for this mission was to gain understanding of these creatures, to help them call for a less aggressive government. You said that if we let you come along, you wouldn't interfere with that process. You're jeopardizing everything we've worked for!"

"My mission is to protect our people from barbaric animals! Animals have no government. Stop treating them as if they were people and just grow up, Roonen Oakshade!" Warford retorts. "Or, by the Lord of the skies, I'll have you charged with reckless behavior leading to potential injury, just as you deserve."

Warford's voice gives way to a clicking sound, and Roonen throws away the communication device in disgust. Dreamspinner and Nightsky come to him offering their support, but the hopha male shakes his fist at the sky and bellows, "I am so bloody enraged at myself for trusting that son of a gargoyle! I just knew he would do something like this. Jo, we are a rotten species!"

"Roonen Oakshade, you calm down this instant!" Jophriel says. "I understand your rage, but it will not help the situation. Let's go to the injured gryphons anyways. Gavin and Indriel are resourceful in finding ways to provide medical care."

Jophriel rubs Sunground's feathered head to reassure her. She picks up a satchel and leaves with Roonen and the two hopha physicians named Gavin and Indriel. Sunground feels that she should go with them, but she knows she must stay behind to deal with the situation regarding Star Sailor and Mountain Rain. She instead delegates the responsibility of accompanying the hophas to Dreamspinner and Nightsky. The two males nuzzle Sunground before they depart, and she returns their expressions of affection. She hopes fervently that none of the gryphons have been seriously injured or even killed. She pushes the thought aside, for she knows that she must not give in to useless anxiety.

She rustles her feathers slightly, regains her composure and returns to the squadron of gryphons. They are now engaged in a scuffle over whether or not to turn in the well-respected Star Sailor. River Wind appears to be losing authority with the other four squadron members, who are squawking in anger over her orders. One of them yells at her, "Let us no longer serve the killer of the oracle! River Wind, you are nothing but a coward. We will not turn in Star Sailor to share the fate of poor Truth Speaker! Let us join Star Sailor and the others!"

"Have you forgotten your oaths?" River Wind retorts. "Would you join these traitors who align themselves with hophas, hippogryphs, and winged horses?"

"It is better to serve them than the great monster Talona!" another squadron member cries. "I would rather have the horse-lover Sunground as our queen than her. What have I to lose? My entire family has been imprisoned!"

Mountain Rain and Star Sailor watch the melee in amazement. "See what you have created, Sunny?" Mountain Rain says as Sunground joins them. "Talona is losing loyalists left, right, and center!"

Sunground shakes her head and explains all that has occurred with regard to Warford's attack on the gryphonic air squadron.

"Jophriel, Roonen, and the other hophas are going to tend to any wounded gryphons," Sunground explains. "I have sent Dreamspinner and Nightsky to accompany them. Meanwhile, we must all move out before the minions of the regime consider us an armed threat. I have decided that we will break into three groups. I will lead the first group, and you, Mountain Rain and Star Sailor, will lead the second and third groups. I hate to interrupt your plans to sacrifice yourselves to Talona's wrath, but I badly need your leadership skills. I am ordering you not to go with River Wind."

"River Wind isn't going anywhere, by the looks of things," Mountain Rain responds. "She's completely lost control of her group. Let's recruit them to our side before they tear each other apart."

To the astonishment of all present, the four gryphons under the command of River Wind agree to join the movement. River Wind is at a loss as to what to do now that she has lost her squadron members. She reluctantly follows them but makes it clear that her loyalties do not lie with Sunground. "I have no choice but to join your foolish movement, Sunground! But make no mistake, I will not hold back any information pertaining to you rebels should I be captured and questioned by Talona's loyalists."

"That's good!" Mountain Rain answers on Sunground's behalf. "Because there's not much to tell other than that we're friendly with hippogryphs, hophas, and horses."

"And that you're planning to overthrow the legitimately installed government," River Wind retorts. "To my shame, I will be known as your traitorous cohort."

"We understand the limits of your involvement, River Wind, and we respect them," Sunground says, glaring at Mountain Rain. "If you like, you can join another group of Air Squadron members who were mistakenly injured by one of the hophas, a male who was acting alone and not under the guidance of the chief leaders."

"Injured?" River Wind repeats the word in surprise. "How did those puny two-foots ever injure members of our Royal Air Squadron?"

"They did it through a technology that allows them to shoot out a kind of lightning bolt. It has the effect of stunning us temporarily. The gryphons of the air squadron had attacked their *airship*, that is to say, the flying nest-shelter, and..."

"What are you babbling about, Sunground, pet of the hopha?" River Wind screams. "It is true what they say about you. You are raving mad! Tell me where the injured gryphons are and I will go to them. If I see any of your hophas near them, I shall tear their scrawny bodies apart!"

Sunground feels a surge of panic within her. She has miscalculated badly in telling River Wind about the injured gryphons. She centers herself, knowing that panic will interfere with her thinking process. She remembers the communication device that Jophriel installed within her areas of hearing and her beak. She turns away from the group and signals Jophriel. "I have foolishly told one of the squadron leaders about the incident, and she now wants to go on a rampage against hophas. Be very careful! Maybe you should all go inside Warford's ship."

"Sunground, calm down," Jophriel responds. "We are tending to the wounded gryphons now. Dreamspinner managed to convince them to let us set their wings. As for Warford, he is nowhere to be seen."

"The gryphons are not behaving aggressively?" Sunground asks. "How is that possible?"

"They seem to be a little intimidated by us and by Nightsky," Jophriel explains. "I think that they believe we will fire on them again."

"Watch out for aggressive gryphons, Jophriel," Sunground says. "We will try to convince the squadron leader not to attack." When Sunground turns around once more, she realizes that Mountain Rain has "convinced" River Wind not to fly forth by pinning her underneath her grand talons.

"You are under arrest, River Wind!" Mountain Rain informs her. "For treason by way of your support for the monster queen."

Sunground reprimands her sister, but it does no good. Mountain Rain refuses to give up her quarry and orders Star Sailor to retrieve some vines so that she can bind River Wind's hind legs and forearms together. Sunground thinks of what they did to Star Sailor not so long ago when they were all fleeing the ground and air squadrons. Because of that act, the squadron members would have killed her had the hopha not intervened and brought her to the enclosure in the lowlands. Sunground knows that she cannot allow her sister to dominate in this case.

"No, Rain!" she screeches, flying at Mountain Rain and beating her wings. "You are not commanding this group, I am! I order you to let River Wind go. Let her go where she pleases. We will not resort to violence of any kind!"

Star Sailor steps forward to support Sunground's command, and Mountain Rain reluctantly relinquishes her hold on the young gryphon. River Wind cries and flaps away into the air unceremoniously.

CHAPTER FOUR

Unexpected Allies

There is no more time to waste. They hurriedly organize the large contingent of diverse beings, separating them into three groups. Sunground divides the three hippogryphs whom Night Lover sent, putting one in each troop. The four squadron members turned renegades divide themselves among the troops led by Star Sailor and Mountain Rain. The former LEO Lionheart leads the wingless contingent within Mountain Rain's group, while Day Minder the kryphon leads the wingless ones under Star Sailor's command. Uncle Ground Paw accompanies the wingless within Sunground's group, although she worries about the elderly keythong joining the march. She would have preferred that he stay with the hophas and Nightsky, but he would have none of it. He is determined to go with Sunground in order to help her challenge the government. She knows that she must not fret too much about her friends and family but keep her eye on the big picture. Still, it seems almost suicidal to be marching straight into gryphonic territory.

She dispatches the remaining hophas to join Jophriel and the others in tending to the wounded gryphons. She does not want to risk the lives of the hophas by bringing them straight into gryphonic territory. Before she leaves, she signals Nightsky telepathically to let him know of their plan, and he sadly bids her a safe journey.

"Dreamspinner and I will look after the hophas and the wounded gryphons," he says. "Do not worry about us, my love, but go forth courageously."

Sunground sends her gratitude. She is unsure of how courageous she will be, but she appreciates the winged horse's blessing nonetheless.

As soon as they are organized, the three groups depart. They each travel different paths up the mountain, with Sunground's company going straight up the center path. Each group consists of twenty-five members, since the renegade keythongs and kryphons have significantly increased their numbers.

As they continue up the mountain path, Sunground wishes that they could fly, as climbing up the mountain by paw and talon is tedious. She knows, however, that in the air they would be too vulnerable to marauding squadrons. *Besides,* she tells herself, *it is better to be in solidarity with our wingless brothers and sisters who cannot take flight.*

The group slowly reaches the upper echelons of the Mountain of the Skies and as they progress, something astonishing happens. Many throngs of bedraggled lower-class gryphons and opinici begin to join them, walking painfully with the flightless ones rather than immediately taking to the skies as is natural for gryphons.

"We heard about the return of Sunsky of the Mountains!" one of them explains. "We wish to walk with you, for we would rather die than live under Talona's reign of wrath."

Sunground is deeply moved by this unprecedented gesture of faith in her. She knows that it is Queen Heartsong's line to which they are loyal rather than her, but it is amazing nonetheless. The issue of her mating with a winged horse and having given birth to a hippogryph does not seem to faze the newest members of the peace march.

Sunground and Ground Paw explain in further detail what they are attempting to accomplish, and that the group must not turn to violence or it will negate the intent of the mission. Surprisingly, the lower-class beings bob their heads in assent rather than arguing. As they continue along the path, the same thing happens, over and over again: the gryphonic people join them, silently and without rancor. They do not quibble about the presence of keythongs, kryphons, or even the hippogryph. They simply march alongside.

"How is this possible, my niece?" Ground Paw asks her quietly. "I have never seen anything like it!"

"It must be the influence of Queen Heartsong and the oracle Truth Speaker from beyond this world," Sunground answers. "They have been whispering into my heart since this whole crisis began, and they are no doubt doing so with the average gryphon. It makes sense, actually, that the lower-class people would be the ones who would listen to the messages of the oracle most intently, for they did not have respect automatically conferred upon them from birth. They've had to work hard to earn social respect and with the reign of Talona, all that has been taken away from them. Look at how ragged they all appear, Uncle Ground Paw! Why, that would never have occurred under Heartsong."

Ground Paw nods sadly, for Queen Heartsong was not just his queen but his mother as well. Sunground feels deeply grateful for the presence of Ground Paw, whose support gives her great hope for young Groundsky. As she thinks of her son, she pines also for the rest of her family back at the caverns. *They are fine,* she thinks. *Groundsky, Moon Wing, Mother Skystar, and the others are safe.* Nonetheless, she fervently asks the oracle to protect all families everywhere from the terror going on around them. Things must indeed be very bad if the lower-class gryphons, normally a staid and contented lot, are joining them.

They make their way up the mountain painfully until they come to the edge of a cliff. To go over to the main political center, they will need to fly. There is a pawbridge further along for the keythongs and kryphons, but the way will be slow for them. There will no doubt be sentinels on the bridge, but the marchers are at a point now where they must engage with, rather than avoid, gryphonic authorities. Sunground hates to send her newest wingless compatriots into a certain trap, but she can think of no other way. Lifting them to the gryphonic city one by one would be too time and energy consuming, and staying here at the edge of the cliff is not an option either.

"I will lead the wingless ones to the bridge, my niece," Ground Paw says, sensing her anxiety. "We will meet Lionheart, Day Minder, and our brethren from the other two teams, for they will also need to travel to the pawbridge. There is no other way for them to cross."

Sunground looks into her old uncle's eyes and confirms the plan wordlessly. She taps beaks with him before he and the other wingless ones leave in silence. After they have departed, she surveys the winged group before her. The addition of the lower-class gryphons has increased their numbers significantly but even so, it will still be a suicide mission to fly straight into the heart of Gryphonia. She looks upon the lone hippogryph in her group, Soul Flower, with great concern. How can she in good conscience lead a hippogryph into this death trap? Surely, her treatment at the talons of the authorities will be most severe. She thinks of Moon Wing when she looks at Soul Flower, who is only slightly older than her daughter is.

"My brave compatriots," Sunground announces. "I cannot let you follow me into this next step of the mission without allowing for anyone who has second thoughts on the matter to gracefully bow out. The likelihood that you will be captured or killed in this flight for peace is great. There will be no shame upon any who wish to withdraw and return to their families."

"Many of our family members have already been captured or even killed, Sunsky of the Mountains," one of the gryphons replies. "There is no turning back. We are all ready to do what must be done."

Sunground feels a surge of love for these brave ones who were betrayed so unceremoniously by their higher-class sisters. They are right: for the gryphons there is no going back. *But what about the lone hippogryph?* She looks questioningly at Soul Flower.

"I am not turning back, Sunground. Perhaps I should start calling you Sunsky now that you are returning home. I have sent a telepathic signal to our leader, Night Lover. Although we are out of normal telepathic range, I have great distance capability, and I have asked for reinforcements. I see an image in my mind of Night Lover sending forth an army of hippogryphs that will join us in this venture. You see, I realized as we progressed along our journey how much momentum is accumulating for the Talonic reign to be abolished. I have had many arguments with your daughter Moon Wing in the past, but I now agree with her firm belief that our people should aid this mission. I intended to send Night Lover the signal only if I believed that there might be a chance of success for this endeavor. The lower-class gryphons and wingless ones joining this cause so fully have finally made up my mind for me."

Sunground gapes at Soul Flower in shock. *An army of hippogryphs?* She knows the beings well enough to understand that they will be peaceful, but the gryphons of the higher mountains will certainly not see them that way. *They will view them as portents of catastrophe, minions of evil that must be destroyed!* She feels her heart flutter in panic, but she tells herself that she must trust in Night Lover's judgment. They do not have the time to get into an argument about it. She only hopes that Moon Wing will be safe.

"Moon Wing and the more vulnerable ones will be brought to the hopha tunnel," Soul Flower reassures her, as if reading her mind. "Do not fret over them. The two-foots will protect them."

Sunground finally nods and gives the signal for the group to take to the skies. One by one, the gryphons and the hippogryph spring into the air and beat their wings mightily. They ascend until they are all one flock in the mountain sky. As they do so, the winged ones from the other two groups join them. Obviously, Star Sailor and Mountain Rain have come to the same conclusion that they have. The flock has increased its numbers dramatically, sailing above the nest homes as one entity, until it arrives at its destination and circles Central City.

To Sunground's profound surprise, there are no gryphonic air squadrons beating down upon them. Where have they gone? She peers through the clouds to the ground and stares down in horror at what she sees. Many gryphons are lying on the ground, being tended to by another gryphon who systematically lays them out and treats them. *This must be the physician, Light Healer!* While Sunground is relieved to see the physician free from her prison cell, she is concerned about what has happened to the injured gryphons. They look as though they have been stunned and have suddenly dropped from the air.

Warford! Sunground remembers the renegade hopha's words to Roonen: *'My mission is to protect our people from barbaric animals. Animals have no government. Stop treating them as if they were people and just grow up, Roonen Oakshade!'*

If Warford believes that the gryphons are mindless savages with no culture, in spite of all evidence to the contrary, then they are all moving targets for him. It will not matter which side they are on. At the edge of her eye, she notices a hophic *airship* closing in on her troop.

"Scatter, flock of sisters!" she screeches as loudly as she dares. "Warford's airship is taking aim at us!"

The gryphons fly in different directions immediately, creating a fluttering chaos in the skies. Five of her comrades go down, plummeting into the hard rock below them. She feels a jolt of painful, stinging energy surge through her body, and she too tumbles helplessly to the ground. She lands with a thud, her wing crushed into the rock. She has lost flight but not her consciousness. The stunning sensation has left her paralyzed, but she can still think and speak. She screeches out the name of the physician.

"Light Healer! This hopha is acting alone! We are here on a mission of peace!"

The physician is upon her immediately. "Sunsky! River Wind told us that you and your group were on the way, but these hopha creatures that you befriended have betrayed you. They have been attacking all of us with their flying nest-shelters, or whatever River Wind called them. Talona has actually freed me from prison to attend to this outrageous emergency. The two-foots are extremely aggressive!"

"No! Not all of them, only Warford!" Sunground screams, as Light Healer turns her attention to working on her injured wing. "Jophriel!" She suddenly remembers to tune in to the listening and speaking device that the hopha had placed within her center of hearing and on the edge of her beak. "We are being fired upon! It is Warford!"

There is no response. Either Jophriel is in trouble, or Sunground's fall damaged the device. Their peace flight has crashed in a most devastating manner. She feels her mind falling into a dizzying spiral, as if she were once more in the midst of that terrible windstorm that brought her into Nightsky's tender care so many sun revolutions ago. Before she loses consciousness, she raises her beak to see Nightsky's form once more, hovering up above her in front of Warford's airship. There is a male hopha on his back, screaming epithets. Together, they are placing themselves between Warford and the flock of remaining gryphons.

Sunground hears the familiar squawk of her noble opinicus Dreamspinner, who lands next to her. Jophriel tumbles off his back unceremoniously, and Sunground feels the warm hand of her friend stroking her head feathers soothingly before she descends into oblivion.

CHAPTER FIVE

Imprisonment

When Sunground awakens, she finds herself in a dimly lit room of rock. She feels a stabbing pain in her wing, the same one that was injured many sun revolutions ago in the windstorm. It takes her a few moments to orient herself to her surroundings. She soon remembers that she has arrived at Gryphonia Mountain City, where she had once departed from Light Healer's den in such a squawking fury in her youth. She believed that she would never again return, yet here she is. She has come full circle and arrived back home, although she and her compatriots were treated to an extremely rough welcome. She peers at the rock bars and rope-web that block the entrance of their rocky den, and she realizes that she is imprisoned. She is not alone, however. Beside her, still stroking her head, is her hopha friend.

"You are awake, Sunground!" Jophriel exclaims. She reaches over to a pile of nuts and seeds, offering her some on an outstretched hand. Sunground nibbles the seeds in a feeble manner, for the searing pain in her wing has eclipsed any appetite that she might have had.

"Jophriel," she says when she has finished her meager meal. "What's happened?"

"You and I were both captured and brought here. I believe it is a prison cell, but we are not in it alone. There is an opinicus here as well, but he is sleeping right now in the corner."

Sunground glances at the dark form in the corner but pays it little heed. She is more concerned about the attacking airship outside. "What is happening with Warford? Is he still shooting people down?"

"No," Jophriel replies. "Roonen finally talked him down and placed him under citizen's arrest for endangering a sentient species. He told Warford that he was taking over the mission due to the man's incompetence and that the new name for the mission is now *Operation Button-your-mouth, Warford!*'"

Sunground caws a chuckle in spite of her condition. The last thing she remembers seeing is Roonen on top of Nightsky, yelling obscenities at the airship. He was a fierce yet comical presence. She is surprised that Warford listened to him.

"Has the airship remained grounded or taken off?" Sunground asks. She is concerned about how the gryphons will treat the hophas if they get their talons on them.

"The airship is completely grounded," Jophriel explains, "and will be for some time. All of your peace delegates flew at Warford's ship under the direction of your sister, Mountain Rain. Warford's wife Clariel and his son Riva were with him in the airship and told him, in no uncertain terms, to halt his attack on the gryphons. Once he landed, Mountain Rain ordered the attacks to stop. Clariel was the one to alert us about Warford's scheme to attack the gryphon city in the first place, so Roonen, Nightsky, Dreamspinner, and I were able to arrive here as quickly as we could to help stop him from acting on his insane plan. As long as the Warford family stays inside the airship, they should all be safe. Dreamspinner is guarding the airship along with some of your gryphons."

"What about Roonen and Nightsky?" Sunground asks. "Are they in danger? We are right in the very heart of gryphon society."

"Roonen and Nightsky are staying by the airship, which has been surrounded by your troop. They are offering protection for them from the local authorities, who seem to be dwindling in numbers, according to Dreamspinner. Apparently, many of the gryphons are calling for your release from prison."

Sunground's mind is whirling. *It seems unbelievable, but somehow this crazy peace plan of Nightsky's is working in spite of all the mishaps with Warford! It is possible that we could succeed, as long as the tensions between the government factions and those loyal to Heartsong's line do not erupt into some kind of civil war.*

She feels a moment of peace and reassurance as Heartsong and Truth Speaker send their unending and beauteous love from beyond. Success will be theirs, but she does not know what to do in the mean time. The prison cell severely limits their capacity for action. Hope remains, however, as many of the gryphons seem to support the idea of replacing Talona. *The only problem is, who will replace her? That will be a most sensitive question.*

As Sunground contemplates the state of her society, Jophriel tinkers with the communication device she has kept hidden under her cloth coverings. There is a beep, and Roonen's voice comes through to break the dullness of their captivity.

"Jo!" he says, his voice strained with worry. "Are you all right? Have those bird-cats injured you in any way? If they have, I'll rip their feathers out!"

"I'm fine, and don't you dare try anything like that, Roonen Oakshade!" Jophriel says. "You're beginning to sound like Warford.'"

"Warford is another creature altogether," Roonen replies. "He's being a real idiot right now. I'm going to change the name of the mission again to Operation-Kick-Warford-in-the-Butt."

"Roonen, what is happening out there?" Jophriel asks. "Is Warford cooperating with you?"

"Just barely," Roonen replies. "He keeps exiting the craft and I keep telling him to get back inside. Luckily, Clariel and Riva are seeing things our way, so they're keeping him under control as best they can."

"And what about the government gryphons?" Jophriel asks. "Is the stand-off still in place?"

"So far, they're keeping their distance from us," Roonen responds. "We aren't telling them that Warford's ship is out of fire power. Do you know, Jo, that moron drained so much energy by firing willy-nilly at every winged thing in the sky that he ran the power clean out of it? He would have crashed it if Clariel and Riva hadn't taken over the controls and brought it down. How do you like that? Even his own wife and son have turned against him, he's so bloody insane."

"All right, Roonen," Jophriel says. "Just try to keep Jack as calm as you can. Don't worry about us—we're in a prison cell, but we're safe at the moment."

"Being locked up in a prison cell isn't what I'd call safe," Roonen grumbles. "Dreamspinner and I want to come up with a plan to free you, but Nightsky disagrees and we've all been arguing about it."

"No!" Jophriel exclaims. "Nightsky is absolutely right. No heroics, Roonen, and I mean it. Tell Dreamspinner that Sunground is fine—other than her broken wing, that is. I'll keep you informed, all right? I love you."

Jophriel snaps her device shut before Roonen can reply. She hides it within the cloak of her lower clothing. Sunground ruffles her head feathers in anxiety. She hopes that Dreamspinner and Roonen do not attempt to break their way into the prison dens. It would be yet another act of violence in what is supposed to be a march of peace. She knows the assault that Mountain Rain led on Warford's craft has been essential in getting the situation under control, but it is not the message that she wants to impress upon the inhabitants of Gryphonia Central.

A stirring in the corner interrupts Sunground's thoughts and she sees a young opinicus stretching his limbs. As he walks out into the limited lighting, she gapes at him in shock. He has similar features to Dreamspinner, such as bands of light gold among mainly dark-brown colored wings and a leonine body that glistens reddish-gold, even in this dimly lit den.

"Sunground," Jophriel says softly, "this opinicus is called Sun Wing. I was communicating with him a bit before you woke up. Do you know him?"

Sunground sits in shocked silence for a minute. This adolescent is her son, stolen from her at birth by Dreamspinner's ruthless grandfather Thundercloud. *How will the youth react to me*, she wonders, *or does he even know that I exist?*

Sun Wing speaks directly to her, nullifying her concerns. "Mother Sunsky!" he exclaims, innocently using her old name. "I have been waiting my entire life to meet you."

Sunground caws plaintively as she draws near to him and envelops him in her wings. The embrace lasts for several minutes, and Jophriel withdraws respectfully into a corner to give them some privacy.

"Sun Wing, the son of my brave Dreamspinner!" she finally manages to croak. "How is it that you know my name?"

"I know it because my great-grandfather Thundercloud spoke it often, although he did so mainly as an epithet. Still, curiosity always filled me. Ever since I was a young cub, I have yearned to know the truth about my mother and my father Dreamspinner as well. I have seen him before, but he has kept a strict distance because of the decrees of my great-grandfather. Thundercloud forbade me to have anything to do with either of you, but that has only fueled my desire to find you. Grandfather Windsinger told me quite a bit about my father, but I could coax little out of him regarding my mother, she who has been so mysteriously absent in my youth. I knew from hearing all of the rumors that you had gone to give birth to a hippogryph in the Valley of Outcasts. I was determined to know more, so I took a flight to the valley when I was just a few sun revolutions younger. Unfortunately, Grandfather Windsinger apprehended me before I could find the hippogryph settlement. Is it true, Mother Sunsky—oh yes, I suppose that you are now known as Sun*ground*—that I have a hippogryph sister?"

"Yes!" Sunground exclaims excitedly. "Her name is as the night-time moon to your day-time sun. She is Moon Wing, and she is your sister. I know she would be thrilled to meet you, my son. You are about to become an uncle, for she is due to give birth."

"I wish that I could meet her," Sun Wing whispers sadly, "but that is impossible at present. My entire family and I are in prison. My grandfather Windsinger is in an adjacent cell with the opinicus Sun Quest, who apparently is my maternal grandfather."

Sunground's heart skips a beat. *Father Sun Quest is in the adjacent cell!* She caws loudly but to no avail.

"They are out in the work yard chiseling stone statues for Talona with their beaks," Sun Wing explains. "They will be there until night time. We, on the other wing, must endure constant cell confinement. I believe that we are here to be tortured for our traitorous thoughts and activities. I was jailed for speaking in defense of my great-grandfather, Thundercloud."

Sunground stares at him in horror. Has her unknown yet beloved son been tortured? She feels rage welling up inside her for Talona.

"I have not been physically harmed," Sun Wing says. "But I have been made to witness the torture of my great-grandfather. He was arrested for attempting to lead a rebellion against Talona. He intended to install an opinicus, his son Windsinger, as king of Gryphonia. He wanted a male to be the chief ruler for the first time in our history, but not enough gryphons supported the uprising and so Talona jailed us all. My once proud grandfather must endure the humiliation of being a ground slave. His wings have been clipped and Talona has given him the name "Ground Chiseler" to teach him a lesson as to his "proper" place in society. Few gryphons supported his bid to be king, but his treatment at the claws of Talona has turned many against the regime."

Sunground's body and mind are numb with shock. She is

horrified to learn that Thundercloud was tortured in front of his helpless great-grandson, and she is astounded by Talona's cruelty. *Does this vicious predator know no bounds? She asks herself. I don't particularly like either Thundercloud or his son Windsinger but even so, they have been the ones to raise my dear Sun Wing.*

"Sun Wing," she says gently, fearing his response, "where is Thundercloud now?"

"He is dead," Sun Wing replies mournfully. "His old body could not sustain multiple torture sessions. He lasted for ten horrible days, having all sorts of painful treatments inflicted upon him. He finally died in this prison cell last night. He said that it was time for him to leave this world and that he was going to join his old nemeses King Lightning Bolt and Queen Heartsong in the Otherworld. He intended to make his peace with both of them. I know not whether he encountered the king and queen in the sky beyond this one, but my main consolation now is that he did not die alone. I was here with him when he passed away."

Sunground coos a mourning call, heartbroken that her adolescent son was forced to endure such a terrible ordeal. She taps his beak and rubs her head against his to comfort him.

"Mother Sunsky," he says, withdrawing from her caresses. "You do realize that Talona will be torturing you next and that I will be made to witness your death?"

Sunground's heart turns cold with fear. Of course she will be subjected to Thundercloud's fate. She has been the reluctant leader of this peace movement that now, thanks to Warford's foolish actions, will be seen as an uprising similar to that of the old opinicus. The worst part is that Sun Wing will be left with the horrible memory of her torment. The terrifying thought of young Sun Wing himself being tortured enters her mind and she shivers painfully.

"You do not need to worry about me, Mother Sunsky," Sun Wing says, sensing her thoughts. "And I refuse to call you anything but your original name, now that I am about to lose you."

"Sun Wing!" she cries. "You may lose me but not your own life! I will plead for you to be spared. I will ask that Talona do her worst to me, if she will spare you this horrible fate to which she subjected poor old Thundercloud."

"You don't understand, Mother Sunsky," Sun Wing replies. "I will never share your fate, although I wish I could. I will only ever witness it being done to my friends and family—Talona has assured me of this. You see, I am her first mate."

"What?" Sunground croaks miserably. "Sun Wing, you are too young! You cannot be Talona's king."

"Yes, Mother, I am," he counters, shaking his head. "I agreed to the arrangement to spare Windsinger's life. He now wishes that I had left him to Thundercloud's fate, for he cannot fly and he says his life is now worth nothing. Your father Sun Quest keeps pecking at his tail to try to drive some life into him, but I think that he too is slowly fading. The mighty opinici were never meant to be ground slaves."

"Oh, my dear," Sunground exclaims. "No one was ever meant to be a slave of any kind, not opinici, gryphons, keythongs, nor kryphons. Oh, how I wish we could restore sanity to this world!"

There is a rustling noise in the corner, and Jophriel suddenly pops out from the shadows. "Sunground, you can restore sanity to your society! Most of the gryphons have tired of Talona's reign. I'm sorry to have eavesdropped, but I couldn't help but overhear your conversation. No one wants this *tiger canary* in power! Why are you all kowtowing to her?"

"Jophriel, you foolish two-foot!" Sunground screeches. "You must know that it's not that simple. There are laws in place to protect the reign. There must be a clear majority in opposition to the government if the gryphonic people are to challenge the reign under section eight of the Gryphonic Code."

"Oh, blast the Gryphonic Code!" Sun Wing declares. "Your two-footed friend is right. Why do we stoop in fear to Talona? I am the king! I will challenge her for the right to rule or at least on behalf of our daughter Sky Talon's right to rule when she is fully grown. Until she grows up, I will be the sole ruler."

Sunground momentarily forgets the argument as she takes in this latest piece of news. "Sun Wing! You and Talona have a daughter? She has been birthed?"

"Yes, Mother, or maybe I should say 'Grandmother' Sunsky. The gryphon chick Sky Talon was born this very morning. Talona came and informed me herself. She showed me my new-born daughter before letting me know that I was banned from ever seeing her again."

Sunground growls. It is happening to her son just as it had when she was banned from Sun Wing many revolutions ago. *It is history repeating itself*, she thinks ruefully.

"Sun Wing," Jophriel asks. "Why are you, as Talona's official mate, in prison?"

"Because Talona does not trust me. My father's family and my mother's have turned against her, and she does not want to take a chance. As long as I am imprisoned on some petty charge, I cannot challenge her reign from my position as king consort. In fact, my position is rendered null and void by my arrest, as stipulated under some obscure little by-law in the ever-infallible Gryphonic Code. That dictatorial legislation really needs to be replaced by an Opinical Code, as far as my grandfather Windsinger and I are concerned. To tell the truth, we want the opinici to one day rule as kings over the gryphons."

Sunground senses the anger and disgust in her son's voice and although she understands it, she is also disturbed by his words. She knows that he has not emerged unscathed from his upbringing by the angry old Thundercloud. The combination of his being raised by two rebellious males, together with the unhappy mating experience with Talona, has created chaos in his mind. Sun Wing's dark tone is tinged with the same anti-gryphonic sentiment as his great-grandfather. She hears the unmistakable voice of Thundercloud booming from her son's beak. *Blast Thundercloud and Talona to the skies,* she thinks furiously but does not say aloud.

She chooses her words to her son carefully. "Sun Wing, I know that my actions long ago caused a great rift between us, especially since we were torn apart at the time of your birth. Perhaps you will not wish to listen to me, but I hope you will at least hear what I have to say. This gryphonic queendom, under which you have lived most of your life, is not like the reign of your great-grandmother, Heartsong. Gryphons are not terrible creatures, in spite of what Thundercloud may have told you about us. We need the opinici to support us and if we all work together, we may successfully challenge the reign of Talona. An angry king consort who desires the forceful take-over of a rule for himself or even for his young daughter, will never truly reign. You must not challenge Talona in that regard, as it will place your own life in too much jeopardy. I beg of you, do not follow the path of Thundercloud! He became so obsessive in his anger toward gryphons that he engaged in violence to overthrow the government. His rebellion did not garner support because of it. Do you understand what I am trying to say, Sun Wing?"

"Yes," the young opinicus snarls in contempt. "You want me to support a purely gryphonic power structure with opinici as mindless puppets of whichever new regime crawls into existence. But how can we be sure that the next gryphon will not behave exactly as Talona has?"

"I think that is your great-grandfather speaking, Sun Wing, and it is not coming from your own voice!" Sunground snaps. "This is not about either gryphons or opinci but about a collective cooperation between all, including keythongs, kryphons, hippogryphs, winged horses, hophas..."

"It is true what Thundercloud said about you!" Sun Wing explodes. "You are still a hippogryphin' horse-lover!"

Sunground shrieks at her son, her heart seeming to splinter into a million pieces. "Is this what my son thinks of his sister, Moon Wing?"

"No!" retorts Sun Wing. "I can forgive her for being born a hippogryph, but I cannot forgive you for mating with that portent of death and disaster, Nightsky! He is the reason that death and disaster have been visited upon us all!"

"Winged horses are *not* portents of death and disaster! They are gentle, peaceful creatures. Your dear old great-grandfather was truly a portent of death and disaster if ever there was one. Why, he killed your paternal grandmother, Wing Dreamer, just for mating with Nightsky!" As soon as the words are out of her beak, she regrets them.

"My grandmother Wing Dreamer's name is never to be spoken!" Sun Wing screams in response. "Thundercloud said so. How dare you criticize Thundercloud, you horse-loving hypocrite! I don't believe what you say about him killing Wing Dreamer because he would never do such a thing. She was the former mate of Grandfather Windsinger, even if she did mate with a horse as you did. He may have banished her to the Valley of Outcasts, but he did not kill her!"

Sunground stops herself from vocalizing her next screeched reply, realizing with great shame what she has just done. Sun Wing has almost certainly not been told about Thundercloud's murder of Wing Dreamer. He will have been told only that she mated with a horse and that she was banished for it. Sun Wing retreats to the shadows of his nesting spot in the corner.

Jophriel cautiously places a hand on Sunground's back. "I'm not sure I understand all of the happenings in your family, Sunground," she whispers, "but I know these things take time to work through. Give Sun Wing that time. He's had an awful lot to take in at once. Do I understand correctly that his elder family member was killed in front of him?"

"He was tortured and died later in this very cell," Sunground replies, extremely weary. "Sun Wing witnessed the torture. Now, unless we can all overcome our differences, the same thing will happen to me."

Jophriel nods, her featherless face turning paler than its usual light-pinkish shade.

There is silence in the cell for a long time. Sunground travels inside herself to feel the strength of the oracle, but she finds nothing except her heart beating rapidly in anxious trepidation.

Where is the voice of the oracle when she is so badly needed? Sunground wonders as her terror of the approaching night grows.

"Do not seek my strength, Sunsky of the Mountains," a quiet voice within her answers, "but rather seek your own. You will find it in the silence of your own heart and mind."

As Sunground feels the beating of her heart, her wild mind simmers down to a raspy whisper until all is bathed in stillness. She does not think but simply exists in this quiet state of no-time. Jophriel and Sun Wing nod off to sleep, but soon she is aware of a familiar presence that arrives into the cell as night falls. Sunground opens her eyes to behold a wondrous sight: there before her is Father Sun Quest.

CHAPTER SIX

The Tormentors

"Father!" she cries, muffling her caw of relief as best she can.

"My dear and courageous daughter," Sun Quest whispers. "I have begged the oracle to let me see you this one last time before I am taken."

Sunground's feathers ruffle furiously at this statement. "You will not be taken! We are going to challenge the Talonic government under section eight of the Gryphonic Code."

"The Gryphonic Code," Sun Quest laments. "It has been thrown into the dust. That creature of mine whom I can no longer call daughter pays it little heed."

"Then we will bring it back!" Sunground cries. "No gryphon may completely do away with the Gryphonic Code. It is permissible to make changes as needed but only with the supervision of the lawgivers."

"The lawgivers have been tossed in prison," Sun Quest replies, "and Chief Magistrate Queenstar has been placed under home den arrest. None of them holds any legal power at this point, and they cannot prevent us from being executed. But I will try one more time to plead with Talona for your life, daughter."

"Talona cannot execute an opinicus!" Sunground exclaims. "There are too few, and they are all needed for mating."

"If I am in this cell, it means that I am awaiting execution. Old Thundercloud, by the way, was also an opinicus but was executed without a second thought."

"He was very old," Sunground reminds him, "and the leader of a violent rebellion."

Sun Quest looks surreptitiously toward his sleeping grandson, of whom he knows so little. "Don't let the young prince hear you say that," he whispers. "He has been corrupted by Thundercloud's thinking and does not listen to reason on the subject of the gryphonic reign. I heard your argument with him as the guards led Windsinger and me to our cell. Just a little while later, the guards received an order to move me to this cell, leaving Windsinger on his own. I have seen young Sun Wing only from a distance, but that blasted cellmate of mine refused to tell me anything about him. It is indeed a cruel irony that this will no doubt be my last night of life and the only opportunity I will ever get to talk to him, and now to hear that he thinks opinici should be reigning leaders... *r-aaaaa-kk!* What a squawking mess that would create! Old Thundercloud was a fool to think that we males could be in charge of an entire society."

Sunground chirps at her father in irritation. While she is glad that he has not lost his old feistiness, she sees that he is just as stubborn and opinionated as ever.

"First of all, Father Sun Quest, this is *not* the last night of your life. Second, Sun Wing is not wrong. There is no reason why an opinicus or a gryphon or both could not be entrusted with the reign, if they are so suited. For that matter, keythongs and kryphons could also be rulers."

"Now, my daughter, I know that the hippogryphs have made you mad," Sun Quest replies, shaking his head. "Keythongs and kryphons in charge as well as opinici? If we ever do succeed in dethroning Talona, you will turn the whole world topsy-turvy!" Sunground makes a plaintive cooing noise and rubs her head against his. He returns the gesture, enveloping her in his soft, giant wings. It feels so wonderful to be back in her father's strong and protective presence. They stay close together for a long while, dozing and waking periodically, each checking that the other is still there.

Sunground does not know where the moon sits in the sky when she hears the sound of talons scraping the stone floor. She peers into the darkness and sees a group of gryphons approaching them. She rises with a start, waking her father in the process.

"It is the Tormentors," he murmurs softly. "I can feel their odious presence. Be still! I will deal with them."

Sunground is about to reply but is interrupted by the lighting of a torch nearby their cell. Jophriel has awoken and is by her side immediately.

"My father has joined us, Jophriel," she explains, "and he calls these gryphons 'the Tormentors.'"

Jophriel's hand grips the back of Sunground's feathered neck tightly. *She has certainly proven herself a steadfast friend,* Sunground thinks, *and no matter what happens next, I am honored to have known her.*

She squints as her eyes adjust to the new light in the cell. She peers more closely at the gryphon nearest to her and gapes in shock. There before her is her half-sister, Queen Talona. She has grown larger since Sunground last saw the fearsome gryphon sibling. Her beautiful white-gold feathers shine in the light, but her eyes appear wild and crazed.

She is not well, Sunground thinks. *I can sense it. If Talona is insane, then there is another clause in the Gryphonic Code that allows for her removal from the head of the government—but how to implement it?*

Talona stares icily at her for a long time. Sun Quest steps forward to begin his plea for Sunground's life, but Talona silences him.

"Enough, Sun Quest!" she screeches, holding up one talon. "I do not wish to hear you defend your favorite daughter's life. I know you no longer consider me your daughter, so I will not pay you the disrespect of calling you 'Father'. I must tell you, however, that I am not here for you. I would like you to witness Sunground's torture so that you can keep my dearest little first mate company, he who is so loyal to the dead traitor, Thundercloud."

Sun Quest screams at Talona, but to no avail. The vicious queen finally turns her attention to her hated sister.

"Well, well, Horse Lover!" she taunts, cackling snidely. "You have dared to return home to challenge my reign. Oh, my dear, I trust you know that we cannot have a member of the hippogryph clan as our queen."

"Talona!" Sunground says with as much courage as she can muster. "I know you and I have had many arguments in the past, but let us put those aside and work together. You know that you are losing the support of just about everyone in the community. It is not too late for you to change course, to be the leader that your mother Soundringer hoped that you would be."

Talona lets out a rasping, wrathful wail. "Don't speak to me of my mother! Lecture me not about how to reign, Hippogryph-Bearer! I would rather mate with a dozen horses than share my power with you. Do you really think that the community will follow one who creeps about with horses and hophas?"

"Talona," Sunground replies, attempting to keep her tone level. "It is not important to me that I be the ruler. My followers and I only want wise governance. You have not shown the wisdom that Heartsong tried to impart to you."

"Spare me that old vulture's name!" Talona shouts. "I have made it illegal for anyone to say that name publicly, so here is another charge upon your sorry head. You are a traitor, Sunground of the Valley, and I will listen to you no more. I grow weary of your reconciliatory pandering. Don't you know that we are no longer silly adolescents, jealously guarding our secrets? Let the torture begin! Ring Screecher, go forth and do your worst to this rebellious fool."

Sunground's body freezes with fear, but her mind remains surprisingly clear and calm.

"We are with you," whispers the spirit of Queen Heartsong. "Do not be afraid, dear Sunground, for Talona is still a chick with great pain in her heart. Remember the way of compassion!"

The old gryphon, Ring Screecher, enters the cell as the guards struggle to bring the enraged Sun Quest under control. They finally succeed in binding his four leonine limbs with strong cords, wrapping the ends around his beak. His eyes glare at them with fiery contempt, his sides heaving and his body bloody and scratched. Sunground's heart feels as though it is about to break as she watches the elderly opinicus floundering helplessly.

The young opinicus, Sun Wing, requires no such binding. He sits in the corner of the cell, now awake but seemingly indifferent to what is about to occur. He turns away forlornly at the sound of his mother's reassuring coos. She knows that he does not want to witness yet another family member being tormented and is withdrawing to protect himself emotionally.

The guards turn their attention to Jophriel, who has been standing by Sunground and whispering into her communication device. Sunground can hear Roonen's voice only slightly, as the device's volume is not high. She can imagine how upset he must be upon hearing of their new danger. She hopes that he and Dreamspinner do not resort to violence in order to break into the prison cave.

The communication device is snatched from Jophriel's hands and given to Talona, who examines it with curiosity.

"Please, let Jophriel go free! She is not a threat to anyone," Sunground begs, to no avail. Jophriel is bound, arms to feet, and deposited roughly beside Sun Quest.

"Sunground!" she cries, her voice heavy with anger and sorrow.

"Jophriel," Sunground says softly. "Do not be afraid. My spirit grandmother and my oracle are with me, as they are with us all."

Jophriel calls out the name of her own hophic oracle, the male who lived long ago in the ancient hopha lands.

"May the divine prophets bless you, my gryphon friend!" she coos in return, struggling somewhat to translate her spiritual thoughts into the gryphonic language.

Ring Screecher steps forward, ignoring all pleas and coos. She places a cord around Sunground's neck and beak while the guards stand by in case Sunground puts up a fight. She does not fight but remains still, and a peaceful calm descends upon her. She regards Ring Screecher and notices that the old gryphon is missing an eye. She remembers as a young chick meeting a member of the Royal Flock of Hunters, one of those who hunted meat for the rest of the community. At that time, the hunter had recently lost an eye, and Sunground remembers feeling repulsed at the sight of the red, raw, empty eye socket.

She looks at the gryphon as she is now, summoning compassion for this one who was once a hunter but has since become a tormentor for the Talonic regime. The eye socket is now scarred over, a dark purple color that blends easily with her black head feathers. The old wound seems to have become a part of her, no longer quite so repulsive; yet it is disquieting to Sunground, seeing this empty space that returns no gaze. A name suddenly jumps into her mind: "Night Hunter!" she cries, her words stifled by the cord around her beak. "Why are you doing this, you who were once a brave predator?"

"I am Night Hunter no longer," she rasps, her tone dead. "My name is now Ring Screecher, and you are about to find out why."

The guards insert a stone-carved ring around Sunground's neck that feels uncomfortably tight, almost cutting off her breath. The ends of the cords run through the ring on either side of her neck. Each of the guards takes the ends of the cord in their beaks while Ring Screecher inserts a hook onto the top of Sunground's beak, with a tough and thorny vine attached to it. She runs the vine over Sunground's head and through the neck-ring, the thorns sticking painfully into her feathered skin.

Sunground listens to the beat of her heart and senses the presence of Truth Speaker. She feels the oracle's spirit wings enfolding her, together with the wings of Queen Heartsong and Queen Grass Grazer. The three sets of wings form a kind of spiritual nest for her heart. She enters a profound moment of deep silence, a place where she understands that all is love and that life is continuously connected within an infinite source.

"Begin!" a voice cackles. It emanates from that being known to her as "Talona" but whom she now sees as a beauteous creature of light. *Talona's understanding of life has become terribly distorted because she believes herself to be separate from Creation.*

Ring Screecher slowly pulls Sunground's head back, the thorns on the vines piercing her neck and head in an agonizing fashion. Sunground feels the urge to screech, but the guards are now pulling on the other two cords, causing the ring to tighten slowly around her throat. The pain is unbearable, and she feels herself being strangled by the ring and cords.

She fights to keep her mind centered on the nest of love that the oracle built with the help of her grandmother and Grass Grazer. She comprehends that her heart has always been in this place of love, but her mind has not yet realized it.

Suddenly, the tension lets up. Sunground feels herself dropping back into consciousness. Jophriel is screaming while Sun Quest flops mutely on the ground, his beak tied firmly shut. He is enraged and heartbroken at the same time.

Sunground does her best to send them a reassuring wave of spirit from the oracle's soul nest. The anxious pair seems less than reassured, and is unable to receive the gift.

Ring Screecher and the guards give Sunground a brief reprieve, releasing the cords and allowing her to regain limited head movement. A few moments later they intrude upon her relief by roughly yanking the cords back once more, strangling her almost into unconsciousness before relaxing the cords yet again. This treatment continues interminably until finally Sunground feels the spirit lifting her from her misery.

She is now above her own body, looking down upon it as a detached but deeply compassionate observer. She feels profound empathy, not only for her friend and family members but also for the guards. She knows the hatred they feel toward themselves and their actions, as if she was the one who had performed the deeds. She feels sorrow for Ring Screecher as she carries out her odious task in a sullen torpor, and for Queen Talona, who in her blind rage orders all of this.

Talona, she realizes from her perch in the soul world, has been marginalized since birth and shunned because of many gryphons' contempt for her mother. Soundringer, known by the sarcastic title, the queen of gossip, has been hated for the vicious rumors that she once delighted in spreading throughout the community. This unfortunate tendency on the part of Mother Soundringer to speak ill of others has long held tragic and unintended consequences for her only daughter. The people ostracized her, and that included Sunground and her family members. She recalls in deep remorse that they have rejected Talona repeatedly for a long time. Sunground now understands that they are all responsible for the terrible state into which their society has descended. Talona alone does not bear the entire burden of blame.

Sunground is astounded that she sees everything from her position, viewing events simultaneously. She observes the mother of Talona as she pines in grief for her wayward daughter. Soundringer lies, thin and bedraggled, in a cell just a small distance away from their own.

At the same time, Sunground is aware of a great eruption of chaos outside the prison cave. Dreamspinner angrily demands her release while Roonen brandishes a small, sharp weapon, waving it at the fearsome yet diminished gryphonic forces that still guard the prison. One of the gryphons scratches Roonen's arm with her talons and red blood pours from his wound. Nightsky chases the gryphons away, biting and kicking at them furiously. She sees that the gryphons still loyal to Talona are beginning to lose their fear of the winged horse, and they peck at him with increasing strength and frequency.

Around them, the rest of the peace contingent remains firm, led by Star Sailor and Mountain Rain, who stand their ground. They are joined by Uncle Ground Paw, Day Minder, and Lionheart, who have managed to lead their three groups of keythongs and kryphons across the pawbridge. A growing throng of gryphons from every level of society gather around, screeching and flapping their wings, demanding an end to Talona's reign. They are led in a chant by Mountain Rain, who slyly encourages them to repeat, *"Free Sunground! Free her to the skies!"*

From the chaos of the ground to the freedom of the skies, Sunground is aware of it all. She sees a flock of hippogryphs, led by Night Lover, descending upon Gryphonia's Central City. They surround Nightsky, Dreamspinner, and Roonen, forming a protective circle around them. The two hophas, Jack Warford and his mate, Clariel, dash from their still-grounded aircraft to drag the bleeding Roonen to safety. The hippogryphs intervene by helping the injured male onto Nightsky's back and the winged horse, himself badly scratched, trots over to the airship with Warford and Clariel running along beside him to steady Roonen.

Sunground feels Roonen's seething rage without being drawn into it. He screams epithets, arguing with Warford that he needs to find Jophriel rather than to receive medical care. He is weak from loss of blood and is swiftly overpowered by Warford and Clariel, who between them lift him by the arms and feet up the ramp and into the craft. They are welcomed by the Warfords' son Riva, who feels immensely relieved to have them join him. He helps his parents tend to their colleague.

From the skies, there is a mighty screech as the young hippogryph, Moon Wing, flies into the throng with Jophriel's daughter, Halona, perched on her back. In front of Halona, a keythong is balanced most precariously over Moon Wing's body: It is Groundsky, Sunground's keythong son. Accompanying this unlikely trio are Mother Skystar, Cloudhopper, and the two young gryphons, Rainbow Dreamer and Luck Wisher.

Sunground feels the thoughts and emotions of all of these beings flood her awareness until finally, she enters a blank state of nothingness.

CHAPTER SEVEN

Redemption

Sunground's body is in intense pain, especially around her neck. It has been stretched backwards so many times that she can now barely move her head without experiencing deep discomfort. Jophriel tends to the wounds that were caused by thorns. She administers a substance to her skin on the spots where the feathers have been rubbed off. It stings, but it is nothing compared to the torment that she has recently endured.

"Sunground," Jophriel murmurs. "I am here and so is your father, Sun Quest. He is still tied, but I managed to cut the cords around his beak so that he can speak."

Sunground raises her head slowly to lessen the pain. She looks at Sun Quest, his four leonine limbs still tightly tied.

"My courageous daughter," he says. "You have won the battle—for now. That cave bat, Talona, has given up for a while. Apparently, you did not succumb to her in the way that she had hoped."

"Father Sun Quest," Sunground says, her voice hoarse and rasping. "I have had a glimpse of the otherworld, the sky beyond this one. I learned that we must treat Talona with compassion, as she became the way she is partly because we taunted and rejected her as a young chick."

Sunground's mind turns to the painful memory of when Talona and she were young chicks of only eight sun revolutions. She remembers how she and her sister Mountain Rain assailed young Talona, plucking her feathers out and calling her names.

"Father Sun Quest loves us but not you!" she remembers Mountain Rain cawing gleefully.

Even at that tender age, Sunground felt a great deal of guilt for participating in the melee because she had done nothing to stop it. She wished that she could have shown better leadership skills but at the same time, she knew that she must forgive the young chick who was once known as Princess Sunsky. She had possessed neither the wisdom nor the maturity to act as a better role model to her sister. Still, the memory haunts her because she knows that Talona's past torment was repeated time and again, not only by her and her sister but by other young gryphlets all over the queendom. Talona had been almost universally disliked from the moment she was born, because the adults in the community so disliked her mother. The gryphlets had picked up on this intense dislike from the adult gryphons and had collectively applied it to the once young and innocent Talona.

Her memories of the past are suddenly interrupted by Sun Quest's caws of derision. "That is no excuse for this kind of barbarism!" he screeches. "I was also teased by gryphlets when I was a young opinclet cub, because I had front paws instead of deft, creative talons! This is a natural part of life. Are you suggesting that the bullying of Talona when she was a young chick somehow justifies her present adult behavior?"

"No!" Sunground replies. "No, I am simply saying that we must find a way to forgive Talona for her present actions, through apologizing or acknowledging the pain of her past."

Sun Quest grumbles to himself but says no more.

"Our oracle taught us that forgiveness of our enemies is essential," Jophriel says, "so I can understand what you're saying, Sunground. I guess the only problem is, will we be executed before we have a chance to acknowledge Talona's past hurts?"

"No," Sunground says firmly. "I have seen what is going on outside this prison, when I was having my revelation in the otherworld. Jophriel, Roonen is injured, but Warford and Clariel took him into the airship for medical treatment. He will be safe there."

Jophriel gasps in shock. "He will be safe if he stays in the airship but knowing Roonen, he will not. Oh, I wish I could communicate with him! He needs to be told to stay where he is—not that he'll listen, the stubborn goat."

"It's all right, Jo," Sunground says. "I felt strongly when I was in the place beyond this one that Clariel, Warford's mate, is a strong-minded female. She will keep Jack and Roonen right where they're supposed to be."

Jophriel appears surprised. "You're right, Sunground. Clari is a tough bird and once she puts her foot down, there's no defying her. You really must have been in a state of heightened awareness to glean that about her, because when you first meet Clariel, she seems quiet and subservient to Warford."

"She is not," Sunground says. "She will take good care of Roonen. So stop fussing, Jophriel."

Jophriel nods, tussling Sunground's head feathers playfully. She is truly a great friend, and Sunground is infinitely thankful to her for being willing to undertake this fearsome journey with her. There is, however, something else that Sunground needs to tell her. *What is it?* Her mind has difficulty remembering what she saw after Roonen was wounded and taken to the ship. She searches her memory, but it is lost in the blankness of the oblivion that overtook her. They all remain silent for a time, each contemplating his or her life within the sanctity of their own hearts.

Sunground's newly discovered son has said little to them but nonetheless moves nearer to derive some comfort from them. He has spoken no more about his great-grandfather, Thundercloud, nor about his plan to become king. Sunground finds little ways to include him in their circle, such as cooing at him or simply speaking his name, with no expectation of a response.

As Sunground contemplates Sun Wing within the silence of her heart, she feels a presence beside her. She opens her eyes to find that Sun Wing is lying beside her. She nuzzles him, tapping his beak lovingly. He says nothing but taps back.

"I am so sorry, Sun Wing," Sunground says. "I should never have spoken to you about what happened to your late grandmother, Wing Dreamer."

"Do not be sorry, Mother Sunsky," he responds. "I knew this in my heart, even if my mind denied it. Thundercloud did not speak of Wing Dreamer often but when he did, it was with such venomous hatred. I had the feeling that he had something to do with her death but at the time, I pushed it aside. My step-grandmother Stormspeaker once alluded to the murder, but she would not answer my questions about it when I pressed her for information. I asked the physician

Light Healer about it as well, and she arranged for me to have an appointment with the oracle."

"You went to see Truth Speaker?" she asks incredulously. "What did she say?"

"She told me that the mysteries that surrounded my life would be revealed to me when the time was right," Sun Wing replies. "I grew impatient and left the meeting screaming epithets. Now I know that she was right to have withheld the information from me. I would not have been able to manage, knowing the truth about Thundercloud being a murderer when I was at such a young age. Even now it confuses me, for I did love Thundercloud in spite of his nasty nature."

"We cannot help but love those who are close to us, Sun Wing," she says. "It is only natural. Thundercloud, for all his anger, was still one of us. He was a gryphonic being. He did not do anything that was not agreed with collectively, within the dark silence of our own minds. We have all been infected with the venom of hatred, my son—hatred for winged horses, hippogryphs, keythongs, kryphons, hophas, and ultimately for ourselves. We cannot hate another without also hating ourselves."

Sun Wing nods slowly, as though processing this.

"You listen to her, Sun Wing!" says Sun Quest. "Your Mother Sunsky is very wise. She has just been to the sky beyond this one. And, my daughter, I must tell you that I will be the one to speak with Talona. I will attempt to apologize to her, as you suggest. After all, it was because of my rejection of her that she is like this. I have never really considered her my daughter, and I now realize that I was wrong. This whole mess is my fault and my responsibility to remedy, although Talona will likely kill me in the process."

"No, Father Sun Quest!" Sunground screeches. "You are not going to apologize to her alone. This is something that must be done by the whole community—*after* Talona has been arrested and prevented from causing any more harm."

In answer to Sunground's statement, a familiar cackling sound echoes through the prison dens. From the shadows, Talona emerges. "So, Sunground! Now that you have had to endure some degree of torment, as I did when I was a chick, you wish to issue an apology to me! I'm terribly sorry, but I'm afraid that it's far too late for that. We aren't chicks anymore, and I know the real reason you're here. You would illegally usurp the queenship that you so irresponsibly abandoned long ago. I have been listening to your conversation, my dear half-sister, and I have just heard evidence of your treason. You, the outlaw, planning to arrest me, the legally installed and rightful queen of Gryphonia! You are pathetic. I believe I shall be merciful to you, in light of your statement that you hope to issue a community-wide apology to me for your actions. You must forfeit your life, however, to truly repent the past. If you want to save the lives of your family members and friends, you will issue the apology publicly and call for the rebels outside these walls to stand down. Order the hippogryphs, hophas, and winged horses away and then stand ready for your public execution. You, like Thundercloud, will serve as an example to the community of what happens to traitors of the regime."

Sun Quest roars at her in rage. He is helpless in his sorrow and fury.

"Thank you for your acknowledgement that you have been wrong to reject me all these years, Father Sun Quest," Talona continues. "Isn't it amazing how much love one wins when one asserts authority? I think that I will reward you by keeping you alive, just like my dear little mate, Sun Wing. You shall have the privilege of observing the execution of your wayward daughter and her malevolent counterpart, Mountain Rain. She, along with the traitor Star Sailor, has agreed to come into custody in exchange for Sunground's freedom. They shall have their wish, although it will not be quite as they think. Sunground will be freed, only to go to her beloved sky-beyond-this-one that sadly does not exist. Sorry, dear Sister Sunground! Oh, how I hate being the bearer of bad news! Sunground's execution will be followed by those of Mountain Rain and Star Sailor, and any others who decline to stand down from traitorous activity."

Sun Quest's vocalizations become louder and more rage-filled by the minute. Sunground and Jophriel attempt to calm him but with limited success. His screeches are echoed further along the prison chamber by a voice Sunground knows can only belong to Mountain Rain. There is a calmer voice as well that attempts to quiet her.

Talona is correct: Mountain Rain and Star Sailor are in prison!

"Mountain Rain!" Sunground calls. She is silenced when Ring Screecher and the guards enter the cell and tie her beak shut, along with those of Sun Quest and Sun Wing.

"Shall we ready the prisoner for another torture session, my queen?" Ring Screecher asks Talona.

"No," Talona snaps. "The time has ended for quaint, quiet little torture sessions. I want her taken immediately to the city center for execution! You are to be the executioner, Ring Screecher. The hoards are growing more rebellious by the minute, and we cannot afford to wait. Gryphonia must have a demonstration of what true power is all about!"

Ring Screecher bows her assent, gesturing to the guards to secure the prisoner. The guards peck roughly at Sunground. One places a collar and leash around her neck, while the other opens the webbed netting that bars the entrance to their prison den. Together, they push and pull her through the opening of the den. Jophriel moves to follow, but one of the guards bites her arm savagely.

"I must accompany Sunground!" Jophriel screams in the gryphonic language.

"Let the hopha go with her!" Talona orders. "Once her friend is dead, she and her mate will leave our mountains with their flying thing and its magic lightning! And, if the hopha truly wish to have peace with the gryphons, they will also take their dark winged horse with them and never again return."

Jophriel nods in silent agreement, helpless to do anything else. She follows Sunground and the guards cautiously.

As they leave, Talona orders a new group of guards to bring the other prisoners out: the three opinici, Sun Quest, Sun Wing, and Windsinger, along with the two gryphons, Mountain Rain and Star Sailor, are herded out of their cells. They are accompanied, to everyone's dismay, by Talona's own mother.

As Soundringer joins them, disheartened and bedraggled from her time in prison, the others stare at her in contempt. Sunground turns to her and attempts to speak, but her beak is bound too tightly for her to vocalize anything more than a throaty croak.

"I am so sorry, Sunground," Soundringer says wearily. "I have now realized my mistake, and I want you to know that I have done everything in my power to convince Talona to stand down. I have been unsuccessful, as you can see."

Sunground presses her beak close to Soundringer's in a reconciliatory gesture, but the guards yank upon her chained neck, forcing her head to straighten so that she will focus on the way ahead. Mountain Rain squawks angrily at the guards, until they yank her own chain in warning. She mutters something in a disgruntled fashion but is pecked for it by her fellow leader, Star Sailor.

"Keep yourself calm, Rain!" Star Sailor whispers. Sunground is thankful to her old friend for looking after Mountain Rain during this terrible ordeal.

They ascend the steps to the top of the prison complex, as it opens up into a bustling common area. It is equipped with many stone perches that are built into the mountainous terrain and upon which gryphons normally negotiate various transactions with each other. On this day, however, it is filled as far as the eye can see with a flapping, squawking flock of avian felines, all of them arranged around the prison den demanding the demise of Talona's reign. As the group is paraded in front of the screeching mob, the noise increases substantially.

"Free Sunground!" some of them chant.

"Free Mountain Rain and Star Sailor! Down with Talona, the killer of the oracle!" scream others.

The guards caw in furious terror at the throng as it edges collectively closer to them, pecking at their feathers. When Talona emerges from behind them, accompanied by Ring Screecher and a still-protective Mother Soundringer, the din becomes overwhelming. A squadron of gryphons still loyal to the regime surrounds the trio, and insults are hurled at them.

"Make way for your legally installed queen!" shout the squadron members, now led by the youthful gryphon, River Wind.

"No more executions, River Wind!" a group of young gryphons shout in unison, "Free the prisoners! Abandon the monster Talona!"

The group makes its way slowly to the main perch in the center of Gryphonia City. They ascend additional steps to arrive at the apex and arrange themselves in a small semi-circle.

The perch overlooks the crowd and to her astonishment, Sunground sees a large band of hippogryphs standing quietly amid the ruckus. At the center of the herd, standing proud, is Night Lover, the queen of the hippogryphs. Beside her stands an equally proud Moon Wing. On top of her back, Halona sits resolute and seemingly fearless.

"Halona!" Jophriel shouts, shocked. In response, Moon Wing flies forward and lands upon the stone terrace, with the young hopha still on her back. Sunground realizes that this is the memory from her beyond-sky vision that she had been unable to recall earlier. It was the memory of their beloved daughters descending into the madness taking place on the mountainous ground below. Not far behind his sister is the young keythong Groundsky, who is climbing up to the main perch in spite of his winglessness. He had, Sunground recalls from her vision, flown into Gryphonia balanced and held in place by Halona, on top of Moon Wing.

Halona dismounts from Moon Wing and rushes over to her mother, giving her a hug. "Papa is fine, Ma. We're here to help."

"Halona, Moon Wing, and Groundsky!" Jophriel says as they arrive, Moon Wing tapping beaks worriedly with her mother. "You were all supposed to stay behind at the tunnel to keep the young ones safe! This is a *very* dangerous situation that we are all involved in."

"That's why we came," Moon Wing explains. "The hippogryphs had to leave the cavern, as it was about to be breached by a large squadron of gryphons. The hopha sentinels, Seth and Sharriel, warned us of the invasion before it happened. We were able to accompany the youngest ones, along with Mother Skystar and Aunt Cloudhopper, to the hopha tunnel. Seth and Sharriel and a few of the other hophas were guarding them before we departed to come to Gryphonia. We left the two newborns at the tunnel in the capable care of Egglight, Pegasus, Grass Hopper, and Fluff Feather."

Sunground stares at them in awed wonder. *Both Moon Wing and Grass Hopper have given birth in our absence! It is a beautiful gift to all of us, before I leave this world for the sky beyond this one.*

She fears, however, that her family members may be in terrible danger. *Talona may want them executed as well!* She peers about in frantic horror, searching for Mother Skystar, Cloudhopper, and her two nieces. They are nowhere to be seen, but Sunground can now remember that she had seen them fly in also when she was in her altered state during the torture session.

Moon Wing senses her thoughts. "Fret not about Grandmother Skystar, Aunt Cloudhopper, and my two cousins," she bleats. "Papa Nightsky and the Warfords are guarding them and keeping them safe, not far from here. Look, Mother Sunground, Talona's regime has fallen! The gryphons are all demanding changes, and they are not even attacking the hippogryph group. Take those silly ropes and chains off and celebrate!"

Sunground regards her youthful daughter with great pride in spite of their dire circumstances. Out of the corner of her eye, she sees Talona creeping close to her. The wrathful queen was flustered at first by the appearance of a hippogryph and a hopha on the terrace, but she is now determined to take back her power.

"Do you see the guards next to Mountain Rain and Star Sailor?" Talona croaks softly. "They have orders to kill your sister and friend if you do not immediately order the hippogryphs, hophas, and their ilk away."

Sunground nods her reluctant assent. Talona is obviously terrified of the strange creatures around her, for they represent a direct threat to her reign. With her beak still bound, Sunground can say nothing to Moon Wing verbally, but she attempts to send a thought message: "I love you, Moon Wing. Remember that."

Moon Wing stares intently at her and sends her own thought message:

"Take charge, Mother Sunground! Order the guards to arrest Talona on the basis of section eight of the Gryphonic Code!"

Sunground wishes it was that simple. She looks at Mountain Rain and Star Sailor, and she can see the guards' talons at their throats, ready to rip them out at a second's notice from Talona. Moon Wing also realizes the dilemma and steps back a bit. She murmurs something to her brother, Groundsky, who has managed to climb up onto the public terrace. Together, the siblings look at their mother and aunt helplessly.

One of the guards approaches Sunground, ripping the cord off her beak so that she can vocalize once more. Talona gives her half-sister a warning glance.

Sunground screeches at the crowd, asking them to be silent. The throng, anxious to hear what the returning rebel will say, ceases its noise.

"My fellow gryphons," she calls out, her voice trembling. "I must first address the hippogryphs who have recently joined us. My dear friends, I must now order you to leave Gryphonia for your own safety. I am grateful to you for your support, but this is a gryphonic matter, and I must insist that you leave this place now."

There is an excruciating silence as all the gryphons turn to the group of hippogryphs still standing in their midst to see how they will react to Sunground's order. The hippogryphs do nothing. Finally, Night Lover speaks. "Sunground of the Hopha-Equine Gryphonic Alliance, I regret to inform you that we do not take orders from gryphons. We are staying here until the gryphonic government agrees to stop all hostilities toward our people."

Sunground's mind spins in panic. She cannot blame Night Lover for standing her ground, but at the moment the only thing she can think of is saving the lives of Mountain Rain and Star Sailor. Knowing how resolute and stubborn hippogryphs can be, Sunground changes tactics.

"My fellow gryphons," she cries out, shocked at how easily she is giving in to Talona's threats. "I would like to tell you that I apologize to Talona for all that I have done to reject and marginalize her in the past. Her regime is, I believe, a direct result of the pain she holds in her soul because of this rejection."

Sunground is interrupted by jeers, hoots, screeches, and whistles. "Don't give in to the monster, Sunground of the Valley!" some of the gryphons cry out. "Seize the moment! Seize the power!"

Sunground closes her eyes for a moment, going within to consult her own heart. "*Remain firm,*" comes the response. She opens her eyes and the throng quiets, curious as to what she will say next.

"I must remain firm," she says, reiterating her heart's statement, "and insist that we owe Talona a community-wide apology for our treatment of her..."

More hoots, jeers, and screeches assault her senses. Sunground dares not look behind her to see what is happening to her sister and friend.

"'Tell them all to stand down and support my regime,' Talona croaks, "or face the consequences."

Sunground's body is taut with tension. If she orders them to stand down now, there is a distinct possibility that mob violence will break out. "My fellow gryphons!" she calls out at last. "I ask that you be peaceful in your intentions. Violence will solve nothing but rather will cheapen all of our lives in its destructive rage."

"Where is *your* rage, Outlaw Sunground?" a member of the crowd screeches.

"I..." Sunground stammers, faltering. She does not wish to aggravate Talona any further, for she can hear the angry queen snarling at her.

"Kill Mountain Rain!" she shrieks suddenly at one of the guards.

Sunground whirls about in sheer terror. The talons of the guard are piercing her dear sister's throat, slowly strangling the life from her.

"Don't be a fool, Sunground!" Mountain Rain croaks, managing to pull her head fiercely out of the guard's grip for a fleeting moment. "Call... for... a change..."

Suddenly, from above, an enraged cry peals out and a mighty gryphon swoops down from the skies, her maternal talons drawn. She neatly takes out the guard, pecking at her furiously as she does so. Sunground gapes in astonishment: It is Mother Skystar!

"How dare you do this to my family, you rotten imbecile!" Skystar roars thunderously at the befuddled guard.

"I was just following orders!" the guard stammers.

The second guard, having seen the menacing sneer from Talona, grips her talons into Star Sailor's throat, preparing to rip it out. She hesitates for a moment as the crowd urges her to save Star Sailor's life and disobey the raging queen's directive.

Another screech sounds from above and in swoops yet another gryphon matriarch, attacking the offending guard savagely. It is Queenstar, the mother of Star Sailor.

"We gryphon mothers will tolerate the mistreatment of our daughters no longer!" she bellows as the crowd roars its approval.

"Take out Talona!" they scream. "Down with the Talonic Regime!"

"You traitors!" Talona screams back at them ferociously. "You will be made to pay for your treachery!"

The executioner, Ring Screecher, is hastily brought forward.

"Ring Screecher!" Talona yells in a terrified rage. "Execute Sunground!"

Ring Screecher steps forward ominously, bringing her deathly beak close to Sunground's throat. Sunground hears her family members clamoring and cawing in horror, but they cannot attack Ring Screecher for she is now surrounded by royal squadron members.

"No, Ring Screecher!" a voice calls. Sunground recognizes it as that of the physician Light Healer. "Don't do it! Remember who you are! You are Night Hunter of the Royal Flock of Hunters! You are no executioner!"

"*Remember, you are Night Hunter!*" the throng echoes the physician.

Sunground is eternally grateful to Light Healer for injecting a more peaceful message into the hostile crowd's mentality. Ring Screecher, however, is engaging her talent for torture by slowly tightening her beak's grip on Sunground's throat. As the grip grows tighter, she can feel her breathing become more and more restricted until she collapses, her talons scratching helplessly in the air. As she feels her consciousness slipping from her, a familiar male screech call sounds from above. She feels a rush of wings accompany the vocalization, and the pressure on her throat vanishes. She gasps and rasps, raising her head to behold the noble opinicus Dreamspinner tussling with Ring Screecher, his mighty leonine paws now upon her throat.

"No, Dreamspinner!" Sunground croaks. "Remember... peace..."

"I remember, my queen!" Dreamspinner replies, "and I will not harm this reprobate cyclops, but I do urge you to call an end to this regime!"

The throng is once more growing volatile in its demands. "Execute Ring Screecher, mighty Dreamspinner!" it shrieks collectively, as if from one body. "Execute Talona!"

"No more executions!" Sunground rasps, unable to be heard above the din, except by Dreamspinner.

"My queen, and your true queen, Sunsky of the Mountains, informs us that there are to be no more executions!" Dreamspinner cries to them.

While Dreamspinner engages the crowd, Mother Skystar and Mountain Rain take advantage of Ring Screecher's incapacitation to talk to the squadron members surrounding them. Skystar uses her old authority as a former council member to convince the squadron leader, River Wind, that Talona's reign is over and that she will need to take her orders from them now. River Wind peers at Talona, who is engaged in a shrieking tantrum whilst her mother, Soundringer, attempts to calm her.

"Let them through, River Wind!" Soundringer calls, her voice regaining some of its old authority. "I plead insanity on behalf of my daughter. Take this poisonous power away from her before it kills her."

Soundringer is clawed by a panic-stricken Talona for this remark and Soundringer returns in kind, bellowing vociferously at her to stand down. Talona lets out a chickish wail.

Skystar and Mountain Rain rush in to the circle of confused Royal Air Squadron members to attend to the beleaguered Sunground.

"My cherished daughter!" Skystar exclaims. "Are you able to stand?"

Sunground struggles to stand up, weakened by the attempted strangulation. Mountain Rain calls for the physician, Light Healer, who flies up to the terrace.

Upon examining her, Light Healer declares, "She needs rest. Lie down, Sunground."

Sunground taps beaks affectionately with the physician, relieved to be once more under her compassionate care.

"I will, physician Light Healer," Sunground assures her. "I promise you. First, however, I must address the crowd."

Mountain Rain lets out a gargantuan bellow, silencing the throng.

"My sister is now free of all threats and ready to address you!" she calls. "The one who should have been queen in the first place will speak her truth!"

Sunground steps forward, uncomfortable about immediately being pushed into the queenship role without the consultation of a council of some kind, but Talona had dispersed the council and declared it to be too interfering. She closes her eyes, feels her beating heart, and with it hears the sound of her grandmother's heart song. She feels the presence of the oracle within her as she draws herself up, ready to speak the truth as she understands it.

"Gryphons!" she calls to an expectant crowd. "Opinici, keythongs, and kryphons! I call for a regime change, under section eight of the Gryphonic Code: When a gryphon leader is failing to perform her duties properly, according to the code, she must step down and allow an interim leader, namely the chief magistrate, to take her place until the council has found a replacement candidate for the reign. I also direct your attention to the insanity clause that states, 'a leader must have rational capacity in order to govern'. Soundringer, the brave mother of Talona, has declared her daughter to be insane..."

"And I, as chief physician of Gryphonia, heartily concur with that assessment!" Light Healer cries.

"Now that we have heard the physician's statement, I must remind you that anyone within our society who has been declared insane will receive only the most compassionate care and treatment. Light Healer will be in charge of Talona's rehabilitation program and *not* the Royal Squadron. As for the squadron, the prison guards, and any other gryphons that worked for the previous government, they cannot be executed either. I stand before you all and declare that *no one* shall be executed, but instead we will work with the old regime's loyalists in order to create a peaceful transition to new governance. I ask all of you to consider the future of Gryphonia. Is there anyone who does *not* agree that Talona's reign shall be terminated?"

An eerie silence follows. No one speaks in support of the queen—not the guards, nor the Royal Air Squadron members, nor Ring Screecher. The silence is broken by another pain-filled wail from Talona. Soundringer attempts to comfort her but is bitten for her efforts. The once-loyal squadron members slowly close in on the former queen, preparing for the inevitable order to place her under arrest.

"And so, Gryphonia," Sunground says, "do we all declare Talona's reign to be rendered null and void by virtue of her unsustainable and insane actions toward gryphonic society?"

The throng roars its approval, screaming at River Wind to place Talona under arrest. At long last, River Wind gives in and issues the fateful order. The former queen is bound, talons-to-paws, and the two guards who once followed her orders are put on duty to guard her. Soundringer lies down beside her daughter, tapping beaks with her and cooing tenderly. Talona does not push her away this time.

"Let us reinstate Sunsky, Queen of the Mountains!" some members of the crowd crow.

"No! She is still a horse-lover!" others cry.

As soon as the word "horse-lover" has been uttered, they witness the spectacle of a black winged horse flying down to the public terrace with a male hopha on his back. As Nightsky lands gingerly beside Sunground, a fearful silence grips the crowd once more. The hopha male, Roonen, jumps off Nightsky's back and runs over to his mate and daughter, embracing them protectively. Sunground looks at Jophriel, whose eyes speak encouragingly to her.

Nightsky walks over and nuzzles her. Sunground feels her confidence sagging once more, but as the love from Jophriel and Nightsky fill her, she finds a renewed sense of well-being. She steps forward to address the crowd. "My people! Do not be afraid of my lover, Nightsky, for without him, there would have been no peace march to Gryphonia. He and my beloved daughter, Moon Wing, have encouraged me in my actions every step of the way. I would have abandoned the plan as ludicrous if it had not been for them and for my hopha friends as well."

A rustling of feathers from the throng and muffled squawks greet her words.

"Before the oracle was executed, Sunsky," Light Healer explains, "she foretold that the Talonic regime would end, and the first sign of its demise would be your return as queen, accompanied by a female hopha and gryphonic beings from all levels of society. The second sign, the oracle informed us, would be a flock of hippogryphs landing in the middle of the city center and refusing to leave until you were installed as rightful ruler. The third and final sign was that a dark winged horse, with a male hopha riding on its back, would descend onto this public terrace in the same spot where the oracle was executed. Nightsky has done just that—the three prophecies are fulfilled."

The majority of the throng echoes Light Healer's words. "The prophecies are fulfilled!" they cry. "Let Sunsky rule as queen!"

Sunground—now being referred to with increasing frequency as 'Sunsky' in spite of her former renegade status—is awe-struck. She has difficulty believing that all of this is truly occurring.

Nightsky's familiar voice enters her mind: "Take charge, Sunsky! You must be Premiere Queen now, before they appoint someone far less capable than you of making the necessary changes to your society."

She twitches her tail in response. *She cannot simply declare herself premiere queen! There must be some kind of diplomatic process put into place, or the issue will divide the gryphonic populace.*

"Gryphons and opinici!" she booms, mustering as much vocal authority as she can. "Keythongs and kryphons! I must have a clear majority of you supporting my reign before I can agree to occupy this position. I cannot ignore the fact that many of you are uncomfortable with the idea of my becoming queen because of my association with a winged horse, not to mention hippogryphs and hophas. We are at a turning point in our society. I believe that we must establish rules that will prevent the absolute abuse of power, and I believe that we must be willing to take a hard look at our traditions and laws that have, over the ages, empowered some elites at the expense of others in our society—such as our wingless brothers and sisters."

An enthusiastic crowing erupts from the group of keythongs and kryphons who have gathered near the terrace, led by Uncle Ground Paw, Lionheart, and the kryphon Day Minder. The lower class gryphons and opinici who joined their peace delegation earlier, when they were but a wayward group climbing up the mountain, echo their cheers. The gryphons who occupy higher positions in society peer at them with uncertainty.

"Gryphon sisters and opinicus brothers," Sunground says to them in an urgent tone. "I know that our ideas of equality may cause you anxiety. I will not force them upon you, but I do intend to slowly introduce these changes. I promise that you will not be punished or put down if you happen to be, as my family and I once were, of a higher position within gryphonic society. In order to give us some time and space to consider our options, I hereby declare that a council of gryphons, opinici, keythongs and kryphons be chosen by you to determine the path that we wish to follow.

"I suggest that we begin by reinstating Queenstar as chief magistrate and putting her in charge of guiding this process. I also want to declare my intention to establish diplomatic relations with the hippogryph community, so that we may move quickly to abolish any threats of violence toward them. To my hippogryph compatriots, I apologize whole-heartedly for all past actions perpetrated against you by the gryphonic society that have caused you to fear for your safety. We all owe you a debt of gratitude for your steadfast support in ending the reign of terror."

Night Lover steps forward, peering at Sunground silently. Neither she nor the others say anything, but Sunground feels their love and compassion nonetheless. The many members of gryphonic society are reacting differently to Sunground's speech, some cheering encouragement for the new vision that she is articulating and others voicing fear and consternation.

Night Lover, Queen of the Hippogryphs, finally breaks her silence. "We will establish diplomatic relations with Gryphonia only if you are queen, Mother Sunground," she states. "If anyone else is appointed, we will engage only with you. We make no demands other than to be left alone in our home valley."

A ripple of approval reverberates throughout the throng. Obviously, they are in agreement with Night Lover's statement.

"We shall honor your wishes, Queen Night Lover," Sunground announces, "and I now announce an amnesty for all prisoners held by the former regime. I move that they be unbound and freed!"

This time, there is a roar of unanimous approval for Sunground's assertion. So many gryphonic citizens have had family members arrested and imprisoned, either in the prison den or under home den arrest, that the news of their freedom is greeted with an outpouring of joy and relief.

The joyous mood is interrupted by a question from Sun Wing, the king consort of the former queen. He stands proudly beside his father Dreamspinner, reunited with him at last. "What is to become of Talona?" the young opinicus calls, his beak now unbound as are the beaks of his two grandfathers Sun Quest and Windsinger. "Surely we are not simply going to care for her and require no consequences of her for her actions!"

The elder opinicus Windsinger steps forward, adopting a challenging posture. "I, Windsinger, reclaim my true name! Talona not only dared to rob me of my wings by clipping my flight-feathers, but she also shamed me and my family by renaming me as 'Ground Chiseler' the slave, just as she dared to enslave all you of noble birth! Therefore, *Talona must be executed*, just like my father Thundercloud, our oracle, and many others!"

The crowd is silent for a moment, before suddenly transforming once again into an angry, vengeful mob. "*Death to Talona!*" they cry. "*Death to Ring Screecher and all of the Talonic loyalists! It is they who are the traitors now!*"

Chaos erupts into a cacophony of screeches, hoots, wails, and caws. One voice, however, wails loudest among all of them. "Please, Sunsky of the Mountains!" Soundringer begs, placing herself in a subservient position before the former outlaw. "Spare my daughter Talona's life, and I will give you my own in return! It was my fault that she turned to madness—I pushed her too hard to claim the queenship, and she was not ready. She did not really know what she was doing! Please, Sunsky, I beg you to appeal to the crowd for mercy!"

"Execute both of them!" Windsinger jeers, further inciting the crowd of gryphonic beings to demand revenge. "Even the Gryphonic Code allows execution in cases of mass murder. Section ten sanctions the killing of a wicked one such as Talona and any who have aided and abetted her!"

The crowd takes up the call, chanting, "*Section ten! Section ten! Execute Talona and Soundringer!*"

Sunground flaps her one working wing in anger. "*Silence!*" she booms, surprising herself with the strength of her conviction.

"Section ten of the Gryphonic Code also makes an exception for those who have been declared insane, and after what we have been through, that would be *all of us*. I tell you, no one is to be executed! No more torture, no more executions! Have we learned nothing from this error-prone reign? What kind of wicked creatures are we if we have not?"

The throng subdues itself slightly, as if it was acting out of one big mob-mind and is now dwindling back down into individual thinking units.

Sunground turns to the father of Dreamspinner. "Windsinger, I know that you are enraged at the torture and death of Thundercloud, and I agree that your rage is justified. We have all endured the terror of not knowing when our beloved family members might be targeted for death, and we have done things in service to that terror that we would never have done otherwise. That is precisely why we must not give in any further to our own rage and terror. If we do, we have truly lost ourselves."

Sun Quest steps out beside Windsinger. "C'mon, my old enemy," he urges. "You know you're not your father. Stop pretending that you are Thundercloud."

Dreamspinner, who still holds the former tormentor Ring Screecher, sets her free and walks over to join Sun Quest. "Father Windsinger, you know that I loved Grandfather Thundercloud, in spite of the fact that he heinously murdered your mate and my mother, Wing Dreamer, for the crime of giving birth to a hippogryph in the Valley of Outcasts."

"How did you know that?" Windsinger asks his son, his voice tinged with guilt and sorrow. "I never told you about it because I felt that you would not be able to handle it."

Sunground is likewise shocked that Dreamspinner knows the truth about Thundercloud having killed his mother. Like Windsinger, she had kept that piece of information from him because of his overly excitable nature. *Could Father Sun Quest have told him?*

"It is Sun Wing who informed me about it just now, as I held Ring Screecher to the ground," Dreamspinner explains. "But I have always known, at some level, what my grandfather did. Know that I love you, Father Windsinger, in spite of your silence about the murder for all these sun revolutions. Know that I love you regardless of your abandonment of me when I supported my one true queen and her family, and when she left to give birth to her own hippogryph daughter in the same Valley of Outcasts to which my mother was exiled. You also supported Thundercloud's expulsion of me from my son Sun Wing's life. I choose to forgive you for this and for all the other wrongdoings, but I must insist that you stand down on this vengeful call for execution. Remember, the executions of Talona and her loyalists would also include Sun Wing, for he is king consort to Talona."

Windsinger stares at Dreamspinner, obviously astounded at his son's newfound courage in standing up to him. He regards his grandson Sun Wing with great affection and then hangs his head in shame, his body beginning to tremble until he collapses in grief. He yowls like a cub. "This was not my intention, Dreamspinner! I agreed with none of Thundercloud's actions—not the murder of Wing Dreamer, not your abandonment, and not Sun Wing's harsh upbringing, deprived of his true parents! I know I should have stood up against Father Thundercloud, but I was so afraid of him. I have lived in fear of him ever since I was a young cub and now that he is gone, I am struggling to find ground of my own to stand upon. Certainly, I do not want my grandson to be executed! I ask you though, to consider who will raise his daughter by Talona. What of young Sky Talon? She must not be tainted by her mother's wrath!"

"My queen Sunsky and I will help to raise Sky Talon," Dreamspinner says. "With Sun Wing's help, of course. We will raise her to be a gryphon of great kindness and compassion. I am quite sure that her grandmother, Soundringer, will also be willing to help."

"Soundringer!" Windsinger and Sun Quest sputter in dismayed unison. Sun Quest beholds his damaged daughter, Talona, together with her mother Soundringer.

"As long as Windsinger is big enough to acknowledge past wrongs, I guess I'd better do it too," he exclaims finally, ambling over to tap beaks with Soundringer as a gesture of reconciliation.

"Talona's behavior is as much my fault as yours, Soundringer. I sired her because of a courtesy mating with you, but I've been anything but courteous. I should have supported you more with her upbringing. I am truly sorry."

Soundringer is so astonished at this unexpected apology that she cannot speak. She flutters her wings nervously but does not back away from her former lover.

"Sun Quest," she murmurs. "I forgive you if you and your family will also forgive me for my obnoxious behavior toward all of you—and especially you, Skystar. I engaged in much vicious rumor mongering against you and Sunsky. I now know that I was wrong. Sunsky should have been queen in spite of the hippogryph birth."

Mother Skystar moves toward her mate slowly until she is standing with him, facing their former nemesis together. "All is forgiven, Soundringer," she tells her without a trace of bitterness. "We will all support you in Talona's rehabilitation, as well as in the raising of your newborn granddaughter, Sky Talon."

Soundringer looks sorrowfully at Talona, huddled in a position of dejection and defeat. She is surrounded by her former minions, who have all turned against her. She glares in a sullen fashion at her mother but offers no further resistance.

The crowd has been listening intently to the dramas unfolding on the terrace, as if transfixed by them. Sunground is just as flabbergasted as anyone else by this sudden flurry of reconciliation. She decides to take the opportunity that the lull in passions has provided her, and she pushes herself to address the crowd once again. "Sister gryphons and kryphons! Brother opinici and keythongs! The time has come for you to decide. Will you support all of us on a path of forgiveness and reconciliation, as Queen Heartsong and the oracle Truth Speaker would have wanted? Or will you give in to your ravenous desires for revenge, as buzzards who feast on long-dead carrion?"

"I support you to the skies!" the physician Light Healer cheers. "Let the healing of our society begin! Let the light guide us into wisdom!"

"Come on, you idiots!" Mountain Rain shouts. "Support the new path! You know it's the only way to go if we're to recover from this madness."

The throng is silent for a moment. Then, one by one, each gryphon, opinicus, keythong, and kryphon proclaims individually his or her support for the new path into the future, each voice escalating into the next until they chant a chorus of "Yes! We support you!"

Sunground is deeply moved by their astounding collective resolve to venture forth into the unfamiliar skies of a new society, one that will eventually be based upon freedom and equality rather than upon privilege and power.

CHAPTER EIGHT

The Circle of Gratitude

The process of creating a new society is a slow and arduous one. Queenstar, the mother of Star Sailor, was reinstated as chief magistrate and tasked with creating a new governmental structure to unite the winged and the wingless, male and female, and bringing them together on an equal basis. She requested the aid of Skystar in interviewing all concerned parties and drafting a proposal.

Meanwhile, there is an almost unanimous belief among the gryphonic population that Sunground—now officially re-named Sunsky of the Mountains—should be queen, as prophesied by the oracle. Sunsky insists that they wait before proclaiming her leader.

"There must be power checks and balances before anyone takes over the reign," she explains. "I do not wish to engage in a selfish power grab."

"Don't worry, Sunny," Mountain Rain says. "With this slow-moving rock ball of a process you've put in place, we get it."

Sunsky is deeply grateful to both her sisters, Mountain Rain and Cloudhopper, who have acted as advisors to her. *It feels so wonderful to be home again,* Sunsky thinks. *Especially without fear.*

It is a feeling that Sunsky never thought she would ever experience again. Indeed, the inhabitants of Gryphonia are all experiencing such a deep sense of well-being that they have spontaneously formed groups to express their gratitude to the oracle and old Queen Heartsong for guiding the society into a new and hopeful age. These gratitude ceremonies have been held every morning since the Talonic Regime ended.

Sunsky waits patiently for her family members to arrive while she offers her own prayers of gratitude to the oracle. She knows they must choose a new oracle, but whom? Who could possibly fill such a sacred position? The only one who comes to mind is Light Healer, but she is already busy with her duties as a physician.

Her musings are interrupted by a whinny. From the skies, Moon Wing swoops in and lands near her mother, followed by the new foal, Moon Drop. Sunsky marvels at how proficient her new granddaughter is in her flight skills. After the crisis was over, Moon Wing and Groundsky traveled back to the hopha tunnel to collect their newborns.

The hophas transported the two babies back to Gryphonia in their airship, accompanied by old Egglight, Groundsky, and his newest mate, the young kryphon Fluff Feather. Grass Hopper, Pegasus, and Moon Wing accompanied the airship, each flying nearby it to allay any fears the gryphons might still hold toward the hophic airships.

From the time the two young ones toddled out of the airship, Sunsky has delighted in them. They are exquisite. Moon Drop is both black and white, having inherited the colors of her father, Pegasus, and her grandfather, Nightsky. As her mother predicted, the tiny foal had dropped into this world by moonlight, to everyone's surprise.

Moon Wing was outside the cavern at night, collecting grasses for the herd with the hopha sentinels, Seth and Sharriel. Suddenly, with very little warning, the filly plopped out upon the grass, the lunar beams of light shining on her piebald coat. Sharriel helped to rub down the filly. Thankfully, the female hopha was familiar with equine births, as she had attended many of them at her family's stable. The hopha male, Seth, ran back to the caverns to alert Night Lover and Pegasus, who rushed to the new mother's side. They soon determined that Moon Drop is a rare being indeed: She is a winged filly, perhaps the only one of her kind. Until her birth, all female horses were born wingless.

"When she is older and ready for the journey, Pegasus and I will take her to the hopha flatlands to see Papa's mother, Goldmare," Moon Wing tells them.

In the mean time, Moon Wing has chosen to remain with her mother Sunsky in Gryphonia, in spite of the fact that Night Lover and the other hippogryphs have long since departed to return to their home in the Valley of the Hippogryphs (no longer referred to as the Valley of Outcasts). Night Lover wished them all well but before she left, she participated in a family ceremony to honor the life of her gryphon mother, the late Wing Dreamer. In it, she and Dreamspinner acknowledged each other as brother and sister in a moving hippogryphic family ritual.

Even Windsinger, the father of Dreamspinner, attended the ceremony to atone for his silence in the face of Wing Dreamer's murder by Thundercloud. In a deeply gracious gesture, Night Lover unconditionally forgave Windsinger for his passive part in the sordid deed. Night Lover's generous act of forgiveness, Windsinger told them, had changed his heart forever.

As Sunsky contemplates the wonder of forgiveness, she is interrupted by two rowdy, rollicking youths. Groundsky chases his newfound opinicus brother, Sun Wing, who annoys Groundsky by flitting up into the air every time the keythong is about to pounce on him.

"No fair, Brother Sun Wing!" Groundsky grumbles. "I can't follow you into the air."

Sun Wing caws merrily in response. He is so much happier since he regained his freedom, Sunsky observes with deep relief.

The two young males are joined by the females Fluff Feather and Grass Hopper, who concentrate their efforts on a young cub with some very distinct physical characteristics. Amazingly, Grass Hopper gave birth to the cub inside the cavern, at the same time that Moon Wing was giving birth to her foal outside in the moonlight with Night Lover and Pegasus by her side.

Mother Skystar, having had experience birthing hippo-chicks when Moon Wing was born many sun revolutions ago, attended the birth of the new cub inside the cavern with the aid of Egglight and Fluff Feather. Meanwhile, Cloudhopper attempted to keep Groundsky as calm as possible under the circumstances.

The birth was a success, and Grass Hopper referred to the youngster as her little "cub-colt". The physician Light Healer told them, upon examination, that he is a "hippopinicus". In all her experience as a physician, she told them, she has never before seen such a combination of opinical-equine traits. The new little hippopinicus cub-colt was named Kingdreamer by his proud papa, Groundsky. He has the rear body of a winged horse, like the hippogryphs; but unlike them he has two rather elongated leonine forelimbs, similar to those of an opinicus except for the greater length of the front legs. He is a stark contrast to his sister hippogryphs, with their aquiline forelimbs and razor-sharp talons.

Young Kingdreamer, however, is oblivious to his highly unusual physical traits. He bounds in and pounces at his equally odd cousin, Moon Drop. The two of them gambol about, Moon Drop lifting herself off the ground every once in a while with her strong wings to avoid Kingdreamer's pounces. Kingdreamer growls in irritation at this, for although he has wings, he has not yet figured out how to use them.

"Don't worry, Kingdreamer," his mother Grass Hopper calls. "You will be flying after Moon Drop soon!"

Groundsky and Sun Wing stop their own game of tag to watch the youngsters engage in the same activity. Sky Talon, Sun Wing's tiny gryphon daughter, jumps into the fray fearlessly. True to her name, she extends her talons and leaps mightily into the air after Moon Drop, plopping back to the ground when her wings fail to keep her aloft.

"No tag for Sky Talon!" Egglight cries, hobbling along behind her charge. "Her wings are still far too tender—they could be damaged playing with those two big hippo-choals!"

Sunsky fondly remembers her old nanny's piercing screech from her own chickhood days. Egglight has always been extremely protective of her young charges.

"Fret not, Nanny Egglight!" the kryphon Fluff Feather says. "I'm sure Sky Talon is tougher than she appears."

"Now you listen here, young Fluff Feather!" Egglight scolds. "The way you and Master Groundsky have been carrying on, you'll be the next to give birth to one of these little creatures. You need to learn proper caretaking techniques!"

Fluff Feather groans. She originally ran away to the hopha lands to avoid being sterilized for life under the oppressive old regime, yet she is in no rush to have young ones of her own. Groundsky, however, jumps for joy at the prospect.

"Yes, my queen Fluff Feather!" he caws at her. "You are to be my first mate when I become king of the keythongs. It will be a true delight to provide my son Kingdreamer with a brother or sister! Rug-a-bug-bug!"

"Oh, humph-a-dumph-dumph, Groundsky!" Fluff Feather replies in consternation. "You as king and me as queen? When is that going to happen?"

"*If* you become king and queen, Master Rug-a-bug-bug and Mistress Humph-a-dumph-dumph!" Egglight chirrups at the pair. "You are both still young, and neither of you are ready for such lofty postings!"

"The oracle foretold it! The oracle foretold it!" Groundsky sings back at her. "Rug-a-bug-bug! I will become king one day, and Fluff Feather will be my kryphon queen! No more subservience for keythongs and kryphons, Nanny Egglight. No more sterilization. We may *all* mate, now!"

Egglight mutters to herself, not at all certain that she approves of certain aspects of the new equality.

Old Ground Paw joins her in her commiserations. He was recently chosen as chief advisor to the newly reinstated Council of Keythongs, along with the kryphon sage Fish Beak, who is creating the foundation for a brand new Council of Kryphons.

"These changes are a shock to the system for us elders, Egglight," Ground Paw says gently. "I hope you will join Fish Beak in her endeavor with the new kryphonic council. Your participation would be an asset to all of us, for the keythongs have never before had a sister council of wingless ones that we could turn to for support in our governance."

"A council of kryphons!" Egglight grumbles. "We wingless sisters are far less numerous than our wingless brothers. What need have we of our own council, separate from the keythonic one? What is next, a Council of Hippopinici for young Master Kingdreamer? A-aaaa-aaaa-kkkt! We all seem to have become kingdreamers and queendreamers. What folly!"

Sunsky overhears the conversation of the two elders. "Is that such a bad thing, Nanny Egglight?" Sunsky asks. "Now, all the youngsters may dream of great things!"

"I think, Mistress Sunsky," Egglight responds crisply, addressing her in the same manner that she did when Sunsky was a chick, "that every society needs its ordinary grounded folk. We cannot all be taking off on flights of fancy, thinking we will be queens or kings. We cannot all be rulers! Some of us must focus our energies on the needs of others rather than on our own individual dreams."

"Oh, Nanny Egglight! You haven't changed a bit. Didn't you have dreams, back when you used to care for Mother Skystar?"

"Certainly not!" Egglight says. "My only dream was to raise your mother properly whilst Queen Heartsong attended to her reign and then to mind you and your sisters, young scamps that you were, followed by your sisters' two saucy chicks, followed by the great whopping escapade that we have recently managed to survive. My only task now, at my advanced age, is to advise your own youngsters in the raising of their newborns. That has been my life, and I care not a hoot for the council!"

"Still, Egglight," Ground Paw persists, "we would benefit so greatly from your experience, and you would not need to give up much of your time with the youngsters, no indeed. We are working on the creation of an Elders' Advisory Council, so that all we who have grown up under the old rules can advise those younger on what is of value and what has been less than useful. I can tell you that from what I have heard, there is amongst the keythongery and the kryphonery an almost unanimous agreement on banning compulsory sterilization. Who would have thought that could ever occur?"

"R-kkk-t!" Egglight chirps. "I'm afraid it's far too late for you and me, Ground Paw."

"Perhaps for reproductive purposes, but..." Ground Paw's voice trails off, leaving the rest unsaid.

"Ground Paw, you are far too sly for your own good!" Egglight admonishes.

Sunsky peers at the two elders in amazement. Was it possible that Ground Paw and Egglight had harbored dreams of a secret courtship all these sun revolutions? She knows better than to ask Egglight, but perhaps Ground Paw might tell her now that the social barriers between the winged and the wingless are lifting.

Sunsky is excited. Everywhere she turns, she sees evidence of new life. Chicks and cubs are being born, new councils are being created, and elders are re-kindling lost desires. For the first time in ages, she feels great optimism for all their futures.

"Sunsky!" her elder sister, Cloudhopper, clucks. "Are you off in the mind sky again? We've been calling your name repeatedly."

Cloudhopper and the rest of the family gathers around her, all of them finally reunited after their grueling ordeal.

"I'm sorry, Cloudhopper," Sunsky says. "I was just marveling at the new changes in our society and the new life with which we have all been blessed! It's almost like a dream."

"Listen, Sunsky, Queen of the Mountains," Mountain Rain says. "Being a ruler is serious business. You can't be dreaming all the time! You'd better get ready to do some reigning and leave the rainbow dreaming to my chick."

"I can be the queen, Mama!" Rainbow Dreamer chirps. "And you can help. You can get ready to do some mountain reigning."

"Chuckle, chuckle, caw!" Mountain Rain replies dryly. "Everyone's a jester these days."

"We're all in a cheerful mood, Rain," Skystar says. "It's been so long since we've all been together and our family seems to be ever-expanding, what with Moon Wing, Groundsky, Grass Hopper, Fluff Feather, and the youngsters joining us here in Gryphonia. I'm glad that Moon Wing and Grass Hopper have chosen to stay here rather than return to the valley."

"And don't forget our young kinglet, Sun Wing," Sun Quest says. "Since Windsinger and I have become friends, there's no stopping us from spending time with him and little Sky Talon, our newest addition."

"Of course, Dear One, of course!" Skystar replies. "We have so many of them now that it's hard to keep track, but Sunsky is right. We have so much to be grateful for."

"The only one who isn't grateful for all that's come to pass is Talona," Cloudhopper says. "I've just been to visit Soundringer. She says that Talona is still depressed because she's lost so much power and must now be held under home den arrest."

"Well, she needs to be under some kind of arrest," Mountain Rain says. "She's lucky to have the luxury of a mere home den arrest after what she did to destroy just about everyone's lives! Why, she would have killed Sunsky, Star Sailor, and me if she'd remained in charge."

Sunsky rustles her feathers slightly at the mention of Talona. Like Cloudhopper, she visited Soundringer, but Talona refused to see her hated half-sister. Soundringer told her that she flies into a rage every time someone mentions the name "Sunsky".

"I'm sorry, Sunsky," Soundringer told her sadly on one such occasion. "I'm afraid that Talona will only let me and the physician near her. Light Healer has been helping her with some ancient soul-healing measures, but she says the rehabilitation will take a long time. We must all be patient."

Sunsky thanked Soundringer for making the attempt and went on her way in great disappointment. She had so hoped that, with love and forgiveness, Talona would recover from her madness. Unfortunately, it did not seem quite as simple as that. Light Healer advised both Sunsky and Cloudhopper, the only family members with any inclination to reconcile with Talona, to focus instead on their own healing and that of their family.

"The only way you can help Talona," Light Healer told them, "is to heal yourselves. Remember, you and your family members have been through a terrible trauma."

The physician gave them all meditative exercises to practice so that they could care for their own souls in the wake of what is now referred to as the Talonic Reign of Darkness. Sunsky's great consolation is that the rest of her society is responding well to the changes.

Even the terrifying tormentor, Ring Screecher, has success-fully rehabilitated her life. Light Healer insisted that, although she would be kept under strict surveillance, Ring Screecher should also be given an opportunity to return to her old occu-pation of hunting for the community. The physician realized that, to atone for her torturous actions, the one-eyed gryphon must begin to make a positive contribution to society. She was therefore allowed to reclaim her old name, Night Hunter, and return to her true calling as a nocturnal predator.

Indeed, all Talonic loyalists receive an amnesty under the new government. Everyone will get the chance to right the wrongs that they were forced either to permit or to perpetrate in the name of loyalty to the queen. After enduring Talonic practices for what seemed like an eternity, Gryphonia is finally ready to evolve into a somewhat more enlightened society—or so they all hope. Indeed, hope is what inspires Sunsky at this moment, watching the young ones play and listening to the old ones chatter.

They are now ready to arrange themselves into the Daily Circle of Gratitude. Before long, Nightsky and Pegasus, together with Jophriel, Roonen, and Halona, arrive for another visit in their by now less-feared airship. Today, they have brought along two other hopha family members: Roonen's mother Andriel Oakshade follows the family with the couple's younger child, a little male named Falcon.

Falcon gives a squeal of delight and runs to play with Moon Drop, Kingdreamer, and Sky Talon, his reddish-gold mane flapping in the breeze. The tiny two-foot mixes fearlessly with the youngsters of other species, hardly seeming to notice the vast difference between them and him.

Andriel, an older hopha female with graying hair and a kindly sparkle in her sky-blue eyes, brings a large container of fruits and grasses that she puts in the center of the circle as a gift. The youngsters jump in to nibble at it straight away, but they are shooed away by Egglight and their parents, who tell them to wait until the ceremony finishes.

Andriel directs Jophriel to translate her speech into the gryphonic language: "O, great and noble gryphons, opinici and others!" she says. "My family and I have come to join your Circle of Gratitude, if you will permit it."

Sunsky nods her assent.

"We, the Oakshade family, pledge our support for your new government," Andriel continues. "Please accept the small gift that we have brought along as a peace offering. Know that we will continue to work tirelessly with our own hophic government to ensure that it is rendered illegal to use any form of airship weaponry to attack gryphons, hippogryphs, or anyone else. The hopha Jack Warford is now being held accountable for his deplorable actions during your crisis, and he and his family send their most heart-felt apologies."

Sunsky bows before the Oakshade matriarch, signaling her acceptance of the gift, the pledge, and the apology from the Warfords. "All is forgiven, Mother Andriel, and we are truly grateful to your family and all the other hophas who were willing to help us, including the Warford family."

Andriel returns Sunsky's gesture. "Goldmare, the mother of Nightsky, sends her greetings, and we invite you and your family to visit us in the flatlands to meet her when you are ready. We will prepare the surrounding populace so that there will be no fear of your arrival."

Sunsky is overwhelmed by emotion at the thought of gryphonic beings traveling freely to visit hophas. Jophriel and Roonen have acted as unofficial ambassadors to Gryphonia since the fall of the old regime, helping to work out the territorial boundaries of areas where hophas may travel and sacred places where they may not.

One of the conditions that the newly formed Council of Gryphons and Opinici insisted upon with regard to hophic air travel is that their "magic lightning" technology be disabled when flying within gryphonic territory. Jophriel and Roonen went one step further and made a rule within their own research team that no airship used for flight within the gryphonic territory can be equipped with weaponry of any kind. Sunsky proposed to the chief magistrate that the reverse also be true, that a gryphonic law prohibit any winged being from attacking hophic airships.

The hophas position themselves within the circle, and they all begin to chant a gryphonic prayer of gratitude that Light Healer taught them. As the chants echo throughout the mountain skies, Sunground feels a healing wind pass through her twice-injured wing. She remembers the stormy winds that deposited her long ago into the gentle care of Nightsky, and the stormy violence of the hophic weaponry that shot her down into the vicious clutches of the Talonic regime. Both events resulted in the disabling of her wing, but now the wind rustles softly through her.

She feels the presence of those in the Beyond-Sky, of Queen Heartsong and King Lightning Bolt, Truth Speaker, Grass Grazer, and Mountain Pounder, the courageous father of Nightsky. She even senses the presence of old Thundercloud, the once-ruthless opinicus, who is now deeply humbled in the Beyond-Sky by the forgiveness of his one-time prey, Wing Dreamer.

Wing Dreamer's presence now fills her. She feels her deep and generous spirit as soft feathers surrounding her in a nest. "You shall be the next oracle," her quiet voice whispers, "and you shall aid in bringing peace and healing to all our societies."

Sunsky opens her eyes, shocked. "What?" she asks aloud. "How can I be the reigning queen and the oracle at the same time?"

"It is true," the voice of Truth Speaker agrees. "You have already been functioning in the role of visionary for your people. I choose you, Sunsky of the Mountains, as my successor. I choose you with the blessings of your heart's song and the truth of your speaking, and I choose you as the dream of your own wings."

As the chants of gratitude around her give way to the profound silence of spirit, Sunsky surrenders to this mysterious poetic voice that has arrived at the entrance of her heart through the voices of the sky beyond this one.

CHAPTER NINE

Ground and Sky United

As the gratitude ceremony ends, the great Chieftain Star Sailor of the Flock of the Sacred Feather, the replacement organization for the now-defunct Royal Gryphonic Air Squadron, swoops in.

"My friends!" she announces, "The chief magistrate, my mother Queenstar, wishes to see all of you—especially Sunsky. She will be landing here, within your family circle, to share with you a proposal."

There is much excited chirping and cawing amongst the family members as they anticipate Queenstar's mysterious proposal.

"It's about the queenship, Sunsky, I'm sure of it!" Cloudhopper says.

"How is Sunsky ever going to be ready for all the administrative tasks that a queenship entails?" Mountain Rain complains. "She needed to receive the training that Grandmother Heartsong wasted on Talona."

"It wasn't Grandmother Heartsong's fault, Rain!" Cloudhopper cries.

"I never said it was!"

Mother Skystar screeches to halt the skirmish of words. "Stop it, both of you! This is about the present and future, not the past. I suggest that we leave the past behind us and concentrate on what the chief magistrate has to say. We all know that her position of leadership is only temporary, until we have a governmental structure we can all agree upon. I have been working with her long and hard on drafting this proposal, so you all need to listen up!"

"Excuse me, Skystar," Star Sailor says politely. "I have another announcement before my mother arrives to discuss the proposal. The former members of the Royal Air Squadron who were attacked by Warford's airship and who have been rehabilitating near the caverns under the care of the hopha physicians, are now ready to come home. They will be escorted back by my flock members. I have explained to them that Talona's regime has collapsed under the weight of public resistance and that a new government will be formed to take its place, this time with much more emphasis on justice and equality. I am proud to report that they are jubilant about the change and are eager to return to duty under the Flock of the Sacred Feather."

There is a chorus of congratulatory clucks and caws toward Star Sailor, who has regained so much of the pride and dignity that Talona's regime stole from her.

As they celebrate the formation of the Flock of the Sacred Feather, a large golden-feathered Gryphon lands in their midst. The excited beings all gather around her.

"The Chief Magistrate, Her Honor, Queenstar!" Star Sailor intones, drawing herself up into the dutiful pose of a flock chieftain.

"Your Honor!" they all cry, bowing before her.

"All right, all right!" Queenstar replies impatiently. "There's no need to bow. I'm not the queen, nor do I have any intention of taking over that hallowed post. I intend to return to the judicial branch of this government as soon as gryphonly possible. We have a mess of new laws to process, the lawgivers and I. To that end, I am here to announce our new proposal." She pauses to regard the hophas present.

"We, Your Honor, would like to request that Jophriel and Roonen Oakshade and their family be present to hear of this proposal. They have become family members to us," Sunsky declares. "And also the hippogryphs Moon Wing and Grass Hopper, as well as the winged horses Nightsky, Pegasus, and Moon Drop."

"Yes, yes," Queenstar replies. "As well as the hippo-opinicus and the whoppo-whip-pingagus, and whatever new combinations of beings your mad brood is planning to sweep on into this creative new social experiment of ours. Believe me, Sunsky, it has not been easy for your mother and me and the rest of the council appointees to implement some of the changes that you want."

"I realize that, Your Honor," Sunsky responds. "I am truly grateful to you for being willing to take on this complicated task. Have you any recommendations on how we should handle the queenship question?"

"Yes, I do. What do you think we have been spending our time trying to determine? We have interviewed hundreds of gryphonic beings and conducted a poll among thousands more. Everyone believes that you should have some sort of visionary role because of your special Beyond-Sky relationship with the oracle. Where there is disagreement, however, it is over the fact that your practical and administrative skills are almost non-existent. You have spent most of your adult life in exile with the hippogryphs, whose society is a simple tribal one, and you have not even been a part of *their* governing system. Still, we all believe that the queenship should go to Heartsong's line, and that is why I have come up with the idea of a trinity queenship."

"A trinity queenship?" Sunsky echoes. "What in the name of Gryphonia is that? A queenship of three?"

There is much flapping of wings and cawing as the family reacts to the possibility of a three-part leadership.

"There will actually be a six-point leadership structure, with the contribution of the two opinicus consorts, Dreamspinner and Sun Quest," Queenstar explains. "They will be given specific and active leadership roles with respect to the other opinici in our society, and they will be training the former king consort, Sun Wing, on the duties of a future king. You did request a structure that includes both genders, did you not?"

Sunsky bobs her head, dumbfounded, as Sun Wing and Groundsky jump about in sheer jubilation. "We will both be kings, Brother Sun Wing!" Groundsky caws. "Rug-a-bug!"

"Rug-a-bug-shush, Groundsky!" Egglight hisses. "That goes for you too, Sun Wing. Listen to the rest of the magistrate's proposal. What of the queenship, Your Honor?"

"The queenship," the Magistrate continues, "will be divided into three parts—a trinity, as its name suggests. Skystar, the daughter of Heartsong, has a much better grasp of the daily administrative tasks that take up a ruler's time, so she shall be named Administrator Skystar, Queen of Practical Tasks. You, Sunsky, have a gift for seeing the overall vision of the new path on which we will be embarking, and we know that you have been in contact with the oracle and the old queen in the sky beyond this one. We have been struggling with what to do about the appointment of a new oracle. Light Healer has been performing the roles of both the physician and oracle ever since Truth Speaker's death and she is utterly exhausted. We therefore propose that you take on a kind of dual role, minus the administrative tasks that are the responsibility of your mother. We ask you, Sunsky of the Mountains, to be our new oracle queen."

Sunsky stares at the magistrate, flabbergasted and speechless. It is as Wing Dreamer and Truth Speaker told her. She is to be oracle and queen, all without her having done or said anything to bring it about! This proposal to the magistrate came from the gryphonic people, she realizes with humility, and somehow they have all come together in the formation of this conclusion by some mysterious, collective spirit.

Sunsky closes her eyes for a moment and sees Queen Heartsong and King Lightning Bolt, handing her the ancient Scepter of Rulers that has been handed down queen to queen for generations. She opens her eyes and, filled with renewed purpose, grants the magistrate's request. "I accept in all humility this sacred responsibility, Chief Magistrate."

"Good," Queenstar replies in a business-like tone. "You will be the one to receive the Scepter of Rulers in the upcoming coronation."

After the cheering caws have died down, Mountain Rain asks an important question. "What about the third part of this thing? Is it going to be you, Magistrate? Or Star Sailor?"

"Certainly not!" Queenstar snaps. "I have told you, my intention is to return to my legal duties. As for my daughter, she has absolutely no desire to leave her new posting as chieftain of the Flock of the Sacred Feather. She is a gryphon of the sky, not a ruler!"

"Who then, Magistrate?" Cloudhopper asks.

"Mountain Rain," Queenstar answers. "You have shown great leadership in your role as one of the three leaders of the peace delegation, together with your sister Sunsky and my Star Sailor. Therefore, I propose that you be the third member of this trinity, as you are a granddaughter of Heartsong. You will be the royal ambassador to the Gryphonic-Opinical Councils, once we have determined which appointees will be accepted by the collective as councilors. I understand from Star Sailor that you, like your Mother Skystar, possess a strong sense of the practical and a most assertive way of getting your point across. You will be the perfect liaison between the oracle queen's visionary proposals and the various councils' practical implementations of such."

"But am I a diplomat or a queen?" Mountain Rain stammers, overwhelmed by a crisis of confidence for perhaps the first time in her life.

"You will be both," the magistrate explains. "You will be the premiere oracle queen's appointee to the councils. Your job will be to explain in practical terms the spiritual wing-ding-ding that the oracle queen has been spouting. Do you accept this task, Mountain Rain, queen sister?"

"I..." Mountain Rain hesitates as her sisters huddle around to encourage her. "Yes, I will, but I'll need a queen's appointee advisor, a kind of liaison between the queen's appointee to the councils and the oracle queen, to prevent the queen's appointee from tearing the oracle queen to pieces when she churns out too much spiritual wing-ding-ding. I nominate queen sister Cloudhopper for that job."

"What?" Cloudhopper squawks. "I thought this was supposed to be a trinity queenship? Would this not be turning it into a quadrinity queenship or whatever? I mean, I'm completely confused by it all!"

"You'll get used to a permanent state of confusion when you enter into this leadership business," the magistrate responds drily. "Mountain Rain, you may appoint as many queen advisors as you wish, but they would still come under the auspices of the third leadership. You and Cloudhopper may share that responsibility, while Skystar will form the second queenship. Sunsky will be at the pinnacle of the structure, as she forms the premiere queenship. You will all be connected, like a triangle—is that as clear as a thundercloud in a windstorm?"

The three sisters bob their heads in unison, thunderstruck. Who would have thought that they would *all* inherit the duties of the queenship?

Sun Wing has been hopping up and down as the magistrate explains the queenship trinity.

"What about the three opinici, Magistrate?" he asks. "Will we have any *real* ruling power?"

"Yes," Queenstar says. "The triple kingship will operate in concert with the queenship trinity. Sun Quest will be the senior king, Dreamspinner the intermediate king, and you, Sun Wing, will be the junior king in training. You will all have input, but you must do so in a way that supports your queenship counterparts. They, in turn, have a duty to support you.

Your part of the rule will include the concerns of all opinici, as you will be working closely with the new Council of Opinici. You will also have the responsibility of consulting with your brother keythongs on the Council of Keythongs. Likewise, the gryphonic queenship will be responsible for consulting with not only the Gryphonic Council but also with the soon-to-be-created Kryphonic Council and queenship trinity."

"What of the keythonic kingship, Your Honor?" Groundsky shouts, unable to contain himself any longer. He is as excited as his brother Sun Wing.

"Likewise, a keythonic kingship trinity will also be created, and it will function as the gryphon-opinicus structure does. The keythong kings and kryphon queens will be responsible to both the councils of the keythong and to that of the kryphons. When we bring the winged and wingless governmental structures together, they collectively become a twelve-point process in four partnerships—gryphon, opinicus, keythong, and kryphon. Simple, eh?"

"Clear as a thundercloud in a windstorm, Chief Mag!" Groundsky cries. "Rag-a-bag-bag, three caws for the Mag!"

"Groundsky!" Egglight scolds him. "How dare you behave in such a raucous fashion toward the chief magistrate! Ground Paw, take charge of this youth!"

Queenstar interrupts any chidings that Ground Paw was about to give the rambunctious young keythong.

"Actually, Egglight," the magistrate announces, seemingly invigorated by Groundsky's cheers, "I should mention that you were nominated by Ground Paw and your old kryphon friend, Fish Beak, to be on the Elders' Advisory Council and furthermore, that your nomination was accepted."

Egglight clucks in consternation. "That sly old buzzard, Fish Beak! She never even gave me a choice about it. And as for you, Ground Paw! You knew about this all along when you pretended to convince me to join the council voluntarily."

"Fish Beak made it clear that she wanted you," Ground Paw stammers. "You know how hard it is to deny Fish Beak what she wants."

Egglight grumbles a response but offers no more resistance to the idea. Sunsky believes that the elderly nanny is secretly pleased to be included in the council after all this time, although she hates to admit it.

Skystar and the magistrate confer for a moment before Queenstar continues to explain the radical changes being made to their society. "All right, then! I have one more thing to tell you, and then I'm going home to have my morning meal with my family for a change. It is concerning all these beings who have not traditionally been friends or visitors to Gryphonia. I have no wish to offend any of you, but I am referring specifically to hophas, hippogryphs, and horses, winged or otherwise. Since we are likely to be spending much more time with these creatures under the reign of the new oracle queen, we need to have a diplomatic structure in place to help the gryphonic beings to better understand the minds of the others and vice versa. Therefore, Skystar has proposed that we have an embassy here in Gryphonia Central, whereby appointed ambassadors to our territory can lay out any issues they may have with us."

"But what if we don't have any issues with you?" Moon Wing interjects, not wanting to be left out of the conversation. "After all, hippogryphs are partly gryphonic."

"There are bound to be issues that come up between our peoples, Moon Wing, and during those times when there are none, the ambassadors can educate us as to the ways of their people. Jophriel and Roonen have been the acting hopha ambassadors, but they will need to go home again to tend to their family."

"I will be the hophic ambassador, Grandmother Skystar!" the young hopha Halona says. "I'm single! I can do it!"

"I nominate you, Halona!" Moon Wing agrees. "And I'll be the hippogryph ambassador..."

"Not so fast, young ones!" Queenstar says. "Neither of you are prepared for such postings, but we will keep you both in mind for the future. As for the present, Skystar has already spoken with Queen Night Lover, and she has agreed to send an ambassador, Soul Flower, as well as two assistants, Nectar Sipper and Joker. I hope Joker takes this assignment seriously."

"She will," Sunsky says. "All three of them will. They joined us in our peace march up the mountain, and they have all earned my highest recommendation."

"Excellent!" the magistrate replies. "You are showing promising leadership skills, Queen Sunsky. Skystar will, of course, continue to provide you with additional training in this matter."

Sunsky chuckles inwardly. Mother Skystar has been providing her with 'additional training' all her life, and she doesn't expect that the matriarch will stop doing so in this matter or any other.

"But Magistrate!" Moon Wing bleats, interrupting Sunsky's thoughts. "What about an ambassadorial team from the hopha? I highly recommend Jophriel and Roonen."

Queenstar turns to Jophriel.

"Roonen and I will be advisors to the new team," Jophriel explains, "but we cannot live here indefinitely. Roonen wants to return to the farm, and we need to spend time as a family with Halona and Falcon, although both of them are insisting that we visit here frequently. Of course, we will do that, but Halona will need to catch up on the education that she has missed while accompanying us on this journey."

"I would have missed the most important education of a lifetime had I not come with you!" Halona exclaims. "But do tell us who the hophic ambassadors will be, then."

"We have decided," Jophriel responds, "in concert with Nightsky, that the hophas and the equines should form a joint embassy so that the horses have some form of moral support. Many gryphons, after all, still fear them due to the various myths and superstitions that surround winged horses. Nightsky agreed to be the equine ambassador, and he will work closely with the hophic team to advise them on gryphonic thought and behavior."

"And the hopha ambassadors?" Halona persists.

She is interrupted by her little brother, Falcon, who jumps up and down cawing like an opinicus, calling out, "Uncle Jack! Uncle Jack! Uncle J-aaaa-aaaa-kkk-raaa-kkk-ttt!"

"Falcon!" Roonen chides him, before turning his attention back to the assembled group. "You all better rest on your haunches for this one. The Warford family has volunteered to be the new ambassadorial team, should you agree to it."

"What?!" Dreamspinner squawks. "Jack Warford? The one who shot down my queen and many others with his magic lightning? Surely you won't support this idea, Roonen?"

"It wasn't me who thought it up!" Roonen replies. "Don't start your feathers flapping at me, Dreamspinner! This embassy posting is a governmental thing, and therefore we had to file a request with our own government. Since Warford is the only one of us to already have a role within the government, he was deemed the best one to do this, along with his wife."

"The actual ambassador to the gryphonic peoples will be Clariel Warford," Jophriel informs them, "not Jack. He will be the liaison between the hophic embassy and the hophic government. With regard to gryphonic affairs at least, he will be taking orders from his mate now. Also, they will be aided by their adult son, Riva, who is like his mother—fascinated by the gryphonic culture."

"But will Warford not be punished, then?" Dreamspinner asks. "After what he has done, how can we trust him, even as a liaison aide?"

"Believe me, Dreamspinner, he's already received his punishment from his wife," Roonen says. "He's going to issue a formal apology to the gryphonic society as soon as he arrives."

Sunsky voices her approval of the plan. "This is good news, Dreamspinner! It means that Warford will have the opportunity to learn that we are not the savage 'tiger-canaries' that he thought we were. We now have an opportunity to change the minds of hophas such as Jack Warford, and I believe that we will work well with his mate Clariel and their son, Riva. Remember, it was Clariel and Riva who helped convince him to cease his hostilities."

"Very well, my love," Dreamspinner says. "If this is your wish, then I will obey it in spite of my misgivings about Jack Warford."

"Very well, indeed!" Queenstar echoes. "Now that we have announced the new changes, let the ground and sky be united in an unprecedented alliance! And, I am leaving to join my family for our breakfast. We shall see you all at the Changing of the Scepter Ceremony!"

The chief magistrate flaps breezily out of their presence, followed by her dutiful daughter Star Sailor.

CHAPTER TEN

The Scepter of Rulers

It is unbelievable to Sunsky what has transpired in gryphonic society within such a short period. Here she is, back at the same public terrace upon which she was to have been executed. Now, she is here for a far nobler purpose: to accept the Scepter of Rulers and to be sworn in as the first oracle queen.

Her mother and two sisters are by her side. Behind her stands her opinicus king, Dreamspinner, whom she has taken as her official first mate. Her noble father Sun Quest stands proudly behind Skystar, while Sun Wing the young opinicus stands behind his Aunts, Mountain Rain and Cloudhopper. Surrounding all of them is the rest of the family: Moon Wing, Groundsky, Grass Hopper, Pegasus, Fluff Feather, Rainbow Dreamer, Luck Wisher, old Ground Paw, and the newly appointed councilor to the Elders' Advisory Council, old Egglight. Egglight is at present fulfilling her usual role of nanny, tending to the newest members of the clan, Moon Drop, Kingdreamer, and Sky Talon.

She will have quite a job on her talons, Sunsky thinks, *trying to keep the young ones still during the ceremony.* Already, she has enlisted the help of Ground Paw in keeping the infants entertained while they are waiting for the hallowed ceremony to begin.

The terrace is lined with royal members of the Flock of the Sacred Feather, led by the Great Chieftain Star Sailor. The mother of Star Sailor, Queenstar the chief magistrate, stands in front of them ready to perform the ancient rites. Beside her is the physician and acting oracle, Light Healer.

A crowd of gryphonic beings has gathered, and it stretches far out across and beyond the central gathering area. Within the crowd there are not only high ranking members of gryphonic families, but also those from the former lower classes, as well as the newly enfranchised keythongs and kryphons.

To Sunsky's immense joy, Night Lover and her troop of hippogryphs have also arrived for the coronation, responding to her earlier invitation relayed to them by the new hippogryph ambassador, Soul Flower.

It is unprecedented in the entire history of Gryphonia to have such a diverse population in attendance, and it also includes hophas and horses. Jophriel, Roonen, and Andriel Oakshade stand among the other beings, together with the two children, Halona and little Falcon. Both treat the occasion of being surrounded by so many gryphonic beings as a perfectly normal occurrence.

In fact, the entire group of hophas that were a part of the peace delegation attends, including the new ambassador, Clariel Warford and her aides, Jack and Riva.

Standing beside Jophriel and Roonen is the dark, beautiful Nightsky, an unofficial mate of the new queen, and his wingless mother, Goldmare. Goldmare, an exquisite golden mare as her name suggests, made the arduous trek part way up the mountain in order to be here, but it was necessary for the hophas to fly her in the rest of the way in a large airship.

The gryphonic populace has been dealing well with this odd assortment of beings, to Sunsky's immense relief. There have been no skirmishes or tussles between the various groups and for that, she is eternally grateful.

Jophriel, Roonen, and Clariel have done a great deal to help prepare gryphonic society for the event. Educational talks were arranged, whereby members of the various groups speak to gryphons about their ways and culture. Ambassador Soul Flower of the hippogryphs was the first outsider to speak at one of these information sessions. The sessions were well attended, for many gryphonic beings are fascinated by the hippogryphs, ever since the whole flock landed bravely in their midst to stand in solidarity with them over the governmental change.

Gradually, although there is still much more work to be done in the area of education, the gryphons have nonetheless been learning to accept the new beings in their midst. Not everyone is pleased with the changes but most realize that it is much preferable to the Talonic Reign of Terror.

Groups have also sprung up among the gryphons that are dedicated to preserving the "good old traditions" of gryphonic culture and to advocating for a more conservative approach to outsiders. These conservative groups fear the influence of the other species.

Sunsky realizes that she must, as queen, reach out to these groups and create a dialogue, so that they feel that the governing body is willing to listen to their point of view and consider it. It is vital that they not feel isolated from the rest of society.

She knows that it will not be an easy task to bring all the differing viewpoints into the councils to arrive at compromises, but at least they have begun to build the groundwork for such cooperation.

And, she thinks, *I will have Mother Skystar and my sisters to help guide me, as well as the three opinicus kings. I will not be alone in this queenship.* Indeed, she has never really been alone, for she has been guided from within by the voices of her grandmother, the oracle, Grass Grazer, Wing Dreamer, and above all, her own heart's song.

A bellow sounds from above, and the crowd members flap their wings in appreciation. The sound of their feathery applause is like a mountain wind rippling through the morning air.

The chief magistrate, followed by the physician-oracle, Light Healer, ascends into the air and flies around Gryphonia Central three times, as tradition dictates must be done at a coronation. They both land after they have flown their third circle, the magistrate giving another screech as the pair lands in front of the new queen-to-be and her family.

Star Sailor follows the same pattern of flight, leading her honor guard of twelve members of the Flock of the Sacred Feather three times around the mountain. They land upon the terrace, surrounding the royal family members. The flock members and their leader then snap into an attentive and dutiful pose. Star Sailor, her full plumage having grown back to its former glory, plucks a feather from her wing and gives it to Chief Magistrate Queenstar. She takes the feather and gingerly lays it before Sunsky.

The feather signifies the support of the flock for the new queen and her royal family. Sunsky takes it in her beak and gives it to her keythong son Groundsky, whose job it is to hold the sacred feather for his mother while the ceremony is in progress. He holds it in his beak proudly, standing stock-still as the family awaits the presentation of the scepter.

"Gryphons, opinici, keythongs, kryphons, and all others assembled here!" Queenstar intones. "We are here to accept and witness the ceremony of the Scepter of Rulers, which will officially recognize Sunsky of the Mountains as our queen. Before we do, however, I ask all of you assembled if anyone here has just cause to believe that Sunsky should not be queen."

A period of silence ensues that seems to go on forever. Many of the assembled beings cast furtive glances around, as if expecting some interruption. The tension is unbearable. Sunsky knows that there must be some traditionalists who oppose her reign, but they seem hesitant to express this in front of the throng.

"Fellow gryphons!" Sunsky finally bellows, taking an assertive step forward. "I know that the prospect of my being the queen upsets some of you. I ask you to make your viewpoints known to us. I assure you, I will not mistreat any who oppose my reign. Rather, I want to include you and listen to your voices so that when we do move forward, we may do so in such a way that no one feels excluded from the process."

The majority of gryphons flap their wings in approval, but one former leader of the now-defunct Royal Gryphonic Air Squadron does not applaud. River Wind steps forward to speak. "Sunsky of the Mountains!" she calls, amid screeches of disapproval from the crowd and cries to *keep quiet*. Many gryphonic beings remember how River Wind remained loyal to Talona until the end of her reign, and they resent her for it.

"Listen to River Wind, sisters and brothers!" Sunsky says. "We were all once unwitting allies of the old regime. None of us can claim complete innocence except for the very young. Speak, River Wind!"

"Thank you, Queen-Designate Sunsky," River Wind says. The hoots of derision die down. "I now realize that I once supported a cruel dictator, but you all know that loyalty is important to me and to my family. I therefore pledge that I will be as loyal to this queen as I was to the last one! The great majority of people want Sunsky as their queen and I bow to their wisdom, in spite of my misgivings about this new system of government. As a traditionalist, however, I believe that gryphons should not mate with any but opinici, and I firmly feel they should not mate even with keythongs. Once the new laws are approved, I worry that many kinds of unorthodox pairings will occur with increasing frequency."

Out of the corner of her eye, Sunsky can see her keythong son Groundsky trembling. He is obviously fighting to stop himself from bursting into caws of triumph. He knows that to open his beak and to drop the sacred feather would not bode well for the reign.

"River Wind!" she calls, preemptively interrupting Groundsky before he can give in to temptation. "I respect your point of view and I know that many of you feel this way, although none but River Wind has had the courage to state it."

River Wind cocks her head in surprise. No one has described her as "courageous" since her service to Talona ended. She has been granted complete amnesty from her role in serving the old regime, as have all the others who served under Talona. Nonetheless, the greater society has derided all traditionalists who reluctantly supported Talona's reign.

"One of the reasons we have begun the process of creating ambassadorial postings for other beings such as hippogryphs and hophas," Sunsky explains, "is that we wish to help all of our peoples to understand each other so that there will be no violence between us. Will there be more matings with hippogryphs or horses as a result? Perhaps, but as we get to know our sister hippogryphs and the equines, this will seem less and less threatening to us. My Moon Wing has been a joy to me ever since she was born! I would make the same decision to birth and raise her myself if I was given the chance to return to the past."

Moon Wing utters a cry of joy and steps forward to join her. "We are nothing to be afraid of, great and noble gryphons!" she calls to the astounded audience. "Did we make war upon you when we came to support the end of Talona's reign? No! We stood peacefully amid the chaos. We held the space between peace and war, as my father Nightsky says. We are born of you! We are a part of you, whether you choose to accept it or not."

A rustling of feathers greets Moon Wing's bold impertinence.

"We no longer quibble with the fact of your birth, Princess Moon Wing!" River Wind says. "But, my sister gryphons, do we really want to have hippogryphs joining our society and perhaps ruling over us one day?"

Sunsky realizes that she cannot allow Moon Wing to take over the proceedings, so she gently nudges her back a bit with the help of Mother Skystar.

"My apologies!" Sunsky calls. "My daughter would certainly like to rule, but today is not the day."

The throng bursts out in laughter, and the tension is broken. The chief magistrate, however, is not amused. "All right, all right!" she booms, irritated with the delay. "Enough hilarity for one day! The traditionalists' point has been taken, but the law-givers have determined that in this case, the queenship must be offered to the one who was originally first-in-line to the Stone Throne. In addition, the law has now changed with respect to a gryphon who births a hippogryph: The clause within section nine of the Gryphonic Code, that forbids such a gryphon to reign, has been struck down as archaic and discriminatory."

"I have spoken my piece, O Magistrate!" River Wind replies. "I shall speak of the matter no more, yet the issue I have raised will still be present in spite of the new laws."

"We thank you for your concerns, River Wind," Sunsky says. "We will all work through them together, over time."

"Very well!" exclaims the magistrate crisply. "Now, if there are no other statements, let us get on with it!"

There is silence as they wait for another interruption. When none comes, Queenstar takes it as unanimous agreement and recommences the ceremony.

"This ceremony will not only be the coronation of one queen but of a trinity of queens. Sunsky will be reigning monarch, but her rule will be divided into three parts. The first part is comprised of the administrative tasks of the reign that will be carried out under the authority of Queen Mother Skystar; and the second part is under the jurisdiction of the royal appointee to the councils, which position shall be held jointly by the sister queens, Mountain Rain and her advisor, Cloudhopper; and finally, the third part will be held by the oracle queen, the one who resides at the pinnacle of the structure and who provides us with vision and overall leadership."

The sound of a multitude of flapping wings greets the magistrate's words.

"The queenship trinity," Queenstar says, "will be complimented by a kingship trinity, comprised of the king father, Sun Quest; and the king son, the young opinicus Sun Wing; and finally, the spirit king, Dreamspinner.

"The three kings together will operate in conjunction with the concerns of the Council of the Opinici, while the queens operate in conjunction with the Gryphonic Council. On matters pertaining to both genders, the Council of the Opinici will join with the Gryphonic Council to become one body, the Gryphonic-Opinical Council."

Queenstar pauses a moment to let the information penetrate the minds of the audience. Sunsky knows that it is a lot for everyone to take in, but she agrees with the magistrate and wants to make sure that the population at large has some understanding of the new, more complicated governmental structure.

"There is, in addition to the gryphon-opinicus structure, a twin keythong-kryphon consular structure which will operate in the same manner: The keythongs and kryphons will choose their own kingship and queenship trinities that are to cooperate with the Council of the Keythong and the Kryphonic Council."

The sound of many feathers rustling at once threatens to drown out the sound of Queenstar's formidable voice.

"The keythong kings and kryphon queens will be chosen and crowned in a separate ceremony for the grounded ones, to which we are all invited. They tell me that I may announce the appointment of one keythong king who has been unanimously voted in by his colleagues. It is someone with wise and fatherly qualities, someone with an outstanding record of service. Ground Paw has agreed to take on the role of the king-father of the keythongs. He will still maintain his posting on the Elders' Advisory Council, along with his new official mate, Egglight."

Hoots of surprise and delight interrupt Queenstar, not only from the crowd but from the royal family as well.

Uncle Ground Paw has become a king, while the nanny Egglight and he have taken each other as official mates! This is so wonderful and amazing that Sunsky wants to go over to old Egglight and Uncle Ground Paw right now to embrace them both in her wings. She restrains herself, however, because she knows that Queenstar will not be happy with another breach of protocol, especially not from the reigning oracle queen.

"In addition," Queenstar continues, "Groundsky, the keythong son of the oracle queen, will be the Son King or junior-king-in-training, like his opinicus brother Sun Wing. He is the only keythong that we know of who has the capability to produce offspring, along with the kryphon Fluff Feather, who similarly resisted compulsory sterilization. These two, I am told, are to become official mates to each other and will therefore represent a future where sterilization for the wingless is unlawful."

This time, Queenstar cannot control the chorus of jubilant hoots and caws that culminate in a song known as "*The Lament of the keythong/kryphon*", followed by a new rendition, which celebrates the dawn of their mating freedom.

Groundsky, to his mother's relief, has miraculously refrained from joining in the vocal merriment. The sacred feather remains firmly in his beak, and he maintains his dutiful pose. She looks upon him with great pride.

At long last, she thinks, *I have seen the beginning of my keythong son's dream to become king one day! It is indeed a historic moment for all of us.*

Sunsky moves toward his mate Fluff Feather to tap her beak in a congratulatory gesture. The two youngsters will need much support in learning to fulfill these grand new leadership roles, as Sunsky knows well.

The chief magistrate clucks irritably at Sunsky to move back into her formal pose so that she can conclude her exposition and get on with the ceremony.

"During those times when decisions must be made affecting all four groups of beings, the Gryphonic-Opinical Council will meet with the Keythonic-Kryphonal Council and together all four partnerships will comprise the *Gryph-Opini-Phon-Key*, or the Grand Council."

There is an excited quivering of wings, as the throng collectively contemplates the numerous changes.

"The Scepter of Rulers," Queenstar continues, "at this point in time, can only be presented to one, however. I decree by unanimous consent and by the hallowed traditional law that this honor shall go to Sunsky, as will the oracle's Crown of Leaves. The Crown of Leaves will be presented by the acting oracle, Light Healer, while I will present the scepter."

A solemn silence greets the magistrate's pronouncement. Slowly, a chorus of chirps and whistles begins, increasing in volume and speed until it blends into a harmonious song of joy and triumph. It is the "*Song of the Gryphons*" and Sunsky trembles at the singing of it.

She feels the presence of Grandmother Heartsong and the oracle close by, as well as many others in the spirit realm. She has resisted this moment all of her life, yet it is no longer bathed in fear of the future. As the *"Song of the Gryphons"* ends, she bows her head to the magistrate. She feels the loving presence of her entire family, including the hophas, the hippogryphs, and the equines.

Light Healer steps forward and places the Crown of Leaves on Sunsky's head before embracing the new oracle in her wings. Sunsky feels a surge of inner spirit power, and she welcomes the wisdom of the ages into her soul.

With her proud family looking on, the chief magistrate steps forward and places in her talons the Scepter of Rulers. Sunsky feels the majesty of all the former queens pass from the scepter into the present awareness of her mind and heart. She is now prepared to take on her sacred destiny.

The End